BLOOD & SILVER

NICOLE MCKEON

TOWER ROOM
publishing

www.towerroompublishing.com

Protect Your Mental Health

BLOOD AND SILVER IS an adaptative fairytale reimagining that explores themes of self-identity, and how the people who love us can help us see ourselves as worthwhile even when guilt and shame make us feel like monsters. More than that, it is the story of two people who cannot forgive themselves until their enemy teaches them how.

These are adult themes expressed in a manner that will not be suitable for all audiences and includes but is not limited to:

- Violence and violence including minors (no minors die in this novel)

- Animal death

- Mild gore

- Death and dismemberment

- Drugging

- PTSD

- Depression

- Discussion of suicide

- Mercy killings

- Graphic sexual content

- Self-surgery

Blood and Silver is a companion novel and part of The Gwen St. James Affair universe.

1

Alix

"DID YOU HEAR THAT?" the priest squeaked, clutching the silver cross to his chest with shaking hands.

Alix refused to roll her eyes or snap at the man. It wasn't every day a priest offered himself as bait to catch a werewolf, and that act of bravery deserved respect.

So as she scanned the shadowed undergrowth, she said, "Of course, I did. Just as it intended me to. They want you to hear every cracking branch, see shadows move in the dark, smell the musk of their pelt. They need your fear, Père Henri. They want you to run."

The wide-eyed young priest gulped and edged closer to her on the dirt path. He breathed in short, quick bursts and stank of stale sweat as his heart galloped like a panicked horse.

The combination of mortal fear and adrenaline was difficult to resist. If the werewolf didn't attack soon, she would need to put some distance between the father and herself.

Pére Henri muttered in a constant litany, his voice low as the buzzing of bees. "Why did I agree to this? Lord, why would I put myself in this foolish position?"

"Because," she said, calculating her words for effect, "your parishioners are in danger and they need a man of God to protect them from being torn to bloody pieces in their beds."

His heartbeat redoubled and the scent of his terror billowed out in an invisible cloud. No mortal, human, elf, or dwarf, was brave enough to use themselves as bait for a monster without fear. But the priest didn't break, even when a shadow passed between them and the full moon, throwing the forest path into momentary darkness.

She slid her hands over the pistols hidden beneath her red cloak and listened to the sounds of the night. Crickets, owls, and frogs ceased their symphony. A westward wind rose, making the shadows shift beneath the trees as it carried the scents of the night toward her. Damn. She'd planned to capture one werewolf, but another scent on the wind changed everything.

"It has been a quarter of an hour," Père Henri whispered. "Why does it wait?"

"Because"—she thumbed back the hammers on her revolvers—"there is more than one wolf. And"—she gave the frightened man a predatory smile—"because they know who I am."

Père Henri began praying in a quavering voice, stumbling over the words of the Lord's prayer as his courage broke. His steps faltered. A twig snapped and his panic hit a crescendo, exactly the combination that would drive the werewolves to attack.

A blood-curdling howl split the silence, and the air filled with the sharp stink of human urine.

Poor Pére Henri.

The proof of his vulnerability was too much for the wolves. A large female broke cover from the road, and a second, smaller male joined from the opposite side.

Instead of capturing a werewolf for the Sisters of St. Christophe, she would have to kill them both. So much for the search for a cure. Alix gritted her teeth and formulated a new plan as the wolves stared them down. The beasts were similar in build, like dire wolves with longer, more flexible limbs, both a sandstone red with white socks. Relatives, perhaps?

That was unusual, but she didn't have time to worry over the strange circumstance because at some unseen signal, both wolves snarled and hurtled toward them.

"Run!" Alix barked.

The priest hiked his skirts above his knees and fled back down the moonlit path with the panicked speed of a hare. He could not outrun them, but he made a distracting target. Fleeing prey was irresistible.

Alix wrenched her eyes from his retreating figure, spun, pulled the revolvers from beneath her cloak, and fired with both hands. The wolves leaped aside into the trees under the thunder of gunfire, disappearing into the shadows.

She creased the male, who crashed into the bushes, thrashing as he tried to cope with the pain of a silver-inflicted wound.

Ten bullets left.

The female spared a glance for her companion but didn't stop running. Her instincts took over, and Pére Henri was a mouthwatering target she couldn't ignore, not to defend her partner, or to protect herself.

Alix leveled both pistols and opened fire again. The first bullet took the wolf in the foreleg, breaking the bone with an audible crack that sent her tumbling through the underbrush with a yelp of pain. The second shot went wide, but it gave Alix plenty of time to drop out of the way as the male leaped at her from the shadows.

These two were clearly inexperienced. Alix rolled to her back and fired two shots at his underbelly as he sailed over her head.

Six bullets left.

He hit the ground and somersaulted to a stop, a crumpled heap of blood and fur and twisted limbs. She spun to her feet and sprinted after the priest, but he was nowhere to be seen.

Damn.

He was faster than she thought, and that meant no distraction for the remaining wolf, who limped back onto the road. Moonlight glinted off an impressive set of teeth as she snarled and circled. Only a fool would think the wolf any less dangerous with a broken leg, and Alix was not a fool.

She angled her body to keep both wolves in her sights. The male wasn't getting up, and the female was still fast enough to dodge before Alix could squeeze the trigger. She had to anticipate the female and fire where she would be instead of where she was.

Blood matted her fur and stained her muzzle, and her yellow eyes burned with ravenous hunger. With the spell of Pére Henri's fear broken, she was free to focus on Alix.

The werewolf circled slowly, far enough away to dodge if Alix raised her arm, and kept her left ear cocked toward her fallen comrade, who whimpered and twitched in the dirt.

Following an instinct, Alix turned both pistols on him. The female lunged, throwing her body between the woman with the guns and her dying partner. Gunfire roared, but Alix didn't wait to see where she'd hit the female because Père Henri screamed in the distance, and the coppery scent of human blood wafted toward her on the breeze.

She turned and sprinted toward the screams.

The priest had climbed an ash tree, but height wouldn't save him from the werewolf slavering beneath the branches. Alix's mind spun. That made three wolves, an unthinkable number given that the beasts were solitary creatures.

In hundreds of years, Alix had only faced two werewolves at once a handful of times. But never three. The wolf leaped fifteen feet and sank its claws into the bark, snapping at Père Henri.

The father screamed again and scrabbled higher as teeth clacked shut centimeters short of his feet.

Alix aimed as she ran and fired, but something hit her from behind, sending her sprawling into the dirt. The female. How was the creature still on her feet? The silver wounds should have incapacitated her, if not killed her outright. If the wolf hadn't been seriously wounded, the impact of her attack could have broken Alix's back, and she would never have healed from such an injury fast enough to save the priest.

Pére Henri screamed again.

They were in trouble. The priest was a fool for volunteering for such a hunt, but he was a courageous fool who deserved to live. She only had two silver bullets left, and she was going to use them to get him out of this forest alive.

Taking the best option available, she sighted down the length of the barrel and fired at the female. The first shot blasted through her left eye, and the second took her in the chest.

Alix didn't generally aim for the head; it was too small a target to track and hit reliably, especially on a creature as fast as a werewolf. But it was three to one and she was injured. Her only chance of keeping Pére Henri alive was evening the odds.

The female dropped without a sound and didn't move.

The male wolf sent a heartbreaking howl tearing through the forest. Alix holstered the empty pistols, drew her silver daggers, and spared a glance for the embattled priest.

He had climbed high into branches too slim to bear the weight of the hungry wolf, who stood on its hind legs, snapping and clawing at the bark in frustration.

Pére Henri didn't have long.

Neither did she. The wolf closed the distance between them faster than she would have thought possible and struck her like a runaway train. She wrapped her arms around his thick neck and clung to his body with her legs as they hit the ground. He rolled, snapping and scratching, but she held on.

All she needed was a single opening, and her dagger would slide be-tween the creature's ribs, and—the wild, musky scent of another werewolf broke her train of thought and her heart dropped.

Another wolf?

This job had only been for one werewolf, and she'd brought enough bullets for two on the unlikely chance another wolf hunted this forest. But not four. She couldn't fight so many at once, not without a better plan and more silver bullets.

She didn't have time to wait for the perfect opening, so she released her grip on the creature's fur, planted her feet to stop them rolling, and stabbed his broad rib cage with both daggers.

The scent of the other wolf grew stronger.

Beneath her, the injured beast twisted like a snake and struck. His teeth sunk through her forearm from one side to the other, locking her right arm in place. The fool didn't know it, but he'd sealed his own fate.

While his jaw was clamped on her arm, she shifted her grip on the dagger in her left hand, jerked it out, and drove the full length of it through his throat at an angle. Hot blood covered her hand in a silent rush.

The wolf released her arm and jerked away, pulling the handle out of her slippery fingers and writhing on the ground like a worm. The dual pain of his poisoned injury and of the silver wracked his body.

If the blood loss didn't kill him, the wolfsbane would.

There was no time to bind her own wound because the biggest werewolf she'd ever seen crashed through the bushes at an impossible speed. He was huge but sleek, his tawny body more elegant, more like a true wolf than the brutal form she'd just destroyed.

His gaze flashed across the scene, eyes catching the moonlight with a glint of green. Human intelligence burned in those eyes, not the animal madness she expected in a werewolf. The stomach-dropping recognition of death stopped her breath. If this wolf attacked, they were doomed.

The beast picked up speed, its gaze locking on the tree where Pére Henri's grip was faltering.

She jerked her knife free of the dying wolf and sprinted toward the tree at an angle to intercept the newcomer, daggers held low. Planting one foot on a fallen log for leverage, she leaped.

They collided mid-air and hit the ground in a tangle of thrashing limbs. Pain shot up her forearm but she ignored it and held on, scoring a deep cut on the wolf's left haunch. Instead of attacking her, he twisted away and launched himself at the werewolf beneath the tree.

The scent of Pére Henri's fear was thick in the air, sour and sharp, like a good beer, mixed with the unmistakable tang of human blood. Her mouth watered, but she gritted her teeth against the temptation and pushed it out of her mind with the familiarity of practice.

She had to get to the priest.

Both werewolves hit the ground in a swirling, slavering ball of fur and teeth. She dodged them and leaped to catch the bottom branch, hauling herself up with bloody fingers and ignoring the throb of her injury.

The father clung to a high, thin limb with desperate strength, his face white in the moonlight. One leg dangled uselessly beneath him.

"Pére Henri, hang on!" she shouted.

He grunted, but his arms shook.

Balancing on the branch beneath him, Alix set her hip against the trunk and raised her arms. "I've got you."

He squeezed his eyes shut and shook his head.

"Dammit, Father! If you fall, I won't be able to save you, and you can't hold on much longer. I'll catch you, I promise."

And if he didn't hurry, whichever wolf won the fight would be snapping at their heels.

He opened one eye a slit to glance down at the fight and his face paled further. The huge wolf was vicious, tearing chunks of flesh from the smaller male and spattering the forest floor with dark blood. The struggle wouldn't last long.

They had to hurry.

"Come on," she said, reaching toward his waist. "I'll catch you."

Père Henri released the branch only reluctantly, slipping low enough for her to grab his belt. He shrieked when his grip broke.

Alix jerked his flailing body upright, catching him as his feet hit the fork in the branch and his knees buckled. "I've got you."

He wrapped every available limb around her and held on with the last threads of his strength. At least the tree was wide enough here that he wouldn't fall into the tangle of wolves.

"The fight is almost over," she whispered. "I'll drop on whichever wolf wins, kill it, and we'll get you out of here."

"No," he begged, tightening his grip until his whole body shook. "If I don't, it will come up this tree, and I cannot fight it here."

"I can't..."

The scent of his blood was too close, too dangerous. In this heightened state, she was as much a danger to the priest as the werewolves. She should never have allowed him on this hunt.

Biting back self-loathing, she pried his arms off, made sure he was safely balanced against the trunk, and swung out onto a limb. She would drop on the winner and kill him before...but the fight was over. With a powerful twist of his body, the large wolf tore out the throat of the smaller creature and spat the flesh on the ground.

That was a wound even a werewolf couldn't heal from.

Chest heaving, he glanced around the clearing, and then up. Their eyes met and a thrill of unaccustomed dread ran up her spine. He did not stare at her with the magic-induced madness of a monster. The cold intelligence in his gaze told her he knew what he was doing.

With a dismissive flick of his ears, the large werewolf turned and staggered toward the tree line, disappearing into the shadows. Père Henri still stunk of prey, so once the beast killed to protect his hunt, he should have been slavering at the foot of the tree.

When the magic was on them, werewolves fought and hunted as long as there was blood in their veins. But she didn't have time to complain. This was the chance she needed to get Père Henri to safety.

Maneuvering him out of the tree was nearly as hard as fighting the werewolves had been, and he clung to her like a child once they were back on the ground.

"There," she said, trying to untangle his arms from around her neck. "We're safe. You can let go."

He did but crumpled to the ground in a heap of black cloth and clutched his leg, rocking back and forth.

"Oh God, my God," he prayed, "protect me from evil."

"Don't worry, Father," she said. "People only turn if the wolf savages them unto death."

He turned his face up to her, panic in his eyes, and then looked back down at his leg. For the first time, Alix noticed the wound. She'd smelled the blood but was too focused on the fight to realize what it meant.

She sank to her knees next to the priest and pulled his robes aside. A gaping wound, like a dark, hungry mouth, opened along the inside of his thigh and a stream of blood spurted to pool on the ground beneath him. The fight by the tree had lasted less than a minute. Unless she did something, Pére Henri would be dead in less than three more.

2

Alix

SHE RIPPED HIS BELT off and applied the tourniquet, though she knew it was useless. Once the wolf damaged his femoral artery, there was no saving him.

She tied off the leather but kept pressure on the wound. "Listen to me, Father. I can staunch the bleeding for a while and try to get you to the village, but there is no equipment there for a transfusion. By the time–"

He shook his head, cutting her off. "I understand."

"If you die like this, from the wound..."

"I will turn. I know. You warned me before we came here."

They locked eyes and dread condensed like ice in the pit of her stomach.

His shaking increased, silent tears spilling down his pale cheeks. "Can I–can I pray?"

She swallowed. "Of course, Father."

He was halfway through his prayers when his voice weakened. "There's no time." He fell back against the trunk of the tree. "You must do it. You must–" He swallowed, his delicate Adam's apple bobbing. "Must do it."

Her stomach knotted in protest and Alix had to lock her jaw against the horror building in her chest. It would do no good. What must be done *must* be done. Better now than when the magic turned him into a monster. She could grieve him later when there was time.

"I'm sorry, Father," she whispered as she clenched her jaw and drew the silver dagger.

He placed one cold, wet hand over hers. "You helped me protect them. We protected them, didn't we?"

She hadn't cried in more years than she could count, but tears stung her eyes. "We did. *You* did."

He nodded, then took a few quick, shallow breaths, and said, "I feel it, the darkness. It's like a blanket rolling over me. Do it, my lady. Do it now!"

"Forgive me," she breathed.

The smile on his face was small and weak, but real. "There is always forgiveness for you."

Alix closed her eyes and plunged the dagger into his chest.

His heart fluttered around the blade, trying to reject the foreign object, trying to beat, perhaps even trying to change, but the silver prevented all of it. She sat there with his body in her lap, fingers curled around the blade, till all chance of his changing was long past.

He had been a brave man, braver than she'd given him credit for. And he had protected his village. The people of St. Michelle would no longer cower in the night, afraid of disappearing, or of losing their children, because their parish priest used himself as bait to draw the monsters away.

Her fingers reached for the jeweled pendant beneath her shirt and curled around the familiar shape, closing tight. It brought her no comfort, tonight.

"Well, Alix," she said, voice heavy with disgust. "You've earned your coins."

The priest was a hero, but after being savaged by a werewolf, the village would never allow him to be buried in consecrated ground. So she dug his grave beneath the tree and fashioned bent branches in the shape of a cross to mark his faith, misplaced as it might have been.

It was the only last rights he would receive and more than she'd give to the wolves. Magic deserted them in death, leaving their human bodies nude and bloody on the forest floor. She avoided looking at them as she waited.

Dawn bled color and light into the sky, stealing the darkest shadows and turning the world silver-grey. Exhaustion and grief dragged her toward the ground like lead weights. What she wouldn't give for a soft bed and a door to close out the world.

But the rumble of cart wheels on the hard-packed dirt of the road forced her to put away those thoughts.

"You're late, Mason," she called to the scruffy dwarven man.

He hauled on the reins, pulling his mules to a stop, and brushed a meaty fist beneath his nose. "Three, eh? You get too casual with those silver bullets and catch a couple of travelers?"

"No. They were hunting together."

Mason's red brows rose to the brim of his slouch hat. "You're serious?"

She turned a steely gaze on him, and the dwarven man raised his hands, palm out. "I don't mean to question your integrity, Lady Hunter, but...I've delivered quite a few werewolves to the Sisters over the years and these"—he flicked a finger at the bodies—"ain't usual."

"No," Alix said, considering the corpses. "No, they're not."

Werewolves were solitary monsters, too violent and single-minded to cooperate. That made them easier to track and kill. Sometimes a bond between spouses was strong enough to keep a hunting pair together after the magic changed them, but that was rare.

"A family, then?"

"What are the chances they'd all survive the transformation?"

Mason ran his hand down his braided beard and scowled but didn't answer. Even if a family managed to survive a werewolf attack, they would be more inclined to attack one another upon waking than work together.

Something was very wrong with these three.

Mason glanced away from her, cleared his throat, and gestured with his chin to the empty cart behind him. "Might as well load 'em up. Suddenly I don't feel so safe in these woods."

Alix rolled her tired shoulders and nodded. The adult male had the solid, sinewy build of a laborer, but she lifted him with ease. "I thought this one might be a miner, judging by the calluses on his hands and the muscles of his arms and upper back."

"Mining grinds a man down," Mason said as she deposited the body in the back of his cart. "Almost can't blame him for turning to dark magic for a little more power."

Alix considered the children lying side-by-side in the dirt next to the road: a boy no more than eighteen, and a young woman barely into adulthood. Both had snub noses, freckles, and red hair. "I can. The hunger for power got four people killed."

"Four?"

"The priest didn't make it."

Mason shook his head, pulled a knife from his belt, and kissed the metal. "May the earth accept and keep him."

"And the blade never forget his name," Alix said, finishing the ancient dwarven prayer.

She arranged the bodies in the cart, tied dried wolfsbane to their ankles, and used a special match to heat the ring on her forefinger.

Mason leaned over the backrest and peered at her as she held the flame beneath the metal. "What happened to your signet?"

The symbol on the flat face of the ring began to glow. "One too many fights. The runic sentence was damaged. It won't heat anymore."

He grunted. "You'll burn yourself, that way."

"When I find time to visit an artificer, I'll have it repaired. In the meantime"—she gritted her teeth and pressed the hot metal against the right palm of each body—"this will have to do."

Once she applied the hunter's mark, Alix dropped the dirty ring into her pocket to be cleaned later, rubbed a handful of dirt between her palms, and brushed them off on her trousers.

"Want a ride to the convent?" Mason asked as he readied the reins. "I won't charge you extra."

She'd worked with Mason enough that he wasn't quite as afraid of her as other mortals were, and the promise of comfort and conversation was tempting.

But her job wasn't done.

Another werewolf hunted this forest, one far more dangerous than the beasts she already killed. "Not this time, Mason. But I'll be along behind you."

"Take care, then, Lady Hunter." He clicked to the mules and snapped the reins against their flanks.

The wagon trundled down the road as the first rays of sunlight pierced the canopy, falling in slanting pillars across the forest. She pulled her hood up, sighed, and slogged into the underbrush in the direction the green-eyed wolf had disappeared. Luckily he was already traveling toward the convent, and since she'd been heading there for her next assignment, she considered that a fortuitous circumstance.

Broken twigs and disturbed leaf mold were the only signs she had to follow until the underbrush cleared and the ground hardened. Then the trail simply vanished. Scouting the ground in wide arcs revealed nothing.

It was mid-afternoon when Alix stopped to chew a piece of jerky and stretch her muscles. The wind picked up, blowing a lock of hair across her face and carrying with it the familiar stink of wolf pelt.

Her daggers jumped into her hands, and a thrill of recognition ran up her spine. She followed the scent farther into the trees, picking up the rasp of heavy breathing and a long, drawn-out groan. Something moved beneath the branches of a scrubby bush butted against the granite face of a cliff.

She adjusted her grip and pushed the branches aside.

A man lay curled in a fetal position on the ground, long, dark blonde hair covering his face. He had several wounds, scratches and bruises, and blood plastered his shirt to his skin. Another victim of the werewolves? No wonder the wolf stink clung to him.

She slid the daggers into their sheaths and nudged the man's shoulder with the toe of her boot. "Are you alright?"

He only groaned and curled more tightly, arms wrapped around his middle.

All she wanted was a warm place to sleep, something to eat, and maybe some wine to drink away the vision of life leaving Père Henri's eyes. But she couldn't leave the mauled man to die of exposure or lie there till the scent of his blood drew more mundane predators.

Besides, if he'd managed to survive the beast she was tracking, he may be able to help her find it.

She bent and pressed her fingertips against the pale column of his neck. A strong heartbeat, though his skin was shockingly cold. He should survive until she found a safe place to nurse him back to health.

With a sigh, Alix slid her arms beneath the man, wincing when he sucked in a pained breath, and hefted him onto her shoulder.

The brute must have been well over two hundred pounds, far too big to carry any distance in her current state, but she should be able to get them to better shelter than the underside of a bush before her strength gave out.

His blood soaked through the shoulder of her cloak and seeped into her shirt, warm and wet against her skin. She swallowed hard against the sensation and let the sights, scents, and sounds of the wood distract her as she hurried to find shelter.

The man groaned and tried to roll off her shoulder.

"Nope," she said as she tightened her grip. "I know it's uncomfortable but you're going to have to put up with my shoulder in your guts for a little while. I think I hear..."

The wind picked up and a hollow humming echoed to their left. A game trail led her to a cliff face where, behind a stand of saplings, the thin crack of a cave opened in the rock.

She squeezed through, relieved to find the place shallow and relatively clean, if not musty and damp. A fire would make it downright cozy. The man grunted in pain when she plopped him down against the cave wall.

"Sorry," she muttered, then turned to forage some firewood, but he reached out and caught her ankle with surprising strength for someone so battered.

"Wait," he croaked.

She jerked her ankle out of his grip. "If I don't warm you up, you'll probably die. And if I don't get away from you soon...we'll both regret it. I'll be back with firewood."

If she were a normal person, or even a good person, she'd try to staunch his wounds first, make sure he was out of danger and comfortable.

She was neither of those things.

But she was tired, tempted, and too weak to trust her self-control. Alix didn't need another death on her conscience tonight, so she crept back into the lightening woods and searched for dry wood.

By the time she returned, her self-control was firmly back in place. She started a fire, boiled water in her travel pot, and dug an old shirt from her pack. When the torn pieces were thoroughly boiled, she wrung the extra water from the steaming cloth, and stared down at her patient.

He was handsome, with broad cheekbones, a long, straight nose, and a short blonde beard that didn't disguise a strong jaw and full lips. And though his clothing had been torn, it was well made, if not flashy.

What was he doing alone in the woods this far from civilization?

She could ask him that when he woke, which he might do when she began cleaning his wounds, if they were serious enough. But she found no scrapes beneath the smears of blood she mopped from his face.

Odd. And his scent wasn't quite right, something too wild and rich for a mere human.

She jerked open his shirt, where the fabric dried and stuck to his pale skin, and found only a fine pink scar along the flat muscle of his chest. He'd bled enough to soak his shirt and hers on the walk to the cave, and now there was no wound?

Several creatures that looked human healed faster than mortals, and all of them were dangerous. Luckily, most of them were rare and reclusive. And when she added up everything that happened since last night...dread and suspicion tightened her muscles and made her breath catch.

Alix carefully turned the stranger's body toward the firelight, searching for what she was afraid she would find. An open cut glistened red in the firelight.

Exactly where she'd cut the huge werewolf.

Alix scrambled backward with a muttered curse, drawing a dagger as she went. She had to kill the creature before it woke and attacked her.

He shuddered and curled into a fetal position, wrapping his arms protectively across his chest, brows furrowing in pain. If he was still alive after the beating he'd endured, and hours of suffering through the wolfsbane oil that coated her knife, he was impressively strong.

Perhaps strong enough to serve as a test subject for the Sisters. Since werewolves destroyed her life, the least she could do was provide the Sisters with a creature that might help them unravel the dark magic for good.

Alix dug the silver manacles from the bottom of her pack and glared down at the creature with a grim smile.

3

Cyrus

CYRUS SHIVERED AS THE cave floor leached the warmth from his battered body. He instinctively tried to turn on his side so less of his skin was exposed to the rock, but a broken rib sent icy shards of pain crackling through his chest. He froze, breathless. Every muscle cramped, a constant stream of dull fire burned from his hip down to his knee, and a dozen cuts, bruises, and contusions combined to create a pain that overwhelmed his ability to think.

He could handle pain and continue to fight, but when his life was in danger his body monopolized every available resource to heal itself, stealing heat, energy, strength, even his concentration. The magic would heal his wounds if they could be healed but left him no defense against the pain. He couldn't even hide in the oblivion of sleep.

Fighting only made the healing process longer, so he lay helpless as wave after wave of torment broke over him. Time faded in and out. Light flared to life somewhere nearby, turning his eyelids dull red. Fire? Blessed warmth on his face. Pressure on his forehead. A steady, low, melodic humming. More pain as someone jostled and jerked his body. Something cold against his lips. He clutched the water skin with blind desperation and gulped until he couldn't hold his head up. All the while pain seared and scalded every nerve ending.

But the low humming sound was strangely soothing. He hung onto that sound through every wave of agony until, instead of ocean breakers that pounded him into the rocks beneath, the pain receded to a calm lake, lapping at his feet. The experience became a haze of disconnected thoughts and observations, dissipating like morning fog in the sun, as indistinct as a dream.

When sleep finally claimed him, the last sound he heard was the humming.

The scent of roasting meat dragged Cyrus out of the darkness, leaving him sore and disoriented, with a mouthful of drool. Where was he and who the hell was cooking? A low, honeyed voice hummed somewhere nearby, and the crackling of fat on an open fire made his stomach ache with hollow need so powerful his abdominal muscles clenched.

Only instincts honed by years hunting monsters in the wild were strong enough to stop him from leaping to his feet and searching out the food. *We are vulnerable,* his wolf screamed. *Information and safety first, food later.*

He sank back into himself, retreating from the pain to let his senses gather information and try to remember how he'd ended up...wherever he was. Judging by the echoing quality of the sound, it was either a cave or a stone cottage with an open door. A woman was cooking an animal over a small fire, and there was only one heartbeat, so she was alone. The birdsong told him it was nightfall.

Had he truly been unconscious for an entire day?

He'd been on the road, headed toward his next job, when he'd caught the scent of a werewolf. Bits and pieces of the fight emerged from the haze of his memory, someone screaming, and then he'd hidden beneath a bush to wait out the pain of healing.

If he'd been asleep since last night, the wounds must have been life-threatening. They certainly hurt enough.

"You had better eat some of this," the woman said. "You'll need your strength if you plan to survive."

There was no point in trying to fool her. If she hadn't killed him while he slept, he'd likely live through the next few moments. His wolf relented, and Cyrus opened his eyes, letting the world swim into focus.

A beautiful woman crouched on the other side of a small fire. Her black braid hung over one shoulder, nearly reaching the floor, and she regarded him with amber eyes that glowed in the firelight. Her features fit together with a symmetry and elegance that was arresting: thick lashes, a stubborn chin, and olive-toned skin on the pale side of tan.

It wasn't a face that took one off guard, but became more fascinating the longer one looked. And her close-fitting menswear–snug trousers paired with a work shirt and leather vest–did nothing to make the rest of her less interesting.

Had *she* brought him here?

Cyrus made to push himself into a sitting position only to realize his leg was on fire. Gasping, he grabbed for the wound, but his wrists were bound. His heart jumped into his throat and he bore down to break the slender manacles but they bound him as if they were inch-thick iron.

"What is this?" he demanded, voice rough.

"That," the woman said with barely concealed disdain, "is insurance, wolf."

"Wolf?" he asked, controlling his expression to mask his shock. How did she know what he was?

The woman's head tilted to the side, her unblinking eyes like smoldering coals. He'd seen hawks move exactly the same way. "I've killed enough of your kind to know what you are, so please do not patronize me with that innocent expression."

"I don't know what you're–"

Before he could finish his sentence, she loomed over him, one foot on the chain that bound his hands, the other jerking away the red wool blanket that covered him.

"There," she said, gesturing to the bloodstain on his hip. "The only wound on your body that hasn't healed, made by a silver knife coated in aconite."

A pained breath hissed through his teeth. He tried to roll away from her hands and condemning eyes but she held him pinned.

Aconite. *Wolfsbane.*

No wonder the pain had been so extraordinary and he'd almost died. He was weaker now than he could ever remember being, even before his transformation...and *she* had done it.

Hazy memories returned from the night before, of a cold-eyed woman between him and the werewolf he hunted. He'd tried to avoid her but she attacked and cut him.

"*You,*" he spat.

Dark amusement twisted her features into a rictus of disgust. "I don't forget a single cut I make, wolf. So thank whatever dark gods you serve you are still alive and not rotting with the rest of your kind. Yet."

Fury awoke in his chest and stretched, unfurling its claws. "Do not compare me to those beasts."

Though his voice was as cold as the blade of a knife, their relative positions robbed his threat of its edge. Moon help him, he was powerless and she knew it.

One dark brow arched in derision. "I'll do as I please. And you," she turned, sliced off a steaming piece of meat, and held it out to him on the point of her knife, "will eat what I've generously cooked for you."

His mouth watered and his stomach nearly turned itself inside out, but he didn't accept the offering.

She rolled her eyes and said, as if reading his thoughts, "You're worth nothing to me dead, and I've already eaten half of it. There is no poison on this blade. Eat the rabbit."

If she wanted to kill him, he supposed there was nothing he could do about it. At least, not until the wolfsbane was fully out of his system. *And then*, he thought, with a hunger that had nothing to do with food, *they'd find out whether her chain could still hold him.*

"Afraid, wolf?" she taunted.

Cyrus gritted his teeth, slid the meat from the knife, and sniffed it, finding no traces of anything other than healthy young rabbit. The meat was gone before he could think twice, leaving a sheen of fat on his lips.

She tossed him a water skin. He sniffed that, too, then drank until it was empty. The woman watched his every movement as if she could burn him to the ground with her eyes. Her hatred heated the small cave more than the fire.

"Why?" he asked.

She leaned back against the stone wall opposite him, one knee bent and the other leg stretched out in front of her as she played with the end of her braid. "Why what? Why are you still alive? Why am I feeding you when I'd prefer to slide my dagger into your gut and twist?"

"I'd settle for an answer to either question."

She considered him for an interminable moment, the end of her braid running through her fingers. She was probably imagining him spitted over the fire.

At last, she said, "I'll answer your questions if you answer mine."

"That's fair," he said, weighing his first question carefully. "Why hold me hostage? Why am I alive, when you clearly want me dead?"

"You're alive because I'm curious."

"That's not an answer."

"It's more of an answer than you deserve."

Cyrus clenched his jaw against an angry response. He was in no position to fight his way free, and he didn't think she would respond well to intimidation. He would have to use whatever psychological weapons he could forge, and being reasonable might be the best place to start.

Forcing patience into his voice, he said, "You attacked me. You've chained me when I've done you no wrong. In fact, you are the only transgressor here. A full answer is not too much to ask."

"You are alive because I thought you were a man," she said, through clenched teeth. "When I happened upon you, you appeared to be a victim of the wolves, so I found a safe place to tend your wounds. It wasn't until I uncovered the cut I made that I realized you were one of the monsters."

So, the woman had a short temper and a hatred as deep as his own. At least she also had a sense of honor. Those were tools he could leverage if given the chance. So he used every bit of his hard-fought self-control and inclined his head, accepting the answer.

"What drove you to hunt in a pack?" she asked.

"What?"

"This arrangement of ours only works if you honor it, wolf."

He forced himself to ignore her patronizing tone. "I'm not dodging the question. I don't know what you mean."

"Werewolves don't hunt in packs. Last night there were four of you. Why?"

How much truth should he share? Given her responses so far, learning the truth about him wouldn't make her any less hostile. And she claimed to have killed werewolves but she wore no hunter's ring. By the dictates of his clan, he kept his own identity a secret long enough that, even if she were a hunter, she likely wouldn't know who he was.

To have a hope of getting out of this, he needed more information and time to heal. So he said, "I doubt you will believe me."

"Humor me, then."

Cyrus sighed and shifted his weight, trying to find a sitting position that didn't cause the fire in his hip to shoot blazing arrows down to his knee. His shirt slipped open with the motion. She must have been telling the truth about checking him for wounds. He reached toward the buttons, but the silver bound his hands too closely to fasten them.

When he raised his eyes, she was staring, her eyes fixed on his chest, nostrils flared as if pulling in his scent. Was that...fascination in her gaze? Their eyes met and her expression darkened to furious disgust.

"Have the decency to cover yourself," she spat and threw the red blanket at him.

No, it wasn't a blanket, he realized as he caught it. It was a cloak. He pulled the fabric against his chest and settled back against the wall. If he gave her some truth, would it convince her to release him, or only make her want him dead?

"I wasn't hunting with them," he said, at last, "I was hunting them."

"Why? Did they violate your territory?"

"You haven't earned that question, yet. You told me why you did not kill me on sight. Why did you leave me alive afterward?"

She pulled a dagger from the top of her boot and began cleaning her fingernails with it as she eyed him. "I told you. I was curious. Too many things about last night were wrong, irregular. Like werewolves hunting in a pack and shrugging off silver wounds that should have incapacitated or killed them. I want answers, and you are the only person who can give them to me. Why were you hunting the other werewolves?"

"Because they deserve to die," he said simply.

She scoffed and pointed the knife at him. "And you don't?"

He started to respond but his tongue stuck against the roof of his mouth. It felt as if his head were stuffed with cotton, floating somewhere above his body. Memories tickled the edges of his mind, memories of broken bodies and smoking ruins. "Aye, I do," he said, his voice thick. "Just not for the same reasons."

The amused censure faded from her face, and she narrowed her eyes at him. She was beautiful, like a bird of prey or a hunting cat, and she'd kill him just as happily. But he had been honest with her, and maybe she recognized it.

"You demanded full answers from me," she reminded him.

Cyrus took a deep breath and tried to pull his mind back together, ignoring pain in his leg so he might concentrate, but the insistent fire only grew as the exhaustion of recovering settled back in his bones, like a bird returning to its nest. "What is the point in giving you an answer you will not believe?"

"Why are you hunting your own kind?" she repeated.

"You won't–"

"Why?"

"Because they are not my kind," he snarled, rolling half to his feet, pain forgotten. "They are unnatural, an aberration distorted and twisted by dark magic, and they all deserve death, every one of them."

She leaned away from his fury, surprise and confusion drawing her brows together. "Do you think you can fool me? Me? Do you not realize whose cloak you are using to shield your nakedness?"

The adrenaline from that short bout of fury drained him as if someone had been slowly pouring him out of his body, like an emptying wineskin. What was happening to him? He collapsed against the wall, breathing hard. "I've no reason to lie to you."

"No? Saving your own life isn't a reason?"

"I'm no' really worth saving," he mumbled. His native Scottish accent, muddled by living abroad so long, had seeped back into his voice as conscious though fled. The cave darkened and, in the shadows, familiar memories of death stared at him with hollow eyes. His limbs grew heavy and his tongue didn't seem to want to cooperate.

Had she drugged him, or was this merely the exhaustion of recovery pulling him back into a healing sleep?

He managed to slur, "Wha're your plans for me?"

Her smile, as wicked and sharp as the dagger in her hands, was the last thing he saw as darkness overcame him.

4

Alix

ALIX STARED DOWN AT the sleeping monster and grimaced. Even weak from injuries and poison and bound with silver, there had been strength and intelligence in his eyes, and a calm calculation that was intimidating.

That he was conscious at all was disconcerting. Most werewolves slept through the day during the full moon cycle because the involuntary transformation drained their resources. Instead, he sat there looking more like a lion than a wolf, with his mane of dark gold hair and green eyes, and tried to reason with her.

Like a normal person.

He should have been frothing, cursing, and threatening to rip her throat out. Thankfully, the alchemical tincture of valerian root she spiked the water with had finally put him under, though he resisted far longer than she would have liked.

Perhaps she truly found a specimen strong enough to help the Sisters cure lycanthropy. No more children would ever suffer her fate and be left alone in a dangerous world.

As soon as the moon set and the forest was safe for travel, she would load the wolf on the makeshift litter and drag him to the convent before the drug wore off.

Alix cleaned her ring until not a trace was left of the grisly job it had done and slid the mark of her profession back onto her finger. She cleaned and reloaded her pistols, refilled her water skin, cut down a couple of thick young saplings, and bound her cloak between them. With all in readiness, she had an hour or so to rest before moonset. And she'd need it if she was going to drag that heavy body twenty-five miles to the convent.

Pulling the small leather embroidery pouch from her bag, Alix settled against the wall and let the tension drain from her muscles. Being half-vampire meant she didn't need half as much sleep as mortals, but after days of hunting and fighting, she was nearing the end of her reserves.

Sleeping with the monster so close would be stupid, however, so embroidery would have to do.

The wolf groaned in his sleep. His big body jerked now and then, like a horse twitching off flies, back and shoulder muscles straining against the thin cotton of his shirt.

A line of sweat darkened the fabric between his shoulder blades.

Alix clenched her jaw and focused on the thread. There were only four strands of the green silk left, not enough to repair the damage to the hem of her cloak.

The wolf spasmed again, this time accompanied by a low cry of pain, his dark blonde brows drawing together as his hands tightened into fists. A moment later, he whimpered, "I'm sorry. Mam, I'm so sorry."

Her fingers froze and the icy fist of memory curled around her heart. How often had she wished she could tell her mother she was sorry?

Sorry for leaving, and sorry for making her wonder what happened to her daughter and the woman who protected them both when no one else cared.

Sorry for never coming home.

But she had no business empathizing with a monster, even if his dreams echoed her own.

"Nooo," he whined, body arching as if he could pull away from something. In sleep, his light Scottish brogue deepened. "It wasnae my fault. I–it wasnae...Lyrus...och, god the blood..."

She was suddenly nine years old again, kneeling in a warm crimson pool on the cottage floor, her fingers locked around a knife as she cried, "It wasn't my fault," in an anguished voice no one would ever hear.

Alix blew a frustrated breath through her nose to dismiss the memory and stuffed the pouch back into her pack. Concentrating on the only thing that ever brought her peace would be impossible while he thrashed about. He should be deeply drugged, not having nightmares. Of course, the damned creature wouldn't do anything easily.

The wolf rolled to his back, chest heaving, a sheen of sweat standing out bright on his forehead and upper lip as he whispered in a horrified voice, "They're dead."

In the echo of his nightmares, Alix saw the specter of the werewolf who destroyed her life as if it stood before her, mad yellow eyes rolling as her knees shook.

"No' Effie," the wolf moaned, and his broken voice echoed her own remembered cry of *Grand-mère, no!*

"Shit." She lunged to her feet and pushed his shoulder with the toe of her boot. "Wake up, wolf. It's a dream. Wake up!"

But he only flopped to his side, face twisted in agony as runnels of sweat ran from his temples. Nightmares emerged from the dark corners of her mind and extended hungry arms in her direction.

Alix bent and shook him roughly. "Wake up!"

He gasped and jerked upright, catching her left arm in both hands before she could leap away, faster than he had any right to move, especially after sleeping off the poison. The blade of her dagger was pressed to his throat before she consciously thought to draw it.

His eyes locked on hers but they were unfocused, opaque with nightmares, his entire body thrumming with so much energy she felt it in her bones. He was far too strong. Waking a dangerous person from a nightmare was never a good idea, but she couldn't bear the pain of both his memories and her own.

Gritting her teeth, Alix increased the pressure of the blade and growled, "Release me, wolf. Now."

Sense stole back into his eyes like sunlight in the dawn sky. He took in their relative positions and several expressions chased one another across his face: surprise, realization, and finally, calculation.

Better to put an end to whatever he was thinking before he did something stupid. She twisted the knife enough to draw a bead of blood. "You cannot break my arm before I cut your throat. Release. Me."

His jaw muscles clenched, daring her to do it, his face inches from hers as his fingers tightened like iron bands. Then something seemed to click in his mind. He released her in a rush and collapsed back onto the floor with a groan. Alix bounded out of his reach, heart racing.

"I feel like hell," he said from the flat of his back as if he hadn't been preparing to rip her arm off moments before. "I should have let you kill me."

"I still might, if you don't stop making my life harder," she said, irritated that she'd managed to feel any emotion other than anger toward the monster, and angry she had been stupid enough to put herself within reach of the beast.

He must have been in the grip of memories, otherwise, he never would have released her, not with his freedom on the line. But the risk had been worth it. Now that he wasn't suffering, her memories retreated back to the dark corners she banished them to years ago.

He lay on his back, staring at the ceiling, his breath coming easier and more slowly. Stupid. She should never have woken him. Transporting a drugged werewolf would have been so much easier than dragging a conscious prisoner who could argue and fight back.

He sat up, shifted until he was comfortable, and stared at her with curious calculation.

When he'd woken the first time he looked drained, hollow-cheeked, and disoriented. Now there was color in his skin and the dark circles beneath his eyes were gone. The alchemical drug should have left him dizzy and disoriented, but he sat there with firelight in his hair, green eyes glowing, looking at her like a predator staring down a potential meal.

"You don't seem to be struggling against the moon," she accused, discomfort forcing her to break the tension somehow.

He glanced at the silver around his wrists and raised an eyebrow. True, silver would stop the magic from forcing him to complete the transformation, but it should not be a comfortable experience.

In the past, seeing a werewolf in silver chains during the full moon had been like watching someone try not to cough in public. Their body demanded relief but they fought it back, shaking with muffled grunts until the urge passed. He did not do even that.

"A question for a question?" she asked.

"Water first? Clean water, if you don't mind."

With a wry grin, Alix tossed him the skin. He sniffed the mouth of the bottle and gave her a narrow-eyed glance.

"I suppose you'll have to trust me."

With a resigned shake of the head, his Adam's apple bobbed a few times, and he wiped his mouth with the back of his hand before replacing the cork. "I'm not struggling against the moon because I am not her slave."

Alix snorted. "Of course you are, that is what it means to be a were-wolf. But I have some time to spare, so"—she crossed her legs at the ankles and made a sweeping gesture with one hand—"please. Entertain me."

A light kindled in his eyes as he looked at her, something feral and hungry that made her breath catch. The corner of his mouth quirked in a grin that would have curled her toes if he was a man and not a monster.

"Unlock this chain," he coaxed in a low voice, "and I'd be happy to entertain you, minx. All night long. Or, as long as you can handle me."

A hot rush ran from her breastbone to her knees, of surprise or anger or something else, she couldn't tell. She'd seen his body, lean with corded muscle and impressive power, and his words conjured a vision of them together, one so potent that heat pooled low in her belly.

But the sensation was followed by furious disgust that made her lip curl into a sneer. She drew the knife and pointed it at him. "Don't forget that killing you would please me much more than keeping you alive, wolf. So watch your tongue."

"I could certainly please you with my tongue if you wish it."

"Not if I cut it out first," Alix spat as her cheeks flamed and her heart jumped into a gallop. A self-satisfied smile crept across his face. That smile said he found a weapon that penetrated her armor, and he would use it. He did not want her, not really. But he was happy to disconcert her if he could.

Her fingers curled into fists, but he threw his head back and laughed. "You certainly are a violent prude, minx, I will give you that much. Throw me a bit of that meat and I will explain why the moon does not rule me. Unless you have a better idea for something I can do with my mouth?"

Waking him had been a mistake. If she had to put up with his vile suggestions much longer, they were definitely going to fight.

She hacked the rabbit in half and flung the hot meat at him. It took a serious act of willpower to bring her temper under control. She wouldn't give him the pleasure of knowing he had succeeded.

"I am not a prude," she said, sliding back into her seat. "I'm just not attracted to *dogs*."

He froze, the steaming rabbit halfway to his mouth, and looked at her through a haze of heat and anger. "Oh, yes you are," he said. "I can smell it. *Minx*."

"Don't call me that!"

She tried to sound intimidating but it was hard to do while fighting back another blush at the thought that he could smell her arousal. Likely he was only lying and trying to make her uncomfortable, but she refused to admit that a monster was capable of making her feel desire. The very thought of her body betraying her that way made her stomach turn.

"Then what should I call you?" he asked in an infuriatingly reasonable tone.

Damn. She'd handed him that one. What the hell was wrong with her? She pulled out her knife and began cleaning her nails to give her hands something to do that didn't involve killing the only werewolf she managed to capture in years.

She would get him back to the sisters alive. And when he realized they were using him to destroy the rest of his kind, she'd watch the smug condescension melt off his face.

"You may call me La Cape Rouge," she said, confidence seeping back into her voice. If he could play the game, so could she.

He paused mid-chew, fat shining on his lips. "You? *You* are the Red Cloak?"

"At your service," she said, sketching a bow. "Or did you fail to notice the blanket under which you slept?" She jerked her head toward the sled leaning against the wall, the one she'd built using her famous cloak.

"And you have the gall to call me a monster? You have more blood on your hands than any three hunters. Who knew the Red Cloak was such a hypocrite?"

She pulled out her silver dagger and threw it before she had time to think or feel anything other than fury. How dare this murderous creature call *her* a monster? In an instant of disorientation, she felt her grandmother's blood hot on her hands again, hotter than the tears that streamed down her cheeks. She didn't even have time to regret throwing the knife.

But that didn't matter, because he caught it.

He *caught* it. By the handle. While she watched in shock, he flipped the dagger around, studied it, then saluted her with the blade and said, "Violent."

"If I am violent it is your fault. Give me back the dagger."

"Come and take it."

"If I do, you will not leave this cave alive."

He raised a brow and his expression communicated his thoughts as clearly as if he had spoken them. *Violent.*

No one knew how she dreamed about living a life without violence; of being safe, of never having to pick up a gun or a knife, of sleeping in a bed in her own home, and waking to tend a garden in the sunshine. But those were not possibilities her father left to her.

She would never have that safe, warm life. The only safety she would know is the safety left when she was more violent than the monsters who lurked in the dark.

Perhaps she was violent, but that was the only thing that kept her, and many others, alive.

So, she could either prove to him how violent she was—and prove him right—or respond calmly despite the hot blood pumping through her veins. This was a game of emotional chess, and Alix refused to lose it.

Sharing her father's blood didn't mean she had to share his nature. When she chose violence it was careful, purposeful, and used for the good of others, not for her own pleasure. Besides, if she shot him now, she'd lose any chance of turning him over to the Sisters.

"My name is Alix."

After a beat of silence, he replied, "Mine is Cyrus."

"I would say it is nice to meet you, but–"

"No need to start lying now."

If he hadn't been a monster, she might have smiled at him. He tore into the meat again, then tossed the dagger back across the fire. She had not expected that show of good faith, but caught the knife and sheathed it, then waited while he finished his meal. When he was done, he tossed the bones into the fire, wiped his greasy fingers on the hem of his shirt, and shifted until he got comfortable.

He was obviously making her wait, seeing how long her patience would last before he finally started talking. "I am not a slave to the moon because I am not the same as the creatures you hunt."

"You are a werewolf," she said, emphasizing each word.

"Of course I am. I am a man who changes into a wolf. For someone who claims to know so much of my kind, you seem woefully uninformed."

It was a struggle to force her jaw to unlock enough to say, "Enlighten me, then."

"The creatures we killed last night are abominations. They have taken the gift and turned it into something evil."

"A gift, is it?"

"Do not scoff. My people accept the gift to protect life and to have strength for battle. We prepare and train for it so we can become servants of our people. Those"—he jerked his head toward the cave mouth—"*take*. They take the gift by force and the power of it twists them until they cannot balance man and wolf. Instead of being a partner with the magic, it rules them. They give themselves over to the power to satisfy their own desires. And the rare few who are turned against their will do not remain innocent long."

She stared at him in disbelief. "I have never heard more ridiculous nonsense in my life. Chosen? Trained for *protection*? Did you truly think this fairy story would convince me to do—what? Trust you? Set you free? As if the magic itself were not evil! Werewolves are monsters," she said, pointing at him with her knife. "They serve nothing but their hunger. But, by all means, save that charming story for the Sisters of St. Christophe. I'm certain they will find it very entertaining."

Dammit. He made her so angry she'd just revealed her plan without thinking. Her hand settled on the hilt of her pistol. If he knew of the Sisters and their mission, he would attack her to save himself. With a casual step back, she put enough space between herself and the monster that she could draw and fire before he crossed half the space between them.

His jaw muscle worked a few times, as if he was either trying not to smile or chewing over the words he wanted to say until they were soft enough to swallow. Finally, he lay back on the stone floor and pillowed his head on his folded hands.

Alix let out a slow breath and relaxed muscles primed to draw and shoot. If he wasn't trying to fight his way out of the cave, he didn't know about the Sisters. If she played this right, she may be in the clear. If not...there were always the pistols.

"Care to make a deal, wolf?"

5

Cyrus

ALIX CROUCHED ON THE other side of the fire and rested her elbows on her knees, as if she were picking a flower and not manipulating him to accept a deal she believed would end with his death.

The Red Cloak was one of the most renowned monster hunters in Europe. She had killed more werewolves than anyone living, save perhaps himself. The hunter's signet ring on her right hand glowed orange in the firelight, a symbol she burned into the palm of every monster she killed.

How had he not seen the ring before? Knowing she was a hunter could have changed everything. Then again, given her response to the truth he dared to tell, maybe not. Maybe she truly hated him that much.

Under other circumstances, and with a bit of time, he might have tried to slip past her guard and challenge her assumptions, but Alix had an impenetrable shield around her emotions. She did not seem to care for his honesty *or* his persuasion.

Her control only slipped during moments of anger or embarrassment, and nothing seemed to irritate her more than a few sensual suggestions. Who could have guessed that sex was the only chink in the Red Cloak's armor?

Of course, his chance of using that weapon was slim; he had smelled her desire, like a potent drug thickening the air, but her fury was far stronger. If she lost control of herself, it wouldn't end with her riding him like a newly broken horse...it would end with him dead.

And he found that despite her plan to turn him over to what she believed was a horrible fate...he had no similar desire to kill her. She rescued him when she thought him human, did her best to clean and heal him, and fed him when she would rather have given him the sharp end of her knife.

Of course, she'd also chained, insulted, and attacked him. But he would have his revenge. His lips curled back, bearing his teeth in a wolfish grin as he imagined the look on her face when she discovered that the very people she expected to be his downfall were, in fact, his employers.

They were headed to the same place, but it suited him well to make her work for it. So he asked, "What deal?"

Alix picked up the makeshift litter and laid it on the ground next to him, then gestured at the famous red cloak tied between thick saplings. "I will deliver you safely to the Sisters of St. Christophe. They study lycanthropy, and if what you say is true, they will be interested to hear of the way you differ from other werewolves. Let them interview you, and I will free you from these chains."

Cyrus fought back a snort. She was willing to free him from these chains only because the Sisters would use stronger ones to secure him to the wall. This bargain offered nothing but truth, twisted as it was.

But laughing in her face was likely to earn him a knife in the belly instead of a free ride to the place he was already headed. Taking her deal and seeing the shock on her face when the Sisters welcomed him would be sweet revenge for spending two days chained while she insulted him.

"Very well," he said. "I accept."

She blinked as if she'd expected more of a fight. Throwing her off balance was more enjoyable the longer they played this game. But she recovered quickly and gestured to the litter. "Good. We are agreed. Get on."

"Why not unchain me? Now that we have an accord, I'll walk."

She snorted. "No, you will run. Or attack me. I care for neither option, so get on."

"I thought we had an agreement?"

"The agreement was that I would deliver you. I never specified how. Are you breaking your word so soon?"

She was baiting him. Cyrus ground his teeth and reminded himself he was getting what he wanted. But the litter looked...rather small. Alix was tall enough, perhaps eight inches above five feet, and leanly muscled, but he was at least a head taller and twice as wide.

"I appreciate your determination," he said, "but you won't get as far as you think carrying me on that. I am heavier than I look."

She raised one dark, patronizing brow. "I know how heavy you are. Who do you think carried your unconscious carcass in here?"

No one could say he hadn't tried. With a sigh, Cyrus shifted his weight until he sat in the middle of the fabric. The wool was fine, both thick and soft, and edged with swirling embroidery of vines and leaves. It would be a shame to ruin such fabric.

He couldn't stop himself from trying one last time. "My bodyweight will rip your lovely cloak."

"Let me worry about that," she said, positioning herself between the carrying handles.

He shrugged and prepared himself to fall off, or fall through, but she lifted him with no noticeable effort and dragged him out of the cave and into the forest. He sat stiffly for several minutes, but she never dropped him, never wavered, and never stumbled despite the darkness of the early morning.

The scent of her sweat, sweet and sharp and tinged with spearmint, floated back to him, but her breathing stayed rhythmic even as the sun rose and climbed into the sky. No human, not even a well-conditioned one, could carry such weight for so long without stopping.

Canopy passed overhead in a steady, soothing flow: shifting leaves and reaching branches punctuated by patches of blue sky and the occasional bird or squirrel. Even the rhythmic footsteps and the steady drag of the sled skids on the dirt road were relaxing.

Last night, he had been weak enough to doubt his ability to do more than bargain with his captor, but as he breathed the clean air, strength and vitality flowed back into his body. The magic had finished cleaning his blood, destroying the last of the wolfsbane while he slept. He could break the chains now if he chose. But the thin silver made his captor feel safe, and he was getting a free ride in the bargain. So Cyrus lay back with his hands behind his head and dozed, wondering what manner of creature Alix was.

At least, until she dropped him. He struck the ground with a yelp and sat up to find himself in a dirt clearing off the road, the kind of pull-out travelers used to camp or stop for a meal. He swallowed back a curse, replaced the gruff tone he wanted to use with one guaranteed to annoy her, and said brightly, "Time for lunch, is it? I can catch something for us if you'd like to just—" He raised his wrists and jingled the chain enticingly.

She tossed him the water skin fast enough that it would have hit him in the face had he been a normal man.

"I'll take that as a no."

"We won't eat again until we reach the convent," she said, stretching her arms up and behind her back and groaning as she worked the soreness out of her muscles. The motion pulled her shirt tight across her chest, outlining her breasts against the straining fabric.

She groaned in pleasure, and the darkly sensual sound made him flinch in surprise, spilling water down his chin. He cursed and wiped the drops, then tossed her the skin, waiting to fix the fit of his trousers until she turned away. It hadn't been so long since he'd had intimate company that a simple groan should have made him hard, yet here he was, trying to hide the uncomfortable bulge in his pants. That was almost more infuriating than her insults.

A wagon trundled by, creaking rhythmically behind the steady clop of the donkey's hooves. A bearded elfin farmer with a floppy cap on his head sat on the bench with reins in hand. His pointed ears peeked out of a cloud of curly white hair, and he turned curious eyes on them as he passed.

A human boy of perhaps ten years rode in the back, wielding a leafy branch to protect the produce from birds. He smiled and waved, showing a pair of dimples.

"Why not ask for a ride?" Cyrus suggested as the wagon passed. "It would save you the trouble of hauling me."

"I don't want your stink to scare that poor donkey."

"Or you are afraid to answer questions about why you have an innocent man shackled."

"The day I fear a farmer is the day you can put me in the grave."

Cyrus snorted. "Only a fool doesn't fear a farmer. They are tough, smart, practical, and resilient people. Otherwise, they wouldn't be farmers long."

"Smart people do not scare me," she said as she slung the water skin over her neck and shoulder and positioned it diagonally across her torso. "Cruelty and stupidity are much greater dangers. Be glad you are not stupid, or you'd be dead."

She positioned herself, lifted the sled, and dragged him back out onto the road. They bumped along for another quarter of an hour when the report of gunfire echoed through the woods and sent the birds in the canopy scrambling for safety.

Bandits.

The farmer's wagon was the only traffic they saw on the road for hours. Highwaymen didn't always attack their victims, but if the farmer or the boy were injured, he and Alix were too far away to help.

Alix adjusted her grip on the handles of the sled and started running. What had been a comfortable and lazy ride turned into a challenge. Cyrus braced his feet against the bottom crosspiece of the travois as his stomach lurched from side to side. "Release me!"

"Now is not the time, wolf."

Why was she so damnably obstinate? "What if they are members of The Revenant? You'll need help. You can replace my bonds when the farmers are safe. I swear it."

"No."

"Then leave me and run faster. I will not move until you return."

"Shut. Up," she grunted.

Alix lowered her head and sprinted, faster than any human should have been capable of, especially when pulling over two hundred pounds. For a moment Cyrus considered rolling off the sled so she could run without a burden, but he knew she would only turn around for him.

He could break the chains now and reach the farmer's wagon in seconds but, if he did, she would think he was trying to escape and fight him. Then no one would help the farmer. Making the run easy for her was the only conscionable answer.

She was panting hard when they pulled around a bend and jerked to a stop that almost flung Cyrus from the sled. After she set the handles down, he spun to take in the scene and cursed under his breath. Sure enough, the highwaymen wore the red fingerless gloves of The Revenant.

Alix muttered, "Shit."

The notorious outlaw band stretched across Western Europe and resisted the push of civilization through sheer brutality. As a hunter who worked primarily in the untamed countryside, he'd put food in his belly more than once using the standing bounty on dead members.

They'd dragged the farmer and boy out of the cart and roughed them up enough to make them pliable, judging by the fresh bruise on the farmer's face. The terrified man dug into his pockets for coin while one member, a hulking brute wearing a black hat, pointed a pistol at his chest with one hand, and held the boy by his neck with the other.

"Please," the farmer begged, "don't hurt the boy."

With a sneer, the bandit shook the child like a rag doll, making his teeth clack together. "If you don't want him hurt, you'll pay the toll and fast."

The farmer fumbled a measly handful of coppers from his pocket, his face wracked with conflict as his eyes flicked between the boy and the bandit. "This is all I have. If you'll only wait until I sell—"

The bandit backhanded the farmer with the butt of the pistol and rage electrified his body, making Cyrus's muscles tense to spring.

One of the highwaymen dug through the cart, stomping on vegetables as he searched for other valuables, while the third monitored the road in the opposite direction. He snapped the end of a carrot off between his back teeth and said over his shoulder, "Come on, they've got nothing worthwhile. Kill the bastards and leave them."

"Stay here," Alix ordered before he could suggest simply shooting the bandits from cover.

She approached the tableau silently, leaving him screened by roadside bushes, and stood on the hard-packed dirt with her cloak thrown back and her feet braced. Both hands rested loosely on the butts of the knives sheathed on her thighs.

"Release them," she ordered. "Leave the wagon, drop everything you've stolen, and I will let you live."

Five sets of eyes snapped up and locked on the lone woman. Cyrus's muscles tensed in anticipation. Alix was clearly something more than human, but warning three men with guns was an act of suicide. Even he could be taken down with enough bullets.

"Do we kill this bitch," asked the man in the back of the wagon, "or keep her?"

If their actions hadn't already made Cyrus's blood run hot, those words would have done it. He'd seen what happened to men and women taken by The Revenant.

The bandit holding the boy said, "Kill her. She'd be too much trouble."

Alix leaped forward and the motion was so fast it was like watching a magic trick. One second she was in the center of the road, and the next she was halfway to the wagon. There was no in-between moment where she took the steps required to put her there. Cyrus had seen werewolves move that fast, but never a human.

The bandit in the back of the wagon swore and fought to dig his gun out of his pants as Alix blurred toward him. But the weapon stuck on his belt and by the time he raised it to aim, she was upon him.

The black-hat bandit raised his pistol, but he was too late to save his compatriot. Alix sprang into the bed of the wagon, pushed the gun barrel toward the sky as the bandit pulled the trigger, and buried her knife at an angle under his breastbone. She turned, dragging the body with her as a shield.

It happened so fast Cyrus hadn't even the time to consider breaking his chains to help her.

The farmer and his boy were veterans of the road and hit the ground as soon as they heard the first shot. Cyrus hoped that kept them out of danger. As Alix moved, dragging the dead body with her, she stripped the pistol from his limp hand, sighted over his shoulder, and fired on the bandit wearing the black hat.

The farmer flinched as the man hit the ground in front of them with a dull thud, legs bending the wrong way.

"Luc!" the last bandit yelled. He circled the wagon, gun trained on Alix as he squeezed off careful shots. The dead man's body twitched with each impact, but Alix held him upright with the knife planted in his chest and waited for her shot.

The woman was quick, cold, and accurate; as soon as the bandit gave her an opening, she fired. Her bullet struck the center of his forehead with a wet crunch. He stood for a moment, eyes wide in surprise as a dribble of blood trailed down the side of his nose. Once his body realized his head was no longer working, his legs crumpled, and he collapsed to the dirt like a bird struck with a stone.

The entire affair lasted perhaps five seconds.

Alix tossed the body of the dead man out of the wagon in disgust, wiped her blade clean on her pant leg, and sheathed it before hopping down. She checked the farmer and boy for injuries, but the farmer flinched away from her as if she hadn't just saved his life. He was not ungrateful, only scared.

Cyrus understood why they feared her. Alix was a magnificent predator: fast, efficient, and lethal. But those skills did not save her from emotion. She stiffened in response to their fear, and the corners of her eyes tightened in a manner that spoke of old pain, long ago accepted and endured.

The farmer offered her his coppers, but she refused the money with a gentle smile and shake of her head. As they returned to their seats in the cart, she dragged the dead bodies to the side of the road and pulled a red glove from each.

"Take this," Alix called, tossing the farmer one of the bandit's pistols. "And these." The red gloves followed. "Send the constables back for the bodies, and keep the bounty to pay for the goods they destroyed."

He caught the pistol with characteristic elfin grace, but set the weapon carefully away from himself on the bench, his face twitching with disgust. He nodded his thanks before flicking the reins.

Alix grabbed a handful of dirt, rubbed it between her palms to clean most of the blood, then brushed it off on her pants.

He was suddenly glad he had not tried to help her. If he'd snapped the chains and rushed in, she would have seen it as breaking his word and attacked him with the same ferocity. His decision not to irritate her more during their short stay in the cave proved to be wisdom of the highest order.

As it was, she strode confidently toward him, her long, dark braid swinging behind her. Her clothing clung to the curves of her body in a rather distracting manner, and her cheeks were pink from exertion.

It didn't appear to be blood lust that made her amber eyes glow, merely the heightened state of battle that made one feel more alive. She was both dangerous and compelling as hell, drawing his eye with irresistible force. At least, until she opened her mouth.

"The good boy knows how to stay," she said, bending forward to put her hands on her knees as if talking to a dog. "Do you want a treat, good boy?"

"You might want to be a bit nicer to me, minx," he warned.

"Really? Why is that?"

"Because you've been shot, and I'm the only one left to help you.

6

Alix

SHE LOOKED DOWN AT her torso. Two holes marred the dark fabric, which was already wet and clinging to her skin; one was high on her chest, below her left collarbone, and the other was low on her right side, just above the hollow of her hip bone.

The bullets must have traveled through the dead body and passed into her.

"Dammit." She turned and asked over her shoulder, "Are there exit wounds?"

"I will tell you that on one condition."

"The condition is that I let you live."

"The condition," Cyrus said, "is that you let me treat your wounds."

She snorted. "You are in no position to be making bargains."

As if she could trust the word of a werewolf? That was precisely why she'd left him in chains. The bargain she offered was meant to keep him docile for easy transportation, not give him freedom.

"And you're in no position to turn them down, unless you would prefer bleeding to death."

Alix would not bleed to death, but she couldn't tell him that. He might be rare as a werewolf with some self-control, but even he wouldn't guess that a half-vampire was roaming about the wilds of France, saving farmers from bandits and killing the monsters that preyed on mortals.

Her kind was a myth, a legend cooked up by frightened peasants. In three hundred years, she'd never met anyone else like her. And if she wanted to protect her anonymity, she must keep it that way.

Vampires were even more feared and hated than werewolves, and when the time came for pitchforks and torches, no one would care that she was merely half. Keeping her secret outside the convent had become second nature, and with so many monsters in the world, it wasn't hard to let people draw the wrong conclusions.

But Cyrus had already been too close for too long. And with senses as acute as his, letting him operate on her was a terrible idea. Of course, he would shortly be in the care of the Sisters, which meant he'd never leave the convent again. What did it matter, then, if he knew what she was? He'd already seen enough to know she wasn't human.

But the thought of this monster knowing about the blood running through her veins made her guts twist in dismay.

"I'll wait for the next traveler," she said.

"That wagon was the only other traffic we have seen since this morning. How long do you think you have?"

"Fine," she said, "Fine. We are agreed, you may treat them. Are there exit wounds?"

"No."

She closed her eyes for a moment and took a deep breath. That meant he would have to remove the bullets. Superhuman healing abilities did not make her immortal. Leaving a bullet inside one's body was never a good idea if it could be helped. And while the pain was manageable now thanks to the energy of battle, that would change quickly when he started digging about inside of her...particularly if he wasn't gentle.

She would also be wounded, vulnerable prey to his werewolf senses, and putting herself in that position would be idiocy of the worst sort.

"Get on the sled," she said as she walked around to position herself between the pull bars.

"You shouldn't be pulling–"

"Shut up and get on the sled! God's breath, you are contrary. I'll pull you to somewhere safer for this farce of a surgery."

"If you unshackle me, I can walk there."

"That was not part of the arrangement."

He gritted his teeth and scooted back onto the cloak, bracing his feet against the crossbar at the bottom. Alix set her shoulders and pulled, ignoring the first threads of pain radiating from the bullet holes as her muscles took up the stress of Cyrus's weight.

Clean, boiling water was required for surgery, and if she remembered correctly, a stream flowed nearby. An infection could not kill her, but her body took longer to heal from infections than it did from wounds. Being laid up with a fever for several hours or, heaven forbid, several days, was not a luxury she could afford.

"We are close to water," the wolf said.

"Where do you think I am dragging your heavy carcass?"

A stream, perhaps four feet wide, tumbled down a pair of mossy banks beneath a huge weeping willow. Alix dragged the sled to a flat spot near the roots of the tree, dropped it with a satisfying thud, opened her pack, and pulled out supplies.

Thanks to her father's immortal blood, Alix healed several times faster than humans, elves, or dwarves. The recent werewolf bite on her forearm healed in less than an hour. And a few hundred years of life taught her to ignore pain when it could be ignored, and cope with it when it could not. As a result, she rarely carried medical supplies, and certainly not the kind needed to fish bullets out of her muscles.

Which meant that this would hurt.

Cyrus watched as she grabbed dry twigs and leaves, filled her travel pot with water from the creek, and started a small fire. His steady regard made her skin hot and the hairs rise on the back of her neck. So she took a fallen branch as thick as her arm and jammed it a foot into the ground, drew her pistol, and said, "Hold out your wrists."

"Why?"

"Because I told you to."

He glanced between her eyes and the pistol, then snorted and held out his wrists, glaring at her as she secured him to the stake. It wouldn't stop him if he decided to attack her, but it would slow him down long enough for her to shoot him.

With that accomplished, she went back to preparation for surgery, creating a sort of tripod with three oblong river rocks, and balanced the pot atop them over the flames.

Cyrus's voice sounded very reasonable when he said, "I could help, you know."

"What happened in the last two days to make you think I trust you?"

"Have I done anything to earn your distrust?"

"You have done nothing to earn it," she countered.

"How can I, when you have me tied up like a common criminal?"

"Why do you care to try?"

He threw his hands in the air, or tried to, but since they were still chained to the post, the gesture looked ridiculous. "Perhaps I don't want to see you die."

"Doubtful."

"You agreed to let me treat your wounds."

"So I did," she said as she peeled a springy green twig, then split it up the middle, stopping about an inch from the end. "But I never said how much."

He growled; actually growled, and not in a frustrated human way, but in an angry werewolf way that made her want to grab her pistols. But instead of lunging at her, he demanded, "Do you want to die?"

Alix stuffed a smaller piece of wood between the tongs she'd just cut, then bound the end and the crosspiece with a bit of twine. The result was a serviceable pair of tweezers that, she hoped, were long enough to reach the bullets.

They had almost no grip compared to their metal counterparts but were better than using her fingers, so they would have to do. After a quick sanitization in the boiling water, they were ready to use.

"You made a promise, minx," Cyrus said.

"You can bind the wounds after I dig the bullets out," she told him, then stood and wiggled out of her pants.

He made a choking noise. "Why are you taking off your trousers?"

"Because I only have one pair left, and I don't want to bleed all over them. Be quiet and let me focus."

"You agreed to let me treat your wounds, not lie on my back while you further injure yourself. What about keeping your word?"

"I am keeping it," she said as she lay back, using her pack as a backrest so she had the proper view of the small entrance wound just above and inside her hip bone. "I said I would let you treat my wounds. I never said how. It's not my fault if you are terrible at negotiating. Next time, make clearer expectations."

Cyrus made more growling sounds, but she ignored him and pressed on the flesh around the wound, hoping to feel a lump somewhere beneath. It hurt, but after a moment, something hard and pea-sized shifted an inch or so beneath her skin. That wasn't as bad as she expected. The bullet must have lost quite a bit of velocity before it hit her.

Alix positioned herself, readied the tweezers, double-checked the location of the bullet, and plunged the tip into the bullet hole.

She bared her teeth against the pain and tried to pinch the ball between the tips of the makeshift tweezers. There it was. She had it. Fresh blood oozed from the wound, making it hard to see, so she focused on the feeling, letting the pain make her senses sharp.

The metal was misshapen from its journey through a body and a half, and fit awkwardly between the carved wood. But she had it. She just had to pull—the bullet slipped to the side. She lost it.

Growling in frustration, Alix wiped the sweat from her brow with the back of her forearm, dabbed away the blood with a clean cloth, and readied herself to try again. The effort was making her dizzy, and every time she gripped the bullet, it slipped from between the smooth wooden ends of the tweezers.

She fell back against the pack and pulled in deep breaths, promising herself never to travel without standard medical equipment again.

"Alix," Cyrus said in a low, persuasive voice. "Let me help you. You can hold one of those silver daggers to my throat if you like, but this is pure stupidity."

She eyed the wolf. He squatted where she'd chained him with his elbows on his knees, as if he was just waiting for an excuse to break the chains and lunge. If he got close enough to extract the bullet, he'd also be close enough to figure out her secret.

Close enough to kill her.

Alix rolled onto her side, unsheathed a dagger, set it on the ground within easy reach, and said, "You'll stay where you are if you want to live long enough to see the next sunrise."

The wolf swore, muttering something about incompetent idiots, but she ignored him and readied herself for another attempt. She could do this. Once the tweezers were sanitized with boiling water again, she dried them and started digging.

Blood oozed and tissue swelled as her body attempted to protect itself from invasion. The muscle fibers healed so fast that she had to tear them to make the bullet accessible, but finding it was getting harder. Every movement made the pain burn hotter. Her vision swam and her breath came in great gasps as her body tried to shut down to heal.

She'd gone too long without sleep or enough food, and after the exertion of the last two days, the bullet wounds tipped the scale. A frustrated mewl of pain escaped as she fumbled the tweezers.

"Son of a bitch," Cyrus growled.

Then he leaped and the silver snapped with a metallic *ping*.

He was faster than he should have been, far faster than she expected, and pain and exhaustion made her too slow to react. Mind fuzzy, she reached for her dagger as she thought, *he shouldn't be able to do that*.

He landed on her before she could raise the knife, sitting on her thighs and trapping her legs with his own as both big hands pressed her shoulders down.

"Your leg is spasming," he said, in the voice an angry father might use with a willful child. "It is causing your stomach muscles to clench and shift. That's why you keep losing the bullet. Be still and I will remove it."

Alix had been too groggy to react before he sprang, but she was fast enough to jerk the silver dagger up and jab the tip into his skin just below his breastbone. It sank in a quarter of an inch, but he did not flinch.

Instead, he leaned down, forcing the blade further in, and said, "You can stab me if you like, but I am going to remove these bullets."

A simple twist of her arm could kill him, but the pulse beating in the hollow of his throat was strangely compelling, and as her mind drifted from reality, she found herself staring inexplicably at the line of his jaw where the muscle tightened as he concentrated.

He still stank of wolf, but also grass and sharp sweat, and the way his thighs flexed against her legs was...distracting.

Cyrus frowned as he prodded the edges of the bullet hole with his fingertips. "You've damaged yourself even worse than if you'd just left the bullet inside."

"I had to hurry or the skin would have healed over the bullet," she murmured.

His head snapped up, eyes locking on her face. They were very green, his eyes, like sunlight on grass, surrounded by long golden lashes. Men always had long lashes, which was ridiculously unfair. Weren't women supposed to be the fairer sex? What right did this wolf have to be so beautiful?

His fingers pressed harder. Fiery sparks of pain shot outward from the injury and she winced, turning the blade in warning, but he ignored the pain, licked his full lips, and fastened his mouth over the wound.

Alix's body and mind froze. She hadn't expected the wolf to try sucking the bullet out. His hair spilled across her bare stomach, silky and cool. But his mouth was hot and the fresh beard growth on his chin scratched as he pressed down on the edges of the wound with his fingers and drew on it with a deep sucking motion of his lips and tongue.

In an insane moment of tingling pleasure mixed with pain, Alix's back arched, and the bullet popped free. Cyrus leaned back with the metal clamped between his white teeth, her blood on his lips and chin. A single drop slid down the column of his throat and into the hollow beneath his shirt.

Alix watched, transfixed, as he spat the metal into the dirt, casually knocked the dagger from her grip, and shifted to get a look at the wound on her chest. He gripped her shirt in both hands and tore the fabric to expose the hole. The dagger fell from her fingers as if in slow motion.

She ought to catch it, but couldn't think of why.

Cyrus spat and wiped her blood from his lips with the back of his hand as he examined the second injury. "This one is deeper, and you're going into shock," he said, then swiped her dagger off the ground and plunged the tip into the boiling water. "I need to be fast. Try not to move."

Before she could respond, there was a burning pain in her chest. She groaned through gritted teeth and fought to stay still despite feeling as if she was sinking into deep, warm water.

"There," he grunted, holding something small and bloody between his fingers for a moment before tossing it away in disgust.

Her head rolled back, too heavy to lift, as her body took over and cannibalized all of her energy to heal itself. She was powerless to stop it or protect herself from the werewolf looming over her. His angry face was probably the last thing she would ever see.

7

Cyrus

She fainted.

He was free. He could lope into the woods and never worry about being chained, again...so long as he was willing to leave the unconscious woman on the ground, bleeding and alone by the stream.

She had held him hostage, was foul-mouthed, stubborn, prejudiced, and suspicious. She also intended to turn him over for experimentation.

Leaving her would be the smart thing to do.

But she'd also thrown herself into danger to help strangers and killed two werewolves to save a priest. She cared for him when she thought him a man and fed him even when she claimed she would rather have let him starve. No matter how he felt about her, she deserved to live.

Even if that meant she would only try to hunt him down, again. Even if her blood was too light and sweet to be strictly human. Besides, she was working for the Sister as well, and if one hunter could not trust another, his profession was in a sorry state.

With a resigned sigh over his own idiocy, Cyrus bound her wounds in strips of the cleanest cloth he could find, wrapped her in the cloak, and used a fallen log to elevate her feet. Moving her wasn't a good idea until she recovered from the shock...*if* she recovered.

But as he examined her, he realized she hadn't lost much blood, her wounds were shallow, and her heartbeat was strong. Why had she gone into shock in the first place? Perhaps her body was reacting to something he did not understand or could not see.

That left him two choices: he could either monitor her here and hope she recovered on her own, or risk moving her to find help. If she wasn't purely human, human treatments may not do her any good.

Either way, he could do nothing for her by the bank of a stream. If he remembered correctly, the convent wasn't that far away, so Cyrus packed her bag, loosened the straps to slide on over his shoulders, and lifted her limp body. Time to find help.

Unlike humans, who used to rely on the sun and stars and now relied on maps and compasses, Cyrus had an infallible sense of direction. He oriented himself toward the convent, looked into the pale, clammy face of the woman who would have preferred him dead, and ran, calling on his wolf for speed.

He was fast, but the convent was nearly twenty miles away if he remembered correctly, and he wasn't certain she would last the two hours he needed to cover that distance. He could have made it in half that time as a wolf, but dragging Alix on the sled would have bounced her about dangerously. She was already as heavy and limp as a dead body and, though she was still breathing, her heartbeat had slowed significantly.

How had she gone from being so violently alive to the edge of death in a matter of minutes? When he saw her proud, fierce expression melt into dazed confusion, his stomach sank with sick fear. It was like watching a tiger prowl back and forth in a small cage at the zoo instead of slinking through the jungle. Whether or not one liked the tiger, imprisoning it felt wrong. And it was partly his fault.

If he had stepped in during the fight, he might have saved her. Instead, his poor judgment resulted in another failure, another person hurt because he made the wrong call, and struck the wrong balance between man's logic and wolf's instincts.

That was why he avoided getting deeply involved with people, as a rule. He could not stop himself from caring, and caring came with heavy consequences. Every time he failed or made a mistake it was catastrophic. Visions of his village, of his brother's broken body, flashed across his mind like a lightning bolt, nearly making him stumble over an exposed tree root.

For such an old wound, the memory was still painfully tender. He couldn't let this woman die, too. He pushed the memory out of his mind, double-checked his patient's condition, and pushed himself faster.

Her olive skin had gone a sickly shade of grey that made his stomach muscles clench.

Why he should care about keeping this woman alive didn't bear examining, not when keeping himself breathing steadily required all of his concentration.

Heart pounding heart, lungs sawing, Cyrus covered the miles in a blur of passing trees and shocked travelers who weren't quite certain what they had just seen. Alix was heavier than she looked, and his muscles burned as he pushed them to the edge of exertion.

The winding forest path forked, and Cyrus followed it to the right, where it widened and slowly became busier. Wagon ruts cut deep by years of heavy loads made for dangerous obstacles and soon forced him to slow enough that his fellow travelers recognized what passed them on the side of the road.

Sweat ran from his forehead in rivulets, and calls of, "Do you need help?" followed him around nearly every bend. If they did not reach the convent soon, he was going to need a break, and from the look of death on Alix's face, she didn't have time to spare. If the woman died on him after all of this trouble, he would kill her.

At last, the sound of bells echoing through the forest made his heart give a painful lurch of relief. He put his head down and pushed himself for whatever speed he had left. The walls of the convent of the Sisters of St. Christophe came into view through the trees, grey stone weathered by time and covered with moss and clinging vines.

Relief washed over him. He'd made it, and Alix was still alive.

He stumbled to a stop before the old double door and kicked the wood with his boot, panting and using his shoulder to rub the stinging sweat out of his eyes. A moment later, a panel slid open and the beatific face of a nun appeared. Her eyes widened as she looked at Cyrus, then at the burden in his arms, and slid the panel closed with a snap.

Several clicking and clinking sounds came muffled through the door before it swung open and a woman in a brown habit said, "Come, come, bring her this way."

He followed her through a courtyard, past a flock of chickens scratching about in the dirt, and toward the longest of the buildings. To an unsuspecting eye, this convent looked like every other: tidy, relatively poor, and full of women doing the chores of daily life between prayers.

Only, the Sisters of St. Christophe were anything but ordinary, and they certainly weren't poor. A series of very wealthy, very secretive benefactors had a distinct interest in funding research of the supernatural, and no one was better or more secretive than the Sisters. They specialized in the monsters of Western Europe, with particular emphasis on one of the most dangerous and prolific: werewolves.

This meant that the simple-looking infirmary they entered was out-fitted as well as any hospital in Europe. Several older, more experienced nuns who acted as nurses, saw to their patients at the back of the building where large windows let in light and fresh air.

"Sister Mary Thérèse!" his guide called, "It's Alix!"

A mature woman, perhaps somewhere in her mid-seventies, appeared from the back room wiping her hands on the skirt of the white apron that covered most of her habit. Her iron-grey hair was pulled back in a tight bun, and she walked with all the grace of a falling tree. But there was an air of competence about the woman that made Cyrus grateful she was in charge.

"Put her down, here, carefully," she ordered.

He slid Alix onto the table, then flexed his arms to force blood back into his hands. Sister Mary Thérèse didn't give him a second glance. She began her examination, pressing her fingers against the pulse beneath the corner of Alix's jaw and asking in a deep, businesslike voice, "Who are you?"

"Cyrus. The Mother–"

She cut him off by raising one hand and saying, "That's enough, I know who you are. What happened to her?"

Cyrus explained the events of the afternoon.

The sister snorted in disgust as if mere bullets should not have caused such a response. "She captured you, you say?"

He couldn't quite hide the embarrassed tone in his voice when he replied, "In a manner of speaking."

"How long were you together before this robbery?"

"Two nights."

"Did she sleep during that time?"

"I assume she must have."

"Did you witness her sleep?"

He thought about it. "No, I suppose not. But I was busy healing."

"From?"

"A knife wound."

"Silver?"

"Yes, coated in aconite."

She chuckled, which seemed rather inconsiderate, and asked, "Did Alix do that to you?"

"Yes."

"Hmm. And after she was wounded, what did you do?"

"I removed the bullets and treated her wounds."

One grey brow raised. "How did you remove them?"

His cheeks heated. "I removed one with a makeshift pair of wooden tweezers, and I–sucked the other one out."

Her hands stilled, and she turned to regard him with an impassive face that made him more nervous than her anger or incredulity might have.

"Did you just say, *sucked it out?*"

"It was very shallow," he said in his own defense.

"Do you have these tweezers?"

Relieved not to be discussing the sucking of bullets, he opened the pack, pulled out the tweezers and handed them to her. She turned them over in her hand, sniffed the wood, and picked at it with one clean fingernail.

Cyrus interrupted her examination of the crude tool and said, "Shouldn't you be helping her?"

"They are rather large but this isn't bad work for an emergency," the nun said, then stopped and looked up at him. "I'm sorry, what?"

"Shouldn't you be helping her?"

"Oh, she will be fine."

"What do you mean she will be fine? She's in shock, she should have been dead an hour ago!"

Sister Mary Thérèse paused and eyed him. "I see. Well, if Alix has not seen fit to explain, it is certainly not my place to do it for her. Come along."

The sister turned to lead him out of the infirmary, but he folded his arms and planted his feet. He wasn't leaving until someone did something. He hadn't just run the woman twenty miles to watch her die while help stood by and did nothing. "Since when are the Sisters so unmerciful to the wounded?"

Mary Thérèse turned on him slowly. "Pardon me?"

"You have done nothing to help her, and she is in shock. By the moon, simply look at her skin!"

She raised a single eyebrow and put her hands on her ample hips. "Are you questioning my ability to do my job?"

"No, but I–"

"Alix will be fine. I have known and treated her for years. You can trust me in this."

When Cyrus still didn't move, she rolled her eyes and said, "Mary Sofia, will you watch over Alix, please?"

A stocky nun with red hair and round cheeks left her patient sitting up and eating in the back of the infirmary and hurried to the front. "Of course, of course," she said, flapping her hands at them. "I will watch over her."

Cyrus followed Sister Mary Thérèse from the infirmary knowing there was nothing else he could do but still feeling reluctant to leave.

Mary Thérèse gave him a sly look as they crossed the courtyard. "So, Alix captured you, in a manner of speaking, eh? What was this manner?"

"She found me healing," he admitted. "The fight was closer than it should have been."

"You said she cut you."

"Aye, with a poisoned blade."

"She always was a clever girl. Well," she leaned toward him and said in a conspiratorial tone, "don't tell anyone else she snapped you up so easily, or it will ruin your reputation."

He snorted. Being poisoned by both silver and wolfsbane would have killed other werewolves, but she already knew that, so he said, "I haven't got a reputation worth protecting, Sister."

She patted his arm and made a *tsking* noise. "That is probably best, in your line of work. I take it Alix does not know who you are? No, of course not, or she would not have attacked you. Then again—" She tilted her head to the side as she reconsidered. "Perhaps she would, at that."

The second building they entered was as plain and spartan as the infirmary, but equally well-made and appointed. Sister Mary Thérèse led him to the guest wing and unlocked the door to his cell. Everything was in its place, neat and clean.

A bed, table, and chair were the only furniture in the room, and if one were to give a cursory glance at the furnishings, one would think them as humble as they appeared. But the beds were solidly made of good quality wood, the mattresses were stuffed and well-sprung, and the wool blankets were of the finest quality, soft and supple.

The only thing that was not in its place was Mother Superior, who sat on the bed with her hands folded, her homely face beatific and solemn.

"I see you have arrived in one piece," she said.

"It was a close thing."

She narrowed her eyes at him. "I see that, too. Thank you for answering my summons."

"The Sisters of St. Christophe confirmed my appointment," he said. "It was the least I could do."

The Mother nodded and stood. "I am grateful my predecessors were wiser than their contemporaries. We have great need of you now."

"I was intrigued by your request. What can you tell me?"

"You need rest," she said, placing an affectionate hand on his shoulder. "And I would rather explain the circumstances only once. When I introduce you to your partner will be soon enough for details."

He frowned and folded his arms. Partners were dangerous, especially for the likes of him. Alix proved that. Even more cosmopolitan hunters were uncomfortable with the idea of partnering with a child of the moon. That made protecting the secret of his blood much more difficult.

"Your letter said nothing of a partner," he said.

"The situation has worsened since I sent it. And she was out of the country."

Alarm made him take an involuntary step back. She couldn't be serious, and yet he was terribly afraid she was. "She?"

The woman had the gall to give him a gently amused smile. "Yes. In fact, I believe you've met her."

8

Alix

"Pay them no mind, my love," Maman said as she crouched and brushed Alix's hair out of her eyes. It had come loose from her braids again and hung in long strands outside the careful confines of her red hood. "Country folk are superstitious, that's all."

"But why are they only superstish–superstitious about me?"

Maman made sure the hood of Alix's cloak still shaded her face from the sun, then took her hand and resumed their walk through the village. "People fear things they do not understand, and they have never met someone who must always wear a hood."

"Everybody gets sunburned, sometimes," Alix muttered, glancing back over her shoulder at the angry woman who had kicked her and Maman out of the shop.

"That is true," Maman agreed. "But not everyone gets sunburned so easily as you do, or as badly."

Alix sighed and her stomach growled. "Will I grow out of it, as I grew out of my milk teeth?"

"Maybe. Some people do grow out of such things. Did you know my hair was as yellow as a dandelion when I was your age?"

Alix considered the wealth of Maman's dark hair, braided down her back past her waist, and decided that the yellow hair was just another story she told to make her daughter feel better. It didn't work, but she would never tell Maman that.

"Maybe if you let me stay home," Alix said, repeating the same argument they had just that morning, "the people would let you shop in the village. And then we wouldn't be so hungry all the time."

Maman did not answer.

Alix jerked upright with a start, hands flashing to the small of her back, but her blades were gone. Instead, she felt a thick bandage of some sort. Her eyes flew around the room as she rolled into a defensive crouch, prepared to spring in any direction.

"There you are, my girl. I wondered how long you would sleep. How do you feel?"

The familiar, low, husky voice had the same calming effect as a shot of whiskey. Alix's muscles relaxed, and she turned to see Sister Mary Thérèse standing from a nearby chair, a smile in her eyes if not on her face.

She was at the convent? How?

"Groggy," Alix said. She swung her legs out and sat on the edge of the bed. "And confused."

"Shall I have a bit of blood brought in for you?"

"No need. How did I get here?"

Sister Mary Thérèse smiled and hooked a thumb in the direction of the door. "That wolf carried you in. At a run, no less."

Alix blinked, startled. With a frown, she thought back over the past day, swimming through a fog of sleepy memories. One hit her hard enough to make her teeth clench: Cyrus leaning over her with a bullet between his teeth and her blood on his lips and chin. He brought her here?

"Why?"

"He was concerned for you," the sister said, amusement roughening the edges of her voice.

"I doubt that."

"I do not. Here, let me look at you." Sister Mary Thérèse examined her eyes, her gums, and checked her pulse. "You should have some blood."

"I don't want any."

"Oh yes, you do. It will make you feel better."

"Sister–"

"And what were you thinking, anyway, to go so long without proper food and sleep? It is no wonder your body shut down. You are only lucky that wolf has a conscience."

What had Alix been thinking? That staying alive and keeping the unusual wolf contained was worth losing a few nights of sleep she didn't need. Of course, she had not factored in the intensity of the fight and the grief of failing Père Henri, nor being shot. She had only eaten enough during their stay in the cave to keep the worst of the hunger at bay because she did not trust leaving the wolf alone long enough to hunt for anything bigger than rabbits.

"Sister Mary Thomas?" Mary Thérèse called.

A short, plump woman with salt and pepper hair popped her head above the edge of the bed she had been making. "Yes, Sister?"

"Will you fetch Alix a cup of goat's blood? She is still feeling poorly."

Alix sighed and lay back on the bed. It was useless to argue with Mary Thérèse.

"We will need the fresh meat anyway, now that the wolf is here," the older woman reasoned. That was true. They could not study the creature if he starved to death. Still, it was impossible to picture him carrying her here, to the one place he should want to avoid at all costs. Especially not when he could have used her death to free himself.

The sisters were indirectly responsible for the death of more werewolves than almost any other society in Europe, and Alix was their most capable blade. He would be a fool to come here, and an even bigger fool to bring her willingly.

"How did you manage to contain him?" Alix asked. Cyrus was a large man and an even bigger werewolf. The Sisters of St. Christophe had many ingenious gadgets, but combat was not their specialty.

"Oh, nothing could be simpler," Sister Mary Thérèse said. "I simply asked him to stay."

Alix glared at the old woman, unsure whether she was being teased. But the scent of fresh blood suddenly lit up the room like a lightning strike, and Alix's head spun with desire.

She hated the smell, hated the way it made her mouth water and her throat feel like it had been dry for a thousand years. More than anything else, she hated the way it made her feel like a monster. So, she rarely drank blood, preferring instead to subsist on human food, which worked well enough, unless she pushed herself to the limit of her endurance for too long.

Not enough rest, too much healing, too long without sleep, and then the bullet wounds... It was no wonder she was weak, hollow, and shaky. She should have known better, but it had been a long, long time since so many extraordinary things happened all at once.

Sister Mary Thomas offered her a shy little smile as she handed her a stout wooden mug, then retreated.

"Drink up, girl," Sister Mary Thérèse said.

She persisted in calling Alix 'girl' despite being younger than her patient by a couple of hundred years. But it was nice to feel looked after and fussed over, so Alix pressed the cup to her lips.

The blood made every one of her senses come to life with painful clarity; the light was too bright, almost burning, and each sound might as well have been screamed in her ears. Even the scents in the room—lavender, lye, wood oil, beeswax, cotton, chicken shit tracked in by a careless boot—were almost overpowering.

But the dull headache disappeared, the soreness drained away from her muscles, and she felt as if she had slept for three days.

"There we are, right as rain," Sister Mary Thérèse said when Alix lowered the mug. "Your color is back to normal already. Now, your pack and what supplies the wolf rescued are on that bed, just there. Get yourself cleaned up. Mother Superior will call for you before long. You know where the baths are."

Of course she did. Alix had been using the bathhouse of the Sisters of St. Christophe's Convent since they were first built. Like a dutiful child, she gathered up a novice's robe, took a towel from the linen closet, and crossed the courtyard to the bathhouse with her dirty clothes in hand. She kept to the shadows without thinking, avoiding the beams of late afternoon sunlight that broke through the canopy outside the convent walls.

While she no longer burned on mere contact, like she had as a child, years of habit made hiding from the sun an almost unconscious act. She did burn faster than normal humans, and those burns were often more painful and slower to heal than any other wound she suffered. Since her cloak was too dirty to protect her, she crept from shadow to shadow until she was safely beneath the roof of the fragrant bathhouse.

The sisters made their soap of lavender and hyssop, and the scent lingered in every crevice, mixed with the mineral tang of the hot spring over which the house was built. Alix stripped, dropped her dirty clothes into the wash bucket, and stepped down into the steaming water wearing nothing but the simple silver chain and ruby teardrop pendant her mother had given her as a child.

She lifted a soap cake from the bench, lathered up, and luxuriated in the first full bath she'd had in weeks. Afterward, she dressed in novice's robes and carried her clothes to the hot end of the pool, which was the perfect temperature for laundering, crouched next to a novice who was scrubbing aprons, and got to work.

With her clothes hung on the drying lines, she sat on a large rock under her favorite plum tree to brush her hair and let the lingering warmth in the air dry the long strands. The convent was the closest thing Alix had to a home and the only place she had ever felt truly at ease. Unlike the towns she passed through or worked in, everyone in the convent knew what she was, and none of them feared her. Nowhere else in the world could she lay under a tree with her hair spread in the grass and let her mind wander peacefully.

About an hour later, a light tread on the grass made Alix open her eyes from a comfortable doze. The footsteps were confident but soft, favoring the right leg, and the scent of paper, ink, and leather floated toward her.

"Sister Mary Paul," Alix said without looking at the woman. "How are you?"

"How did you know? I changed my gait, this time."

Alix smiled and rolled over to watch the small elf woman approach. She had rich brown skin and delicately pointed ears that peeked between strands of long braids kept tied back. The novice uniform was several sizes too big for her and stayed on her slender frame only with several belts and ties. Ink stained her fingers, and she carried a book in her right hand.

"It was your scent," Alix admitted. "You always smell of libraries."

Mary Paul raised her hands in defeat. "Well, I cannot change that, so I suppose I shall never fool you. Unless I spend all day with Sister Mary Matthew in the Kitchens. Would lard and lemon throw off your senses?"

"No way to know unless you try, I suppose."

"I shall take it under advisement," she said with a smile. "You know why I'm here?"

"Mother Superior sent for me?"

Mary Paul bobbed a little nod. "When you're done getting orders, come visit me. I have a few things you might find interesting."

The office of the Mother Superior of the Sisters of St. Christophe was located in the central tower of the convent that had been a bell tower some hundred years ago. The woman liked high positions from which to stare down at the world. Her clothing had not had time to dry, so Alix knocked on the thick wooden door still wearing novice's robes.

"Come."

Alix pushed the heavy door open and froze. Mother Superior was an imposing woman, tall, with wide shoulders and broad hands. Her nose had been broken at some point, and she had a slight underbite that made her stubborn jaw even more prominent. Everything in the office was neat, organized, and scrupulously clean...except for the werewolf sitting in one of two chairs before the Mother's desk.

Cyrus turned to watch her, one corner of his mouth quirked in amusement. Her blood had been on his lips not twenty-four hours ago.

"Alix, if you cannot control yourself, tell me now," Mother Superior said in her incongruously airy voice. "I don't wish to replace any more door handles or furniture."

Alix released the handle, leaving dents in the metal.

"What is he doing here? Mother, you realize–"

"Of course, I know what he is. Do not be tiresome. Either come in and shut the door or leave."

Turning around and slamming the door behind herself was tempting. "That creature should be in a cell, not in your office."

"That's a fine way to thank someone who saved your life," Cyrus said.

Alix started to snarl a reply, but Mother Superior stood up and cleared her throat, then spoke directly to Alix's mind. *Three hundred years and you still have not learned to control that temper? Alix, the Convent of the Sisters of St. Christophe has been a haven for you since you were a girl. Do not disrespect it now. Trust me as you have trusted me in the past. This mission is, perhaps, the most important mission we have ever assigned, and no one is suited for it as you are. But if you cannot control yourself, I will ask you to leave.*

The mother's gift of speaking to the minds of others was handy for one who wanted to convey secret information, but it was also far more convincing than conventional speech. It seemed to reach down into her and pull on every emotional lever in her chest.

Alix gritted her teeth, closed the door with every bit of self-control she could muster, pulled the extra chair as far from the wolf as possible, and sat on the edge so she might be ready to spring into action at any moment.

Mother Superior was not a foolish woman, but she did not know what this wolf was capable of. He must have broken silver chains to bring her here, because that was the only way he could have carried her.

Any werewolf who could not only abide the touch of silver but break it at will was something to be feared, even by one who killed as many monsters as Alix had. It was probably not a good idea to leave him alone with the Mother. So Alix forced herself to stay and listen.

"Now, children, if we can focus on the task at hand? Good. I regret the two of you met under such circumstances. Things may have progressed more smoothly if I had the chance to introduce you to one another first. Alas, here we are."

Alix doubted anything she could say would make her acquaintance with a monster any more bearable, but she kept her mouth stubbornly shut.

"In the hopes that it may still do some good," Mother Superior continued, "allow me to introduce you. Cyrus, this is Alix La Rouge. She is our very best hunter and has worked for the Sisters of St. Christophe countless times. I trust her *explicitly*." She gave Alix a warning glance. "And I commend her to you with the highest esteem."

Alix kept her eyes locked forward, though she felt the wolf's regard like heat on the side of her face.

"Alix, this is Cyrus Campbell. He is also a hunter and a member of an ancient and pure line. His people stretch back millennia, and he is one of the last. He has worked with our sister convents and other organizations for over two hundred years, and"—she narrowed her eyes at Alix—"his record is spotless."

Alix blinked, her mind whirling. "What? What does this mean, a pure line? There are no *lines* of werewolves, only those unfortunate enough to turn after an attack, and those who choose to bind themselves to malevolent powers."

"You are mistaken," Cyrus said, speaking before the mother could respond.

"Like hell I am."

9

Cyrus

A MORE PIGHEADED, SHORTSIGHTED, foul-tempered woman had never been born. Cyrus ground his teeth as she glared at him with her arms folded over her chest and her nostrils flared, probably imagining gutting him on the floor before the Mother Superior's eyes.

He was a fool to save such a resentful woman. He should have left her in the woods.

"I would not ask this of either of you if the matter were not of the gravest importance," the Mother Superior said, drawing their attention. "So allow me to lay the case before you. Several months ago, we received reports of a deeply concerning nature: werewolves ravaging whole towns in packs.

"Of course we doubted such claims at first, they were simply too outlandish. Werewolves are solitary creatures by necessity. We assumed the reports were superstition or misunderstanding. Until survivors appeared to tell their stories."

"The werewolves I encountered were also resistant to silver," Alix said.

Mother Superior nodded gravely. "This further confirms the accounts I have heard. Cyrus, I know you will not like to hear this, but I can see only two possibilities."

"My people would never commit such acts, sister," he reassured her.

In truth, not enough of his extended family was left to be considered a pack, and the last he knew, they were spread from the Scottish Highlands to East Asia.

Alix snorted, and he restrained the impulse to snap at her. His family had been very careful to keep knowledge of their existence contained, particularly as their numbers dwindled while the monsters thrived, so it wasn't surprising she did not know of the True Born.

Even the Mother Superior could not share knowledge of his family without explicit permission...which he was beginning to regret giving her. But if they were going to work together, Alix's hostile suspicion was a thorn he had to remove from his shoe.

"Is there any chance another family might have given way to the darkness?" the nun asked.

He frowned. "There aren't many families left. While I would like to say no...I cannot guarantee it."

She nodded, seeming to understand how much that admission cost him, and steepled her fingers on the desk. "Then we cannot rule it out. I do not know which is worse, a corrupted family or someone tampering with the infected. I cannot imagine how anyone might manage such a thing. We have been searching for a cure for hundreds of years, and even we have no luck driving out the magic or changing it without killing the host."

"Families? The infected? Mother, why do you draw such distinctions? Werewolves are only made through magical infection. Whether by being savaged, or inviting the magic, the mechanism is the same. Is this to save his feelings? Because I can guarantee you, he has none."

Cyrus flexed his hands, imagining wrapping them round her throat. That would shut her up.

The mother said, "Do you truly believe me misguided, Alix? That I could lead the Sisters of St. Christophe for five hundred years and not understand the nature of the enemy?"

"I believe that if such a thing were true, I would know of it."

"Not even I know all the secrets of this world," the nun said in a firm voice. "Be honest. Had you known, would that have stopped you from hunting the True Born?"

Alix clenched her jaw and a spike of anger pounded into Cyrus's chest. No doubt the woman had killed her fair share of True Born in her long career. Members of his blood likely died with her accusing eyes as their last sight.

Memories forced their way to the front of his mind. He saw his brother, just a bairn wrapped in swaddling, as their mother held him up, an offering to the moon and a promise of protection for the future. He had wriggled like a fresh caught trout until he freed his wee fist and waved it in the air. "We are those who partner with the magic," he said, almost without realizing he was speaking. "Who train for the burden, who give ourselves as a sacrifice to protect kith and kin. We are the True Born children of the moon, tied to her by the blood of our ancestors and offered as babes. We are chosen to live with her magic until our service is ended.

"The monsters you hate are twisted by the magic and their own selfishness, grasping for power they never prepared to wield and being destroyed by it."

Her flat gaze and clenched fists made it clear his truth meant nothing to her. "Tell yourself what you like, wolf. You certainly seem to have convinced her." She threw a hand toward the mother. But I will not be taken in by fairy tales so easily. I have seen your kind tear babes from the arms of their mothers, and worse. There is nothing you can say that will convince me to trust you, or absolve you from the guilt of what you are."

When he spoke, his voice shook and his hands curled into fists. "Is that so? And what kind of monster are you, Alix La Rouge? For you are certainly no human. Don't forget that I have tasted your blood."

She shot out of her chair so fast that had he been purely human he would not have even seen the movement until she was halfway across the floor.

But he was no mere human, either, and he was tired of her jibes. She swung in a lightning-fast blow, but he caught her fist and prepared to rear back and kick her through the closest wall.

Enough!

The word rang in his mind, clanging inside his skull with such force it brought him to his knees, and Alix with him.

You will both cease this childishness. Whole villages are dying, ravaged by monsters we cannot understand. If we do not stop them the threat will only spread. You are the most capable hunters on the continent, and the best fit to end this threat. But if I cannot trust you to put innocent lives ahead of your own petty squabbles, say so now.

Cyrus pushed his hands against the sides of his head to stop the pounding as Alix rolled out of his reach, panting, a combination of fury and shame on her face. She wiped the back of her hand across her mouth and stood.

"I have more reason to hate werewolves than most," she said. "But I will never put myself above innocent lives. Even if it means working with the likes of *him*. You know this."

The Mother Superior's eyes softened. "I know it, my child. But you needed to be reminded."

"You truly believe he is the right—*person*—to help me end this threat?"

"I would not have sent for him otherwise."

Cyrus stood, shook off the effects of the mental assault, and brushed his hair out of his face to glare at both women. One had attacked him, and the other used her gift against him when he tried to defend himself. He'd completely lost his touch with the fairer sex.

Maybe he should tell them to handle the problem themselves and walk away.

As appealing as that option sounded, after seeing what these new werewolves were capable of, how could he say no? Did he really want that harridan out there on her own if other True Born were involved?

No. This mission was his responsibility.

Still, he couldn't resist getting in a quick jab, so he jerked his chin at Alix and said, with as much disgust as possible, "You do not ask me if I am willing to work with *her*."

Alix flinched, though she disguised it well. That should have given him a sense of satisfaction, but it only made guilt settle heavily in his gut.

After seeing that damned woman in action he couldn't deny she was deserving of the stories they told about the Red Cloak. And if this threat proved to be true, they would need one another. Had Alix not killed two of the werewolves before he fought the third, he would have gotten his throat ripped out.

Cyrus gritted his teeth. "Where shall we start?"

After being dismissed, he walked the entire circumference of the convent nearly six times before working off enough frustrated energy to relax. It was impossible to close his eyes without seeing the hatred and disgust on Alix's face.

Worse, it was impossible not to admit to himself that he deserved it. The woman had wormed beneath his skin, faster than anyone he'd ever met, and he could not help but respond accordingly, no matter how petty it was.

He sank onto a bench in a patch of sunlight, kicked off his shoes, and dug his toes into the turf. The grass was warm from the sun, fragrant and soft beneath his toes. After a while, the tension in his shoulders relaxed.

He might be as much a monster as Alix claimed, but he didn't have to live like one. He would kill when he was called upon to protect innocent lives, but in the meantime, he could enjoy a sunny afternoon just like anyone else. The burden of death and doom followed him, no matter how far he ran, but he could put it down for a little while and simply be a man sitting on a bench.

He leaned back and closed his eyes, listening to the comforting sounds of honest people working with their hands, of birds plucking bugs from the leaves of the pea plants, and the confident tread of the Mother Superior's rather large feet.

With a sigh he opened his eyes. "Twice in one day? To what do I owe the honor?"

She stopped next to his bench and folded her hands. "Will you join me for a walk?"

"Do you have any plans to shout inside my head?"

A small, apologetic smile curled the corners of her mouth. "Not unless you deserve it." Then she raised a brow in question and tilted her head toward the path.

Cyrus stood, stretched, and joined her.

"You must not blame Alix," she said as they passed beneath the arching stone gate of the convent garden.

"But I would really like to."

She laughed. "She can be difficult. And stubborn."

"And dangerous."

"That, too. But she had a very traumatic childhood."

"Who did not?"

"True enough. She came to us as an orphan with no one in the world. As she grew older, she wanted nothing more than revenge. I am ashamed to say that I took advantage of her need for vengeance. There were more monsters in the world then, and too many innocents died. We needed hunters like Alix."

"I remember," he said, seeing a flash of blood-soaked grass and glassy eyes in his memory.

"She was trained as a hunter from the age of thirteen. She has known nothing else. And because of her profession, she has seen and done terrible things," she added softly.

Cyrus knew firsthand the way terrible things stuck in one's memory, like heavy paving stones that built roads to places one did not wish to visit. "What did she hope to avenge? I have heard so many tales of the Red Cloak I cannot tell which is true; she killed a werewolf while protecting her grandmother, a hunter rescued her from a werewolf attack... Perhaps if I knew what was true, it would help."

The Mother Superior looked at her feet as they walked down an aisle of rose bushes, her brow furrowed in thought. "That is her story to tell."

She turned to the rose bushes and cupped one tender flower in her work-roughened hand. "A rose is a beautiful flower, is it not? The smell draws one in, and it opens with such layered complexity." She ran a finger across the delicate petals and smiled to herself. "It can withstand rather extreme environments and temperatures, even neglect and drought. But the petals are delicate." Her thumbnail left a bruise behind, marring the smooth red surface. "To protect itself, the rose grows thorns. And if you want to pick one, you must beware."

Cyrus frowned at the flower, wondering why the topic of conversation suddenly changed to botany. "I am familiar with the plant, aye."

"Roses that grow in environments where there are many predators develop more thorns," she said, her voice gently patronizing.

"Ahh," he said as her analogy finally sunk in. "Aye, I see."

"You may learn the truth if you earn her trust."

Earn the trust of that harpy? He doubted it. Even carrying her twenty miles to save her life hadn't been enough to earn it. But he respected the Mother Superior's decision. Whether he liked her or not, Alix had a right to keep or reveal her own secrets, just as he did.

So he nodded and said, "I'll do my best."

"All will be well, then. Tell me, how is it that the last and strongest line of the Druids has yet to produce more heirs?"

"Some families still offer their bairns to the moon," he said around the lump in his throat, "but she has chosen no one in a hundred years."

She shook her head, lips pressed together. "First the Romans, and then the British. They knew the Druids were a threat, but they cannot have known what they stole from the world when they killed so many of your people."

It wasn't the Romans or the British that destroyed his family. Guilt washed over him in a wave, making it impossible to respond.

They walked a while in silence, for which Cyrus was grateful. Beneath the sheltering branches inside the high stone walls, the world was peaceful and fragrant, so different from the towns outside that stunk of piss and mud. In those places danger lurked around every corner and monsters wore men's faces. But here, everything was exactly as safe as it seemed.

"You said we should begin in Mont Blanc," he said to break the silence. "Are we looking for anything in particular?"

"First to confirm the testimony. And then to discover what is causing this aberration. A lone werewolf is bad enough, but a pack bent on destruction? Not even Paris could survive such a thing intact."

Werewolves working strategically was a terrifying thought. Even with the advanced weapons mortals created, they were not prepared for that kind of destruction. Modern cities were safe precisely because werewolves were solitary and mindless, especially when the hunger was on them.

Something must be done, and he did not trust anyone else to do it. If that meant partnering with the harpy, so be it.

"It comforts me to know you will be protecting the people," Mother Superior said, placing one hand on his shoulder and drawing him back from his thoughts. "I can sense the kindness in you, the compassion. They have need of it, and so does Alix."

His jaw tightened convulsively. "But does she deserve it?"

She laughed, a light, gay sound that made the nuns near them turn and smile in their direction. "My dear soul, do any of us deserve it? What a sad world this would be if all of us received only what we deserved."

Blood on the grass, glassy eyes staring at the sky, the acrid stench of smoke burning his nostrils.

Cyrus blinked away the memories and swallowed. How many times had he been forgiven when he deserved only scorn and death? "I suppose that's true enough."

Mother Superior looked at him with knowing eyes and nodded once. "Show Alix the kindness you do not believe you deserve. She may surprise you."

"Aye, or put a knife in my back when I'm not looking."

"What is life without a few risks?" She winked. "Think of it as a challenge."

She left him at the intersection of two white stone paths. He caught sight of a red cloak entering the library. Did Alix ever walk like a normal person, or did she prowl everywhere she went? As if she'd heard his thoughts, her head turned in his direction.

Her expression had been pleasant, even peaceful, but as soon as they locked eyes, her lip curled in disgust and she hurried into the building in a flash of red. He was supposed to partner with this woman?

They'd be lucky not to kill one another before nightfall.

10

Alix

AN EXTRA SHIRT, THE cleaning kit, a silver chain, the restocked embroidery pouch, and—this time—a leather medical kit with tweezers. If she must partner with the wolf, she'd make certain he never had another reason to put his mouth on her.

The familiar act of packing to leave the convent once again had settled her nerves nicely...until *that* mental image barged into her mind. Alix sucked in a deep breath and closed her eyes, releasing it slowly through her nose.

A knock on the door. "Alix?"

"Just a moment," she called back.

Her nerves shot through the ceiling at the memory of Cyrus's mouth on her skin and her blood dripping from his chin. He'd noticed that her blood was not exactly human, but either he didn't know why, or he'd decided not to press the matter. Worrying over exposing her secret to the wolf was much better than worrying about her body's ridiculous response to him.

Best to give herself a moment to calm down before she opened the door for Sister Mary Paul. Alix was always aware of the monstrous side of her nature, of the potential that she might harm someone by accident when her emotions were heightened. Being so much stronger than mortals came with significant risk.

Now and then, when lives were at stake or when she was desperate for comfort, she would relent. But experience taught her self-control was easiest when she practiced it in the quiet, safe moments. The ritual had become second nature, as familiar as breathing. So, when she finally opened the door, her nervous energy had been plucked and discarded like a wilted rose.

Sister Mary Paul stepped inside with a small wooden box in her hands and a reproachful smile on her face. "I thought you would come to see me, but Mother Superior says you are leaving right away."

Mother Superior. How had the wolf insinuated himself into the trust of one of the most discerning minds Alix had ever encountered? Earning her trust meant he was clever, which made him even more dangerous than she feared.

"The sooner we begin," Alix said, "the sooner this farce of a partnership will be over." And she could unmask the werewolf who had fooled everyone but her.

She wasn't certain what the wolf truly wanted, or why he went to such lengths to convince people of his good nature, but she would find out. And when he finally snapped, she would be ready.

Disapproval drew Mary Paul's brows low over her eyes. "Don't you trust Mother Superior?"

"I trust that she believes she is doing what is right."

"That isn't an answer."

Alix sighed and turned to tighten the straps securing her wool blanket to the knapsack. "I've given her my word. That will have to be enough."

After a moment of contemplative silence, Mary Paul held out the wooden box. "Perhaps knowing these are close at hand will give you a little peace. I've tested them and, if the rumors are true, I think you'll find them useful."

Alix examined the objects, running one finger over the smooth surface. "Are these what I think they are? You finally perfected the design?"

A mischievous smile made Mary Paul's face look far younger than her thirty years. "You won't know till you try them." Her amused expression faded, and she tucked a loose braid behind one pointed ear. "I know you are apprehensive, my friend. But this world is far deeper and more complicated than we like to believe. Just because we want something to be true, doesn't mean it is. For your sake, I will be praying your partner surprises you."

"And I shall be praying he does not," Alix muttered as she slid the box into her knapsack and tied it shut.

"How far is it to Mont Blanc?" the wolf asked.

Alix tried not to look at him when she answered, but hatred drew her eyes in his direction far more often than she liked. He strode down the packed dirt road with a knapsack twice the size of hers on his broad back, acting as if it weighed nothing, while his shoulders and biceps strained against the confines of his white shirt.

"Three days," she said. "If we don't sleep."

"I asked how far, not how long."

"I have not bothered measuring it in miles. Pull out the map if you need numbers."

"You know, minx," the bastard said the word so casually, "we will be in one another's company for at least a week. It would not kill you to be civil."

"Don't call me that."

"Whatever you say, Red."

She stopped, one hand gripping the butt of her pistol, the other resting on the hilt of a silver knife poisoned with wolfsbane, and glared at the man until he stopped and faced her. "The Mother's trust in you, and my promise to her, are the only things keeping you alive. Giving me reasons to regret my decision is not wise."

Cyrus's grin was decidedly wolfish. "It isn't my fault if you cannot control your anger. If you should decide to act on it, just remember: I'm no longer weak and in chains."

"More's the pity."

"Why? Do you like your men submissive?"

"It makes no difference to you. You are not a man."

His green eyes flashed with a dangerous spark of heat. "And you are no human woman, so I suppose that makes us both monsters, doesn't it?"

Alix knew who and what she was. She lived her entire, long life at the receiving end of suspicious glares and fearful glances. Simple words should no longer have the power to hurt her, and yet, at the reminder, pain punched a hole in her stomach and wrapped its long fingers around her guts.

No, she was not human and no matter how much she wished, she could not change the truth. It hurt all the way to her soul, but she refused to let it show in her eyes.

Instead, she stepped closer, too close for safety, and said, "Beware of what you say."

"Or what?" he asked, leaning down until their faces were inches apart and she could see the splinters of furious gold surrounding his pupils. "You'll break your word?"

A twist of her arm and a thrust would kill him. The fool had placed himself within arm's reach, and her fingers closed around the hilt of the dagger in anticipation. Her jaw clenched, but her arm remained still.

"Aye," Cyrus said, leaning back and nodding. "That's what I thought. At least you have integrity if nothing else. I'll trust that, minx, and leave the rest to chance."

He walked into the shadow of the trees without looking back.

She stared after him for a long time, regretting her promise, and regretting more not drawing her knife. The reasonable part of her mind knew he was right; as much as she wanted to attack him, Cyrus had become safe from her the moment she made that promise.

So, she would simply have to wait for him to free her from the oath by breaking his word. And he would, if she knew anything about werewolves.

When that happened, she'd be ready.

Night rose from the shadows and sank from the sky to meet at the horizon, but they did not slow or stop. They walked day and night, eating from their packs and disappearing into the trees now and then to piss. The familiar country passed in a comforting blur of shades of green, birdsong, and the clean, earthy scents of dirt and wet grass.

It surprised Alix to find that, despite her bone-deep hatred of the man, traveling with someone else was...nice. Even without conversation, the sound of a second pair of feet was comforting. At least, until he spoke.

"What time will we reach the village tomorrow?"

"Near the end of the day," she said.

"Then we should rest tonight."

"If you are tired, just say so."

"I'm not tired, but I'm not a stubborn fool, either."

She turned to face him, hands on her hips. "Exactly what does that mean?"

"How long did you go without sleep before the bandit shot you?"

"I don't see what business it is of–"

"How long, Alix La Rouge? Three days? Four?"

She worked her jaw and told herself to stay calm. "Four."

"Your body would have healed itself if you slept, wouldn't it? You would not have fainted near the stream."

"I did *not* faint."

He threw his arms in the air. "Then why do you fight me? You're no fool. We'll need all the strength we can muster if we come upon werewolves. Why not care for yourself now, so you will be more effective when we arrive?"

"Because I don't want to sleep anywhere near you."

He rolled his eyes. "Trust me, minx, I'm not looking forward to it, either, but I'd rather die with your dagger in my back than beneath the teeth of a werewolf because I was too stupid to sleep when given the chance."

With that, he turned into the bush, scouting for a suitable place to camp. Alix swore and followed him. This was a stupid idea. She could never sleep knowing he was near. The night would wear on, minute by minute, hour by hour, and she would simply lie there, resenting him when she could be hunting instead.

But perhaps *he* needed sleep. Her exposure to werewolves did not extend to their pattern of human sleeping habits, and if she was going to be forced to fight next to him, then she would rather not have a partner who made stupid mistakes because he was sleep-deprived.

So, she would simply sleep with her daggers in her hands and hope the wolf had no more nightmares. Her memories were heavy enough to bear without adding his to the pile.

Cyrus chose a small, secluded spot screened by a copse of young saplings and protected from the wind by an outcropping of rock. Which irritated Alix, because it was exactly the spot she would have chosen.

He went about the chores of setting up a camp with quiet efficiency, finishing tasks before she could even begin them. In short order, they had a canvas lean-to to protect them from rain, their bedrolls laid out, and dry wood stacked to keep a fire burning through the night.

She considered their camp, and said, "This is rather extravagant for a single-night bivouac."

"Do you enjoy deprivation?"

"No more than anyone else, but I prefer to move light and quick."

"And I prefer to be comfortable when I can. Besides, a night's sleep can only do us good. In fact, we should have a hot meal," he said, dusting his hands on his trousers.

"An open fire will give our presence away to anyone with a nose and half a brain."

"So will the tracks on the road."

Alix smirked and folded her arms, shifting her weight to one hip. "I do not leave tracks."

"We have nothing to worry over. Anyone who comes looking for my camp is taking his life in his hands." He said the words with a casual confidence that rankled her.

Did he think *he* was the most dangerous thing in these woods? "No matter how fast or strong you are, wolf, even you cannot dodge a bullet."

"Are you threatening to shoot me, minx?"

Alix gritted her teeth and told herself that shooting him was not a good idea, and she should rein in her temper before it made her break her oath. "No, but if I were a bandit, I would shoot you while you slept."

"Then I suppose it is a good thing for me you are not, and that I sleep lightly. I will be back. Start a fire, will you?"

With that, he silently disappeared into the forest. He moved gracefully...but so did bears, in their way, so it wasn't really that impressive.

By the time Cyrus returned with a young boar slung over one shoulder, a fire crackled happily against the rock. The stone absorbed and radiated the heat, letting the small fire do double duty of cooking the meat and heating the camp more efficiently while being less noticeable. Though there was nothing to be done about the scent of frying meat. At least he had been smart enough to gut and clean the animal far enough from camp that not even she could smell the kill.

"That is a lot of meat," she said as he began quartering the animal with smooth strokes of a knife nearly as long as her forearm.

"I am a big man if you haven't noticed. It takes more than cold sausage and stale bread to keep my belly button from bouncing against my spine."

At that mental image, a snort of laughter escaped before she could stop it. He looked up, a curious expression in his eyes. Why did she suddenly feel self-conscious? It hadn't been that long since she had laughed, had it?

She dismissed the lapse by saying, "I've never heard that expression."

"Do that again," he replied, his voice soft but insistent.

"What?"

"Laugh. Do it again."

She rolled her eyes to give herself an excuse not to look at the intense green of his eyes, focused on her as if she were prey. "My humor cannot be commanded. Who can laugh on demand?"

He shrugged and went back to skinning their dinner, muttering to himself.

"What?" she demanded, irritated with his comfortable manner and commands, as if he was her friend who could talk to her any way he pleased.

He stopped cutting, looked up again through long strands of blonde hair that came loose from the leather thong that tied it back, and said, "You snorted."

"So?"

"It was...rather adorable." He said the words as if he didn't want to admit them, and she wholeheartedly wished he hadn't.

"I don't laugh to entertain wolves with misplaced senses of humor," she snapped, turning away to grab the long piece of green wood they would use for a spit and forcing herself not to snap the newly peeled branch. "Besides, there is nothing funny about this situation."

"I'll give you that. This is no comedy. It is a tragedy."

They ate in silence, and Alix kept her eyes on the hunk of steaming meat that was rich and gamey. The less she looked at or spoke to Cyrus, the better.

When he held out another piece of meat, she took it without raising her gaze, seeing only his hands, which looked like they belonged to a poet or a musician, not a killer.

If she noticed someone's hands, it was to judge whether they had a weapon, but his were long-fingered and elegant, with clean, short nails. He plucked the last bit of meat from the roasting stick and dropped it into his mouth, licking the leftover fat from his thumb...and caught her looking.

Alix dropped her eyes and angrily chewed the boar meat.

When the last of their dinner was gone, she retreated to her bedroll, but Cyrus sat by the fire, picking his teeth.

"That is a disgusting habit," she said, sliding beneath the blanket.

"What, this? No, this is cleaning my teeth. I have far more disgusting habits."

"Why am I not surprised?"

"Because you are a judgmental shrew?"

That caught her off guard. Judgmental? She had never considered herself so. Discerning, maybe, but she tried to view people within the scope of their circumstances and not place unfair expectations on them.

Alix treated people as what they were; a cat could only be a cat, after all. And a werewolf could be nothing but a werewolf. Expecting anything more or less was asking to be disappointed. With that thought firmly in mind, she decided not to dignify his insult with a reply, but rolled over and tried to sleep.

At least, until Cyrus climbed into his bedroll.

She prepared to draw her daggers, but he made no move toward her, only shifted till he was comfortable and fell into an immediate sleep. She lay for a long time listening to him breathe. He had not changed shape in the cave, but then she'd imprisoned him with silver and wolfsbane.

With no such precautions, and with his guard down, the magic could take over despite the full moon being weeks away. A nightmare or the scent of prey nearby could trigger the change. Instead of a big blonde man, a shaggy werewolf would lie mere feet from her.

She should get up and take her bedroll on the other side of the fire to give herself more time to react, but he would only use that against her. "So much for the brave hunter, the infamous Manteau Rouge," he would say. "She could not even sleep near a human who had not so much as threatened her."

But Alix knew how quickly a human could become a monster, and she vividly remembered the bristly, musty scent of the fur that scratched and tickled her skin, the rumbling growls, and her grandmother's pleading eyes.

But Cyrus never changed or even rolled over in his sleep. He would, though. She knew it. So, she stayed still and kept both hands on her daggers. The clever little box Mary Paul gave her, full of dangerous surprises, stayed within reach, just in case.

11

Cyrus

THE SOFT BEDROLL, THE crackling fire, and cricket song should have made it a perfect evening, but it took Cyrus hours to relax enough to fall asleep. He could not help but imagine his partner creeping from her bed roll to slide a knife into his exposed kidneys. So when he jerked awake to the sharp scent of her fear heavy on the air, he lay for a few moments in disbelief.

Had he been a dozen feet away, he would never have caught the scent, but her nearness let him hear the thud of a racing heartbeat and quick, sharp breaths.

Was she having a nightmare? If so, it must have been a powerful one, for she hadn't reacted so strongly even when she stood before him with bullet holes in her torso. As silently as possible, he shifted until he could see her still form.

Alix lay on her side, the fire painting her face in warm orange light. Her fingers were clasped around the hilts of both daggers so tightly her tendons pressed white against the skin of her knuckles. Those light brown eyes, hawk's eyes, watched him unblinking, as if it was not him she saw but something far worse.

Cyrus tightened the knot of his bedroll with too much force, wrenching the slider rope until it squeaked. Pressuring Alix to camp had been a mistake. He'd thought the proximity and shared chores might build some modicum of trust and force them to open up in a non-threatening way.

But the strain of a night of broken, nervous sleep only made them both tired and irritable. Alix ignored him as she removed all traces of their camp and slung her pack over her shoulders.

They left before the sun rose and jogged down the tightly packed dirt road past cottages, crossroads, and a rowdy-sounding inn with horses and donkeys tethered outside. A brawl spilled out the front door and onto the steps as they passed. Several men threw drunk, looping punches while other patrons stood in the door to point, laugh, and place bets.

"Fun place," Cyrus muttered as they skirted the fighters.

Now and then the trees parted and the mountains lay before them, row upon row, fading into the distance. They did not stop for lunch but kept up a steady jog through the afternoon. Slowly, oak and maple gave way to pine, and the sun sank below the tree tops. The wind picked up, filling the forest with the uneasy whispers of trees that had seen too much...and the scent of dried blood and rotten flesh.

His instincts kicked in, electrifying his muscles and making every hair on the back of his neck stand at attention. A fallen leaf tumbled through the air and plastered itself against his chest as he caught the scent, held his breath, and verified the direction.

"Do you smell that?" he asked.

Alix inhaled, closed her eyes, and shivered. "It is faint, but...I don't think the survivors were lying."

"How far is the village?"

"No more than a mile. Do you need to do anything to prepare yourself?"

"Such as?"

"Such as taking off your clothes?"

"Longing to see me naked, are you?"

She snorted. "I saw more than enough when treating your wounds. Another look might damage my brain."

Judging by the arousal he smelled that night, and the sideways glances he caught when she didn't realize he was looking, she was lying. But now wasn't the time to call her on it. "No, I don't need to remove my clothes."

"Suit yourself, wolf." She shrugged and resumed walking. "If you want to tear your way through your clothing, I suppose that is your choice."

Soon enough she'd see why he did not need to remove his clothing, and he was going to enjoy the shocked expression on her face. In the meantime, since she was at least attempting civility, keeping the peace was a good idea.

As they neared the village, blood, offal, and rot tainted the air until it was almost unfit to breathe. Cyrus pulled his neck kerchief over his nose and tried to breathe through his mouth, but that was a mistake; tasting death on the air was worse than smelling it.

They crested a rise and looked down into a surprisingly large collection of wooden buildings situated at a crossroads near a stream. The town had been relatively well-off, likely making a majority of its income by serving travelers going to and coming from Switzerland. Or they *had*. From the look of the town, there was no one left to sell or trade.

"If this is too difficult for you, tell me now," Alix said, pistols already in her hands. "The stink will only get worse, and not all of the bodies will be...defiled."

What she meant was, *will you be tempted to eat the dead bodies?*

He felt the growl threatening and swallowed it back. "I have never and will never defile a mortal body."

She raised dark eyebrows in disbelief, but only said, "Are you ready, then?"

Instead of answering, he strode into the remains of the village.

Children probably ran down these streets laughing once. Windows once glowed with the warmth of candle and firelight, filled with families and old friends. Now dark windows and hollow doorways turned the houses into screaming faces that wailed in grief.

Cyrus stopped to pick up a broken toy horse, its little wooden wheel missing, yarn hair matted dark brown with dried blood. Claw marks scored the hard-packed dirt of the road nearby.

"This place stinks of werewolf," Alix said in a low voice.

She was right.

He passed the body of a woman who died with a spade in her hand, the digging edges stained with dried blood and littered with long grey hairs. Cyrus closed his eyes. "May the moon welcome you with her light, and keep you in her grace."

"We should check the buildings," Alix said. Her voice was hard, her hands clenched into fists. Speaking to him was clearly the last thing she wished to do. "If the villagers managed to kill any of the monsters we can examine their bodies."

Anger radiated off her in waves. He suspected she included him in the use of the word *monster,* but he couldn't resent her for it. The abominations that ravaged this town were monsters of the purest kind, and even if he was only adjacent to them by sharing a similar gift, guilt wrapped slimy fingers around his heart.

Monster was not a strong enough word to describe the kind of evil that delighted in causing such wanton destruction.

He needed to move, to do something, or he would scream. "I'll take the north side."

Cyrus strode away without looking back.

The death and devastation in the shadowed halls were beyond description. Sharp-edged memories, too like the scenes before him, tumbled out of the dark corners of his mind to cut him to quivering shreds. Instead of walking through the wooden buildings of a remote mountain village in France, he staggered through the remains of smoldering thatch roofs and crumbled stone walls. Smoke stung his eyes, making them water as he choked on the sickly sweet stink of burned flesh. Blood was splattered everywhere: on walls, on the dirt, and in the grass.

The bodies of men and women he had known all his life were strewn about, left in the positions in which they had fallen, like leaves tumbled by the wind. Even Granny Campbell lay face down on the path with her cap loose. Blood plastered her white hair to her head and neck. She had been carrying a basket full of dandelion greens, and the little yellow heads lay about her like scattered stars.

He wanted to run screaming, to call for Effie and Lyrus, but his shocked body only stumbled forward in a numb trance and choked on the acrid smoke hanging over his village.

When he found them, at last, he wobbled to the ground with a strangled cry. They lay in the tall grass at the edge of the village, pale and broken, like discarded pieces of pottery. Lyrus was only fifteen, but he had died with Effie in his arms, protecting her small body with his own. The boy had taken his sister and run with her toward the safety of the forest. But they never reached it. Lyrus had tried to hide the girl in his plaid, but her little foot poked out from beneath the cloth folds.

Her foot? It had been her hand he saw, chubby fingers limp, the rest of her body sheltered even in death by her older brother. So why did he see a foot?

Cyrus blinked away the vision and realized that he was, indeed looking at a little foot. Only this wasn't the foot of his little sister, and she was not dead. This small foot barely poked out from beneath a rope bed, and as he crept closer, it disappeared, scooting farther into the shadows with a furtive rustle. A little heart beat madly and fear, sharp in his nostrils, cut through the scent of rot.

With great care so as not to frighten them, he knelt and bent down. A small body and a dirty face stared back at him with wide, terrified eyes.

"Hello, sweetheart," he said in French, making his voice as kind as possible despite the grief squeezing his throat. "Don't be scared. I'm here to help you. Do you want to come out?"

The child curled up like a little hedgehog, face hidden protectively behind arms and knees. If he reached under to pull the child out or lifted the straw mattress off the bed frame, that would only terrify them. So, he tried to remember what worked for Effie when she was angry or sad.

"I promise I will not hurt you, or allow anyone else to do so," he told the child. "Perhaps I'll sit with you a while if that's alright?"

No answer.

Cyrus leaned against the wall and let his eyes roam over the rest of the room. A small family once lived here. There was a bed, a little cot, a dresser, a table, just enough to get by and no more. Two adult bodies in the late stages of decay lay on the floor near the door, a man and a woman judging by their shape. Someone had covered their bodies with a blanket from the bed.

Moon and stars, the child lost both parents. Mother Superior said the slaughter took place nearly two weeks ago, so the child must be starving. Why had no one come to search for survivors?

He swallowed back bile at the idea of the little one living here, alone, starving among the dead bodies of mother and father and likely everyone they knew. His heart wrenched at the sadness and futility of it.

"Do you follow any religion, little one? Did you pray over their bodies?"

No answer.

Something should be said, something meaningful. A song sprang to his mind that somehow seemed fitting, an Irish song he thought it was, though he could not remember where first he heard it.

> *"Of all the money that e'er I had*
> *I spent it in good company*
> *And all the harm I've ever done*
> *Alas it was to none but me*
>
> *And all I've done for want of wit*
> *To mem'ry now I can't recall*
> *So fill to me the parting glass*
> *Good night and joy be to you all*
>
> *So fill to me the parting glass*
> *And drink a health whate'er befall,*
> *And gently rise and softly call*
> *Good night and joy be to you all*

Of all the comrades that e'er I had
They're sorry for my going away
And all the sweethearts that e'er I had
They'd wish me one more day to stay

But since it falls unto my lot
That I should rise and you should not
I gently rise and softly call
Good night and joy be to you all

If I had money enough to spend
And leisure time to sit awhile
There is a fair maid in this town
That sorely has my heart beguiled.

Her rosy cheeks and ruby lips
I own she has my heart in thrall
Then fill to me the parting glass
Good night and joy be with you all.

A man may drink and not be drunk
A man may fight and not be slain
A man may court a pretty girl
And perhaps be welcomed back again

But since it has so ought to be
By a time to rise and a time to fall
Come fill to me the parting glass

Good night and joy be with you all."

He sang it slowly, letting the sad words of parting linger in the air like a benediction for all the sorrow this small room had seen. When the song finished, he started again. A little face appeared at the edge of the bed, peeking out of the shadows, and in it, a pair of wide eyes, blue as the sky.

By the time he began a third refrain, the small girl child climbed into his lap.

Her body was stick-thin and cold, and she curled against him as one might cuddle a big dog for warmth and comfort. He rubbed her back and arms to warm her and kept singing. The words were in English, so he doubted she understood them, but they were full of bittersweet sorrow, and he thought she understood that well enough.

When he finished the fourth refrain, he said, "Are you hungry, sweetheart? I have food and water."

She did not speak, but she nodded against his chest. He cradled her like a baby bird and rolled to his feet. There was bread in the pack, though she may need it softened with milk. Her stomach was likely in sore condition and he didn't want her to be sick. But he would not feed her here. Not here. The woods were close enough. Cyrus turned to leave but halted and caught his breath.

Alix stood in the doorway, silver knives in hand, her eyes wide, lips trembling. A little chill ran up his spine. Holy hell the woman moved quietly. And she looked as if she could not decide between gutting him or crying.

"We need to feed her," he said in a soothing voice, "but her stomach won't be very strong. Did you happen to see or smell any livestock? Goats or cows, anything that gives milk?"

Alix blinked as if she didn't understand him, as if she did not see him at all but something else, something terrible.

He chanced walking toward her, though she was as stiff as a doe that scented a hunter. "Alix? She needs food, preferably soft food. She's starving."

When he was within about ten feet, Alix raised her arms as if to ward him off, knives out and blocking the door. Just what he needed: two traumatized souls to care for. She shook and her throat muscles worked as if she wanted to speak or cry, but her feet were rooted to the spot.

She was either having a panic attack, or she was about to kill him.

12

Alix

ALIX WAS IN TWO places at once: standing in the doorway of this shabby apartment that stank of rotting flesh, and lying on the ground next to the dead body of her grandmother. She had been nine, a little older than the child Cyrus cradled against his chest, only there had been no one to comfort her.

Blood covered her hands, soaked into her skirt, and stained the cloak her mother always made her wear, filling the air with the scent of copper and making her mouth water. She hadn't been able to help it, and her body's response made her so nauseous that she stumbled out of her grandmother's cottage and got sick in the bushes.

The moon had watched it all in remote, uncaring silence, leaving her to face the horror alone. Only she wasn't alone, and she wasn't kneeling outside in the cold night. She was standing in the destroyed rubble of someone else's life, looking through the lens of their tragedy at her own pain. Past and present formed two impenetrable walls that crushed her between them, locking her body in place.

"Alix," Cyrus said, his voice deep and soft, like a feather bed. "Alix, you are safe. You are safe."

When his fingers touched her cheek she came hurtling back into her body and flinched away so violently that her back slammed into the wall behind her.

Words fought their way up her throat and came out in a ragged whisper. "Don't touch me."

He turned away, sheltering the girl's body with his own as if protecting the child...from her? That startled Alix back to full consciousness. Did he truly believe her capable of hurting a child?

Of course he did.

Because she had. The brother and sister werewolves she killed had been teenagers, barely more than children. Perhaps she was a monster after all. Swallowing back her pain, Alix sheathed her daggers and modulated her voice to sound calm and collected.

"I'm fine," she said. "Yes, let us feed her, but not here. There is a good camping spot outside town. I think we have seen more than enough to draw conclusions about what happened here."

Cyrus's expression was carefully neutral, but he said, "Agreed."

She turned and left the building without looking back or waiting for him. With his long legs and keen sense of smell, he would have no trouble following her, and she needed some time to calm her nerves before she did something stupid.

Upon coming to her senses, her first instinct had been to snatch the girl from his arms. After all, he was precisely the kind of monster that slaughtered everyone she knew and loved. But that would only have terrified the girl more, and Alix was currently in no condition to make a traumatized child feel safe.

Long strides carried her back down the dirt street and out of town, where she turned into the forest. The undergrowth had been cleared by goats and pigs and townsfolk long ago, but a stand of boulders over the rise were big enough to shield a camp from the road and provide some small protection from the wind.

Alix headed for the spot as she tried to clear her mind and regain some sense of peace, which had been in short supply over the last week. Ever since she had foolishly rescued that damned wolf. Letting him walk into that town without a guard went against every instinct she spent three hundred years honing. He could've gone anywhere, hurt anyone if she wasn't there to stop him.

But she promised to work with him. So she had cleared her side of the town and assessed the damage with all possible speed. The villagers had killed at least two werewolves, judging by the state and smell of the bodies, and she was fiercely glad they managed that much.

A man who may have been in his forties lay on the dirt road with several holes in his exposed skull and a broken silver candlestick jammed between his ribs. By the angle of the bullet holes, someone had shot him from an upper window and incapacitated him long enough for another villager to poison him with silver. He shifted back to his human form in death, though the stink of werewolf still tainted his flesh.

His corpse may have provided other clues, but wolves or other scavengers had carried off whatever body parts were easily detached, leaving that trail cold. The rest of the town showcased similar scenes, like grotesque tableaus at a traveling circus.

Alix was intimately acquainted with death, and she had been expecting such things. But then she found the closet door blocked by a chair and table that had been dragged across the floor. Thinking someone might have been hidden inside for protection, Alix had shoved the furniture aside and pulled open the door to see...food.

Canned goods in questionable condition had been stacked on one side of the closet floor, and empty cans lay discarded on the other. Someone without a can opener had crushed the tin with a heavy rock until the contents leaked out onto the thin rug. Little fingerprints left streaks in the stains. Small hands had scooped up the escaped liquid.

Now Alix knew who hid the scrounged food, and why. Imagining the small girl alone, hiding in the dark closet, hammering at tin cans with a rock to keep herself from starving made her stomach heave. When Alix ran away after her grandmother's death, she had at least been fast enough to catch small animals to keep herself from starving. To this day she could still feel the fur and hot blood in her mouth when she remembered those times. The rabbits had screamed and struggled, but they were easier to catch than squirrels.

Alix clenched her fists against the memories and left a trail for Cyrus behind the boulders, where a stand of saplings created a suitable place to tie their canvas tent. She slung her pack onto the ground and began pulling out the cans she rescued from the closet. The mess kit followed. She tore the leftover stale bread into small chunks and dropped them into her bowl. Having something productive to do helped settle her mind, so when Cyrus appeared with the girl, Alix was calm enough to ask, "Peach juice, or condensed milk? The sugar may help."

"Aye but the milk will be more fortifying. How does that sound, lass? Bread and milk?"

The girl refused to respond and buried her small face against Cyrus's chest, which could not have smelled very nice given their days on the road. Alix tore the top off the can of condensed milk and drizzled the syrupy liquid over the bread until it was the consistency of porridge.

After a bit of coaxing, the girl ate like a starved animal, then licked the bowl clean and drank a carefully measured amount of water. In her tiny hands, the cup looked huge, but not so big as the pleading eyes she leveled at Cyrus while holding up the bowl for more.

"I'm sorry, lass. If you eat and drink too much too fast, you'll make yourself sick."

She frowned up at him from her perch on his knee, looking like a fierce little badger with her dirty face and tangled hair. The poor thing was still hungry and debating whether getting more food was worth fighting her rescuer. But she was also safe and fed, and the weariness of her long ordeal overwhelmed her desire for food. With a yawn and a few owlish blinks, the child lay her head against the wolf's chest and fell asleep within seconds.

"Poor bairn," Cyrus said, cupping the back of her dirty blonde head with one huge hand. He could have crushed her skull with a mere flex of his muscles, but he held her as if she were made of glass.

In a way, she was. And if they were not careful, she would break. But, she thought with with a touch of resentment toward the man who abandoned her and her mother, no father could have held his own daughter with more tenderness.

"What do we do with the poor thing?" he asked.

"There are no other villages nearby."

"What about the convent?"

"The Sisters would certainly take the girl in, but traveling at a speed safe for her recovery will take several days, and the trail has already grown cold."

"Perhaps someone at the inn we passed would be willing to care for the girl."

Alix grimaced. "It is a rough place in the backcountry. Not suitable for a traumatized child."

"The convent is the only other answer. And you are right, the trail is cold. If we do not stop these killings, there will be more traumatized children. My vote is for the inn."

Alix stared at a monster who wore the skin of a man and cradled a sleeping child against his chest as he spoke of protecting lives. She wanted to demand how he could speak this way knowing his kind were responsible for orphaning the girl in his arms...but she could not.

Watching him with the child broke something in her chest. Accusing him now felt wrong, and in a strange way that feeling made her more distrustful: a monster she could understand and predict. She knew how to treat a monster, and what to expect from one. How was she supposed to protect herself from a werewolf who had tried to save her life and defended orphaned children?

Could he be telling the truth about his family's origins? Was it possible there were werewolves walking this world that were not ravening monsters?

No. She could not afford to think that way. He may have more control than the average werewolf, but blood always had the last say, and he would show his true colors sooner or later. No matter how many heroic deeds he did, fangs and claws would always be there, just under the surface of his skin, waiting for an opportunity to prove that a monster was always a monster.

That truth settled upon her like armor, erasing her doubts and removing her unease.

"We will bring her to the inn, then, and see if there is a suitable situation for her there. We can pay someone to notify the convent, and have one of the sisters send for her. If she is still at the inn when we finish this mission, we can escort her to the convent ourselves."

Her voice sounded much more like the Alix she needed to be: cool and confident, with no trace of the scared girl who had, once upon a time, believed that a monster could be saved. That lesson was written on her bones in blood, and did not bear repeating.

"Very well," Cyrus agreed. "That won't take us too far from our mission, and innkeepers always hear any news worth speaking of. We can push for information when we find her a guardian."

Alix stood up and dusted off her pants. "Very well, then, that's settled. I'm going to scout the perimeter of the town to see where the tracks lead. I'll be back in an hour or so. If that child is not safe when I return, I will kill you, my oath to the Mother Superior be damned."

His eyes narrowed, his jaw clenched, and his nostrils flared, but Alix was not intimidated by his anger. She turned and loped into the woods without looking back.

Given what he had done, both in trying to save her and in protecting the girl, Alix knew her statement was deeply insulting, but she had to remind herself of what he really was, needed to say it aloud so they both knew where she stood. And he needed to know she had not dropped her guard.

It was far too easy to see him as a man, and that was a danger she could not afford.

After about an hour, she had followed the werewolves' tracks from town and up high onto the slope of the mountain, where she lost them among scree fields and granite boulders. She would have liked to quarter the ground and pick up their trail, but the sun was creeping toward the horizon and she did not like to leave the girl alone with the wolf for too long.

Unfortunately, her walk had not calmed her nerves, and her body was still alive with tension that had no outlet and memories that refused to be locked away. So when the scent of frying meat and wood smoke reached her, anger made her face hot. What was the fool thinking to be cooking meat so close to the site of a recent slaughter? Werewolves had claimed this place with their kill, and their senses were easily keen enough to smell meat and smoke on the air from a mile away.

She crashed through the bushes into camp and demanded, "Are you trying to draw every predator on the mountainside down on us?"

Cyrus did not bother to look up from the skewers he was using to fry the last of their fresh meat, but turned each of them carefully over the flames before responding, "The only predator on this mountain you need to fear is me."

He clearly had not forgiven her last insult. His voice was flat and cold. Dangerous. She had known he was dangerous, but when he looked up with the firelight in his green eyes, a chill ran down her spine. The child lay in a bundle of blankets on the other side of the fire, her little chest rising and falling peacefully. Safe.

"Fear *you*? Do not flatter yourself," Alix said, keeping her voice low so as not to wake the child, but adding as much venom as possible to every word. "Have you no care for how that girl will feel if a predator approaches this camp? If she is forced to witness more violence? Of course you don't. Why I expected a monster to care about the feelings of a child, I cannot imagine. But I will not allow you to traumatize her further, oath or not."

She drew her daggers as she spoke, and stood on the edge of the camp in the twilight with her feet planted. This moment had been coming since she had first captured him. It might as well happen now. After he was dead, Alix would take the child back to the Sisters of St. Christophe and give her the same option she had been given as a child: vengeance, if she wanted it.

Cyrus gave her daggers a dismissive glance, then wiped his fingers clean and stood. Once he was satisfied the girl was fast asleep, he turned his full attention on Alix. No one had ever looked at her that way, with absolute attention, seeing every detail, cataloging every breath. Her heartbeat quickened, thudding against her ribcage in anticipation of the fight.

"You have insulted me for the last time," he said as he stalked toward her, light on his feet, unnaturally graceful.

"On this, we are agreed."

Alix backed away from camp, around the stand of boulders that protected their fire from the road, keeping pace with his advance. She refused to be the source of more trauma to the girl, but she could not allow this madness to continue. It ended here.

But it was foolish to let a competent enemy choose the manner of the fight. As soon as they were safely on the other side of the boulders, she attacked in a silent rush, daggers slicing through the air with lethal speed and accuracy.

Cyrus did not change into his wolf form to fight back. Instead, he sidestepped her first swing, parried her second by batting her hand away as it passed, and blocked a kick by raising his knee and taking the impact on the outside of his calf. He was too fast and well-trained for an easy fight.

She adjusted her grip and changed directions, feinting toward his left side, then gathered her strength and leaped over his head, turning in the air to land facing his back. But he wasn't where she expected him to be when she landed. A fist twice the size of hers shot toward her face in a jab that she barely dodged, but countered with a forward kick to his lead leg.

They fought in silence, attack and counter, jab and parry, in a blinding swirl of movement like a violent dance with no music other than their breath and pounding hearts. Around the boulders, in and out of the trees, without pause or hesitation. Cyrus was too fast and too skilled, and he was not getting tired. If she didn't do something soon, he would capitalize on the first mistake she made and kill her. It was only a matter of time.

Alix flipped her daggers into a downward grip and leaped with all the speed she could manage, but he caught her by the wrists in mid-air, spun, and slammed her against the boulder, trapping her body between the rock and his chest.

The air rushed from her lungs. She raised her legs and locked them around his waist, squeezing with bruising force as she fought to free her arms. But Cyrus was enormously strong, far stronger than she thought. She may as well have fought with the mountain itself.

He leaned in, crushing her against the rock with his chest and hips.

She snarled, "I'm going to kill you, wolf."

"No, you are not."

"You are a fool."

"I am perfectly safe from you. Would you like to know how I know?"

"I would *like* you dead and skinned on my floor!"

Cyrus leaned in farther, until his lips were inches from hers, until there was no air between their bodies and her arms were stretched out and useless as he pinned them against the rock by her wrists. "If you truly wanted me dead, you would have drawn your pistol and shot me in the head from cover."

"What do you know of how I would—"

"Because I know of your methods. I studied your kills years before I ever knew who you were. If you wanted me dead, I would be dead already. No," he said, his eyes roaming over her face, her lips, his breath hot on her neck. "You didn't want me dead when you barged into camp, Alix. You wanted a fight. That's why you drew your knives instead of your pistols. That's why you insulted me."

"I did not want the gunfire to wake the child, you bloody idiot."

"No," he said, voice growing soft. "You are frustrated, scared...angry. Memories are haunting you. You wanted to burn them away, and there was no other way to do it. But you do not want me dead."

The tip of his nose ran down the length of her neck and sent a cascade of shivers down her spine. He inhaled deeply, pulling the scent of her deep into his lungs and making a little sound of pleasure in his chest.

Alix shook her head, straining against his grip on her wrists, trying to free her weapons. The powerlessness was terrifying...and terribly exciting. And she hated herself for it. "Yes, I do want you dead. You are a monster."

"No, you don't," he repeated. "But you do want me. I can smell it. I can feel the hunger on you. You want to be overpowered, don't you? To be forced to submit, because you are too damned stubborn to accept anything else."

In a powerful twist, Alix wrenched her arm free and struck Cyrus across the face. His head snapped to the side, but he caught her wrist again and slammed it against the rock, knocking the dagger free. Her blow split his lip, and his tongue darted out to catch the blood. The scent of it filled the air between them, even as the wound began to heal.

"Violent minx," he purred.

"Don't call me that."

He leaned closer, until their lips were nearly touching. His pupils dilated, his warmth seeped through her clothing, and the hard thrust of his cock pressed against the inside of her thigh. If Cyrus wanted to kill her, he could do it. She was more vulnerable now than she had been in her entire adult life.

His lips were so close, and she was so terribly alone.

In a voice that ran over her skin like warm honey, he ordered, "Kiss me."

The command hit her in the chest like a blow. With a moan of need and despair, Alix obeyed. It was not a tender thing, full of innocence and fearful desire. She kissed him like a drowning person fighting for air, willing to pull anyone close enough down with her.

The taste of him went straight to her head, and the heat of his mouth made her tighten her legs around his hips. Cyrus ground against her, and she felt the hard length of him through their clothes, pressing against flesh grown sensitive with desire. He released her wrists and dug his fingers into her hips as he tore his mouth from hers and bit her neck hard enough to bruise.

The pain and pleasure combined drove Alix mad with need. She had taken men to bed before but had never wanted one like this, enough to tear his clothes off and taste his skin. To beg for more, for anything, so long as the driving need was satisfied.

He kissed her again, rolling his hips against her in a sinuous motion, making the world spin away in a dark tangle of desire so profound she wanted to cry. When his hand curled over her breast, plucking the nipple between thumb and forefinger, her head fell against the rock and her back arched, increasing the pressure, demanding more.

Alix ceased to be, and there was only this moment, this pleasure so intense she thought she might die of it. She did not need to hold herself back to beware of his frailty. She was free to let herself feel and react, and the sensation was all the more powerful because the bastard was right. She wanted him.

A delicate little yawn and a rustle of blankets broke the spell. Cyrus dropped Alix as if she'd burned him and stumbled backward, his green eyes wide with shock and hunger. His shirt hung open, exposing a wide chest covered with short golden hair, his trousers were halfway unbuttoned, and his hands shook.

The deep need that had pooled low in Alix's belly turned to horror. By the gods, what had she done? Disgust and self-loathing turned into a pit beneath her and she fell headlong into the darkness.

A high-pitched voice said in French, "The meat is burning."

13

Cyrus

DINNER PASSED IN UNCOMFORTABLE silence, though it was nearly impossible for Cyrus to ignore the woman across the fire. If he wasn't looking at her, he was listening to her heartbeat, her breathing, the gentle humming she used to convince the small girl child she was safe.

The girl slowly made her way across the intervening space toward Alix, lured as if by magic, until the two lay together on the opposite side of the fire. The child snored with contented little grunts, and Alix curled protectively at her side.

But Alix did not sleep, judging by the stiff set of her shoulders. Good. If he couldn't rest after their heated interlude, she shouldn't either. After all, she'd attacked him, and he was still stiff with violent need and unspent energy running through his body like an electric charge.

The roasted meat had not been flavorful enough to wash the spearmint flavor of her out of his mouth, and the heat of the fire on his face was a warm breeze compared to the scorching feel of her body under his hands. He still pictured her with his waking mind, dark hair tumbled down to her hips, shirt halfway undone, chest heaving, eyes

wide with shock, mouth swollen from kissing him. By the moon, he'd
been tempted to worship her.

But recognition had drowned her surprised expression in horror as
soon as she remembered who they were to one another. For a moment he
thought she might vomit, but she only turned away from him, crouched
next to the girl, and began talking in a low, soothing voice, leaving him
standing alone in the shadows wondering what the hell happened.

Alix was both beautiful and interesting, but he only admired her the
way one might admire a bird of prey. Aside from needling her in the cave
to make her uncomfortable as his captor, he wasn't stupid enough to
think of or even desire more than cold politeness from her. Why would
he? She was hateful, rarely smiled and never laughed, and considered him
a monster.

Until she goaded him into a fight and made his blood sing with such
vital, pulsing excitement, he knew his life would forever be split between
that moment and everything before it. Fighting her had been like dancing with a whirlwind: grace, power, and deadly beauty in his arms. But
she was more than a mere force of nature. She was broken.

The Mother Superior hinted at trauma in her past, and her reaction
in the apartment confirmed it. He recognized the dazed expression, the
frozen limbs, the sweaty palms. He felt all of those things more times
than he could count, especially when the memories were upon him.

Broken recognized broken, after all.

Despite that, she clearly wanted him. For a moment, she wanted him
enough to ignore her hate. Or, perhaps she wanted the freedom to let
go of her rigid self-control, to allow herself to enjoy pleasure she did not
have to fight for or justify. He understood that well enough.

Sometimes the desperation to feel anything other than pain made one
mad.

The predator in him sensed her weakness and wanted to exploit it, to break her to his will, to coax and tease her until she writhed beneath him with need only he could satisfy. But years of training taught him to control the darkness inside him, just as he controlled the wolf, and he refused to let the predator have its way.

Cyrus surged to his feet and stalked toward the road to take the first watch. He needed to be far enough away from Alix that the scent of her and the gentle rustling of blankets didn't make him remember the feel of her. He didn't want it, and she did not deserve it.

Alix hadn't shown vulnerability in a moment of trust; relived trauma and desperation had dragged it out of her. To take advantage of that would truly make him the monster she accused him of being.

So he stood near the road staring into the darkness and wondering...what would happen if he was careful with her, if he honored that vulnerable moment? Would she begin to trust him, to see him as something other than a monster? Would she be free of the hate driving her? A vision sprang to his mind unbidden, one of Alix smiling and laughing, spinning in a fall breeze as bright leaves floated through the air and tangled in her hair. She ran toward him, eyes shining, and threw herself into his arms.

Once he imagined it, the vision would not leave him any peace. He saw her every time he closed his eyes, wanted her with every breath. It made no sense. The woman made him mad with frustration far more often than she made him hungry with desire, yet the vision would not dissipate.

So he stood in the dark, listening to the sounds of the night until he could no longer ignore the pull of the warm space by the little campfire. He crept back but stayed in the shadows watching her chest rise and fall as he tried to remind himself of all the reasons convincing Alix to be his lover was a terrible idea.

Sweat ran in a tickling rivulet down his spine, but the girl clung to his neck and upper back like a tree frog, adding her body heat to the warmth of the sun. They'd been walking for the better part of two days, and while she spoke little, the child had grown bold enough to order the two of them around with pointed fingers, wide eyes, and stamping feet.

After lunch she stood before him, the top of her head reaching only as high as his hip, and pointed at his back with one commanding finger. She accompanied the gesture with a stamp of her bare foot, making a cloud of dust rise around her legs.

"Looks like I'm the pack mule," he told Alix with a resigned sigh before picking the child up and slinging her across his back like a sack of flour.

She wriggled around and locked her arms comfortably about his neck, each foot nestled against the palms of his hands like stirrups. He could have sworn Alix grinned, but she set off ahead of them at a jog, scouting the road and often circling around through the trees. The woman was so quick and quiet she didn't make a sound even when navigating the dense underbrush. Even her scent, the healthy sweat of exertion, only reached him when he was downwind.

After a rather long scouting run, she waited for them on the crest of the next hill, her red cloak silhouetted against the sky, and said, "The inn is twenty minutes away."

"Hear that, lassie?" he asked the girl on his back. "In twenty minutes or so, you shall have a fine room of your own, and plenty of food, and a kind person to take care of you."

She made a sound of distress and tightened her little arms until they threatened to cut off his circulation. He stopped to pry her arms loose, but she clung to him like a burr to a horse's tail.

"What seems to be the problem?" Alix asked.

"Our wee lass doesn't like the thought of staying at the inn, I think," he said, trying to free himself without hurting her.

Alix stepped closer to look up at the girl's face, which was smushed against the side of his neck. "Is that true, little one? You don't want to go to the inn?"

The child squeezed and Cyrus fought not to make a choking sound. The little beastie was strong. Alix stared at her for several long seconds, then reached down and untied the sheath of one silver dagger, lifting it for the girl to see.

"This is my favorite dagger. It is made of silver, and carved with magic runes to keep it strong. Do you know what it's for?"

Her little head rubbed against his neck as she shook it.

Alix pulled the blade just far enough from the sheath to show the metallic sheen. "Silver is for killing werewolves and other magical creatures of the night, but only those tied to the moon. And this dagger has killed too many werewolves to count."

The girl's grip loosened, and she sat up a bit, finally interested.

"I have been looking for someone to take care of it for me for a while, someone who will only use it on werewolves, or to protect themselves.

Silver knives are special, and should never be used in anger, or on the innocent. Do you know of anyone who would keep my knife for me?"

A nod.

Alix smiled at the girl. It was a tender, genuine smile, not one of the smirks she often threw at him like daggers. And her smile, though not aimed at him, was just as potent as he imagined it would be. His chest tightened.

"I am glad to hear it," Alix said, tapping the tip of the girl's nose with one finger. "Who should I give it to for safekeeping?"

The girl released him and stretched out one bony little arm.

"You?"

A nod.

"Well"—Alix tapped her chin, pretending to think it over—"I suppose that might work, but there is one problem. I only lend my weapons to people I trust, and I don't know your name yet."

One arm tightened around his neck, and the extended arm dropped in disappointment he felt through the tension in her body. But Alix waited. After several heartbeats, a tiny voice said in his ear, "Mercedes."

"Mercedes," Alix repeated, holding out her hand. "I am Alix La Rouge."

After a moment of hesitation, Mercedes held out her hand, and Alix took it.

"Nice to meet you. Would you rather hold the knife now or wait until we reach the inn?"

Mercedes's fingers extended, wiggling impatiently, and Alix chuckled before tying the handle down so it could not be drawn. She offered it to the girl.

As soon as she held the knife, Mercedes sagged against his back and sighed. He hadn't realized how tense she'd been. Now she had something with which to defend herself, and her relief was palpable. He wished he'd thought of offering her some kind of weapon two days ago when she was wrapped around him like a boa constrictor.

Twenty minutes later, they entered the yard of the inn. The squat, two-story building crouched on the edge of a clearing near the road, weather-worn grey shingles and cracking plaster making the place look like a grumpy old man glaring down at travelers as they passed. Several horses took turns at a trough while wagons parked along the roadside. Drivers secured feed bags to the heads of their mules as men stained with road dust trailed in and out of the building.

Sour beer, rising bread, sweat, leather, horse shit, and roasting meat combined to fill the air with a smell unique to countryside inns. Cyrus had not stopped traveling since the destruction of his village, and life on the road made inns the next closest thing to home, but this place did not hold the peace and comfort he hoped for. It was bursting at the seams with exactly the kind of people he hoped to avoid.

"This is going to be dangerous," he told Alix, hoping Mercedes was listening. "There are at least two large parties here, and none of them appear genteel. You are a beautiful woman and they are likely lonely, so keep your hood up and try not to..." His words trailed off as he looked at her.

Alix wore men's clothing for practicality, which showed her lean, muscled form to advantage and hugged her body enough to be revealing. Snug clothing made sense from a fighter's perspective, but the kind of men drinking in the inn would not see Alix's clothing as a concession to practicality. They would likely consider it an invitation.

"I appreciate the thought, wolf, but I can promise you those men will bother me no more than they will bother you. And if they are foolish enough to approach me, I am quite capable of discouraging them."

"I never doubted that," he said wryly, imagining her thoroughly dressing down anyone who approached her without respect. "But I would prefer not to frighten the innkeeper away from sharing information with us by killing his patrons."

Alix shrugged and said, "We will simply have to deal with whatever happens, won't we?" before swirling the cloak around her body, covering her tempting curves–and weapons–from view. She spun and led him out of the sunshine and into the dark, fragrant roadside inn.

Despite being alone in the middle of nowhere, the inn was well-built. Sawn wood plank floors, a proper bar with a tap and an oven, and a river rock fireplace with a hearth big enough to stand in made the place a haven of comfort for weary travelers. He took a deep breath: carrots, celery, garlic, rosemary and...rabbit stew? The smell almost made the noise—pints thumping on wooden tables, chatter and laughter, silverware scraping, and a few drunken snores—worth enduring. But every table was full, so Cyrus carried Mercedes to the foot of the stairs and sat on the bottom step so she could climb down while Alix approached the bar.

The men at the edges of the room followed with their eyes, but those closest to her, the ones who saw her face, blanched and looked away. When she pressed in next to them at the bar, they stared at her in admiration for a moment, then leaned away and tried not to look in her direction.

Their reactions were so curious, Cyrus began to wonder if they were looking at the same woman. But before he examined that thought too long, another woman entered the inn. Her hair, the color of bitter chocolate, lay in a braid over her shoulder, and she walked with the graceful confidence of nobility.

She was not striking, like Alix, but had appealing features and an amused, engaging expression. She wore the kind of utilitarian clothing one might see on safari, and carried an umbrella, of all things.

Eyes that followed Alix minutes before now locked on the shorter woman with speculation, roaming up and down her figure as she joined the crowd at the bar. Two burly men with sunburned faces and rolled-up shirtsleeves, miners by the look of their muscled forearms, regarded her with particular interest and nudged one another with raised eyebrows.

"Here you are," Alix said, appearing in front of them with mugs of beer in one hand and a bowl of rabbit stew in the other.

Cyrus drank half the mug in one swallow and watched from the corner of his eye as Mercedes ate spoonful after spoonful of stew.

"Careful, lass," he told her. "Don't make yourself sick now."

She was likely past the danger of harm, and had been well-fed since they discovered her, but still ate as if every meal may be her last.

"The innkeeper agreed to speak with us once the customers are served," Alix said, leaning against the wall and swallowing a mouthful of beer.

"That calls for more bowls of stew then," Cyrus said, standing. "Will you have one?"

Alix raised an eyebrow, as if their coldly professional relationship did not prepare her for the extravagant kindness of being offered a simple bowl of soup.

"Yes, please," she said at last.

The barkeep was a stout elf woman with delicate features and rosy cheeks. She had a businesslike expression, several earrings in each ear, and dark tattoos peeking out from beneath her shirtsleeves. When Cyrus approached, she held up one finger for him to wait while she pulled two more mugs of beer, handing one to the brunette and the other to a dwarvish man with shoulders like a bull.

"I told your woman I'd speak with you once I finished service," she told him as she snapped a hand towel and tossed one end over her shoulder.

"So you did. I've only come to ask for two more bowls of stew if there is any more to go around."

"There is, but it will cost you four copper pennies," she said, turning away to lift clean wooden bowls from a pile.

He counted the money out and waited.

"I'll be slagged," the dwarven man said, looking him up and down. "You're about a giant, aren't ya?"

"As close to one as you are likely to meet," Cyrus agreed.

"And strong, too, I'd wager. How is it the mines haven't snapped you up yet?"

"What makes you think they haven't?"

"Well–" the stranger began, sounding embarrassed, but a soft, feminine voice said with some amusement, "Anyone with eyes can see you are no miner, my large friend, so if you are going to lie, you ought to pick a different profession."

Two bowls of hot stew hit the counter in front of him with a thud, but he ignored them and turned toward the lady, for she could be nothing other than a member of the aristocracy, given her bearing. Alix's eyes were a shade of brown resembling sunlight through dark whisky, but hers were the deep, rich color of newly turned earth, and they sparkled with mischief.

"My lady," he said with a half bow. "What profession should I choose if I want to be a successful liar?"

"Is this a challenge, sir?"

"If you'd like to take it as such."

She folded her arms and took half a step back to get a good look at him. Her eyes cataloged everything, so he raised his arms and did a full, slow turn. One of the men whistled, and his table burst into laughter.

The lady nodded once to herself, took a deep pull from her mug, and wiped the foam from the corner of her mouth with her fingertips.

"Very well," she said. "But if I guess correctly, you owe me something dreadfully valuable."

"Like what?"

"How does your firstborn child sound?"

He laughed. "That's the way they do it in stories, and I would be a cad to deny the sensible request of a lady who has fairly solved a riddle. Alright, my firstborn is yours."

She smirked, which made a dimple appear in her right cheek, and returned his bow. "Challenge accepted, then." She cleared her throat. "Most men with height and brawn like yours avoid boring, indoor jobs, and your tan, as well as the wrinkles at the corners of your eyes, suggest that you work out of doors. Your clothes are worn but well cared for, and the material is rather fine, as is the leather of your boots. Though the soles are worn. So, your occupation earns you more money than the average laborer, and you travel a great deal on foot. The calluses on your hands are not of the thick sort belonging to woodsmen or blacksmiths, and the scars on your knuckles suggest you use your hands for violence, rather than a traditional outdoor trade."

Half of the patrons stopped talking and turned to listen to the woman with raised eyebrows.

"You do not carry the weapons of a professional hunter, though the scuffs on your belt indicate that when you do shoot, you prefer a pistol and are a right-handed draw. If I were to guess..."

Her eyes took on a faraway look, replaced a moment later by a troubled expression. Had she guessed his true nature? Surely not. She opened her mouth, closed it, and winced. "You know, I do believe you have stumped me," she said a moment later with a weak smile. "It appears your firstborn child is safe, sir."

The audience made sounds of disappointment and returned to their conversations, but he didn't take his eyes off the strange woman who had, in fact, read him like a book. But he got the impression she did not like whatever she'd seen.

He bent down and said, "For the record, you were right about every observation. So, chances are, you are right about whatever conclusion you've come to." He picked up the bowls and winked at her. "But I don't bite, I promise."

She chuckled, and the unease drifted away, leaving her smiling as she raised her glass in salute and said, "That is a relief. But I should warn you...I do."

Cyrus threw back his head and laughed. He was still grinning when he rejoined Alix and Mercedes. The former remained leaning against the wall, but her arms were folded over her chest and her eyes glowed with irritation.

She snatched the bowl from him fast enough to spill hot stew over her fingers. "I do not know what you consider professional," she hissed, "but taking strange women to bed on the job does not qualify."

Cyrus did not bother to hide his confusion. "What?"

"We do not have time for you to flirt your way across the countryside, wolf, so try to control yourself until this job is done."

By the bloody moon, was Alix...jealous?

Cyrus shook his head and tried not to laugh, knowing it would only infuriate her. If he pushed his luck, she might add rabbit stew to the road dust already coating his clothes. "That was nothing but a bit of friendly jousting."

"Oh, is that what you call it?"

"Have you never laughed with a stranger just for the pleasure of company, minx?"

"Of course not. And don't call me that."

"What you saw," he said, gesturing to the bar with his thumb, "was a mere bit of fun. I need no ulterior motive to enjoy the company of a clever person. And laughs are hard enough to come by in this world. I will take them where I can and be glad of it." Alix only eyed him as if he were mad, which made him want to nettle her a bit, so he added, "If it makes you feel any better, I would rather gaze at you in unrequited adoration than flirt with a hundred women."

His words had the intended effect. She scowled at him, but her cheeks glowed with color, and she turned all her attention to her stew, ignoring him as if he did not exist.

He was not sure why, but that felt like a victory.

Mercedes handed back her empty bowl and lifted both arms, wiggling her fingers and staring at his stew. It looked like he wasn't eating alone.

14

Alix

IF THE INNKEEPER DID not meet with them soon, Alix was determined to leave the building and let Cyrus handle the rest. The sights and sounds overwhelmed her senses with no escape: squeaking chairs and laughter, thumping mugs, sloshing drinks, scratching flatware, scraping, coughing, and the overwhelmingly sharp stink of sweat, leather, oiled metal, sour beer, bad breath, and yeasty bread.

Her skin crawled with the need to get away and into the open air.

The only thing stopping Alix from taking Mercedes and waiting outside was the trying to figure out what was wrong with the strange, pretty brunette at the bar. She ate her stew and bread if she sat in a fancy restaurant in Paris instead of a backwater tavern in the middle of nowhere. Alix could have ignored that, if the woman smelled like a normal human, if she didn't move so quickly, so gracefully.

She was more like an elf, but didn't smell like elf-kind, either.

Cyrus hadn't so much as glanced in the woman's direction since returning with the stew, choosing to give Mercedes all of his attention, but Alix found her eyes continually drawn to the bar. If the woman was a vampire, Alix would have smelled and sensed it. There were a dozen other rare monsters creeping about the wilds of Europe, but Alix ran down the list of qualities identifying each monster, and none of them fit.

Not elf or dwarf, and certainly not banshee, so what was she? Was she dangerous? Not knowing made her want to hold the woman down and demand answers.

The innkeeper stepped out from behind the bar and motioned to the stairs. "There we are. Let's talk somewhere quieter, eh?"

Alix breathed a secret sigh of relief as Cyrus lifted Mercedes into his arms and led them up the narrow staircase to a small, empty bedroom at the back of the building. He set the girl down on the bed while Alix motioned the elvin into the room, watching the hallway to ensure no one followed.

The innkeeper eyed them both, put her hands on her hips, and said, "What is it I can do for you? Keep in mind, I have customers and little time for idle chat."

Cyrus held out his hand. "My name is Cyrus, and this is my associate, Alix."

The eyed Cyrus up and down once before shaking his hand. Alix didn't blame her for a bit of caution. Cyrus was a big man. "I am Ruby," she said, "and this here is my place. What do you want?"

"This," Cyrus said, gesturing to the child, "is Mercedes. Her village was a couple of days' walk East of here."

"Was?"

"Werewolves attacked maybe two weeks ago, as far as we can tell. There isn't much left."

"A whole village?" Ruby asked, hand on her heart. "Are you certain it was not The Beast?"

After a beat of surprised silence, Alix said, "It was several werewolves. I am certain of this."

Ruby's hard expression melted away and her eyes filled with concern. "Root and stone, the poor dear. That would be Mont Blanc? I wondered why we've seen no traffic from there in the last couple of weeks. How many people... no, don't answer."

Cyrus gave the child a sympathetic glance. "We found Mercedes hiding in the village. She needs looking after."

"She seems comfortable enough with you," Ruby said.

"Aye, but we need to hunt down the monsters before they destroy more towns."

Ruby considered that, sighed, then pulled the dish towel off her shoulder, running the worn fabric between her fingers. "And the woods are no place for a child. You two are Hunters, then?"

Alix shot Cyrus a surprised glance. Hunters had grown less common as the boots of technology and industry crushed magic out of the world, and few modern people knew of them. Those who did were either the ones holding the purse strings or those who lived in particularly dangerous locations.

This Inn was remote, but so far as Alix knew, it was no more dangerous than any other part of the French countryside. So how did an innkeeper know what they were?

"Living apart from society doesn't make me ignorant," Ruby said, noting the glance they shared and folding her arms. "Don't look so surprised. Those werewolves aren't the first monsters to come through here, and you aren't the first hunters, either."

"Fair enough," Cyrus said.

"But you say you're going to stop them?"

"We are. Permanently."

Ruby frowned. "My inn is fairly prosperous, as these things go. But it costs a painful amount to ship goods this far, and I can't pay your rates. Leastways, I can't pay you the rates the last hunters asked for."

"Actually," Alix said, trying to keep the note of pleading out of her voice, "we were hoping to pay you."

Ruby's hands stilled, her brows rose, and she shot a glance at Mercedes, who was turning the silver knife sheath over and over in her tiny hands, seemingly oblivious to the conversation. "I see."

"We intend to send word to the Sisters of St. Christopher to have someone fetch her. She'll be safe there, but we cannot spare the time to bring her. We hoped you might send a message to the convent, and rent a room and board for the girl while she waits."

"That," Cyrus added, "and safety. I intend to make sure this child stays safe. I would be very irritated with anyone who endangered her."

Ruby puffed up like an angry cat and shook her towel in Cyrus' face. "You will watch your tone, sir. And if you insult me again in my own establishment, I will have you thrown out on your ear. I don't care how big you are."

Cyrus smiled. "Your response was all the proof I needed, ma'am. Please forgive the insinuation."

She looked taken aback, and realized too late that Cyrus had merely been testing her resolve. A sheepish expression perched on her face for a moment, then flew off and left resolve in its place.

"I never cared for a child before, but children are only small people, after all. And I suppose she can sit behind the bar while I work. She'll be safe enough while we wait for someone to fetch her. Besides, Horace has a soft spot for little ones and he won't stand for any nonsense."

"Horace?" Alix asked.

Ruby smiled while leaning half out the door to yell, "Horace!"

A series of thumps and scratches echoed up the stairs, followed by a *fwoosh* of huge wings. Those were the sounds of a monster. Alix drew both pistols and set herself between Mercedes and the hallway as a griffin the size of a huge dog padded into the room.

"Oh, don't worry about Horace," Ruby said, patting one of the beast's heavy shoulders affectionately. "He won't hurt you so long as you don't disturb the peace and play nice with everyone."

Alix stared at the animal, unblinking. It had the sleek, muscled body of a hound, with the paws of a big cat. Both hawk-like wings were tucked neatly against its sides, and its head was similar in shape to a cat's but with the curved beak of a raptor and large, gold, forward-facing eyes. A pair of ears, longer than a cat's, were pricked high and swiveling as it listened to the room and looked at each one of them.

"Found him when he was a fledgeling," Ruby said with pride. "Some fool shot his maman, and he wasn't big enough to feed himself. Been with me ever since."

"And he follows commands?" Cyrus asked, eyeing the beast warily and taking half a step to the right, putting himself between Alix and the wickedly curved beak. As if she needed his protection. Alix scowled, but didn't take her eyes off the creature. If it did lunge for the girl, she would put a bullet between it's pretty eyes.

"Oh, well enough," Ruby said. "Leastways, he knows who is trouble and who isn't."

"If he hurts the girl," Alix began, but Ruby scoffed and waved a dismissive hand.

"He's gentle as a mother hen with babes."

They haggled for a while over the price of room and board while Horace slowly made his way onto the bed: first his head, then head and paws, and then his whole torso, giving the girl time to get used to his presence. Mercedes was shy at first, fingers wrapped around the hilt of Alix's blade. But the big gold eyes were almost hypnotic, and soon she reached out with one tentative hand and ran her fingers over the creature's fur. It shivered and closed its eyes with a rumbling purr.

Once she petted his head, no one else in the room existed. And by the time Cyrus and Ruby agreed to a payment, the beast and the girl were curled into a comfortable ball, snoring, with her arms wrapped around Horace's neck.

Ruby leaned down and stroked the animal's sleek head. It raised one ear and opened a single eye, which swiveled around to meet hers. "You protect her," she told him, patting his neck before heading back downstairs.

But Alix was not so eager to leave. She stood in the doorway, watching the rise and fall of the cinnamon-colored hide and noting how carefully Horace cradled the little girl. The two of them looked peaceful, wrapped in a cocoon of warmth and safety.

"We won't get to say goodbye," Cyrus said. Was that a wistful tone in his voice?

"Are you going soft, wolf?"

"For a wee bairn? Aye, maybe. And I do feel responsible for her. Besides, you haven't got a heart of stone, either, minx. The two of you were curled up much the same way by the fire, so don't behave as if you're not a bit soft, as well."

Alix didn't bother to deny it. The girl had needed comfort, and Alix was honest enough with herself to admit she needed it, too. Mercedes' circumstances had dragged to light many memories Alix did not wish to revisit, memories so sharp that living with them forced her to become tough as rawhide.

For a couple of nights, the girl had slept in her arms, and the two of them kept the memories away. It had been a long time since anyone trusted her enough to sleep so close, close enough for the comfort of human warmth. If Mercedes had not just been traumatized, she would likely have shied away from Alix the way everyone else did.

Mortals may not look at her face and see her vampire parentage, but they sensed it, smelled it, felt that the person they were looking at was not right, not normal. Not safe. Ruby the was one of the rare few confident enough to remain unbothered, and Mercedes was likely too traumatized to notice.

Now and then, when she was truly lonely, Alix would wait for nightfall and seek comfort in the arms of anyone who was braver than the rest, a rare soul who found her more appealing than disturbing.

Perhaps they simply enjoyed the fear of knowing, on an elemental level, that they were in mortal danger when she was near. Some people found such things exhilarating, and Alix would accept that so long as it kept the darkness at bay a while longer. But those trysts only lasted an hour or two.

Afterward, she was back to being alone.

"Oh, hell," Cyrus said, and pulled her into his arms.

Alix pressed her knife against his neck as her heart leaped into her throat. He ignored the blade, leaned in until his lips were inches from hers, and paused, waiting. The blade didn't deter him, but the question in his eyes said her voice would, if she told him no.

Did she? His arms were strong around her, his body warm, and the comfort of his embrace held the loneliness at bay. When she did not pull away, his lips brushed hers, so light she might have imagined the touch; a question, not a demand.

She found herself kissing him back, deepening the kiss without meaning to, answering with her lips and tongue. For a moment, the world blazed to life, and the heat of it burned away the lurking shadows haunting the corners of her soul.

At least, until she remembered she was kissing the damned wolf. Hadn't she learned her lesson by now? Alix pulled away, grimacing. Cyrus let her go, watching her eyes drift to the bead of blood running down his neck. She started to apologize, stopped, and scowled at him as her grip on the knife tightened.

"Spearmint," he said.

All violent thoughts ground to a halt. "What?"

"You taste of spearmint."

She blinked and said dumbly, "I just ate rabbit stew."

"Aye, but so did I. The flavors cancel each other out, and spearmint was left over."

"Flavors don't cancel each—no, wait," she shook her head to clear it. What had she wanted to say? Oh yes. A warning. A warning was good, because if she killed the wolf now, that would frighten the child and leave a terrible mess for Ruby, so Alix said, "Let me be clear about this so that I am not forced to kill you before this mission is over: stay away from me."

"Aren't you exaggerating a bit?"

"Look at your neck and ask me again."

He wiped the blood away and shrugged. "It was worth it."

"You're lucky it wasn't worse, you great bloody idiot. "

"I couldn't help it," he said in his own defense, raising his hands but smiling ever so slightly. "If you don't want me to kiss you, don't stand around looking so forlorn. Anyone else would have done the same."

"No, they would not," she said, sheathing the knife. "Everyone else has more sense."

He opened then closed his mouth and cocked his head. His brow raised for a moment before drawing down in displeasure.

"Damn," he said, then passed her without brushing her body with his and skipped lightly down the steps.

A feminine voice floated up the stairs, the same voice that had guessed so much about Cyrus less than half an hour before. "I realize large words can be hard to understand, so let me say this clearly using single syllables: If you touch me, it will be the last thing you ever do with that hand."

Shit.

Alix followed Cyrus to the bar to survey the scene. One of the burly miners had pushed his way up close to the strange brunette woman, much to the amusement of his companions at the table. He must not have realized she wasn't entirely human, because he stared down at her with proprietary amusement and said, "Come now, you did that mind trick for the big fellow. I only want my turn, sweetheart, that's all."

As he spoke, he grabbed the woman's upper arm. Cyrus made a growling noise and started across the room, but long before he reached the bar, the woman changed her posture. It was subtle, like watching a cat about to spring. Her weight and balance changed, becoming more centered, and her shoulders shifted.

Alix grinned. The woman's body language said she was going to punch the miner in the face.

Scars decorated the man's knuckles and face the way bright colors warned of poisonous animals. He had been in enough fights to notice the change in her balance, because his amused expression faded and he let go of her arm. But he wasn't fast enough.

In a blur, the brunette grabbed his wrist with her left hand, turned, and executed some movement Alix had never seen. The man dropped to his knees with a surprised exclamation, his back to her as she twisted his arm up between his shoulder blades with his wrist pressed inward.

"Please don't struggle," she said in a tired voice. "You will break your own arm, and then I shall have to dry your tears, and both our days will be ruined."

Cyrus reached them, gestured to the man, and said, "May I?"

The woman looked up at him with a tired smile. "By all means."

Cyrus hauled the man up by the scruff of his neck and carried him out the door.

Alix watched them go, then turned to the woman and said, "You handled that well."

"One learns all kinds of useful things when one travels," the woman replied with a dimpled smile. "Please thank your husband for me."

"He is not my husband."

"Oh!" her cheeks turned rosy, and she sent a quick, speculative glance out the door. "Please, Forgive my mistake."

Alix nodded in a mixture of acceptance and goodbye, then handed a purse to the innkeeper. Ruby weighed it on her palm and dropped it into her apron pocket. "I'll send a messenger to the convent to-morrow morning."

"If you don't mind," Alix said, turning to see Cyrus still chastising the miner, "may I ask you a few questions before we go?"

Ruby's eyes roamed over the tables. The crowd had thinned significantly as travelers returned to their carts, so she nodded. "Go ahead."

"You said hunters have been through here before. Can you tell me when?"

"It must be three, four months ago."

"Did they say what they were hunting?"

Ruby rubbed a hand on the back of her neck and rolled her eyes upward as she thought. "They said The Beast had returned. And with so many deaths in the country, who was I to argue? Werewolves never kill so many."

"It was not The Beast. That creature is long dead, I promise you. How many have died?"

"Must be more than threescore if you believe the rumors."

Over sixty? That outstripped Mother Superior's estimates by a significant margin. "Did they say where they were going to look?"

"East," she said, "further into the mountains." She scanned the room again, likely cataloging each patron and judging when to refill pints, retrieve plates, and who would need to be refused more beer. Once she was satisfied, she said, "You are certain it was not The Beast? I still remember the fear, though I was young. It seemed to be everywhere, killing and attacking across the countryside. Doing even common things was hard, as you felt the Beast may attack at any moment."

"No, it is not The Beast. You may rely upon me in this matter." Alix knew this because she had killed it long ago, though the credit had gone to another. But Ruby was right about the fear; after nearly one hundred deaths, the countryside stank of it, and the Beast of Gévaudan was all anyone could think about or speak of.

It had, in fact, been a barghest, and a rather nasty one, something like a mix between a wolf and a hyena. Killing it had not been easy, particularly with the King's elderly gun bearer tagging along.

"Well, you would know," Ruby said, snapping her hand towel and settling it over one shoulder. "And so, time for work. Stop in when you are done, if you have news."

Alix nodded and followed Cyrus into the yard. He stood with his arms crossed and feet planted apart, watching the foolish miner and his companions ride away while casting resentful glances over their shoulders.

"You have made enemies of them," she warned.

"How will I sleep at night?"

"Arrogance is foolish. It will get you killed."

"I'm traveling with La Cape Rouge and you expect me to fear a few miners?"

She looked him over with an appraising eye. "Maybe you aren't as stupid as you look."

He barked a laugh and slung his pack over his back. "Let's pester the locals a bit before we head out. I want to learn more about what has been happening."

"I'll leave that to you, wolf." Alix shouldered her own pack and settled it atop her cloak. The locals wouldn't speak to her, anyway. "I'll scout the area."

"Suit yourself, minx."

"Don't call me that," she said as he turned and walked back into the inn. The damned man made her blood boil, so she strode into the trees, scowling. She needed to find something to kill.

15

Cyrus

NOT EVEN THE MOST dedicated gossips in the salons of Paris could match the trappers, hunters, woodcutters, and miners of the backcountry for pure vocal stamina. They spent days and weeks without hearing another voice, packing away their thoughts until a friendly inn and a pint of beer loosened their tongues enough for the words to come spilling out.

The rough men, with calloused hands and sunburned cheeks, talked about the rumors of monsters, sounds in the night, and abandoned homesteads. One garrulous old man with a patchy white beard and a few missing fingers even mentioned watching through the window of his cabin as a pack of dark shadows crept across an open field.

Cyrus heard it all and made sense of none of it. He could think of nothing but how Alix felt in his arms; the heat of her mouth, the way her body molded to his, giving him the answer he'd waited for. He bled a little, yes, but his head was still attached. It was worth it.

What compelled him to kiss her, he could not say. Maybe it was the desolate longing in her eyes as she watched Mercedes and the griffon sleep. The desire to comfort her began when she stood in the doorway of the little apartment in Mont Blanc, memories of pain etched on her face and every line of stiff muscle. And seeing the sad longing in her eyes today as she stared at the child scraped something raw in his chest. He acted without thinking. Now he couldn't focus on the conversations around him because he wanted to lope into the forest and find her.

When had he started wanting Alix more than he disliked her?

Cyrus swallowed the warm dregs of beer at the bottom of his glass, dropped a coin on the table and left. Instead of piecing the bits of overheard conversation into a cohesive story that would give him insight into their mission, he thought of a pair of light brown eyes. What was wrong with him?

That was a stupid question, he knew what the problem was: despite her prickly nature, his partner had gotten under his skin. That was dangerous for them both. The sooner this job was done, the better.

He stood on the packed dirt and took a few deep breaths to test the wind. Spearmint, sharp and fresh, led him into the forest at a jog. Less than half a mile away, he found Alix crouched in the shade at the edge of a clearing, plucking leaves from a low bush. She popped some into her mouth before dropping the rest into her pocket.

As she closed her eyes and chewed, the knife-edged expression she often wore melted beneath the warmth of an unguarded, gentle smile. It transformed her face, revealing beauty that made his chest tight and his breath stop. Seeing her there, peaceful in the dappled sunlight, was like getting a glimpse of the woman she might have been without whatever trauma had stolen her innocence.

The wind shifted, and Alix stiffened when she caught his scent. The carefully guarded mask fell back into place as she stood and brushed off her hands.

"Any sign?" he asked, blurting the words before she could set the tone with something more confrontational.

She sighed. "Nothing worth troubling about, though there are far too many predators in the area. This forest could use a unicorn to keep things in balance."

"I'll be certain to suggest that to the next unicorn I meet."

She either snorted or laughed, but since he saw a flash of amusement in her eyes, he counted it as laughing, and smiled in return. Her amusement disappeared.

"Any luck with the local rabble?" she asked in a business-like voice as she stood and dusted her hands on her pant legs.

He folded his arms and leaned his shoulder against the trunk of a tree. Could he recapture that moment of easy going humor? Was it even worth trying? "Impossible to tell. Wild folk are always superstitious, and a miner may turn an owl into a harpy after being alone for weeks. But they are worried enough to suspect their neighbors. And in a tightly-knit community like this, that is never a good sign."

"The fear has made them wary. Ruby asked me if The Beast has returned."

"The Beast? Of Gévaudan? That monster has been dead for a hundred and forty years."

"I understand her fear, even if it is based on a faulty conclusion," Alix said with a shrug. "The deaths and strange signs, coupled with so many hunters in the area, make The Beast sound like a reasonable explanation. After all, werewolves don't behave this way, and The Beast cast a long shadow."

That creature had been one of his greatest disappointments. Word of the elusive monster spread across the continent, and Cyrus returned early from Austria to hunt it, in part because of the rising death toll, and in part because the king's six-thousand livre bounty would have come in handy just then.

But by the time he reached France, they declared the creature dead, with signs and flyers nailed to every available surface. Cyrus had been rather disappointed. But that was a century and a half ago. And from the way she spoke...he knew Alix was not precisely human, with strange blood and accelerated healing, but was there more to uncover?

He asked, a little too casually, "You don't believe The Beast has returned, then?"

Alix rolled her eyes and passed him, heading for the road and saying over her shoulder, "When I kill something, wolf, it stays dead."

"That was you?

"Someone had to kill it."

Cyrus clenched his jaw as his heart rate picked up. The Beast had been killed around 1760. If Alix was not lying, and he didn't think she was, then she was over one hundred and thirty years old. Dwarves lived that long, and elves longer. Humans did not.

What was she? No werewolf, not even from a true line. She might be half-elven, he supposed, which would account for her speed and grace, but half-elves aged faster than their elven family members, and at more than one-hundred and thirty years, she would show signs of age.

"How old are you?" he asked, catching up.

"What a rude question. Then again, why should I expect manners from you?"

"If you expect me to believe you killed The Beast, you'd better be able to prove it."

"I do not care what you believe."

"Then why brag about it?"

"So you will know what I am capable of when you run off at the mouth."

This woman was going to drive him mad. No one else was so capable of making his blood boil, and the irritation forced him to take a track that usually worked to ruffle her feathers. "The last time we spoke of what I could do with my mouth, you turned my offer down. Am I to understand you've changed your mind?"

This time, it was her heartbeat that picked up, but she disguised it masterfully when she scoffed and raised a derisive brow. "Why on earth would I do that? Your last unwelcome attempt was so unimpressive, I nearly cut your throat. Why not save both of us the disappointment and keep your mouth shut?"

Cyrus could not tell if he wanted to strangle the woman or kiss her senseless, but he found himself leaning down till his nose touched the delicate shell of her ear to say, "I'm going to make you eat those words, minx, and you're going to enjoy every second of it. And so shall I."

Alix pretended not to hear him, but she swallowed, her cheeks flaming, pupils dilated. "I warned you what would happen if you did not stay away from me," she said, but there was a quavering edge to her voice.

"I won't touch you that way until you ask it of me," he said. "And you will ask me. Mark my words."

"Is that a threat?"

"No. Call it a premonition, if you like. In the meantime, I'll race you to Mont Blanc."

She rolled her eyes and said, "I will do no such stupid thing," but she was speaking to empty air.

Cyrus needed to move, to work muscles tense from the mental image his damned impulsive brain conjured up when he said something he should not have said. It appeared he was not smart enough to keep his mouth shut, not where Alix was concerned.

When she flung insults at him he could not stomach, he found himself willing to say or do nearly anything to put them back on an even footing. Even if that meant threatening to spread her legs and bury his face between her thighs.

By the moon, just the thought of it made all the blood rush between his own legs. A good run should work all of that unspent energy out of his system. He focused on the wind in his face, the stretch and pull of his muscles, and relaxed into the comforting motion. Cyrus let the familiar repetition of his feet and breathing dull his thoughts as the mountainous landscape passed by in a blur.

Peace stole over him...until a streak of red shot past, leaving dust and the faint hint of spearmint behind. Alix disappeared around the next bend, laughing, though he could not tell if it was scorn or joy.

Prey, his wolf howled from a chamber deep within his chest. *Chase her, savage her, show her that a wolf was born to run, to hunt.* A spike of adrenaline electrified every muscle as the thrill of the chase sang in his blood.

So, she thought she could outrun a wolf, did she?

With a grin, Cyrus sank into his body, leaving his brain to fend for itself, and ran. He followed her scent: sharp sweat, leather, wool, spearmint and rabbit stew, and the promising musk of her desire. His feet hardly touched the ground. Running? No.

He was flying.

His prey came into sight, a red blur on the path ahead, cape fluttering behind like the broken wing of a cardinal. Vulnerable, and not fast enough to escape him. A growl of pleasure, deep in his chest, made his prey look over her shoulder; her eyes wide, cheeks flushed, lips parted, chest heaving.

"I'm going to run you to ground, minx," he said.

Her amber eyes—hawk's eyes—narrowed, and she smiled, showing him sharp white teeth before darting into the forest. Alix may be fast, but he owned this wild land, was created to hunt beyond the borders of civilization, ghosting through the night on soundless feet with the wind in his fur. His blood sang a song older than time, of pumping muscles and hunger, and the thrill of the chase. They darted between trees as darkness fell, the forest silent but for their breath and pounding hearts, as if nature itself waited in anticipation.

The new moon left the world shrouded in darkness, but not to Cyrus. Every flash of her long legs, of her hair trailing between branches, was clear to him as mid-day. She laughed at him over her shoulder, and in the shadow of the canopy, her pale face shone like the moon, drawing him onward. But she was not fast enough.

He closed in.

They broke from the underbrush less than ten feet apart, flying across a grassy meadow with a million stars overhead. She was close enough to taste, her sweat and adrenaline sharp in the air, heady as wine. The certainty of the kill made his muscles tense, his legs bunch. He sprang and wrapped both arms around her chest.

Cyrus turned in midair, and they hit the ground on his back and rolled in a tangle of limbs. Alix was safe in the cradle of his arms as they tumbled, crushing the sweet grass beneath their bodies and sending forest pixies flashing into the sky, a hundred shining green lights mimicking the stars.

Breathless laughter followed the pixies, floating into the air with their mingled breath as they rolled to a stop. Alix stretched out above him, covering him from chest to knees, her entire body alive with the thrill of the chase, each curve of her body filling a hollow of his, two puzzle pieces shaped to match.

Cyrus wanted to devour her, to kiss her smiling mouth and bury himself inside her until they both died of pleasure. Her hair had come loose during their chase, and hung in a black curtain down her shoulder and across his chest as she stared down at him.

Her eyes glowed like fire through a glass of whiskey.

By the moon, she was beautiful. And when she smiled like that... He reached up and cupped her cheek. The smile disappeared. The fire died.

She licked her lips, but not in anticipation. "You said you would not touch me unless I asked you."

Disappointment tightened his throat, and he dropped his hand. "Forgive me. The chase got the best of me. It won't happen again."

Alix nodded, then rolled off him and disappeared into the shadows.

Cyrus lay in the grass as the disturbed pixies drifted back down to wrap themselves in leaves or flower petals to sleep, the night going dark again as their lights winked out.

What the hell just happened? It was well past midnight, and he didn't even know where they were.

He hadn't lost himself to the hunt since he was sixteen years old and running through the forest for the first time in his wolf form. At least then his elders kept him in check, teaching him how to balance man and magic, how not to lose himself in the physical joy of overwhelming sensations. But no one had been there to protect him tonight. He would have heeded no warning, anyway.

Running with Alix as freely as flying, the smell of her mixed with grass and pine, had been as addictive as any drug. The thought scared him, but he was very much afraid it was too late to pretend he didn't like the taste of it.

How much time passed since they started running?

His body had not been his own; it belonged to her and the night and the thrill of being alive. And when she laughed and smiled down at him–he wanted that feeling back, wanted it enough that his chest felt too small to contain it.

Now she was gone, and he was alone, and this time he would not chase her.

At least, not yet.

16

Alix

FOLLOWING WEREWOLF TRACKS OUT of the village of Mont Blanc and further into the mountains turned out to be harder than she expected. They'd lost the trail over a scree slide and found it again halfway up a rocky slope, breaking through an unused pass across the mountain.

Alix crouched, dragging her fingertips across a paw print dug deep into the dirt exposed by a fall of scree. The print pointed southeast when the trail she'd been following was firmly tracking east, but the rest of the tracks were lost in the loose rock. She brushed her hair out of her face and stood to see if there were any other signs.

Instead of catching sight of tracks or broken branches, she saw Cyrus's face as he ran through the darkening forest the night before. When he'd challenged her to the race, she rolled her eyes as he disappeared into the forest. She would not be drawn into a pointless exercise by such a contrived provocation.

But something in her, something young and stupid, rebelled at the idea of letting him win. He was too confident already, and she was faster. But as he bounded through the trees, graceful as a stag with ecstatic joy on his face, her soul cried out with the desire to join the chase; to cast aside worry and self-control, to abandon her constant vigilance and simply run for the pleasure of it.

That night she learned, for the first time, what it felt like to be caught by someone strong enough to challenge her...and she liked it; liked the sense of his presence behind her, the promise of danger, the contest of wills. If he hadn't released her, if he'd kissed her beneath the stars with the pixies all around them, she would have been lost.

Somehow, he had charmed her into letting her guard down. Without meaning to, she'd begun seeing him as a man instead of a monster. That made her vulnerable and was foolishness she could not afford, not if she wanted to protect her secret.

"Any sign?" he called from the track he followed a dozen meters to her right.

She refused to look at him and shook her head. The last thing she needed now was to get distracted by his broad shoulders and well-muscled backside. If they were going to stop the monsters who killed Mercedes's family, she had to catch them before they attacked again.

From the tracks, there appeared to have been at least six distinct creatures leaving Mont Blanc, all large and running, judging by the length of their strides.

Cyrus crossed her track and knelt upslope to examine a break in the rock that led into the bushes. "They began changing here," he said, brushing fallen leaves away. "Must be either young or inexperienced."

When she did not respond, he said in a high-pitched mockery of her voice, "How interesting, Cyrus. Why do you say that?"

"I'm glad you asked," he responded to himself in his normal tone. "See all this thrashing about? It means at least one of them has not learned to cope with the pain of their transformation. They're fighting it.

"Why is that important?" he asked himself. "Ah, because it lets us know who we are dealing with, and knowledge is power."

Alix folded her arms and blew an exasperated breath through her nostrils. Did he think she was some child on her first hunt? She wanted to ask what made him think she needed his explanations, but that would draw her into a conversation, which was exactly what she was trying to avoid.

Cyrus stood and brushed off his knees, then glared down at her. It was an impotent gesture, given that there was at least ten feet of space between them, but that didn't stop him.

"You cannot ignore me forever, minx."

Her hackles rose immediately, and she started to say that yes, she could, in fact, ignore him indefinitely. But that would be playing into his hand, so she snapped her mouth shut and pretended to examine something very interesting about the tracks she followed.

Cyrus grunted in disgust and stormed up the path. She lost sight of him amongst the boulders and pine trees, blonde hair and broad shoulders disappearing around a rock outcropping. No other person had ever made her so–so... She pulled the necklace out of her shirt, clutched the red stone to her chest, and thought, *help me, Maman. I do not know what is wrong with me and I cannot seem to help myself.*

No one answered, of course. If there was anyone up there, they couldn't be bothered. Then again, it had been ages since she spoke to Maman, let alone asked for help. You could only ignore someone for so long before they stopped paying attention. And the gem was cold. With a sigh, Alix dropped the pendant beneath her collar, checked the tracks–larger than her palms and dried into the dirt–and kept climbing.

The path split at the top of the pass, which was broken into a rocky labyrinth of crumbling ravines, scrubby bushes, and sheer cliffs carved by the spring melt. Wind tore down the mountainside and blew her hood back, ripping her hair free to lash her face and get stuck in her mouth.

As she tried to capture and tame the wayward strands, a voice floated back toward her, echoing down the ravine. "Alix! Get up here!"

She rolled her eyes and gave up on her hair to jog up a narrow, steep-sided gully.

Wind and echoes distorted the sound, making it appear to come from everywhere at once, and the ground was rockier here, so the prints were hard to track. Alix closed her eyes and pulled in a deep breath to follow his scent.

The coppery bite of blood tainted the air, sending an electric jolt down her spine.

She belted her cloak around her waist to keep it from flapping about and tested the breeze with every other breath as she sprinted over the tumbled rocks. Fear tightened the muscles of her shoulders, and she held her pistols low as she crested the rise and cut right, following the scent down a deer path toward a stand of pine.

Cyrus crouched in the shade, but there were no werewolves to fight; only a dying man leaning against a tree, his legs stretched out, naked skin smeared with crusted blood and dirt. Alix slid to a stop and her pistols wavered as pity swamped her. He was starved, his ribs stark, cheeks hollow and grey. The wind changed, and she picked up another smell.

Werewolf.

Pity dried up under the heat of fury. Visions of the village flashed through her mind: the mutilated corpses of innocent men, women, and children; Cyrus cradling Mercedes' half-starved little body to his chest; Mercedes again, crying in the night and clenching her small fists in Alix's shirt, trying to hold the world together with white-knuckles.

She trained both barrels on his chest, continuing to walk forward with fingers curled around the triggers.

"Wait," Cyrus said, raising one hand.

"What for? He deserves to die."

"Aye," Cyrus said as she reached him, looking up at her with eyes that had shifted from green to gold. Her heart stuttered. That could mean only one thing: he was close to changing form, closer than she'd ever seen him. And he was a much larger werewolf than the ones they'd been tracking. If he changed and fought her now, she would have a battle on her hands.

But his face and voice remained calm as he said, "He does deserve to die. And he will. Look at him."

"I've seen more than enough."

"Alix. Look at him."

She blinked away the memories and allowed her eyes to focus on the man, then recoiled in a mixture of horror and disgust. He was not simply smeared with drying blood; a hundred small, unhealed cuts oozed from his torso, drawing flies, ants, and other crawling bugs to the feast. Yet he was still alive. The magic had not given up trying to heal him, draining his body as it drew on resources to mend the wounds.

But there were too many to heal. How long had he been there? Long enough for maggots to breed flies that buzzed around him, landing on every exposed bit of flesh.

She swallowed back the urge to vomit and said, "He was tortured with a silver knife."

"So he was. I'm hoping he'll tell us why, and where we can find the people who did this to him."

Alix leaned down, pressed the barrel of her pistol to his forehead, and thumbed back the hammer. "Tell us, and I will give you the mercy of a quick death."

The man's eyes rolled drunkenly in their sockets. He coughed, and wheezed through peeling lips, "Water?"

Cyrus pulled his canteen from the leather thong and tilted it gingerly against the man's lips. He gobbled the liquid, spilling half of it on his chest, then coughed so hard that bright red blood flecked his chin and cheeks.

"How did this happen?" Cyrus asked.

The man fell back against the bark, too weak to move. His arm twitched, trying to make an unconscious gesture, but he hadn't the strength to lift it.

"Please, kill me," he whispered.

"You'll die when you tell me who did this to you and where we can find them." The words were harsh, but Cyrus's voice was gentle, almost comforting.

The man licked his cracked lips and closed his eyes, gathering his remaining strength. "Do you swear?"

Alix answered for him. "I swear it."

The man shuddered. "I was tending the sheep when I heard the screams. By the time I reached the village, it was too late. My mother and sisters were dead, and my father was dying. I hid in the bushes and watched. The werewolves"–he coughed and swallowed painfully–"they sat and waited. My father died. Then a man came. He said–he said 'none were strong enough? That is a shame. But you missed one'."

Cyrus went dreadfully still, as if every ounce of his body, mind, and will were focused on the man. Alix found she could not even force herself to breathe.

"He pointed at me," the man said, "and the werewolves...their teeth. Sun and sky, it hurt. It still hurts." His head rolled to one side as if holding it up required too much strength. For a while, he simply panted. When he continued speaking, his voice was hoarse and weak. "They starved us until the full moon and dragged us to the village. When the moon rose, I–gods, forgive me. I can still taste their blood." Tears filled his eyes but never fell. "The villagers killed François. I wish they would have killed me. In the morning, the other werewolves drove the rest of us out of the village. I tried to run away. They—they punished me. Left me..."

His eyes threatened to roll back in his head and he made a little keening noise of pain.

"Where are they now?" Cyrus asked. "The ones who did this. Where are they?"

The man's eyelids fluttered. He took two quick, shallow breaths, and said, "Looking. Looking for more. It hurts. It hurts. It hurts. Oh gods, what have I done?" He looked up with desperate, glassy eyes. "Please. Please, lady. Have mercy."

Alix's hand shook as she raised the pistol, but she did not hesitate. The report sent birds screaming into the sky and echoed back off the rocks, sharp and final as the striking of a gavel. What was left of the man slumped to one side.

"What have you done?" Cyrus demanded, jumping to his feet. "We needed answers, we–" But his voice died when he saw her face.

Alix did not bother wondering what she looked like to him. The world swam in a haze of tears, and her stomach tried to crawl up out of her throat, but she swallowed it back and holstered her gun. "I gave him the mercy he asked for."

Thunder echoed down the valley as the wind dragged a summer storm across the face of the mountain. Père Henri floated to the top of her memory, the kindness glowing in his tear-filled eyes as he said, *there is always mercy for you.* But the only mercy she and those like her would ever find was at the business end of a weapon.

The dead man killed because he was mindless and had no choice. She killed because she chose to.

"Alix, can you hear me?"

A fat drop of rain splattered against her cheek and ran cold down the side of her face. Then another.

"Aw, hell," Cyrus said, looking up at a sky that had become increasingly dark as they listened to the confession of the dead man. Lighting forked across the clouds, followed by a crack that made the ground shake.

"We need to find cover. Come on." He grabbed her hand, but she jerked it reflexively out of his grip.

"If we don't get under cover soon—" He stopped as the hairs on their arms stood up and the air crackled with energy.

Cyrus snatched her pistols and flung them away, then wrapped his arms around her and dropped, covering her with his body as the world went white, the air crackled, and the earth split open.

It took a long time for her ears to stop ringing. Clouds dragged a steady curtain of rain toward them, with the sharp bite of ozone and wood smoke on the air.

"Come on." Cyrus hauled Alix to her feet and dragged her past the smoking stump of a pine tree, split down the middle, not twenty feet from where they lay.

He dragged her on, but her feet were lead weights. Rain hit in a breaking wave, soaking them and turning the ground into mud. The heavens cried for every innocent life taken and every monster who took it, drowning the world in tears.

Would anyone cry for her when her turn came at last?

For a while, it was impossible to concentrate on anything. Her body moved by pure instinct. One foot, then the other, caught her as she fell forward in a semblance of walking. Somewhere above, her mind floated, detached, watching a big blonde man half-drag, half-carry a slender black-haired woman through a thunderstorm. They were a sorry pair of bedraggled travelers, too stubborn to lie down and die.

It was the jostling that brought her back into her body. She blinked and found herself in a leaky one-room hut that stank of musty pelts, staring into the open door of a cast-iron stove where a fire crackled happily.

"What?" she asked, trying to bring the gears of her mind grinding back into order.

Her body jerked to the right, and Cyrus said, "I need to get you out of these wet clothes."

Her head turned without permission as Cyrus pulled her arm out of the strap of her pack and dropped it in the corner. He lifted the red cloak over her head and draped it on a tanning hook near the stove.

"I won't get sick," she said.

"I'm not worried about illness." Cyrus pulled her boots off and set them next to the fire as well. "I'm worried about shock."

"I don't get shock."

He made an exasperated noise and said, "Not that kind" before pulling his shirt off in a single, swift motion, exposing a broad chest dust-

ed with gold hairs that caught the firelight, and a stomach the novices of
St. Christophe's could have washed their clothes on.

"What are you doing?" she demanded.

He unbuttoned his trousers and worked the wet fabric down muscled
thighs, leaving him in wet drawers that were practically transparent.
"Hanging our clothes up to dry. Now scoot over."

"I'm fine," she said. Hadn't she just explained this? Her body healed
too quickly for worries as simple as illness.

Cyrus slid in next to her on the small bed. "The trauma I'm talking
about comes from killing someone, not cold weather."

"I've killed lots of people. I told you, I'm fine."

"Is that so?" he asked, raising a single blonde brow. "Why are your
hands shaking, then?"

Alix looked down at her hands, which were clenched and trembling,
and not from the cold. In fact, her entire body shook like leaves in a stiff
breeze.

Cyrus positioned himself behind her and tugged the hem of her shirt
out of her pants. She should stop him, but she only sat bemused as he
pulled her shirt and vest off over her head, tossing the garments on the
floor near the stove, leaving her in only her stays and trousers.

After a moment of wrangling, her trousers followed, too.

He said, "Come here" before wrapping an arm about her waist and
pulling her back against him.

She had not realized how cold she was until her bare back pressed
against his chest. Cyrus rubbed her arms from shoulder to elbow in slow,
comforting sweeps, warming her faster than the fire could. Telling him
to shove off would have been smarter, but she said nothing. This was
exactly the kind of danger she had been afraid of, danger she would be
powerless to fight because it felt too good not to be alone.

Slowly, with every stroke of his hands on her skin, her body gave up a bit more tension. Her defenses withered, and with them the emotional barriers she used to protect herself. Giving in to her pain and fear was not an option when she was alone, because if she faltered, people died. And, if she broke again, she'd never be able to put the pieces back together on her own.

But she wasn't alone now.

Alix swallowed the lump rising in her throat and said, "He wasn't a monster, was he?"

It wasn't a question, not really. She knew the answer.

"No, I don't think he was. Not on purpose, anyway."

A tear slid down her cheek as another crack of thunder shook the little trapper's cabin. "He wasn't a monster. But I am."

Her hands stopped shaking altogether, and tears fell instead.

17

Cyrus

"My family was killed when I was twenty-five years old," Cyrus said.

He didn't know why he said it. He preferred to keep the memory safely buried, except that the dead man on the side of the hill had a story far too similar to his own...and Alix was still crying. A week ago he would have said there was not a stronger, more intractable, colder human on the planet.

Now each hopeless, heartbreaking sob cut him like a razor blade. He would have said anything to stop her tears.

"I'm sorry," she said.

He continued trying to rub warmth back into her arms and told himself digging up his painful memories was worth it if it helped her feel less alone. "When I was a lad, monsters were much more common, and protecting our villages fell to those chosen by the moon. At twenty-five, I was the oldest of the chosen, and it was my job to keep our families safe.

"One day, a traveler came from a neighboring village and said monsters were on the hunt. Several shepherds had died, and half a flock was destroyed. Must have been two creatures, at least, they guessed.

"Until then, I had only run off a few bandits and protected our herds from reavers and the occasional starved wolf. Of course, I thought I was experienced and clever, and destroying these monsters would prove me a great hero. Moon and stars, I was a fool." Bitterness made his lip curl in distaste at the memory. "I was no hero. In truth, I was as useful as a fart that thinks it's a stiff breeze."

Alix snorted, clapped a hand over her mouth, and shook with suppressed laughter. But the dam broke and a flood of giggles followed until tears ran. Laughter was just as cathartic as crying, and he'd rather hear that joyful sound, one that lightened his load and dulled the pain of his memories, than her tears.

He held her and tried to absorb her amusement like a plant sucking up sunlight. As the hilarity wore off, she wiped her eyes and sighed, then turned on the small cot and faced him. Her eyes were puffy, her nose red, her cheeks splotchy. How could he still find her so lovely?

She said, "Don't tell me what happened. Not for my sake. But if," –she bit her lips–"if you need to share it with someone, I'll listen."

Damned if he did not want to take her up on that offer. Fear and grief churned beneath her steady gaze, yet she offered him a chance to unburden himself. The greater part of his mind screamed that exposing his past only gave her more ammunition to use against him.

But his memories and failures had been yoked around his neck like a plow for centuries, dragging him down, sowing ruin, and growing pain. He carried them alone because they were too heavy to ask anyone else to bear.

Alix had burdens of her own, but she was still standing, still willing to let him share his despite her distaste for him. If he did not take the offer, it may never come again. What would it feel like to release some of the weight, knowing it would not crush someone?

He swallowed and said, "If you are willing to bear it."

She nodded.

Stone cottages were not built for men like Cyrus; he had to crouch to enter and dodge rafters once inside. Staying out of doors was preferable, even if a smirr covered the highlands with a silvery haze that soaked his plaid and plastered his hair to his head.

But today he had important business with his father. So instead of patrolling the vast tracts of land around the village, he bent to avoid the lintel and squeezed into his parent's house. The air was close and warm, rich with the scent of barley bread and pottage bubbling in the coals.

His sister napped on her pallet by the hearth, cherub cheeks flushed pink. One chubby fist curled around the limp arm of Tally, the rag-stuffed doll he bought her at the market.

"Where's the old man?" he asked.

"Just let him hear you call him that," his mother warned, smiling as she set a small white cheese on the board next to a brown loaf and wiped her hands on her apron. Blonde hair escaped along the edges of her scarf, clinging to her neck and temples in damp curls, and her eyes held a twinkle of mischief.

"Och, you wouldn't tattle on me, would you?"

"I promise not to let it slip over dinner on one condition."

He snorted and bent down to kiss her fondly. "You're a manipulative woman, Mrs. Campbell."

"Aye, well, a mother has some rights," she said, patting his cheek with a warm smile.

Cyrus thumbed a piece of cheese off the wheel and skipped out of her reach as she swatted at him for the theft, narrowly avoiding braining himself on a rafter.

"I fulfilled my filial responsibilities, so tell me: where is the old man?"

"What have I done to be cursed with such offspring? Very well, you thieving heathen. He's away down to the loch, bringing up the fish."

"He's back with the fish," came a gruff voice from outside. "Come help me with the catch, lad."

Cyrus found himself obeying the old man without thinking, then sighed as he lifted the stringer of trout from the woven basket that also served as a pack. He was twenty-five now, more than a man, grown, and a protector of their village. He should not be jumping at orders like some child or well-trained hound.

Still, he carried the stringer to the smokehouse and began hanging the fish in lines just below the rafters. The old man joined him with two more stringers and started work on the next line.

"You've heard of the monsters in Nairnoch?" Cyrus said, as casually as possible.

"Aye. Bad business, that."

"Two nights in a row, no less."

His father hung the last gleaming trout and turned to face him. The building reeked of a hundred smokey fires and the oily stink of drying fish had sunk deep into every fiber of wood and straw. It was an overpowering odor, but Cyrus ignored it and met his father's gaze without flinching or turning away.

Arran Campbell was not as tall as his son, but he was stout and strong, appearing only in his forties though he was more than sixty years old.

Though he'd given up his wolf when Cyrus had been chosen by the pack, his eyes still held the command born of decades of leadership.

The old man sniffed and said, "Well, it is their own fault they lost the last of the moon children when Graeme was killed by the English in that foolish raid. Of course monsters will come if they've only Tam and the dogs to protect them. They should have joined Dunmorrow. Instead, they knowingly squandered their gift and now beg for aid. I take it, you mean to give it to them?"

"If the monsters attack Nairnoch with no resistance, they'll come for the bigger villages next. Better to stamp out the threat now, while we have strength and forewarning."

His da made a dismissive noise in the back of his throat, and left the hut, holding the door open for Cyrus to follow. The damp air was blessedly free of fish stink, and he took a deep breath to clear his sinuses. His Da pulled the edge of his plaid up and over his shoulders to ward off the weather.

"If you take the boys," he said, "you'll leave the village unprotected."

"Protecting the village is the reason I'm taking them. We can stop the threat before it reaches us, and keep Nairnoch safe in the bargain."

"Why do you need all of them? Leave Angus and Will to look after things, if you're determined to hie off and save the damned countryside."

"I've kept our patrols close to home at your suggestion. Had I not, perhaps Nairnoch would be safe and those men would still be alive."

"Your duty is not to Nairnoch, boy," his da said, the purple vein on his forehead pulsing. "The moon gave them guardians of their own, and they misused them. Fewer are chosen each year, and they should have known better. No sense in sacrificing ours for their foolishness."

"You'd sentence our neighbors to death when the beasts return and there is no one to stop them?"

"Call them in. Bring them to our village, if you must, but keep your oath and protect those you swore to care for," the old man said, sticking out his jaw. All the signs were there, warnings Cyrus had learned to watch for as a boy that told him an explosion was imminent: the red nose, the pulsing vein, the stubborn thrust of his jaw.

But he wasn't a boy anymore; he was a leader, he'd made a decision, and that was that. "I am keeping my oath," he said, raising his chin. "We will ambush the werewolves above the loch road. We'll trap them there, against the water, and finish them. Then we'll hang the bodies as a warning."

His da snorted. "Only if it is werewolves, as you suspect. What if you're facing something else that–"

"There are witnesses."

"A scared shepherd will turn a starved wolf into a werewolf and a poor vagabond into a vampire. Never trust an eyewitness. Cyrus, listen to me: our village lives without fear because you and the boys do what is right by us. Leaving now," he shook his head and snatched the cane he'd left leaning against the smoke hut. "It's not fulfilling your duty, it's abandoning it. If I still had my wolf–"

"You don't," Cyrus said, slashing the air with the edge of his hand. "You gave up your wolf and left me to lead, so I'm leading. I didn't come to ask your permission. I came to ask you to keep everyone in their homes and make sure they're armed. They'll listen to you. Trust me to do the job you left for me."

"Boy–"

"The decision is mine to make, and I've made it. That's the end of it."

Cyrus turned and left his father standing by the smokehouse, clutching his walking stick as if he could strangle it.

As he strode out of the village, the rain died and left the sky a dull, angry gray that mirrored his mood. All who saw him gave a respectful nod and scuttled out of the way, not wanting to draw his eye. Good.

"Cy! Cyrus!" The voice calling his name cracked into an adolescent squeak on the last syllable, and some of his anger fizzled.

Lyrus ran down the hill after him, all long limbs and coltish grace. He'd be a bear of a man, someday, but now he had the awkward proportions of one growing too fast for their body to keep up; knobby knees, large hands and feet, long legs, and not enough muscle to fill it all out. But his younger brother had a smile that put the sun to shame.

His name was Leith, but he had started calling himself Lyrus when Cyrus left for training. "Now our names match because I'm just like you," he'd said, hugging his older brother's legs with hero worship in his six-year-old eyes. Cyrus had never been able to forget that moment. The boy refused to be called by any other name for long enough that it stuck, and hardly anyone remembered what it had been.

"Wait up," Lyrus panted, slowing to a walk as he drew alongside his brother. "How'd it go?"

"What do you think?"

"That well, eh?"

Cyrus rolled his eyes, but Lyrus clapped him on the back and laughed. "He's bound to take it hard. He led the Moon Children for a long time, after all. He'll come around."

"Aye, I suppose."

Lyrus squinted at the horizon. "Second night of the full moon. Are you off to kill a few werewolves, then?"

"That's the plan. You remember the job I gave you?"

It was Lyrus' turn to roll his eyes. "Hard to forget. Never thought my first heroic task would be babysitting."

Cyrus laughed and pulled his brother into a hug, slapping him fondly on the back. He was the only man in his family not chosen by the moon, so he was hungry to prove himself any way he could.

"Nothing is more heroic than protecting those as can't protect themselves," Cyrus reminded him. "Watch over them."

"I know, I know. Stay safe, brother."

He met up with the rest of the Moon Children at the crossroads halfway to Nairnoch. They stood in a loose group, laughing and jostling as the last light left the overcast sky.

"There's our fearless leader," Angus said, elbowing Liam and gesturing with his chin.

The frustration of his father's disapproval fell away as his pack enveloped him with good-natured ribbing. He'd spent ten years training with these men, living wild and learning to partner with the magic, to hunt and hide and kill whatever threatened the safety of their village.

And when he'd grown bigger and faster than the rest of them, they deferred to him, followed him, and finally chose Cyrus to lead their pack. And he was about to order them into real danger for the first time.

For a moment he wished he'd taken his father's advice, and that they were all home safe by the fire. But it was too late for such thoughts. This was what they trained for, why the moon had chosen them in the first place.

"Alright, alright, haud yer wheesht," he told them. "Mortals are in danger. We've planned this. You know what to do."

Their humor melted away, and the air filled with an expectant charge of excitement as they shifted. Cyrus took a deep, calming breath, lifted his face to the sky, and called on the moon. With enough practice, changing forms only hurt like a good stretch for sore muscles, a pleasant ache, and popping as tissue and joints shifted and slid into place.

One moment, five young men stood on the hillside, and the next, five wolves sneezed and shook out their fur. It always took a moment to adjust, like walking out of a dark cave into the sunshine, but once they settled into the wolf, their enhanced senses kicked in.

A ground squirrel hid close by, its little heart thrumming with panic beneath the constant hum of the midges. Far back in the trees, a pine marten stared at them from the branch of a tree, its small eyes reflecting the moonlight. Angus had recently lain with a lass, and her smell wafted from him like honeysuckle on a breeze. Every head rose and turned toward him.

'Are you trying for pups?' Will asked by tilting his head and flicking one ear, his tongue lolling out in amusement.

Angus snorted and pinned his ears back, which meant, "Mind your business."

Amusing as that was, they had a job to do. Cyrus growled, reminding them to stay on task, and led them forward at a loping trot. As they neared Nairnoch, wolves broke off in pairs of two, disappearing into the heather and growing darkness until Cyrus was alone.

He crouched on the hill overlooking the flock, hidden in the tall grass, and scented the old blood of the kill, wet wool, and the sweet, thick scent of peat smoke from the crofter's fires... but no enemy. The rain had cleared much of it away. Hopefully, that wouldn't matter, as they were ambushing, not tracking the abominations.

They waited with the patience of hunters as the moon traversed the sky, but no monsters appeared and no warning howls sounded from the woods where the rest of the pack patrolled the shadows. Dawn wasn't far away, and time was short. It was time for the backup plan.

On cue, Angus arrived at the edge of the field, alerting the dogs and making the sheep bleat in terror and bolt for the opposite side of the clearing.

Fear rose like a sweet, invisible cloud that made his mouth water. Will stalked in from the other side, cutting off the herd and trapping them between himself and his partner.

The scent was so strong that no predator, especially no werewolf, could ignore it, yet none appeared. Just as Cyrus decided to call his brothers off, a panicked howl rose from the forest near the road. Angus and Will stopped terrorizing the sheep and raised their heads with pricked ears. That was not a signal. It was a call for help.

He flew across the hillside, claws digging into the wet turf, with Angus and Will on his flanks. They nearly bowled into Liam on the road. He lay on his side with a gaping wound from his shoulder down across his chest. His foreleg hung limp as he twitched and cried.

"What happened?" Cyrus demanded, tilting his head and whining.

Liam's eyes rolled in pain, but he lifted his head and pointed his nose toward... home.

18

Alix

WHEN CYRUS'S VOICE TRAILED off, Alix held her breath. As he spoke, the pain of her memories was reflected in his eyes. The promise of impending disaster cast a dark shadow over his affection for his mother, sister, and brother. Bile burned the back of her throat as he described his desire to prove himself and earn his position as a leader; his hunger for the respect of his father, and the gut-wrenching fear of realizing he made a terrible mistake.

Her heart pounded harder than if she were in the middle of a fight, and her throat tightened until it was hard to breathe.

More than once she wanted to tell him to stop, but she could not deny him this chance to release even a fraction of the weight of his past. Especially not knowing the depth of the scars it had left on him.

But now Cyrus was quiet, his eyes glazed and distant, locked on some faraway memory. Sweat beaded unnoticed on his brow and upper lip, and every muscle was rigid with strain. Echos of retreating thunder rolled across the little hut, shaking the timber frame as wind howled through the eaves.

When she killed the broken werewolf, the reality of indifferent fate–a fate that allowed cruelty to make monsters of innocent men–came crashing down on her like a rockslide. How many times had she been the sword of judgment used upon those whose only crime was being caught in the wrong place?

The guilt of that truth crushed her until simply moving her body became almost impossible. And Cyrus cradled her against his chest with the same tender care he'd given Mercedes. He had reached through the rockslide and pulled her to the surface.

Now he was trapped in the prison of his memories, a prison he'd entered willingly for her sake, and she was the only person who might pull him back out.

What should she do? She'd never comforted someone before, had never been close enough to anyone outside the convent to have even the opportunity to offer comfort. But a vague memory of Maman's hands and her soft, gentle voice called from the dark reaches of her mind. Licking her lips, Alix moved slowly so as not to alarm him, and cupped his face between them. His skin was clammy.

"Shh," she said, stroking his temples. "It's alright. I'm here. I'm here."

His pupils constricted and focused, and he took a gasping breath as if surfacing from deep water. Covering her hands with his, pressing her palms against his cheeks, he closed his eyes.

When he spoke, his voice was ragged and heavy with unshed tears. "We ran until we coughed up blood, but we did not run fast enough. The scent of burning reached us long before we neared the village. I knew, even as I ran, that we were too late. The bodies–" He shuddered and a hot tear slid down his cheek to wet her palm.

"Cyrus," she started, but he kept talking as if the memories must either force their way out or burst through his skin.

"I found my da under the rubble of the smokehouse. While my pack searched the ruins for their families, I pulled the stones and wood beams off him. His chest was crushed, but he was still breathing. He held a bent knife in one hand and blood–there was so much blood. He'd given up his wolf years ago to grow old with Mam, so he did not heal."

Alix wiped his tears with the pads of her thumbs.

"He said, 'Your mam is dead. I couldn't save them.' I tried to clean him up and staunch the bleeding, but he pushed my hands away. He was dying. I smelled it even without my wolf, but it would be a slow death. He said, 'Don't let me suffer, boy. Send me to meet your mother.'" Cyrus swallowed hard, and her ribcage constricted, squeezing her heart like a bird in a fist. "So I did."

In the last month, she had killed two men who did not deserve their fate: one brave priest, and one monster who had deserved pity she wasn't able to give him. But it was not their eyes she remembered, or their voices she heard saying, *You must kill me, Alix darling. Please.*

"Lyrus tried to keep his promise," Cyrus continued. "He hid Effie in his plaid and ran for the forest. He was young and fast as a red deer, but the monster caught him anyway. His throat was ripped out. And Effie–"

"No." Alix placed her fingers over his mouth.

He gently pulled her hand away, but threaded his fingers through hers and held on.

"We buried them. We dug their graves with our claws and our hands, but we never spoke. They would not forgive me. I made the wrong choice when it mattered the most, and it cost them everything. They hated me...I hated me."

"At least you were brave enough to go home," she whispered, imagining her mother searching the forest and calling for her lost child, knowing no one would answer.

"I wish I hadn't. I wish I had turned and run as soon as I smelled the smoke and never looked back. Perhaps then I would not see them broken when I close my eyes. I could pretend Lyrus found love, and Effie grew to be as clever as our mam, and—"

"Shh," she said, and pulled him toward her, scooting until her back rested against the flimsy wall and his head lay on her lap. His hair was damp and tangled from their flight through the storm. She brushed it off his forehead, the way her mother had done when she cried, repeating the gesture while humming a soothing song.

The name of the song was lost in the darker parts of her memory, along with the long-forgotten words, but it was a beautiful tune that reminded her of her mother, so she hummed it, anyway.

Cyrus let out a long, shuddering sigh and wrapped his arms around her hips, nestling against her as his body relaxed. Something tender awoke in her chest at the sight of him, a feeling she'd never experienced and certainly never imagined having toward the wolf.

But pretending was useless now. This man was not a monster, no matter how she wanted to deny it. The beasts she hunted for two hundred years were nothing like the gentle man now curled around her like a lost child. Or, perhaps they were, once. Maybe they had been as wrongly, cruelly used as the tortured man lying dead on the mountainside.

If that was so, then she had tried to escape her past and fought monsters to atone for her blood in vain. One truth remained unchanged and unchangeable: *she* was the monster.

Alix hesitated, then asked, "Why?"

"Hmm?"

"Why tell me this?"

Cyrus tightened his arms for a moment, then sat up, took her hand, and turned it over. He ran his thumbs from her wrist, up her palm, and out to her fingertips, repeating the motion and staring down as he said, "I suppose I thought...maybe you'd feel less alone. And"–he raised his head, eyes searching–"you were crying."

He said the last as if it explained everything.

They stared at one another for a long time as the storm continued to rage across the mountaintop. Water dripped through several holes in the roof to patter against the floor, but the walls were sound and their small corner of the hut was warm and dry.

Cyrus's eyes were as green as a summer meadow after a rain, when the sun comes out and the world looks fresh and new. He did not look at her now with derision, frustration, or even with desire...he simply saw her, all of her, and he did not flinch or turn away.

Instead, he released her hands and held out both arms in silent invitation. She hesitated, her cautious nature repeating every reason why trusting him would be a mistake. But if Cyrus wanted to hurt her, he already had a dozen chances. Trying to convince herself he was waiting for the right opportunity didn't work anymore.

Holding her breath, she scooted forward and let Cyrus gather her against his body, one arm wrapped around her waist, the other cradling her head on his chest and shoulder.

Their trousers were still damp, but he was warm, his bare skin smooth, and even the hair on his chest was soft. How long had it been since someone held her? Her muscles relaxed and her breathing slowed and deepened. Was this what safety felt like?

Alix yawned, finally succumbing to the emotional toll of the last few days. With a graceful twist, He turned and lay back across the cot in the opposite direction, pulling her after him. She was stretched out across him, his heartbeat strong and steady beneath her ear, the rain a constant hum above them.

Alix blinked. Had she fallen asleep? Coals lit the room with a dull red glow, and the only sound was the occasional patter of water dripping from branches onto the roof. Cyrus traced her back with his fingertips in long sweeps from her shoulders to her hip and back. Given that she was lying atop a werewolf, half-naked, on an empty mountaintop in a deserted cabin, she was absurdly comfortable.

So, of course, she ruined it by pushing herself up to see if her clothes were dry, but the position left her looking down at Cyrus. The breath stopped in her throat. He lay stretched out beneath her, all lazy grace and powerful muscles, the ridges of his abdomen and the deep shadows of his hips close enough to taste, if she wished it. His eyelids were heavy, his expression relaxed, his lips...

She tore her eyes away and said, "I'm sorry I fell asleep on you."

A contented rumble vibrated through his chest and against her, which was a potent reminder that their hips were still pressed together, and she wore nothing but stays that only covered half of her breasts.

Cyrus noted this with a hot look of approval but didn't move. "Don't be sorry, minx. It was the best sleep I've ever had."

She opened her mouth to say don't call me that but found she didn't mind it quite so much when he said it that way. He stopped breathing. His grip tightened on her hips. Warmth spread from her chest and down, pooling between her legs.

He licked his lips.

Cyrus wanted her. The hard ridge of his desire pressed against her in silent proof. He did not move or touch her in any way that might be considered breaking his promise to keep his hands to himself...but she wanted him to.

She wanted him to kiss her, to palm her breasts, to touch every suddenly aching inch of her. But that would mean asking him, and she refused to give him that victory. He shifted beneath her to ease the pressure, and a little tingling rush of anticipation made her want to flex her hips in return, to ease the fullness growing between her legs.

That would be foolish, and Alix was no fool.

Then again, a few hours ago, she'd nearly been struck by lightning, and this man had shielded her with his body. She'd been too upset during the incident to realize what he'd done, but the memory made warmth flush from her collarbone to her knees.

No one had ever put themselves in danger for her sake, and she was so tired of being alone.

"Can I trust you, wolf?"

He swallowed and raised a brow. "If you're asking me whether I'll keep my promise, then, aye, you can trust me. But damned if I don't regret making it."

A feral smile crept across Alix's face. Part of her, the instinctive, self-protective part, screamed that being this close to him would get her killed. But that part was nowhere near as strong as the need building in her stomach.

"Let us see how well you keep your word," she said and threw her leg over his hip to sit astride him.

"This, ah"–he cleared his throat–"feels like a trap."

She grabbed his wrists and pinned them to the bed next to his head, leaning over him with a rush of power so intense it made her giddy. Cyrus was a big man, and stronger than anyone she'd ever known. He was both fast and deadly, and he was at her mercy.

"It is a test," she said, leaning down until her lips were a breath away from his. "Will you pass it?"

His swallow was loud in the silence.

Alix ran the tip of her nose down his jawline, along the side of his neck, to his collarbone, liking the sharp musk of dried sweat and the lighter, cleaner scent of the storm that still clung to his hair.

He shivered as she retraced the path with her tongue, stopping at the spot where his lifeblood ran close to the surface. In the past, with mortal lovers, she was forced to balance her desire for comfort with her vampiric thirst. The warm, wet heat always called to the monster in her, making her throat dry and her mouth water.

Thirst never won, of course, but it was a constant distraction when the mouthwatering scent was so near. But Cyrus did not smell like a mortal; his blood was wild, more like that of a bear than an elf, man, or dwarf. So she bit him; not hard enough to break the skin, but hard enough to hurt just a little, testing the resilience of his skin and tasting the salt of his sweat.

He groaned and leaned into the love bite, arching his neck involuntarily. Alix smiled and continued the torture, reveling in the novelty of being this close to another person and not battling a darker desire to do harm.

She nuzzled him a while longer to enjoy the sensation, then kissed her way back to his jaw, stopping at the corner of his mouth. He had not moved so much as an inch. With a low sound of pleasure, Alix stretched out, pressing herself against him from breast to knees, soaking in his warmth like a cat in the sun.

"You're trying to make me break my word," he accused, his voice low and gravelly.

The tip of her tongue ran along his lower lip as her hands left his wrists, trailing up the corded muscles of his forearms to his biceps. "You're not touching me, I'm touching you."

"Semantics."

She dragged herself along the length of him, his cock pressing against her through their thin clothing. "Do you want me to stop?"

"Not for the moon and every damned star in the heavens. God, do that again."

She smiled and rolled her hips. Shimmering pleasure followed the caress, and Cyrus groaned, his whole body rigid with the effort to keep his promise.

The sound went straight to her blood like a shot of whisky, but it was proving much easier to get drunk on Cyrus than it had ever been with alcohol. Purring, she leaned down and kissed him.

His lips were soft, his mouth hot, and the salty-sweet taste of him made her lightheaded as he rolled his tongue over hers in a hypnotic rhythm. When she sat up, putting her full weight on his hips, the sight of him made her catch her breath.

Hunger turned his eyes gold, and they were locked on her face, on her lips, with a smoldering desire that was a hair away from predatory. Her heart kicked into high gear, and he heard it, one corner of his lips curling into a smile so sinful she was wet merely looking at him.

"Aye," he said in a low growl, "I want you–with every fiber of my body. I want you so much I can feel my heartbeat throb between my legs."

The knowledge that all that deadly power was helpless beneath her was an aphrodisiac that made her wild with need. She was more ready for him than she'd ever been in her life, and they'd barely done anything.

She scooted back and began unbuttoning the fly of his drawers. Cyrus pulled a breath in through his teeth, and his stomach clenched, the dim light of coals picking out every ridge of muscle. Even when she hated him, she could not lie to herself about his beauty. Now every curve and hollow was hers to explore.

The last button popped free and, with a tug, so did Cyrus. Her eyes widened and her mouth went dry.

He chuckled. "Don't worry, minx. We will fit together like puzzle pieces, you and me."

That was difficult to believe. Hesitantly, she wrapped her fingers around him and stroked him once, from tip to base. His hips flexed involuntarily, and he said through clenched teeth, "You're going to kill me, woman."

"I might," she agreed, then stroked him again. His pulse beat beneath her fingers as she pumped the hard length of him. His eyes rolled back as he bit his lips against another groan.

When he was sweating and both hands were fisted in the thin blanket, she released him. Her own pulse beat between her legs with a demand she could no longer ignore. She began unlacing her fly, and his eyes locked on every motion with predatory hunger.

"I want to do that," he said as she slid her drawers down over her hips. "I want to undress you, to taste your desire, and feel you squirm as I spread your legs."

She fumbled, the vision his words conjured making her hands shake. Lovers were difficult for her to come by, and while she usually enjoyed herself, it had never been like this. When she finally positioned herself over him, she was almost frantic.

"Let me touch you," he coaxed.

Alix wrapped her fingers around his cock with one hand–how was his skin so soft?–then leaned down and growled against his lips, "Shut up, wolf" as she lowered herself with a gasp. Despite how wet she was, he was too big. She retreated, then lowered herself again, and again, each stroke bringing him deeper.

"You're not...ready," he said between clenched teeth. "I don't want to hurt you."

But she'd already begun and need drove her forward. "I'm ready enough."

"My god," he breathed, his eyes on their joined bodies as she slid down, and down again, until finally seating him to the hilt. His back arched and his hands fisted in the rough blanket.

He filled her, stretched her, reaching so deeply that every pulse of his desire throbbed against her womb. She wanted him to touch her, but couldn't speak. All coherent thought fled. She had to move, had to satisfy the building pressure between her legs. So she rocked her hips and felt the first deep rush as he slid out and back in.

Alix whimpered, but she couldn't stop. She needed more of him, all of him, and every moan that escaped his lips made her pace quicken, rocking faster, harder, until she rode him with a desperate need that made it hard to catch her breath.

But it wasn't enough.

Tension built, tightening her inner muscles. She needed. God's breath, she needed him. She could not get enough.

"Alix," he panted, hands hovering over her hips but not touching as she whimpered, searching for something just out of her reach. "Alix, let me–oh god."

She was so close, on the edge of a cliff but unable to jump. In desperation, she grabbed Cyrus's wrists, pressed his hands against her hips, and cried, "Please."

With a growl of triumph, he surged upright and tore her stays in half down the front, exposing her breasts. Her head fell back as he captured one breast, sucking and teasing her nipple with his tongue and teeth. Her fingers threaded through his hair to lock him in place, but now that she had given him permission, Cyrus would not be controlled.

He rolled her other nipple between his thumb and forefinger, squeezing just hard enough to send a sharp thrill up her spine, watching her with narrowed eyes.

"By the moon, you're perfect," he breathed against her breast as his fingers flexed on her hips, slowing her pace, matching her rhythm so that each stroke dragged her wet, sensitive flesh against the base of his shaft.

She shuddered and sucked in a breath.

"That's it." He leaned back to enjoy the sinuous movement of her hips, to cup her breasts, and flick his thumbs across her nipples. Those golden eyes watched as if he could devour her, his gaze so hot it was like a brand on her bare skin.

She was close, so close it made her want to cry. The tension and the pressure were too much to bear. Little whimpering noises escaped as she pulled at him, unable to satisfy the need.

He made a low noise deep in his throat. "Shh. I've got you."

His hand trailed across her stomach and down between her legs until he found the knot of sensitive flesh. She jerked hard enough to nearly unseat him, but Cyrus held her tight against his body. With rhythmic motions of his thumb, he matched the timing of her rocking hips, sending shimmering waves of ecstasy, one after the other, from her center down to her toes. Every muscle in her core tightened, pulling, and the tension redoubled.

"Cyrus," she moaned, knowing she was about to break under the strain as her legs shook. "I'm–I need–I can't–"

"I'm here," he said, sliding his thumb over her, making bright sparks ignite and burn her insides to ash. "Come for me, minx. Oh god, let me watch you come undone."

Everything disappeared but the heat of his mouth, the lean, resilient muscle beneath her palms, the tightening pressure, the pleasure, the aching, desperate need that suddenly doubled, tripled, then burst.

Cyrus groaned and shuddered. His hands tightened as his body arched like a bow, pushing him deeper until they were locked together, spasming and panting, slick with sweat.

She threw her head back and screamed as release hit her like a series of breaking waves expanding from her core, shaking and shivering, drawing her down and down into liquid warmth.

Alix rested her forehead against his. Their breath mingled for a heartbeat before she sighed, collapsed onto his chest, and tipped gently into the welcoming dark.

"Alix. Alix wake up."

"Hmm?" She blinked and shifted. Hair scratched her breasts and a soft, welcome fullness throbbed inside her. They were still joined, and she must have passed out. She wasn't even embarrassed. In a couple of hundred years, she'd had sex more times than she could count or remember.

But never like that.

Her partners had sometimes been patient, tender, or passionate, but they were only interested in the same thing she was: an hour of forgetfulness and a bit of release. It was a purely transactional experience and, while pleasant, she was content to go months, even years, without, when necessary.

But with Cyrus? She wanted him again. Now. Enough that her hips shifted in anticipation.

His hands tightened on her thighs, stilling her before she began. "As much as I would give for another round," he whispered, "we must get dressed."

"Why?"

"Something is outside, and it is not human."

19

Cyrus

WHATEVER MONSTER LURKED IN the dark beyond the cabin was about to pay dearly for interrupting the best evening he'd spent in the last hundred years. True, the situation wasn't exactly romantic: they lay on a too-small cot in a rickety little cabin that stunk of stale fur and mildew. But when Alix touched him, the entire world constricted down to *her*. They could have been in a cow pasture and he would not have noticed.

She scooted silently off him and stood at the foot of the cot. The weak light of dying coals outlined every curve he wanted to explore with his hands and mouth. Her dark hair, which had been cool and silky on his skin, tumbled to her hips in a tousled curtain.

"You are a glorious creature," he murmured, unable to help himself. If she commanded him to kneel and worship her, he'd probably do it. At least, until he stopped wanting her so much it was hard to breathe.

Her heartbeat sped up and she blushed, looking more like an innocent young goddess waiting to be ravished than a hardened warrior. In a way, she was both. Her response to him, her desperation and hunger, led him to believe she may not have had the most considerate bed partners in the past.

Yet she had been hot and passionate even in her vulnerability, and she still wanted him. They might have spent several more pleasant hours in bed, and he would have taken his time. He wouldn't just make her wet, but ready, hungry, and he'd wait till she sobbed with need before giving her what she wanted. Several times. Till her legs shook.

Yes, Cyrus thought as he ground his teeth and rolled silently to his feet. *The creature was going to pay.*

They dressed quickly and gathered their weapons, casting sidelong glances at one another. When Alix realized her pistols were not in their holsters, she glowered at him.

"What? Would you prefer to have been struck by lightning?"

"Don't be so dramatic," she hissed, but he ignored her and closed the stove hatch, hiding the dim light.

Together, they sidled up to the door and stood listening as something crashed through the undergrowth in the distance.

What is it? she mouthed.

He shrugged and tapped his ear. *Listen.*

Below the normal sounds of a forest night was the noise that had woken him: the *glug-gug, glug-gug, glug-gug,* of an enormous heart. Some beasts in India had hearts large enough to make that noise, but the only animals in France with hearts so large were bears, and whatever was outside was *not* a bear.

She touched her nose while raising a brow, as if to ask *can you smell it?* He shook his head. Not enough scent penetrated the cabin walls to identify the creature. Alix rolled her eyes and sighed, giving him a look he interpreted to mean, *you are really going to make us fight this monster with no idea what we are facing?* but Cyrus wasn't worried.

It wasn't the first time he'd killed a monster that surprised him. Besides, with the two of them working together, there weren't many monsters who stood a chance.

Crashing and snapping, followed by a grunt, told him the beast was getting closer. They stood on either side of the door, listening to the footsteps grow nearer. Alix drew the only weapons she had left: her silver knife and pocket knife. If anyone could make good use of those weapons, it was her.

No use in waiting.

Ready? he mouthed.

She nodded.

Cyrus eased the door open to a cool blast of post-storm wind that brought with it the stink of rotten meat, rancid fat, untanned hide, and bad breath. That specific combination of scents could mean only one thing. His confidence wilted and adrenaline shot through his veins like a blast of electricity.

Alix closed her eyes, bit her lips together, and shook her head. Perhaps they should wait it out and let the creature pass. After all, the mountaintop was empty and the only people in danger were the two of them.

That was wishful thinking. The air was full of the bitter burn of woodsmoke, and as soon as he'd opened the door, the scent of their sweat and lovemaking would also be caught up by the breeze. Whatever else people may say of the brutes, they had excellent noses. One needed a good nose if one preferred to munch on rotting bodies.

Wet snuffling followed by a meaty crunch echoed through the trees. They only had seconds before the monster was close enough to smell them. By then it would be too late to do anything but react defensively. There was no time to run or hide. Fighting was their only choice.

He locked eyes with Alix, who tightened her grip on the knives.

I must shift, he said, soundlessly.

A wave of fear passed across her face like a cloud across the sun. In the heat of the fight, would her hatred of his kind force Alix to see him as a monster as well? She made to shake her head but stopped and took a slow, deep breath. Her expression cleared, her shoulders straightened, and she nodded.

Pride in her strength washed over him. Tonight they would fight as partners.

They slid into the night, spreading out as they flanked the monster. Once Alix disappeared into the trees and the sight of him changing wouldn't frighten her, Cyrus called on the moon. The magic slid over him, submerging him in welcoming heat that prickled across his skin like warm water after winter's chill. He changed between one step and the next, and the night came to vivid life.

He had seen well enough before, and far better than any mortal. But his wolf senses picked up the scuttling of bugs, an owl peering at him between branches, and the sickeningly sweet stink of dead human flesh.

With soundless ease, he picked a path silently through the underbrush, his ears and nose leading him toward the creature. It stood in a clearing, impossibly large, with skin as thick and leathery as an elephant, wearing nothing but a rough bit of poorly tanned hide around its hips. One huge, meaty fist was wrapped around the handle of a crude short spear, and the other held the quivering remnants of a human arm.

It chewed, working a lantern jaw far too big for its head, and pink-tinged spittle dripped onto a chest and shoulders that would have made a blacksmith jealous. It was a foot taller than Cyrus at his full height. A little spike of dread made his breath catch. This was not going to be the easy fight he hoped for.

After all, ogres had killed dozens of hunters over the years. They were brutishly strong and far faster and more agile than they looked. But they were not bright, and their eyes weren't particularly strong. They would have to take advantage of that. He hoped Alix knew it, and adjusted accordingly.

The ogre lifted the arm to his mouth and closed his massive teeth almost delicately over a finger, casually snipping it off and crunching it between his molars as he lifted his head and sniffed the air.

Cyrus crouched behind a fern as the ogre finally caught their scent. It turned its head toward the trapper's cabin, sniffing and grunting, beady eyes bright with interest. Alix's pale face flashed through the trees on the opposite side of the clearing, both eyes locked intently on the beast, her lips pulled into a grimace.

She would wait for him to make the first move. *Speed and accuracy*, he thought, muscles bunching as the ogre began following its nose toward the cabin. Twenty feet away. Fifteen feet. In a moment it would pass him. Ten feet.

Glug-gug, glug-gug, glug-gug.

Cyrus sprang, aiming at the ogre's knees. His teeth ripped across the flesh at the back of the joint where the tendons were close to the surface. But the ogre's skin was thick and rubbery and the gash was not deep enough to reach the tendon. He rolled away as a club whooshed over his head and the ogre let loose a furious howl.

The momentum of the swing pulled the creature halfway around, and Alix used the opportunity to dart past, dragging her silver knife across the back of the wounded knee with a powerful stroke. At least, she had been aiming for the knee, but the ogre was already in motion, and her blade hit the thicker muscle of the lower hamstring, instead.

With a roar that raked at Cyrus's ears, the ogre spun and swung his club, swiping the ends of Alix's hair as she disappeared into the shadows. A wound gaped on the back of its leg, bleeding freely, but it wasn't deep enough to slow the creature. To stop it from following her, Cyrus dashed forward and harried the ogre's flanks, snapping at its legs, then leaping backward while Alix positioned herself to attack from the other side.

Faster than he could have thought possible, the ogre reared back and lashed out with a foot that caught Cyrus on the shoulder as he sprang away. He tumbled through the air and hit the dirt in a roll, digging his claws into the soil to right himself. The monster followed him, stomping enormous feet hard enough to make the ground shake.

Cyrus rolled out of the way just as one massive foot pounded into the dirt where his chest had been a moment before, ducked beneath another swing of the club, and dodged to the ogre's weak side, circling toward the injured leg. If they took out the leg, the ogre wouldn't stand a chance. It spun to follow him, club whistling through the air and taking off the top half of a small tree with a *crack*.

Alix sprinted in from the ogre's blind side and leaped. She soared through the air, both knives held in a reverse grip, and landed on the ogre's back. Each knife sunk to the hilt between the beast's shoulder blades. She twisted them as the ogre arched and bellowed in pain.

It reached back to pull her off, but it wasn't flexible enough to reach her. That was his chance.

Cyrus vaulted off a tree trunk, turned in midair, and hit the ogre in the back of the knee with his shoulder. The joint buckled, and Alix leaped free as the monster fell with a ground-shaking crash. She hit the ground, rolled, and came up running. Ogres were fast, strong, and heavy. They were agile enough on their feet but as soon as their legs were compromised, they were just as vulnerable as any mortal. More so, because of their enormous weight.

Instead of popping up to its feet as he or Alix might have done, the ogre was forced to roll to its side and flail for purchase, digging at the ground to lever itself up.

That position exposed its chest.

Alix's eyes locked on the monster with the single-minded attention of a diving hawk. She dashed forward, dark hair flying behind her like a cape made of shadows. She was aiming to land the killing blow, so he'd have to keep the ogre distracted. Because if the monster wrapped its arms around her, it would crush her chest. Not even she could heal fast enough to survive an injury like that.

Heart pounding, Cyrus growled to draw the monster's attention. The low, vicious sound bubbled in his chest as he bounded toward the ogre's injured leg. He hit the sweet spot, his teeth sinking between muscle and tendon. Bitter blood filled his mouth, but he set his feet and twisted his powerful shoulders. The tendon gave way with a pop. The ogre screamed and batted at him with the back of one massive fist.

White light flashed before his vision as Cyrus's shoulder cracked. It felt like getting hit by a runaway cart. He yelped in surprise and tumbled away. The pain would follow, but for now, his shoulder merely throbbed. But the ploy worked.

Alix had the best opening he could have hoped for and struck the ogre with both knives. She buried one between the creature's ribs, and the other into its eye socket. The eye popped with a sick, wet sound, and the ogre howled, flailing both arms to protect its head.

She was too close to get away in time. As the ogre flung an arm toward its face, the limb–thick as her torso–trapped her between the creature's bicep and chest, like a one-armed hug.

It squeezed.

She screamed.

It was going to crush her. A lightning strike of adrenaline hit his blood, and Cyrus launched himself forward, jaws open.

He barely managed to dodge the flailing fist, sank his teeth deep into the ogre's exposed throat, and kicked away with all four feet. The flesh tore free, the monster gurgled, and Cyrus spat the disgusting mouthful onto the dirt.

The ogre tried to breathe, but the sound reminded Cyrus uncomfortably of percolating coffee as air bubbled up through the blood squirting from the open wound. It spasmed a few times, kicking its feet ineffectually, and finally went limp, lying lifeless in the dirt.

Alix shoved the limp arm off and scrambled away, knives held low. For a moment she refused to take her eyes off the ogre, but once she was satisfied the monster was truly dead, she turned and locked eyes with him. A shiver ran from his neck to the tip of his tail, making every hair stand on end.

She was absolutely otherworldly; perfectly still, pale-faced in the dark, unblinking, as if she did not recognize him. That was the face hundreds of werewolves saw before they died at her hands. Perhaps even his kin. And here he was, in wolf form, standing before the Red Cloak herself.

His shoulder throbbed, and now that the ogre was dead, the heat of battle could no longer keep the pain at bay. With every heartbeat, the ache grew until it was a constant burn. He healed quickly, but not instantly, and until the magic finished its work, he'd be in pain. He wobbled, but righted himself, compensating for his bad leg with three others.

If she attacked him, he'd need every bit of coordination to dodge.

Alix blinked and shook her head as if clearing away a vision, but she appeared no less wary. Perhaps it was time to let her see another difference between himself and the werewolf abominations. Cyrus called on the moon.

A moment later, he stood in his human form, still bloodied with an arm hanging limp, but no longer the beast she hated. Unlike werewolves who attached themselves to the magic like parasites and were corrupted by it, his transformation was neither long nor painful.

She stared at him, clenching and unclenching her fingers around the hilt of her blades as if she could not decide whether to attack him or cry. Should he say something? Offer a bit of comfort?

"He didn't put up much of a fight for an ogre," she said.

The statement was an olive branch of sorts, a chance to ignore the fact that his wolf form was still a dangerous topic between them by focusing on something else. He took it, gladly.

"Aye, he was a wee thing. But he still broke my shoulder."

"If he has a bounty or any booty, you can keep it."

"That's kind of you," he said, and meant it. Hunters never gave up their share of a dead monster, even if it only meant pennies in the end. The job was too dangerous to be generous. "But why do I have the feeling that's just your way of asking me to search the bloody thing so you don't have to get your hands dirty?"

She smirked and shrugged. "Take it however you'd like."

Those words were like being dunked in cold water. He narrowed his eyes and pinned Alix to the spot as visions of the trapper's cabin played in his mind. He saw her so vividly in his memory, riding him with sinuous movements of her hips, pupils dilated, lips parted, breasts bouncing in the dim light. But he hadn't had time to enjoy her properly. Now was not the time to bring it up, not after what they'd just done, but he never seemed able to do the right thing with Alix.

"I intend to take it however I would like, minx," he said in a low, growling voice. "It will be slow, and you'll be screaming my name before I'm done. Count on it."

Alix shivered and swallowed.

After a moment more of monopolizing her gaze, he turned and limped toward the fallen body. If he didn't control himself, he'd be grabbing at her like some inexperienced boy. Better to focus on the task at hand, which lay in a battered pile and stunk enough to make his gorge rise.

Ogres were opportunists who liked shiny things, like giant, carnivorous magpies. They stole and looted from the mortals they killed and bodies they discovered, often keeping whatever they hoarded in a sack tied to a cord around their waists.

Cyrus pushed the Ogre onto its back to expose the pouch, grunting as his healing shoulder blazed with pain. The poorly tied sack flopped open, spilling half its contents onto the blood-soaked dirt.

"A key, a pocket knife, a few coins," Cyrus said, nudging the pile with his foot. "Not much worth keeping." He pulled the mouth of the bag open with one finger and peered inside, but even his eyesight wasn't good enough to see to the bottom. With a sigh, he plunged his hand in, then pulled it out, swearing.

"What?" Alix asked, joining him.

"Something poked me."

She raised an amused brow, reached into the bag, and pulled out a broach or pin of some sort. "What is this?"

A symbol he'd never seen before lay on her palm, something like an *S* with a line through it from tip to tip and a circle around the outside that changed it from a letter to something else. "I don't know. A lady's broach, perhaps?"

"Perhaps. I think it is pure silver."

Cyrus shrugged, and instantly regretted it as his shoulder screamed. The joint was on the downward slope of healing, but his muscles still weren't happy with the situation. "Silver. No wonder my finger is still bleeding. Might be worth selling, if you don't mind carrying it around. The metal doesn't hurt me on its own, but if I injure myself with it—well, I'd rather not stain my clothing."

Alix frowned, shuddered, then slipped the pin into her pocket. "I don't like the feel of it. But perhaps Mercedes could use the money."

"Aye. I like that idea."

They stood for a moment and stared at the enormous corpse. They would have to destroy the body so common wolves did not drag the diseased pieces across the mountainside. Ogres were not wholesome meals. It had been years since he'd seen one, as they'd mostly been pushed into the northern mountains by growing populations. What was it doing so far south?

When Alix spoke, her voice was uneasy. "Hard to believe this was a small one. Do you ever feel–do you ever regret their deaths?"

"Sometimes," he said. "But it helps to remember they are called monsters for a reason. They are not easily relocated or driven. If killing them keeps mortals alive, that is a price I am willing to pay."

It was hard not to think of his family, his village, and the monster he had not been able to kill. But the memories were not quite as sharp, now that he'd shared them. Perhaps he could live at last without so much pain.

"Even if it is not their fault? Like the–the man I killed?"

He did not miss the painful uncertainty in her voice; it was so different from the righteous fury she'd flung at him for weeks.

"Abominations–werewolves like him–cannot be saved, Alix. I kill them because they have stolen a beautiful gift meant to protect, and use it for death and destruction. I should say, that malevolent magic uses *them*. It is not the same as an ogre, who is merely living the life nature designed it for. It followed the scent of the dying man and made a meal of his body, as any scavenger would do. Unlike the ogre, however, the abominations are unnatural. They chose their fate."

"Not all of them."

"No. No, not all. But even the innocent ones cannot be saved, not once the magic attaches itself. If there is any selfishness, any darkness in their hearts, the magic will exploit it. You might say their own demons destroy them, in the end. Not even the Sisters have discovered a way to stop it and they've been studying lycanthropy for centuries. Death is the only mercy we can offer. But I take no pleasure in killing them."

"Not even the wolves that destroyed your village?"

She sounded truly surprised. He understood that. Operating from a place of moral absolutism made hard decisions far easier to make, and left no room for guilt or uncertainty. But nothing was ever truly so simple. Admitting that the world and all the creatures in it were complex and carried both light and shadow meant accepting some level of uncertainty. And living with the accompanying guilt.

Perhaps when he finally took his own revenge, he would stop hunting and no longer have to worry about the guilt. But until then? He could live with the uncertainty.

"Werewolves did not destroy my village," he said. "A vampire did."

20

Alix

"ARE YOU HURT? ALIX?"

She blinked away the shock and focused on Cyrus, though his words still rang in her ears.

It was a vampire.

Breath of god, she should have known. The warmth of companionship, of trust between equals, such things were not for the likes of her. She blinked to see Cyrus frowning down at her, standing close enough to see the line of concern between his furrowed brows.

Her stomach heaved, but she swallowed back the bile and shook her head. "No. No, I'm fine."

But she was hurt, just not in the way he thought.

He eyed her a moment longer, taking stock of her limbs as if looking for damage. Satisfied she was telling the truth, he said, "Very well. Let's clean up this mess, shall we?"

They disposed of the body in a hole too deep for even the wolves to dig it up. Alix found the gruesome remains of the ogre's snack, and tossed that into the hole too, before covering the carcass with dirt.

If the scent of death and blood drew any more monsters, it was safer to have walls to hide behind, so they spent the remainder of the night in the trapper's cabin. But the room was cramped and there was no escaping the intimacy of Cyrus's breath, his heartbeat, his smell...so Alix pretended to be tired and ignored every searching glance he sent her way, as if asking her whether the delicate cord of trust and passion that stretched between them mere hours ago still tied them together.

But she could not force herself to look at him. If she did, he would see the truth in her eyes: that his family was dead because of monsters like her. How could she have let herself make the mistake of getting close to him? It was unforgivably stupid.

Her self-recrimination and his confusion mixed to fill the air with so much tension that sleep was impossible, and the little cot with rumpled blankets remained conspicuously empty.

Cyrus swore and kicked the head off a low-growing edelweiss. The small pale flower flew through the air and landed on the dirt, its leaves limp and dusty.

"Cursed storm washed away whatever was left of the trail," he said, then sighed in resignation. "It was a miracle the traces lasted so long, I suppose. We'll have to start quartering the mountain for signs."

"I don't think we have time for that. It could take days and we may still find nothing."

"You have a better idea?"

"I think we can make some educated guesses, now that we've exposed more about our quarry."

Cyrus laughed and the tension on his face eased. His eyes roamed from her shoes to her breasts and settled on her mouth with enough hunger to make her knees weak. "There are a few more things I'd like exposed, but I don't think that will help us catch werewolves."

Heat rushed up her neck and settled in her cheeks. Damn him, how did he do that? Once the itch for companionship was scratched, she was used to waiting months, if not years, between lovers.

But all the wolf had to do was stand there and she found herself unwillingly remembering the taste of him, his hands on her body, the hard length of him filling her with heat. One look was enough to make her want him.

His words leaped to her mind again, echoing off the inside of her skull with painful finality: *it was a vampire.*

Alix swallowed past the lump in her throat and ignored the way his eyes twinkled with mischief when he knew he'd discomposed her. Last night had been a mistake made in the aftermath of emotional turmoil. She'd needed the comfort of touch, nothing more. Cyrus was no different than a hundred others.

She could not afford to think of him, or their intimacy, as anything other than a momentary lapse of judgment. Better if she didn't think of it at all.

"If we believe the tortured...man," she said, storing away her misgivings and bringing her mind back on topic, "the werewolves are ravaging villages, infecting the inhabitants, and rounding up whoever survives the change. They starve the new wolves until they're mindless with hunger, then lead them to the next village to repeat the process."

Cyrus folded his arms, serious again. "Aye, *if* we can believe him. Though his account does match the evidence we found in Mont Blanc. Most of the bodies were not even defiled, simply killed."

"Exactly. So, if that truly is a pattern and not an aberration, we should scout the nearest village on the other side of the mountain in the direction they were traveling. They may already be preparing their next attack. If they are, there should be signs of it."

"Even if they retain more human intelligence than the average werewolf, they won't be able to hide a whole pack. If nothing else, the stink of death will give them away."

That was true enough. Now they just needed an area to search. "How far can a werewolf run before feeding? I don't want to waste time hunting in unlikely places."

He frowned. "I don't know that the standard expectations apply to these creatures. They already break so many rules it may be dangerous to assume. But in good condition, I would expect a healthy wolf to range fifty miles. Perhaps a bit more before it needs to feed."

"Let us start with the closest village then. If we learn nothing, we can spread out from there."

Cyrus searched her face for something she could not guess at. She held her breath and tried not to look as fragile as she felt, but that was surprisingly difficult when the concern in his eyes made her feel about as tough as a china cup. She should tell him. He deserved to know what she was. But the words stuck in her chest and festered.

Finally, he released her from his gaze and clapped. "Well, let's retrieve your pistols and be about our business, then."

"Let's."

Unfortunately, finding the pistols took longer than anticipated. The storm had blown debris across the open ground and created runnels in the dirt that disturbed the topography she remembered from the day before. Cyrus had been so focused on stopping them from being struck by lightning that he hadn't paid much attention to where he threw her weapons.

"Perhaps we should leave them," he said as he bent to inspect the crevices in a fallen log. "We're already behind."

"Perhaps you shouldn't fling other people's valuable property into the forest without noting which way you've thrown them," she snapped. "Besides, those are particularly expensive pieces of artifice filled with silver bullets. You will be glad we found them when the need arises."

"If I hadn't thrown them, you'd be as crispy as that tree."

The tree in question was split down the middle and blackened, half of its crown lying in a tangled heap on the ground. Hadn't they been standing near that tree when the lightning struck?

Sure enough, Alix spotted a bit of silver peeking from beneath a bush not far from the blasted tree. She stowed the filthy pistols in her pack, reminding herself to clean them soon, and followed Cyrus down the far slope of the mountain.

Darkness came on early with the approach of another bank of clouds that blocked the golden sunset light from reaching them. Where had the day gone?

"No good for tracking," Cyrus muttered, squinting at the horizon.

Alix scanned the trees for a likely candidate, settling on a pine tree that must have been around eighty feet tall. It would make a perfect lookout. "Maybe not. But we can take advantage of the elevation."

She took a running leap and caught the lowest branch, swinging herself up in a single, fluid motion.

Cyrus whistled and applauded, and a silly little ember of pride warmed her chest as she climbed. How long had it been since someone was impressed or proud of her for being good at anything? Maman had praised her, of course, and Grand-mère, but adults praised all children.

The huntsman who trained her and brought her to the Sisters had been sparing with his praise, but he was long dead, and there wasn't much call for acrobatics at the convent. It was a stupid reason to feel pleased, but she let herself feel it anyway. She deserved at least something to hang onto.

The top of the tree was thin and limber, swaying in a fitful breeze that forced Alix to wrap her arms around the trunk. The upper branches were far too delicate to bear her weight, but three-quarters of the way was high enough to command a clear view from horizon to horizon.

Darkness covered most of the sky with only a hint of pale blue where the last reflected rays of sunlight glowed against the bottom of the cloud cover. Mountainous silhouettes stretched into the distance in layer after layer, creating a jagged line against the velvet night.

If there were any villages nearby, she should be able to see the light of candles, lamps, and fires. She scanned the peaks and valleys with narrowed eyes. There, nestled in a fold in the land, was the barely concealed light of a town.

Alix dropped to the ground on silent feet and said, "There is a village perhaps twenty miles that way."

"After you, then."

She narrowed her eyes. What was he playing at? His nose was better than hers, and he'd likely be a more accurate guide once they were close enough to scent the village. Then again, wondering about his motivations only made her want to ask him questions, so she adjusted the straps of her pack and strode into the darkness beneath the trees.

But she had not taken twenty paces before the heat of his gaze began to burn a hole in her back. Suddenly the easy sway of her hips and the confident, long-legged stride she took for granted felt less like a mere function of movement and more like her body was singing a siren song.

It wasn't. She was only doing her job. If he stared, that was his problem and not hers. But warmth settled low in her belly as she imagined him watching her walk while thinking about what they'd done last night.

God's breath, if he didn't stop staring, she was going to go up in smoke. *Get ahold of yourself*, she thought furiously, but she said, "Stare too long and I'll be forced to charge a fee."

"I'd pay it without complaint."

The ember in her chest flared bright, lighting her body for a moment with a welcome glow. But it was smothered seconds later by the reminder that accepting attention from Cyrus was dishonest and unfair. He deserved to know what she was.

Suddenly, she wanted nothing more than a private room at an inn with a real mattress, a thick blanket, and a door she could lock.

"If they did come this way, we are already days behind," Alix said. "Let's see if we can catch up a bit."

She broke into a comfortable run, confident he could follow her even if she pulled away. Pulling away would be smart. Every time the wind changed his familiar scent washed over her, only now it was mixed with a hint of spearmint.

Cyrus smelled of *her*.

Visions assaulted her: his powerful body stretched beneath her, his pupils dilated in pleasure, the heat of his gaze like fire on her skin, the feeling of him deep inside—she tripped over a tree root and caught herself before stumbling into a bush.

"Are you tired?" he asked, joining her and keeping pace.

"No."

"You don't stumble, Alix."

Thankfully, even his eyes were not sharp enough to see her blush in the dark. "Apparently, I do."

"What's bothering you, minx?"

You are making me want things that aren't safe for either of us, she thought acidly, *things I shouldn't want. And I still can't stop remembering–* "Nothing, wolf. I'm fine."

Cyrus's jaw clenched, but he dropped back and didn't speak to her again until she slowed to a stop on the crest of a hill overlooking the village. Night swallowed up everything beyond the reach of torch and firelight, making the isolated collection of buildings a beacon in a sea of nothingness.

"A village that size ought to have an inn," Cyrus said. Perhaps he, too, needed a bit of solitude. "There are at least five hours left of darkness. We can find out if the pack has been near or if anyone saw them pass through in the morning."

Loreau was a wealthy village located on the east-west road near the Petite Risle River. It was larger than Mont Blanc, which had in truth been more of a hamlet, and densely populated thanks to constant traffic from Switzerland.

Silence wrapped its soft wings around the place, and there was a sense of well-regulated peace and prosperity in the neatly maintained streets and flowering window boxes.

"This place is too large to be a likely target," Cyrus said as they neared the glow of the lanterns hanging outside the inn.

"Agreed. There are enough people here to endanger the pack, even without silver. And so far the attacks have focused on isolated settlements that may go unnoticed for days. Destroying a village this size would bring every hunter in France down upon them."

As they passed the stable, dozens of large hearts beat in a syncopated rhythm.

"The stable is full," Cyrus pointed out. "Plenty of travelers to question in the morning."

They stopped outside the inn and stood unmoving at the foot of the stairs. If the werewolves were unlikely to attack this village, there wasn't much point in staying the night. Then again, there were quiet rooms inside with comfortable beds and solid doors that could close out the world.

Should they move on and keep tracking, or give in to the desire for just a few hours respite? Alix cleared her throat. "Do you need sleep?"

"You don't?"

"I can go another day, at least. Two, if needed." The nap in the trapper's cabin hadn't exactly been sleep, but it had been enough.

"You won't be much good in a fight if you get injured and your body shuts down to heal itself, again."

She blew an irritated breath through her nose. "Do you need sleep or not?"

"It certainly wouldn't hurt."

"Fine."

She pushed the door open to see a young man with a cloud of red hair sitting behind the bar. His dark skin and freckles made his pale blue eyes shocking by contrast, and his smile was several times brighter than the lamp on the table.

When he saw Alix, his smile faltered and grew stiff, but he recovered, though his heart sounded like it might leap right out of his chest and flee down the main street.

"Welcome to Loreau," he said in a voice that only shook a little. "Do you need a room for the night?"

Alix answered, "Two," just as Cyrus said, "Aye."

The boy's Adam's apple bobbed. "Ah, we are—that is—we only have one room to offer, tonight. The races are tomorrow, you see, and—"

"One room will do," Cyrus said.

Alix started to object, thought of what it would be like trying to sleep in the same room as Cyrus, and left the building. If she had to spend hours with his scent perfuming the air, listening to his breath and the furtive rustling noises as he shifted in the night, feeling the warmth of his body heating the space between them, she'd go mad.

Or, worse, be unable to stop herself from doing all the things she'd been trying not to think about for the last day and a half. Truthfully, she did not *want* to stop herself. And that was terrifying.

"Alix? What the hell was that?" Cyrus jogged up and paced alongside her, his long legs keeping up easily as they strode out of town.

"Nothing. I cannot stay there."

"It would have been nice to know that before we scared the desk boy half to death."

"You didn't scare him, I did."

"How do you know which of us—"

She spun on him, hands curled into fists, fury making her cheeks hot. "Because I am a monster, Cyrus, and mortals know it. They have the good sense to stay away from me."

"What does that mean?"

Tell him, her conscience whispered. *He deserves to know.*

But if she told him, he would look at her just like the boy had, just like everyone always did; everyone except the people who hired her to kill other monsters. Only she did not feel that way around Cyrus, not anymore.

The thought of going back to the hatred and insults and uncomfortable silences, made her heart feel like a bird trapped in a cage growing slowly smaller. So she turned and strode out of the village, cloak flapping around her legs as she left the dimly lighted streets behind for the cool darkness beneath the trees.

"Alix?"

His earlier words echoed in her mind again with ringing finality. *It was a vampire.*

She ran.

21

Cyrus

SWEAT SOAKED THE BACK of his shirt and tickled down his spine as he bent over the stream to refill his canteen.

"We don't have all day, wolf!"

The breeze that carried Alix's voice to him through the trees wasn't strong enough to alleviate the heat or disperse the biting flies. Cyrus swore and batted at the swarm. They scattered for one blissful moment, then returned to buzz hungrily in his ears.

He hadn't been able to soothe Alix's foul temper, and the wee bloodsuckers were unimpressed with his threats, but the heat was an enemy he could defeat...at least for a while. Freezing water stung his skin as he dunked his head, then soaked his shirt.

The flies took full advantage of his naked flesh, but a few bites were a worthy price to pay for relief from the heat. Would that he could find some relief from the sharp side of Alix's tongue. Since the night before she'd been short and distant. He'd gotten too used to the intimacy growing between them, liked it too much, and now that she had withdrawn, he felt her loss like a small hole in his gut.

But there was nothing to be done about it this minute. Perhaps, with a little time, he could soften her temper and find out what was wrong. With his shirt plastered to his chest and water dripping from the ends of his hair, he leaped across the small stream and jogged back to the road.

As he pushed through the bushes, the low lilt of Alix's voice floated toward him. "...going to leave the damned wolf if he doesn't get his arse out here in–"

"Keep your knickers on," he said, stepping into the sunlight.

Alix stood in the shadowed grass at the edge of the road, arms folded over her chest, hood pulled up despite the temperature. Her eyes fixed on him and she opened her mouth to scold him for taking so long, but no sound came out.

Her nostrils flared and her pupils dilated as she stared, her lovely mouth open just enough to make him imagine things he should not be thinking. Desire scratched down his spine with pointed claws. The force of those hawk's eyes trailing across his wet chest and down his abdomen was as hot as any caress. She bit her lip, and though the motion was unconscious rather than flirtatious, it damn near brought him to his knees.

He could not help imagining her making that face as he slid into her, or better yet her mouth on him, her lips wrapping around...

With an internal curse, he wrangled his mind away from daydreams and back to reality. Luckily he hadn't soaked his trousers in the stream, or he wouldn't be able to hide the cockstand throbbing between his legs.

He cleared his throat, but couldn't disguise the rasp in his voice. "You alright, minx?"

A business-like expression replaced the naked longing in her eyes. "Fine. See any tracks by the water?"

He told himself he wasn't disappointed she hadn't crossed the distance between them, but he'd never been good at lying to himself. If she was going to pretend she didn't want him, he could return the favor. "No, nothing. Just like the rest of the countryside around Loreau. I think we chose the wrong direction."

"You mean *I* chose the wrong direction."

"I didn't say that."

"I make mistakes as often as anyone else, don't patronize me."

"There are a lot of things I would like to do to you, Alix. Patronizing isn't one of them." Apparently, he was just as bad at pretending as he was at lying, but she didn't rise to the bait.

Instead, she turned to look back in the direction of the village. "Either the pack did not come this way, or the sign is so old we've lost them."

Cyrus scooped up a handful of dirt and rubbed the grains between his thumb and fingers, letting the bone-dry dust float away on the breeze. "Even if the wolves have been this way, the ground is too dry to hold tracks long."

They'd been searching for signs of the pack since Alix inexplicably ran from him early that morning outside the inn. Despite her grim determination, they found nothing.

Was it seeing him change before their fight with the ogre that had broken the delicate threads trust wove between them? Did she regret their night together?

If she had regrets, she wasn't sharing them. But the tight line of her mouth and the smudges beneath her eyes said she was nearing the end of her strength.

"A good night's sleep wouldn't be amiss," he said, gesturing back toward Loreau with his chin. "And we could both use a hearty meal.

With so many people in town for the races, at least one traveler is likely to have news we can follow."

Alix chewed her lip, a line forming between her brows. At last, she shrugged and blew out a breath. "Might as well. We aren't making any progress my way."

Loreau teemed with mortals of every description: dwarves selling artifice-powered toys that danced and sang, human merchants displaying bolts of cloth, and elvin musicians playing lively melodies or selling food so delectable that not even the stink of sweating bodies ruined the scent.

All of them swore and laughed and jostled and kicked up road dust that settled on his skin and made the gritty air stick in his throat. Next to him, Alix stood as still and taut as a drawn bowstring, her eyes slightly unfocused as she tried not to take in everything at once.

One of the first things Children of the Moon learned was how to filter their senses. Without that discipline, every sight, sound, and smell was overpowering. If Alix was on edge, she was likely too worn down to maintain her normal discipline.

Cyrus maneuvered through the crowd to walk in front of her, making himself a wall between her and the sea of people crowding the street. They parted for him like placid water cleaved by the prow of a ship, leaving a calm space for Alix in his wake.

They edged around an open circle in the center of the road that had been cleared for performers. A pale-skinned elvin woman in gauzy white silk danced to a lyre, bending and turning like a lily in the breeze. Spellbound, the crowd completely missed a pickpocket that worked the edge of the press, moving casually as her fingers darted into pockets. She reminded Cyrus of a hummingbird sipping from several flowers as it fed, choosing only those wearing the most expensive clothing.

For a moment he considered grabbing her arm and walking her to the nearest constable. But as she dipped her fingers into the silk pocket of a wealthy merchant, her bony wrists stuck out from worn, dirty shirt-sleeves that would not keep her warm for another season.

Cyrus's ribs constricted around his heart.

She would likely leave town having made more money from this one event than she'd steal the rest of the year, and if her thin frame was anything to go by, she needed it. But if she was caught? The consequences didn't bear thinking about.

So, he said nothing, hoped she took in a healthy haul, and headed for the inn. When he pulled the door open for Alix, she was gone.

A lightning bolt of panic shot up his spine before he spotted her red hood glowing like a drop of blood in the dirt. She stood at the edge of the crowd deep in conversation with a socialite in a wide-brimmed hat smiled at him as she passed between him and Alix, blocking his view. He leaned around her to see the thief he'd spotted earlier.

Alix spoke in a voice too low to overhear and the woman respond-ed with nods, fidgeting, and the scuffing of feet. Screening her inten-tion under the appearance of an embrace, Alix pulled a leather satchel from her bag, stepped close, and stuffed it into the inside pocket of the woman's tatty jacket. Her eyes were wide and panicked, but Alix whispered something that calmed her expression.

The woman's lips trembled, but she turned and strolled away from the crowd, one hand clutching the bulge in her pocket. She tried to walk with a nonchalant stride, but every muscle on her thin frame was strung as tightly as strings of the lute that filled the air with heartbreaking melodies.

"I don't know whether it's better in here or worse," Alix said as the door closed behind them.

Unlike the rough-and-ready interior of the inn where they'd left Mercedes, this place reflected the prosperity of Loreau in stained wood floors, matching tables and chairs, a polished bar, and several servers carrying trays of ale and steaming plates.

An upscale establishment it was not, but it was clean and full of tourists who laughed and made bets about the upcoming races. As the door closed, fully half of them turned to look at the newcomers. Eyes roamed over him with vague interest or appreciation, then slid to Alix and locked onto her face. Appreciation slowly melted into apprehension, the way one might watch a tiger in a zoo when one realized only a few measly bars stood between tender flesh and tearing claws.

He saw the instant they unconsciously categorized her as a threat and jerked their gazes away, returning to conversations with backs and shoulders slightly stiffer than they had been. The air soured with the faint tang of discomfort that didn't quite reach fear.

Alix's jaw clenched, but her expression did not change. She watched the room with cool detachment, but her heart pounded faster than it had while fighting the ogre.

"I'll find us a table," he said.

She nodded and folded her arms, putting her hands within easy reach of the knives strapped beneath her cloak. Once the hilts were close enough to touch, her shoulders relaxed.

Cyrus slipped between the tables and milling guests, keeping half of his attention on the door in case someone stupid decided to approach Alix despite her withering glare.

"Take whatever table space you can find," the barkeep said as he slid a full pint down the polished counter and began pulling another.

"Rooms?"

"Depends on how much coin you're willing to part with. There isn't much left in the whole of Loreau, but Marcel can usually find space. I'll send him over when he is free. Ah"– he pointed at a table without seeming to look–"they are leaving. If you want the space, you'd better take it."

Wasting no time, Cyrus grabbed the chair as soon as the elderly gentleman stood to help his wife to her feet. He gave the couple a polite nod and raised one hand to signal Alix. She joined him a moment later, much to the chagrin of a party of elves who entered the room behind them.

"They are staring daggers at your back for stealing the last table," she warned in a low voice.

"As long as they're not throwing them," he said, holding out her chair with a flourish, "they can do whatever they like."

One corner of her mouth curled in an unwilling smile as she sat in the proffered chair and pulled her hood back. "Does it not bother you?"

"When people stare? No. It is hard not to look at someone so damnably handsome. I don't blame them."

"Are you certain it isn't your enormous ego that draws their attention?"

"Large things *are* hard to ignore," he agreed, taking his own seat.

She snorted, but her reserve cracked and a hint of true amusement peeked through. "You know, I thought your head was so big because of your thick skull, but it turns out there is a brain beneath all that hair."

"I thought you'd never notice."

The banter was forced, at first, thanks to his effort to distract her from the discomfort, and her effort to pretend everything was fine. But by the time a harried server dropped two pints on their table, the sparkle in Alix's eyes was real.

"We ran out of wine hours ago, but the bread is fresh," the server said, sliding a brown loaf and two bowls onto the table. Whatever steamed in the bowl smelled good enough to eat in a single gulp, and Cyrus took an indulgent sniff: rich, savory, with rosemary, thyme, and plenty of butter. His mouth watered.

Alix tore the bread in half and tossed him the bigger piece. By the moon, had it only been a couple of weeks since she threw a bit of roasted rabbit at him from across the fire? The memory of it was in her eyes, accompanying an embarrassed flush.

Neither of them mentioned it as they used the bread to soak up the broth and scoop tender bits of venison, carrot, and potato from their bowls.

"Whatever they are paying their cook," Alix said around a mouthful, "it's not enough."

He made a rumbling noise of pleased agreement and sucked a bit of broth from his finger. "Anything tastes like a gourmet meal when you've been eating rough for weeks."

When he looked up, Alix was staring at his mouth with open hunger, her bottom lip caught between her teeth. His throat went dry and the last bite stuck on the way down. Several swallows of ale weren't quite enough to wash it down or chill the sudden heat in his blood.

Distraction. He needed a distraction.

"Do you have any pleasures outside hunting?"

She choked on a swallow of ale and covered her mouth with the back of her hand. "What?"

"You know, passions."

She made an unwilling grunting noise like she was either holding back a laugh or trying not to throw up. Heat rose up his neck but he ignored it, and his poor choice of words, and soldiered on. "Pastimes you enjoy, things you do when you're not working."

"Ah."

Cyrus focused on his stew, giving himself a moment to recover from the burning embarrassment threatening to give him away. How in five hells had this woman managed to make him behave like a green lad when he was over three hundred years old?

"I do."

"What are they?"

One corner of her mouth quirked, and she lifted the edge of her cloak to display the embroidery of flowering vines curling around the hem in intricate patterns. Each stitch was evenly spaced, smooth, and fluid, and the threads caught the light like the silvery underside of quivering leaves in the sun.

"That is your work?" he asked.

"It is."

"I admired it when I first saw it. Your skill is something to be proud of."

She ran her thumb over the stitches and her eyes took on a faraway look as she considered the threads of pale flowers scattered amongst the leaves. "When I have a needle in my hand, everything else fades away. My worries, regrets...all of it. Mother Superior used to scold me for using the convent dye on my embroidery thread. She said my fingers looked as if I dipped them in rainbows. I don't think she cared about that as much as she worried I would stain the bibles."

"Did you?"

She blinked, seeming to come back to herself as her eyes focused. "What?"

"Stain the bibles?"

"More than one," she leaned forward and confided. "If I was not training with Jean-Luc, I was embroidering every scrap of cloth I could get my hands on. Mother Superior still has several pillows with my early efforts. The thistles look more like ogres than flowers. They have handed the damn things down from sister to sister, though only St. Christophe knows why."

Knowing the woman she was now, it was hard to picture a young Alix, her eyes less jaded, her smile and laughter closer to the surface, creating lovely little handiworks to give to the sisters. "Who is Jean-Luc?"

Her guarded expression slammed back into place, a door that closed before he got a peek inside. "He was the hunter who trained me. What about you? Any...passions?"

"Fishing."

She choked on a bite of stew. "Fishing? Really?"

"Why is that so surprising?"

"It's not."

"Oh yes, I can tell by the way you nearly killed yourself with a carrot that you are not at all surprised."

"It's just not what I imagined, that's all."

Cyrus sat back and folded his arms over his chest. "Very well, oh famous hunter and embroiderer of cloaks, what pastime suits me better?"

She considered him a moment, eyes sparkling with suppressed mirth. "Carrying around large stones?"

"A very enjoyable pastime, that. Nothing I like better than a few boulders on a Sunday morning."

"Well you must do something to maintain all of..." she said with a vague gesture at his chest.

"That is pure genetics, minx."

"Your humility is astonishing."

"So are the exercises I do to maintain all of this," he said, mirroring her gesture. Then he leaned forward and locked her in place with his eyes. "I can show you a few of them if you like. But they are rather vigorous. You may pass out before we're done."

She licked her lips and swallowed. "Tell me about fishing."

He made her wait, tearing apart his last piece of bread and popping the crust into his mouth. The woman had far more self-control than he did, he had to give her that much. "I used to help my father fish the loch below our village, though that was for sustenance, not pleasure. Still, it's impossible not to find fishing peaceful when the wind is in your hair and the sun is on your face. Sometimes, standing at the water's edge, I still expect to feel his hand on my shoulder and hear him say *we're for home and supper, now, lad*. It's those moments that bring me back to the water."

Her lashes lowered but not fast enough to hide her wistful expression. "I know it must be painful, but you are lucky to have such memories. I would give anything to feel the expectation of hearing my maman's voice. I don't even remember what it sounded like anymore."

Then she looked up and her eyes were clear and transparent as colored glass that sliced him to the bone. "I'm sorry I laughed."

Without thinking, Cyrus reached across the table and took her hands. Her fingers were cold, and he rubbed his thumbs across her knuckles, feeling the ridges of long-healed scars.

"Never apologize for your laughter, Alix. This world needs more of it, and yours is the most beautiful I've ever heard."

Her expression softened like a flower spreading its petals beneath the early morning sun. If he woke up to a look like that every morning, he'd–

"A few dead villagers isn't a plague, Claude," an exasperated voice, loud enough to draw the attention of half the room, interrupted the tender moment. Alix gently pulled her hands away and tore apart another chunk of bread.

"Then what would you call it?" a raspy-voiced Claude replied with a slight slur softening his consonants.

Cyrus eyed the offending table, his interest piqued.

"Will the two of you keep your voices down?" a woman interjected, flapping her napkin at the men. "Are you trying to alarm everyone?"

Claude ignored her attempt to silence them and slammed a palm on the table. "People should be afraid of a plague! And they would listen if they have any sense."

"Where's your proof?" the first voice demanded. "Villagers die all the time from sickness, animals, accidents, or old age. That's nothing worth worrying over."

"Three in a week?"

A shrug. "Bad luck."

"Leo, use your brain, for once. Three in a week is too many, even for chance."

"You don't know what they died from!" Leo said, throwing his hands in the air. "You're a coffin maker, not a medical doctor."

Claude had enough of being disbelieved. He stood, threw back the rest of his ale, wiped his sleeve across his mouth, and pointed down at Leo and the woman. "I can tell you this. I have been making coffins in Loreau for ten years, and I have never shipped three coffins in the same week to the same pla"–he hiccuped–"place. There's a plague, or I will eat my hammer. And you would all be wise to listen!" He flung his arms out and spun, glaring at the other diners. The whole place was silent and staring. "Stay out of Villecourbé, if you know what is good for you!"

Alix watched his face instead of turning to spectate as two men grabbed the belligerent Claude by the arms and dragged him from the inn.

"That was easy enough," Cyrus said when everything settled and people began eating and chatting again. "I bet if we ask another diner, they'll tell us Villecourbé is small and not far from here."

"They will," a stout man with a thick mustache and bald head said as he approached. He walked with loose hands at the end of stiff arms, as if the appendages were only weakly attached. "Orrin tells me you need a room?"

"Aye," Cyrus said, standing to shake the man's hand. "If you have any to spare for the night."

The mustachioed man looked at Alix, his expression hard and inscrutable. "The both of you?"

That question, in such a shocked tone of voice, irritated her enough to say, "Yes. The both of us."

He folded his arms over his chest, glanced between the two of them, and said, "You'll have to look somewhere else. We don't sell rooms to faeries."

22

Alix

"FREAK!"

Alix felt the rock hit, but when she pressed trembling fingertips to her cheek, the slick blood still sent a thrill of shock down her spine.

Another rock struck the ground near her feet.

"She's cursed! Cursed freak!"

The children who had been laughing and playing moments before now formed a wall that separated Alix from the road into the village.

A girl bent and snatched a rock from the dirt path. The freckled bridge of her nose wrinkled in disgust as she said, "She's not a freak. She's a monster!"

This time, the rock hit Alix in the chest.

She turned and ran. *Don't go into the village, don't go into the village, don't go into the village.* Maman's orders ran in a litany, like a prayer, with each gasping breath. She should have listened and stayed safely in their little cottage. But the children's laughter and songs drew her out of the forest as surely as a fish on a line.

Maybe this village would be different from the last one. After all, last time she wasn't careful and didn't wear her hood. If she wore her it, no one *would know she was a monster, and perhaps this time she would finally make friends.*

She should have known better.

Tears turned the world into a blur of greens and yellows and hateful faces as she ran. Alix did not know where she was running to, only that she was running away.

"What's all this, now?" A gentle voice, like a breeze through the grass, stopped Alix's wild flight.

Adults were no safer than children, and sometimes they were worse, but something in that voice quieted her fear. She dashed her tears away with the sleeve of her dress and saw an old woman standing at the wattle gate of a small garden, her white hair caught up in a red kerchief.

"What happened to your face, child?"

Fresh tears threatened, along with rising anger and a sense of injustice that tightened her hands into fists. "The village children. They hate me."

"I'm sure that's not true."

"It is. But I don't care. I hate them, too!"

The old woman knelt in front of Alix and regarded her with eyes as deep and wide as the sky. "They don't hate you, darling. They fear you. But I care for all kinds of fearsome creatures. Would you like to see my hawk?"

Curiosity sprang up to choke out her anger and hurt. "A hawk?"

"Mhmm. She is also fierce, just like you. And people are frightened of her, too. But she is a beautiful creature and her wounds will soon be healed. Then she will leap into the sky and fly again. Come, let us clean you up and I will show you how to feed her."

The familiar pain of inevitable betrayal still stung hundreds of years later. She knew better and still managed to convince herself that this time, maybe the mortals wouldn't notice the indefinable *something* that made her different, dangerous. Perhaps she could have a meal next to regular people and feel she was part of the world, just this once.

It rarely worked out that way. Why should this time be any different just because she wanted it to be?

Cyrus' brows rose as he stared at the innkeeper. "Faerie? You must be joking."

The bald man's expression was as immovable as stone. "You mean to tell me you think she's as mortal as you or me? Look at her!"

More hateful eyes, more sneering faces. She should have been far past feeling shame for what she was, and yet it still soured her guts, making the stew and bread threaten to climb back up her throat.

"You won't sell us a room because my friend is too *beautiful*?"

The owner was not moved by Cyrus's incredulous demand or the growing anger in his face. He did not raise his voice or change his posture, he simply said, "Look at her. She is not natural."

She's a monster.

Angry color stole up Cyrus' neck, and a deep sense of unease filled the room. Backcountry folk would never be convinced faeries were nothing more than myth. They knew something was wrong with her, something that could not be explained by natural means, and a supernatural explanation was better than none.

All conversation had stopped. But the glances that had been amused or exasperated during Claude's tirade now slid toward fear. Monsters were scary but natural. Faeries, on the other hand, were believed to hold strange magic that could ensorcell and ensnare. This fear was spiritual, and the first step down the perilous road that led to mobs and pitchforks.

Alix dropped a coin on the table and grabbed Cyrus' forearm before he could make a scene.

"It is not worth the fight," she said, pulling him toward the door.

"No," he said, unmoved. "I will not stand by while a short-sighted idiot mistreats you."

"Living in the country does not make us stupid," the owner said. "Faeries are dangerous. Inviting them into your home is dangerous. She has been fed, as is proper, but now she must leave. We cannot afford to house monsters."

It was the same detached voice a racer might use when explaining why the horse must be put down.

"If *she* is a monster," Cyrus growled, leaning forward and clenching his fists, "I shudder to think what the rest of you are."

That was the moment, the pivotal tipping point where the mood of the crowd turned from unease to anger. She yanked him down by the elbow and growled into his ear, "Unless you are willing to hurt several innocent people, we must go. *Now.*"

Angry faces stared at them from every corner of a room that teetered on the edge of an explosion. The people were not merely dry tinder waiting for a spark, they were already smoking.

At least he was still in charge of his wits enough to recognize the danger.

Slinging his pack onto his back, he glared daggers at the room as she dragged him out of the inn and back into the crowded street. Sunlight hit her face like a hammer blow, so she pulled up her hood and headed for the outskirts of town at a ground-eating lope.

Cyrus followed and the air around him trembled with anger. When he stopped an unsuspecting villager to demand, "Where is Villecourbé?" the poor man only pointed with one shaking finger.

But she could not stay to watch or apologize to the terrified man for her partner's behavior. If she didn't get out, she would scream until her throat bled.

So much for a warm meal and a door to lock the world out.

Focus; that was what she needed. When she focused on her missions she knew what to expect and what not to hope for. The fear of mortals did not seem so significant when she confronted life and death.

"Alix, wait."

Wait for what? For him to keep showing her glimpses of a life she could not have? For disappointment to crush her like a falling boulder again? The convent was the only place she would be treated like a person.

"Alix!"

She spun, fists clenched and ready for a fight. "What?"

"I'm sorry they–"

"I don't need your pity, wolf. Where is Villecourbé?"

He searched her face, his eyes earnest and concerned, as if he would like to comfort her. But she did not want comfort, so she stared back at him, stone-faced.

Finally, he said through gritted teeth, "That way," and pointed west.

She frowned and scanned the area. How far had she walked? Trees and ferns had swallowed up the noise of the village, and the ripe scent of the crowded streets no longer tainted the air. The only eyes staring at her now were a pair of squirrels and a few wary birds.

She was safe.

Alix closed her eyes and breathed deeply, but relaxation did not follow. Her stomach was still clenched and unspent adrenaline required her to move. "That way, eh? Fine."

She left the road and cut through the trees, leaving Cyrus behind. Good. A brisk walk alone would dampen the emotions roiling in her belly and clear her mind. But a badly felled tree blocked her chosen path, one end so thick with foliage it looked like a stand of saplings. Instead of going out of her way, she leaped the trunk.

Cyrus was on the other side.

"How did you get here?"

"I'm faster than you are," he said with a casual shrug.

"What are you doing?"

"We're making camp for the night."

Alix rolled her eyes. "No, we are going to Villecourbé."

Without taking his eyes off hers, he swung his pack off and placed it purposefully on the ground, one brow raised in challenge. "We need rest. We are staying here, tonight. This tree will make a perfect screen for our camp."

"I don't have time for this."

Cyrus caught her arm as she tried to pass him his. "Alix," he began, voice soft, but she jerked out of his grip.

He stepped in front of her, blocking her escape with his unfairly wide chest.

"Get out of my way."

"You need rest."

"Wolf—"

"I'll rub your feet," he offered, wiggling his fingers as if that was supposed to be enticing.

She sidestepped, and he mirrored her.

Her teeth ground together. "Why are you doing this?"

"Doing what?"

The fear, anger, and guilt of the last few days exploded. "Trying to protect me! I am more than three hundred years old, and I did not live this long by being an idiot. I don't need you helping me and coddling me and defending me and making me want things I cannot have!"

Cyrus went utterly still as she panted and clenched her fists in impotent rage.

"Things you cannot have? Like what?"

"Like a normal life," she said, as if he was stupid.

"Why can't you have it? Because of those idiots at the Inn? Don't listen to people like them, they are superstitious, backwater—"

"They are right! I *am* a monster, and they should fear me. I do not belong among them and they can sense that."

Tell him, the little voice whispered. *Tell him what you are.* But she couldn't. If he looked at her as they had, with suspicion and hate, she wasn't certain what she would do.

He reached for her face, but she batted his hands away. As usual, Cyrus ignored her, backing her up until her pack hit the fallen trunk.

"Who told you," he said, his hands braced on either side of her head, "that you have less of a right to the life you want than they do? Being mortal does not make them more deserving of happiness."

She squeezed her eyes shut, unable to bear the intensity of his gaze. If he looked at her that way much longer, she would kiss him. His forehead rested against hers, the warmth of his body bridging the gap between them.

"You deserve joy but you will not allow yourself to have it because you have let their biases define you. Don't let them win. You can still have the life you dream of, I promise."

Every lesson life carved into her bones was a reminder that peace, happiness, and safety were not for the likes of her. No matter what pretty lies Cyrus told, the truth remained: she was a killer, and blood would always be on her hands.

But, despite her common sense, his promise settled into her chest like stray sparks that kindled a hunger she thought long stamped out. It flared to life, hot and bright, piercing the dark places in her soul. Alix shook her head, unable to clear the tightness in her throat.

Cyrus tilted her chin up with his thumbs and held her there till she met his gaze, his fingertips grazing the sensitive skin on the sides of her neck. "If you won't let yourself believe my words, then look into my eyes. Let them be your mirror. I have seen you fight back your trauma to protect others. I've seen you throw yourself into danger with no thought for your safety, and help those in need when it would not benefit you. Hell, I just watched you give most of your coin to a starving thief. Countless people are alive because you walked this earth. If you cannot believe it for yourself, then I will believe it for you. You need only trust me."

Trust was far too great a risk. She should not try... and yet there was no doubt in his eyes. Somehow, she had fooled him into thinking her a good person, and the warmth of his belief was like the sun coming up on the last day of winter.

Eventually, he would discover what she really was, and hate her for it, but...until then? Maybe she could pretend. Maybe she could let him think she was who he believed her to be. Maybe she could finally learn what it felt like to be cared for, even a little.

At the mere idea of giving in, and of giving in to *him*, the fire in her chest burned out to her limbs, unstoppable, turning doubt and fear to ash.

Suddenly, nothing mattered but basking in the warmth his gaze promised. If she was doomed to spend the rest of her life in the dark, she wanted this memory of light to hold close.

Lips trembling, she said, "You said you would not touch me unless I asked it of you."

Cyrus swallowed and released her, his hands falling away as he took a step back, giving her room to compose herself.

It was one thing to succumb to desire when he lay mostly naked beneath her in the privacy of the trapper's cabin when she needed the comfort and forgetfulness of touch. But here, his blonde hair haloed in dappled sunlight like some godling from a faerie story, looking at her as if she was the only thing he wanted in the world... nerves wrapped their slimy hands around her throat.

If you walk away from this now, she told herself, *you may never have the chance, again. Take this with you, at least; a flame to carry into the dark when you are alone again. Keep it close for as long as you can.*

Alix swallowed back the fear, let herself fall into the depths of those green eyes that looked like the heart of spring, and said, "I'm asking you."

For a heartbeat, Cyrus neither breathed nor moved.

In the next instant, his hands were in her hair, his lips and tongue and teeth tasting and teasing as delicious warmth stole through her. He pushed the pack from her shoulders as his tongue slid over hers, rough and salty and so damn seductive she could barely think.

Threading her fingers through his hair, she pulled him close, pressing her body to his like he was the sun and she'd spent her entire life in the dark.

He groaned against her lips and broke the kiss, breathing hard as he leaned back just enough to see her eyes.

"I promised you I would take my time," he said. "If you can stand when I'm done with you, it will be a miracle. I want to hear you scream my name when you are mindless with passion. I want that more than I want air to breathe. Don't say yes unless you want it, too."

Heat, low and heavy, pooled between her legs at the vision his words created. Mouth dry, breath lodged in her throat, she said, "I want you, Cyrus."

A shudder wracked his big body and his pupils dilated until only a pale green ring remained. His voice was raspy as he demanded, "Say that again."

"I want you."

The slow smile he gave her was so feral that shivers ran down her spine.

"Hold onto me, then, minx."

23

Cyrus

His muscles were so tight with desire Cyrus feared he might snap in two from the strain. As soon as Alix told him she wanted him, blood rushed between his legs until his cock throbbed for the feel of her.

Take her. Take her now, his wolf howled. But the woman haunted his dreams and waking thoughts for weeks, and he meant to enjoy every whimper and cry he dragged from that beautiful mouth.

In the trapper's cabin, she had been hungry and desperate, grasping for release with both hands, but that was nowhere near the kind of pleasure he planned to give her. So Cyrus kissed her deeply, with slow sweeps of his tongue, as if he had all the time in the world.

She wrapped her arms around his neck and curled her fingers in his hair. There were too many clothes between them. He needed to feel the velvet of her skin, to taste the salt and heat of her.

With deliberate care, he ran his hands up the length of her body, over the curve of her hips to her neck, and unclasped the red cloak. It slipped from her shoulders with a rustle to land on the moss.

She arched into his touch, breasts pressed against his chest as she fumbled with the buttons of his fly. The backs of her fingers brushed his cock, making his hips flex toward her hand. If he could not calm himself he would be buried to the hilt before he had a chance to enjoy her.

His forehead dropped to hers, their breath mixing, the air between them thick with desire as clothing slid from sensitive skin. Before long Alix stood in nothing but her torn chemise, and he in his trousers, their discarded clothes in a pile at their feet.

He ran his fingers through her hair and untangled her braid, the cool silk slipping across his skin until it hung in shining waves to her hips. She stood in the shade, her lips swollen from kissing him, nipples pink and pressing hungrily against the thin fabric that did not quite conceal her body.

His mouth went dry as he slid the straps off her shoulders. The wild beating of her heart called to him more than the velvet of her skin or the dark curls at the apex of her thighs.

But it was her eyes that arrested him, luminous amber surrounded by dark lashes, both hungry and vulnerable, hovering on the edge of fully trusting him. A fist of mingled tenderness and desire clenched around his heart.

"You cannot be real," he said, gaze sliding from the crown of her head, down the column of her throat, touching the shadow of her collarbones. A single red jewel hung from a chain around her neck and rested between her breasts, winking in the shifting shadows like a drop of blood.

It drew his eye to the pale scar of the bullet he'd drawn from her chest weeks ago. Other scars, older and more harrowing, were scattered across her body. Those had not been visible in the trapper's cabin. He touched each one with reverence, fingertips sliding across the raised skin that was almost silver in the dappled light.

How many times had she risked her life only to be treated like a dangerous animal by those she fought to protect? Would he have had the fortitude to continue fighting for people if they responded to him the way they did her? That was a strength of character worth admiring.

Such resilience only made the scars more meaningful, made *her* more beautiful. He wanted to kiss each one, as they were signs she was still alive and fighting.

So he knelt at her feet, something he'd longed to do for days, and trailed his fingers up the outsides of her thighs, watching goosebumps break out in a wave across her skin. Leaning in with exquisite slowness, he kissed the scar on the inside of her hip. Alix shivered as his lips grazed the sensitive hollow, her fingers resting lightly on his head and shoulders like a benediction.

By the moon, she was responsive. It was as if his touch brought her to life.

He used the soft curve of her waist to pull her close, reveling in the softness of her, the scent of spearmint and sharp, sweet sweat.

He dipped his tongue into her belly button, and her fingers tightened reflexively in his hair as he nipped her stomach just hard enough to make her back arch. The scent of her arousal, hot and musky, made self-control almost impossible. If he did not take her soon, he'd burn alive.

Abandoning the exploration, he picked up her discarded cloak and fastened it about her neck. Couldn't have his plans leaving marks on her skin. Alix only stared at him in dazed astonishment.

He smiled and bent to capture one breast, sucking the pink tip deep into his mouth. She was sweeter than summer strawberries. He teased her with tongue and teeth as her head fell back and she clutched him to her, demanding more. But he had other plans.

"Trust me," he said against her skin, then crouched, slid his arms between her legs at the knees, and stood.

Alix gasped as her thighs slid over his shoulders and he lifted her with ease, stretching her backward over the fallen tree trunk with only her cloak to protect her naked skin. Her knees rested on his shoulders, forcing her open to his mouth, leaving her with nothing to hang onto but him.

"If I die now with the sight of your legs spread for me, I'd die well pleased," he said.

Her mouth opened as if she would respond, but no sound came out. He planned to change that. Taking his time, he kissed the inside of her thigh, letting his hands roam across her stomach and the hollows of her hip bones as he followed the curve of her leg inward.

The heat and scent of her made him want to howl with need. Instead, he glanced up to see her stretched out before him, arched across the trunk, holding herself up on her elbows as those amber eyes locked on him.

Her expression told him she knew what he was going to do, and she would not stop him but could not look away. His hands tightened around her waist, letting the anticipation sharpen their need to a razor's edge before leaning in and running the tip of his tongue along the cleft.

Alix jerked and sucked in a breath, her hands flying to his head. A thrill ran down to the base of his spine and settled between his legs, hot and demanding, but so small a taste of her was nowhere near enough.

The first time they'd made love she was hungry and desperate, but unwilling to give up control, choosing every aspect of their joining. This time she was absolutely vulnerable, trusting him with the most delicate parts of herself, and he meant to honor that gift.

Cyrus settled to his work with the flat of his tongue, parting her lips in a smooth stroke. Moon above, she was already so wet, slick with need, and as sweet as he dreamed she would be. A low sound of pleasure and the involuntary roll of her hips urged him on.

He gave her exactly what he had not been able to stop thinking about for days, reveling in the taste of her, letting her whimpers of pleasure guide him as he sunk his fingers into her hips and focused on the center of her pleasure with relish.

Alix rocked her hips against his mouth, her head falling back, her skin glistening with sweat. Fingers locked in his hair, holding him tight against her, she rocked her hips in a helpless rhythm. She was close. He purred with pleasure, then released her with one hand and slipped a finger inside of her, then two.

She bucked in surprise, a high-pitched moan escaping her lips, but he held her in place with one arm, continuing the slow strokes of his fingers and matching them with his tongue.

Her unconscious rhythm increased. Alix rode his face as he worked her, breathing as if she'd run a marathon, her inner muscles tightening around his fingers as she whimpered, "Oh gods."

"Come undone for me, minx," he said, and fastened his mouth on her, laving the bud of her pleasure and pumping his fingers. Reaching up with his free hand and taking her full weight on his shoulders, he plucked her nipple just hard enough to add the contrast of pain to her climax.

A series of shudders wracked her body and she arched off the trunk with a cry, her hands fisting in his hair and locking him against her. He did not stop as she broke, tasting the sweetness of her release as her legs shook, knowing it was only the beginning.

Limp and panting, slick with sweat, Alix did not resist as he carefully lowered her from his shoulders and worked his way up her body. He enjoyed every salty inch of her, kissing each scar, and then paying proper homage to her breasts as he re-awoke her hunger one caress at a time.

Finally, he lowered her again till her legs wrapped around his waist. She kissed him, tasting her pleasure on his tongue. As the kiss deepened, Alix's heartbeat increased and her breathing picked back up.

Acquiescence wasn't enough. He wanted her mad with need. He wanted her to know what her body was capable of when they were together, that she did not have to guard or hide herself.

"I'm nowhere near done with you," he said against her mouth, then turned to lower the two of them to the mossy ground with her cloak as a blanket. For a moment, all he could do was stare.

How many times had he imagined Alix beneath him, her hair a wild cloud around her, her eyes heavy-lidded, skin flushed, nipples hard with desire, mouth swollen and curled in a small, satisfied smile?

Leaning down to cover her, Cyrus spread her legs with his hips and kissed a trail between her breasts and up the column of her neck. He slid two fingers between her legs, parted her, and found the knot of nerves at the apex of her thighs.

Alix gasped and dug her nails into his shoulders. He sucked her nipple into his mouth while he worked her, bringing her to the shimmering edge of release once, twice, until her body shook and sweat stood out on her skin, until she pulled at his arms, his head, anything she could reach.

"Cyrus," she groaned, lifting her hips to ride his hand and digging her fingers into his forearm. "Oh god's breath, *please.*"

Again he kissed her, positioning his cock between her legs as he claimed her mouth. The wet heat of her enveloped him as he pressed in, taking his time, torturing them both. Alix wrapped her legs around his waist and tightened them, but he would not be rushed, not when he'd wanted her with every breath for weeks. He was going to fuck her like he'd eat a fresh peach, slow and with relish until the juice ran across his fingers.

Advance and retreat, a little at a time, reveling in the pull of her inner muscles but resisting the urge to thrust home as sweat rolled down his spine and his arms shook with strain.

"Look at me," he commanded, voice raw.

Her eyelids fluttered open, a sliver of amber visible through her dark lashes, and locked on his face. Under the heat of her gaze, he withdrew, then seated himself to the hilt with a powerful thrust.

Alix's eyes widened and rolled back as she gasped, arching off the ground. Wet with her own release and still slick from his tongue, he slid into her with the ease of coming home. A shaft of pleasure arrowed up his spine. She was ready for him, and so tight he nearly came undone. But he had a promise to keep.

He kissed her to give himself time to recover, then bit the junction of her neck and shoulder just to hear her gasp once more.

"By the moon, you make the sweetest noises."

A purring sound vibrated against his chest as she fisted one hand in his hair and dragged his mouth back to hers, kissing him with the kind of wild abandon that made his heart thunder.

Had anything ever felt this good in his entire life? Maybe he should move again, just to find out.

He thrust once more, feeling the pressure of her inner muscles as his cock slid out and back into her. Her legs tightened, forcing him deeper, but those eyes, shining like jewels in the scattered sunlight, demanded he give himself without restraint.

No, he realized as coherent thought slipped away, nothing had felt more right than this.

Writhing beneath him, lithe and powerful, Alix rose to meet each stroke again and again, guiding him home with her body. He shifted his weight, pressing his hips to hers so that when he thrust the friction made her moan and roll her hips.

Waves of bliss beat against him, dragging him under, until he thought he might drown in her. Release built at the base of his spine, tightening his balls. He groaned and tried not to rush. He'd promised to drag cries from her lips and yet found himself whimpering as pleasure raked him with tingling claws.

Alix's eyes were dazed, her cheeks flushed, her muscles taut. She clutched him with both hands, urging him on, and he was powerless to refuse her. With each thrust he became more mindless, unable to get enough of the taste and feel of her, his wolf demanding nothing less than absolute surrender from them both.

"Oh gods," Alix panted as she neared the edge, "don't stop."

Every muscle clenched as he pounded into her and the world constricted until all that existed were her sobbing breaths, the silk of her skin, the wet heat of her, and those damned amber eyes.

"Come undone for me," she said, mirroring his words and rocking her hips as she pulled him down to whimper in his ear, "Cyrus, come for me."

He was lost. Wave after wave of ecstasy broke over him as he rode her, back arching in uncontrolled release so sweet it felt like dying and being born at once.

Alix arched and dug her fingers into his back. Her arms and legs locked around him as she cried in a series of wracking sobs that shook both of them but shattered the very foundation of his world.

Unable to hold himself up any longer, Cyrus collapsed onto his elbows and absorbed the last of her pleasure, her inner muscles fluttering around his cock in helpless spams. He reveled in the musk and salt scent of their joined bodies, the slow, satisfied beating of their hearts.

When he lifted his head, the shining tracks of tears shimmered on Alix's cheeks and ran down the sides of her face into her hair. Her lips were slightly parted and her legs–still trembling–had fallen limp.

The sight of her, peaceful and vulnerable beneath him, utterly without cynicism or fear, broke his heart. He was very much afraid he would never again find all of the pieces.

24

Alix

SUNSET WAS LESS THAN an hour away as they began to set up camp, working like a pair of magnets, moving and responding to one another without conscious thought, connected by a force neither could ignore.

Though often only feet or inches apart, they never touched, both realizing that once the spell broke, the weight of expectation would smother the easy atmosphere. Silence had a price when employed to ignore the future, and Alix was willing to pay it to enjoy the familiar, companionable work. Especially if it helped her avoid discussing whether their lovemaking changed things between them.

It changed something profound for her, though she wasn't sure she could pinpoint exactly how. She'd never been seen that way, been the focus of someone's entire being. No one had ever chased her pleasure, only treated it as a counterpoint to their own. Not Cyrus. Both times he'd focused on her, ensuring she found completion with single-minded determination.

It was as if her pleasure meant as much to him, or more, than his own. Whatever that meant, she didn't want to examine it too closely. Not yet.

For now, she'd take peace where she could find it and not ask for or expect more.

Cyrus dug the pit to keep their fire hidden while she gathered dry wood, constantly aware of his position and where she was relative to it, as if he were true north and she a compass.

When he laid his bedroll next to hers instead of on the other side of the fire, she pretended not to notice, but her heart swelled until her ribs became too small a cage. It was the loveliest pain she'd ever felt.

After the meal in Loreau, Alix expected not to be hungry until the next day, but it turned out that bedding Cyrus required a surprising amount of energy. She ate the dried sausage and cheese as if it were ambrosia. A fresh kill would have been a more satisfying meal, but she didn't want to leave camp–or Cyrus–long enough to hunt, afraid that severing this newly formed connection would leave a rift between them, a hole for doubt to worm back in.

She tried not to look at him and was mostly successful, but not re-membering his mouth was impossible. God's breath, she'd never ex-perienced anything like being touched by him. To be so exposed, bent backward with nothing for support, no control, forced to trust him as her world came undone, feeling the vibrations of his pleasure against her sensitive flesh...

And now, instead of focusing on their mission, she could not stop imagining opportunities for a repeat performance. Which was danger-ous. A lack of concentration was likely to get them both killed if they were taken by surprise.

"A few hours of sleep," he said, drying his mouth with the back of his hand and screwing the lid onto his canteen, "and we can set out for Villecourbé. We can't be more than ten miles away."

She nodded but didn't respond.

Oncoming night sucked all color from the world, draining the sky until velvet blackness crept up the far horizon. It was ten o'clock, or thereabouts. She stretched, forcing muscles that had been tight with both anger and passion hours ago to stay flexible. She pushed herself too far for too long and was dangerously close to exhaustion. Just setting up camp felt like carrying a heavy weight for miles.

And yet, somehow, the idea of sleeping seemed like a waste of precious time.

"You don't like admitting you get tired, do you?" Cyrus asked.

She picked a clover and began neatly peeling the leaves from the stem, never looking up, unnerved that he read her so well. "What makes you say that?"

"You frowned at the sky as if it betrayed you, then glared at your blankets. And you've fought me about it, before."

She shrugged and tried to sound casual. "I don't like admitting weakness."

"Sleeping isn't a weakness."

"It is when your enemies do not sleep."

He raised a brow but conceded the point.

She tossed the mangled clover into the fire where it smoked and sizzled. "Hunts do not usually take this long, not when mortals are in danger. Every moment we waste may cost another life. It is difficult to rank sleep higher than that."

"The average hunt doesn't include a pack of abominations, either. And you won't be good for much if you fall asleep while fighting. Besides, nothing about this hunt has been what either of us would have expected, but here we are."

"Here we are," she agreed.

A tendril of slimy guilt coiled around her guts, squeezing. People were dying and she sat near a warm fire getting ready to sleep. That was profoundly unfair. When she looked up, Cyrus was watching her. Compassion made his expression soft and she suspected he understood her guilt.

Instead of trying to talk her out of it, he rolled himself into his blanket, then held the corner up invitingly and raised a blonde brow. Before she could think better of it, she swung her feet around and joined him beneath the covers.

He wrapped an arm about her ribcage and snuggled her against his chest, her head pillowed on his biceps, back warm from his body heat. Crickets broke out in song as the sky put on a show for them, lighting up along the western horizon with magenta fire as the sun died. Stars winked into existence, visible through breaks in the darkening canopy.

Now and again, a shiver of awareness rolled through her. *There is a werewolf at your back,* a voice warned. Such a thing would have been unthinkable two weeks ago, one week ago. But she had seen him change forms, seen the intelligence in his eyes. He was certainly not the same as the creatures they hunted, no matter how much she had been loath to admit it.

Had it not been for his tenderness, she may have hung onto her skepticism, anyway.

But he held her now the way he held Mercedes when he rescued her from the tomb of her one-time home, wrapped within the circle of his arms as if his body were a shield against the world. Just as he'd done that afternoon, using himself as a bulwark between her and the crowd.

How he'd known the busy street set her nerves on edge she could not guess, but he must have seen her walking the knife's blade between anxiety and escape. The fact that he'd done something to ease her suffering, even something so small, made warmth kindle her belly. No one aside from maman and Grand-mère had cared about her discomfort. The Sisters believed it was something to be accepted and endured, a trial to make one stronger.

But Cyrus had, on several occasions, done his best to ease hers. His consideration warmed her more than his body did, making her muscles relax when she should have been vibrating with wary energy.

She'd never slept next to another person so intimately, not since that night so long ago when her whole life changed and fulfilled the curse of her blood. But Cyrus was not that kind of werewolf. As sleep began to settle on her, it was difficult not to wonder what it would be like when this hunt ended.

Cyrus would leave and she'd be on her own again, managing loneliness as she always had.

But for now, his heart beat a steady rhythm against her back and his breath stirred the hairs at the base of her neck. His arms shut out the world, and she was safe inside them. A sense of peace stole over her, one she experienced nowhere but the convent.

It felt too good to question or fight. So Alix embraced the peace with both hands and slipped off into sleep as one might sink into warm water.

"You must kill me, Alix my darling."

The stink of death filled her nose and mouth, but it was the rasping voice that made Alix's heart try to pound out of her chest.

Her voice came out in a high-pitched, thready whisper. "I cannot."

A ragged breath tore the darkness, one that sounded like it scraped up a raw throat. "You can. The gods have made you strong enough to give me this...this mercy. If you do not, I will try to hurt you. I don't want to hurt you."

Tears ran down Alix's face, leaving pale tracks in the blood smeared there. The handle of the silver knife was too big, and her hands were still slick and shaking. "Grandmere, I am frightened."

Alix gasped and tried to sit up but she was trapped. Someone pinned her to the ground. Terror sent a lighting strike of energy through her veins. *She had to get free.* With a powerful twist of her hips, she hooked a leg around the attacker and rolled until she was sitting astride him, drawing her knife and pressing it to the throat of her enemy.

Familiar green eyes blinked up at her.

Cyrus.

Breathing hard, Alix scooted backward until she was far enough away that there was no chance she might hurt him. Visions still flashed across her sleep-addled mind, hazy against the backdrop of the dark forest; shaggy, iron-gray fur matted with blood, the tatters of a nightgown lying on the wood floor, slavering fangs snapping shut just inches from her face.

"Alix?"

"No," she said, holding a hand up to ward him off. She did not trust herself if he got too close. "Wait till the dream fades."

Cyrus crouched on their tangled bed roll, his eyes clear and patient, pale beams of moonlight breaking through the canopy to make his hair glow. The moon was only a few days from being full. They didn't have much time left. While werewolves did not require a full moon to change shape, they had no choice in the matter when a round-bellied moon sat in the sky.

Which meant any mortals nearby would be in grave danger.

She did not have time to process and discard her memories, so she tried to shove them into a dark corner of her mind. It worked well enough, before. Yet she still felt the warm blood slick between her fingers.

Not even two centuries had been long enough to wash the memories away.

She dragged in a deep breath, held it, and let it out slowly through her nose, but her hands would not stop shaking.

"Have you ever spoken of it?"

Fear clenched an iron fist around her throat. "Of what?"

"The thing that haunts you," Cyrus said. "If you release a bit of it, perhaps it will lose some of its power."

She remembered the way he held onto her in the trapper's cabin after telling her his story, as if releasing the painful memories drained him so he clung to her for support. But Cyrus had not been at fault for the death of his family. He'd done everything he could to stop the tragedy.

He hadn't killed the people he loved, the people who trusted him. A vampire had done that.

A vampire like her.

And she'd almost attacked him mere seconds ago, just as she'd attacked–*No*, her subconscious screamed. *No, no, no, no, no. If you speak it, it will be real. He will see you for what you truly are.*

But didn't he deserve that much for all he had done and sacrificed?

Alix squeezed her arms around her knees and held on tight. She wanted to ask if he would hold her, pull her between his knees, and wrap his arms around her chest, thawing the cold places inside her with the warmth of his concern.

But If he heard her story, he would leave. It was one thing to trust him with her body; if Cyrus intended to hurt her, he had a dozen chances to do so. But to trust him with the truth of what she'd done? Her heart tried to climb out of her ribcage at the mere thought of it.

Alix closed her eyes–memories were never this hard when she was alone and there was no one else to hurt–took one more deep breath to try and steady herself...and froze. Alerted by her body language, Cyrus stopped breathing for three or four heartbeats, then pulled in a long breath through his nose.

Coppery blood, damp fur, and the sour stink of rotten meat wafted toward her on a night breeze. A second later, the rhythmic crashing of running feet tearing across the forest floor with no regard for stealth echoed through the trees.

Werewolves--two at least--were headed straight for them.

"Don't be afraid," Cyrus whispered. "I'll guard your back."

The air warped like heat rising from an oven, making her skin tingle as his magic washed over her. A great tawny wolf stood where Cyrus had been. He nudged her shoulder and she flinched away from his cold nose, biting back an insane urge to laugh. His tongue lolled out of his mouth in a doggy grin.

Alix rolled her eyes and reached for her pack before realizing she had not cleaned her pistols. *God's breath*, what a fool she was. She'd been so distracted by him and what lay between them, by feelings that should not exist, that she'd forgotten to do the one thing she'd been doing religiously for years: protect herself.

At least she still had the box Mary Paul gave her. She dug in the pack but the box was missing. *God's breath.* Her pistols were useless. All she had left was one silver knife.

She turned and leaped, arcing over Cyrus's golden head and landing on the fallen trunk, pulling out her silver knife as she slid into the shadows of the foliage. There would be time to worry about Mary Paul's box after they killed these werewolves. She crouched and sniffed, picking up two distinct signatures on the breeze and something else... a recent kill. Mortal blood.

The thud of running feet neared, echoing the beating of her heart.

They should have stopped outside camp, growled, and prowled in the shadows to strike fear into their prey. Instead, they barrelled through the underbrush with the single-minded determination of intelligent purpose. If her ears were right, there were three of them. Three, and no pistols. This would not be a pretty fight.

Cyrus slunk into the trees to her right with soundless steps, a lighter shadow in the dark, and disappeared as if he'd never existed.

There was nothing to do now but wait.

Alix adjusted her grip on the hilt, and mapped the campsite in her mind, looking for advantages, angles of attack, and potential escape routes. The evergreens here were taller and more slender than the tree Père Henri escaped into. It was a viable option if she was pressed.

But thinking of the late father made images of the destruction of Mont Blanc surface in her mind, of Mercedes' terrified gaze and starved frame... of the man she killed on the side of the mountain and his plea for mercy.

For a heart-shattering moment, the fear of killing another victim of this pack made her fingers numb. Not everyone trapped in a wolf's body was a monster. Not everyone had a choice.

Cyrus's words repeated in her mind. *But even the innocent ones cannot be saved, not once the magic attaches itself...Death is the only mercy we can offer.*

And she would give it to them.

The drumroll of heavy paws grew louder, louder, until a dark form the size of a small pony catapulted from the brush and into the small clearing. It sailed through the air to land on their bedroll with enough force to break bones if they'd still been sleeping. It snapped at their blankets and snuffled with its huge nose, growling low in its chest.

Alix tightened her grip. That was one.

Wolf number two crept out of the shadows on the left. A white blaze glowed between its orange eyes and its fangs gleamed. The beast prepared to catch them if they tried to escape in the only logical direction.

Where was the third wolf?

A crash and a high-pitched yelp of surprise told her that Cyrus found the third. The other two heads snapped up, ears erect, rumbling snarls making the hair on her forearms stand up. The three of them would gang up on Cyrus if she did not intervene.

So Alix did the only thing that made sense. She leaped from cover with her silver knife flashing in the moonlight and landed on the back of the closest wolf.

25

Allies

BLOOD FILLED HIS MOUTH, hot and coppery and slightly sour. The werewolf beneath him twisted and kicked with both back legs, raking his chest like an angry cat. Cyrus tightened his jaw and clamped down, his teeth tearing through fragile flesh.

He'd taken the smaller male by surprise, ambushing him from cover to end the fight without undue pain. But the wolf reacted quickly enough to deflect the killing blow. So Cyrus hauled his prey to the closest tree, pinned it against the bark, and with a powerful twist of his shoulders, broke the wolf's neck.

Unfortunately, werewolves' accelerated healing meant even a broken neck would not remove him from the fight. The creature was still a threat, and if left alive it may attack while he was distracted. He could not leave such danger at his back while Alix fought alone. She was a consummate predator, but fights were unpredictable, especially while outnumbered, and he refused to leave her fate to chance.

So, he tore out the creature's throat and spit the ragged flesh into the dirt. He left the body twitching and charged back into the clearing wishing there was a way to rinse out his mouth. Werewolf blood tasted absolutely vile.

The situation presented itself in a frozen split-second glance; Alix clung to the back of an enormous red wolf, her knife flashing in the moonlight as she plunged it between the creature's ribs. Not far from the battle, another werewolf crouched to leap for her exposed back.

A bolt of terror electrified his limbs. He took two running steps, bunched his legs, and sprang, hitting the beast in mid-air. They plowed into the fallen trunk, splintering wood with a crack like gunfire and driving the breath from his lungs.

Rolling in a tangle of claws and teeth, they slashed at each other until the smaller wolf disengaged and regained its footing. He locked eyes with the creature, a dark female with a white blaze across her chest. She was muscular and quick, and her glaring yellow eyes were not mad with hunger, as they should have been, but full of calculated intelligence.

Shit.

A fight with a crazed monster was one thing; they were strong, fast, and dangerous, but easy to predict and outthink. If these strange wolves maintained their human minds in addition to their magic, this fight would be ugly.

She circled to the outside, trying to open a line toward Alix, but he cut her off, planting his feet and growling a warning low in his chest. She pushed to his right, forcing him to turn to protect Alix's back. He snarled, puffing up his chest as his hackles raised. His body language said *I protect this place.*

She responded but her speech was rudimentary, almost accidental, like a toddler expressing desire for something they did not have the words to explain. But her meaning was clear enough: *I will kill you.*

So be it.

He darted toward her, his teeth flashing. She dodged with a speed that surprised him and his teeth clicked shut just inches away from her hide. Several times he tried to engage, but she avoided him, skirting the edges of the clearing and staying just outside his reach.

Why the hell wasn't she fighting him? She should have been nearly mindless with blood lust by now.

He could not account for the strange behavior until her eyes flicked toward the tree trunk. His instincts screamed a warning and Cyrus leaped to the side just in time to avoid a monstrous werewolf who cleared the fallen tree as if it were a pebble in the road.

The ground shook as it struck, and icy dread condensed at the base of his tail. She'd been baiting him, waiting until the other wolf attacked from downwind and they could take him on together.

The larger wolf was the same size as he, though nowhere near as fast as the smaller female. Its eyes were dull but hungry. If he did not take down at least one of these wolves, neither he nor Alix would make it out of the clearing. But Cyrus was not stupid enough to think he would walk away without damage.

As soon as he attacked one werewolf, the other would hamstring him. He prayed to the moon that Alix would end her side of the fight quickly because this was going to hurt.

With a snarl, he launched himself at his enemy.

Alix

Her knife sank between the werewolf's ribs over and over as she clutched a handful of fur and wrapped her legs around its chest to hold herself in place.

But the wolf twisted and bit at her legs, bucking and bending to throw her off. She could not get a clean strike at its neck, and the wounds healed too fast to bring the creature down. It should have been writhing from silver poisoning, not to mention the aconite coating the blade. The magic should have withered after her first strike with the combination of silver and wolfsbane.

But the red werewolf fought on.

After the sixth cut with no appreciable damage, Alix planted her feet and leaped in a backward arch, watching the world spin beneath her as a fourth wolf entered the fray. Dammit. They were outnumbered. But Cyrus was still standing, so she pushed the other fight out of her mind and focused on her own trouble.

She landed silently, breaking the impact with a roll, and came up running. The red wolf spun and lunged. Alix turned her forward momentum into a slide, passing beneath the wolf's muzzle as two-inch-long teeth snapped together just over her head.

She jammed her silver knife into the beast's underbelly as she slid, opening a long gash from the bottom of its chest to its back legs. The creature screamed and tried to shy away but ropes of wet intestines spilled onto the ground, hobbling its ability to move.

Even this strange magic could not heal a wound that size quickly, and it gave her a valuable moment to retake the creature's back with an efficient leap.

She landed and reached forward to slide the blade across the wolf's unprotected throat, but it twisted its neck and sunk its teeth into her calf muscle, then flexed its shoulders to drag her off. Alix bit back a cry of pain and grabbed a handful of fur as she slid, locking herself in place long enough for a powerful downward thrust of her knife.

The blade sank beneath the corner of the werewolf's jaw and sliced a jagged cut as it dragged her off its back and threw her across the clearing. She hit the ground with a huff of expelled air and rolled to her feet, ready to attack again. But the damage had been done. Lifeblood poured from a gaping wound in the creature's throat, staining the ground red.

It should have been dead at least twice, but these creatures had proven more resistant to damage than average werewolves. She'd have to finish it so there was no chance of it rejoining the fight. But the wolf snapped weakly at her as she approached.

Before she could catch hold of its muzzle, Cyrus cried.

Cyrus

Half a dozen cuts bled freely from various parts of his body, and his breath sawed in ragged gasps. He was weakening and couldn't keep up this game much longer before making a fatal misstep, not with two sets of teeth harrying him from either side. Cyrus spun, his teeth flashing, and opened up a long wound on the large wolf's flank. But the smaller werewolf darted in while his back was turned and slashed at his hindquarters before leaping away again.

As he spun to snap at the smaller wolf to keep her from disabling his legs, he caught sight of Alix sliding beneath the jaws of the red wolf and sinking her knife into its belly.

A sliver of satisfaction lodged in his heart, but he did not have much time to feel it. The large werewolf took advantage of his lapse in attention and hit him like a runaway cable car, bearing him to the ground with a terrific impact. He heard his back leg break, and felt the grinding crunch in the long bone of his shin, but did not feel it. Not yet.

He did feel the beast's teeth sink into his chest, sliding between his ribs and locking in place. The sound that ripped up his throat couldn't be called a howl.

With a desperate twist, he brought his back legs up and planted them against the wolf's chest to push it away. The beast shook him, sending fiery pain radiating out to weaken every limb.

But the wolf was not interested in crunching bones. It wanted tender flesh. When it released him to sink its teeth into his belly, Cyrus kicked and rolled away, scrabbling at the ground with his claws, ignoring the burning pain until his feet were firmly beneath him. The beast scented his weakness and lunged. Cyrus dropped his shoulder to meet the blow.

They collided with a crunch. A whine escaped as Cyrus pushed back and fought for leverage, but his muscles burned and he could not pull in enough air as every breath sent shooting pain through his chest. A current of fiery pain ran up the back of his leg and his injured limb gave out. He had made a fatal mistake and forgotten the other werewolf. True to her nature, she'd waited for an opening and attacked his most vulnerable spot. He'd been hamstrung.

Alix

She wasn't fast enough. Alix abandoned her fight and sprinted across the intervening space but the small, dark wolf darted in and tore the vulnerable tendons on the back of Cyrus's leg before she reached him.

His stability crumbled and the huge werewolf overpowered him, bearing him to the ground as the smaller wolf continued to drag him by the back leg. Fear made her heart pound hard enough to break her breastbone, but Alix launched herself at the dark wolf anyway.

Her knife flashed, and the werewolf yelped and leaped away, giving Cyrus time to stand. Though he balanced on only three feet and his fur was slick with blood, he snarled and launched himself at the larger beast.

The smaller werewolf recovered from the wound and decided Alix was the greater threat. It circled her, head low and lips pulled back in a snarl. Its yellow eyes were bright and malicious, and blood stained its muzzle. Cyrus's blood. He was fighting for his life because of these creatures.

Red fury colored her vision, turning the moon-soaked clearing into a nightmare scene. Alix attacked in a flurry of strikes and slashes, her knife whistling with each stroke, but this werewolf was far smarter and more capable than any werewolf she'd hunted before.

The beast dodged, drew blood, and retreated, moving so fast it was hard to keep up. Her single knife and weak leg could not match four good legs plus teeth *and* claws. Alix needed more weapons. She needed her knives, her pistols, the small box hidden at the bottom of her travel pack. Instead, she dodged an attack, slashed and missed, and risked a glance over her shoulder as Cyrus tore the front leg off of the large wolf.

The whole leg. He wrenched it free like a butcher quartering a hog.

Her stomach revolted and threw herself to the side as the werewolf lunged.

Cyrus

For a moment, all he could do was stand and pant as pain and exertion drove the breath from his lungs. He'd lost too much blood. His muscles quivered and threatened to give out as he watched the werewolf writhe on the ground.

He could finish the creature now, but without a front leg, it was no longer a threat. The werewolf attacking Alix, however, was. He forced himself to turn, forced his muscles to move, and caught his breath again.

Alix and the smaller wolf were engaged in a deadly dance, moving with such speed and accuracy it was impossible not to admire them both, even when he wanted nothing more than to close his eyes and sink to the ground.

But Alix's trousers were wet with blood below the knee on one side, and she wasn't as fast or stable as she should have been. He needed to change the odds.

As quietly as possible, Cyrus slunk around the edge of the clearing, taking up a position on the flank to attack at the right moment. But Alix dodged a snapping lunge, turned her ankle on a stone, and swore as she twisted into a rolling fall. The smaller wolf saw her opportunity, teeth flashing white in the moonlight as they closed over Alix's left shoulder.

Blood pounding in his ears, his vision blurry, Cyrus charged in and locked his jaws around the wolf's back leg. He set himself, digging his claws into the dirt, and wrenched the limb like a dog playing tug.

She yipped and released Alix, turning on him in a flurry of teeth and claws. His back leg gave out and he hit the dirt on his side, barely feeling the flash of pain as her teeth sunk into his neck.

He blinked and everything slowed to a crawl.

Alix struggled to her feet, her left arm hanging useless at her side.

He blinked again. Another figure appeared in the moonlight, a shadow stepping out of the treeline downwind, smaller than Alix but wearing full skirts and a strange hat.

He blinked once more and brought the figure into focus. A grim expression, a set of dark brown eyes, and an arm cocked back to throw...something. It was the woman from the tavern, the one who made him laugh and guessed so much about him.

What was she doing here?

She stepped forward with a graceful motion and hurled something at them. The world exploded in burning pain. His eyes and nose filled with stinging so strong he sneezed and coughed and wretched up his meager dinner even as his body tried to escape into the oblivion of unconsciousness.

Alix

Her knife was pressed against the throat of the strange brunette before the woman could pull anymore...whatever it was from her pocket. The smaller wolf had released Cyrus almost immediately, shaking her head and coughing in whining fits.

The breeze shifted, and Alix bit back a cough as her lungs burned. She doubled over, hacking and rubbing at her stinging eyes.

"I wouldn't do that if I were you," the stranger said, her British accent clean and concise. "Best not to touch them for a while."

"What—what—is it?" Alix said between coughing fits.

"A mixture of domestic chili powders and the crystalized extract of a rather hot variety of chili from India. Highly condensed. The crystals are rather heavy, so you likely only received a bit of the powder. Unfortunately, I cannot say the same for your friend, but I saw no better option."

"Cy—Cyrus?" She rubbed the tears from her eyes to see him lying on the ground coughing weakly, covered in blood and several open wounds.

"Is that his name? Well, we must get you and Cyrus somewhere safe to heal."

Alix tried to scowl at the woman but ended up merely squinting through the watery burning in her eyes. It was the woman from the tavern, the small brunette who was not human—or not quite human. "What are you doing here?"

"I would love to answer that question, but would you mind terribly if we deferred it until we find cover somewhere? My chili grenade overwhelmed the werewolf's senses but will not keep her away for long. And your friend is in grave danger."

Alix dragged her eyes back to Cyrus. He had stopped moving. And he was in his human form. Her heart dropped into her stomach like a lead weight. Werewolves only changed forms involuntarily on two occasions: during the full moon, and when grievously injured.

Which meant Cyrus was dying.

26

Alix

CYRUS LAY LIFELESS IN a pool of blood.

The world stopped for the space of a stunned heartbeat as Alix fell headlong into a stream of icy terror that made her lungs seize and her limbs stiffen. She wanted to run to his side, but she could not move or force her mind to accept the broken body on the ground belonged to the man she knew.

She breathed in short gasps and every one of them was thick with the scent of Cyrus's blood. Why wasn't he healing? He should have started healing within moments of his injuries. He should be grinning at her and saying something flippant about the fight. But the wound in his chest oozed and his leg was twisted the wrong way.

Wait–the wound still bled, and if his blood flowed, he was still alive.

Her muscles unlocked and her mind thawed just enough for common sense to reassert itself. Falling on her knees at his side, she pressed handfuls of her cloak against the wounds. She needed to stop the bleeding until his magic took over.

When the magic took over he would heal. He would be fine.

"Can you lift him?"

Alix blinked up at the strange woman and said through the tightness in her throat. "What?"

"As soon as the pain from the grenade wears off, the werewolf will return. We need a defensible position. If you can lift him onto my horse, we may be able to find a safe place to treat his wounds before they kill him. Or she kills us. Whichever comes first."

True. That was true. She could not treat Cyrus's wounds here and protect him if the wolf returned. She pushed the alarm and confusion away, pulled her pack on, and heaved his limp body onto her shoulder.

Ignoring the pain shooting up her leg and blooming across her torso as she strained under his weight, she followed the brunette to a horse picketed downwind near the road.

A dark mare stood a few hundred feet from their camp, munching the tender shoots growing near a rotted tree trunk. She raised her head and her nostrils flared when she scented them, ears swiveling in their direction.

Alix paused far enough away to keep the horse from feeling threatened. "The horse will shy if I get too close."

The woman pulled a scarf from her saddlebag and tied it around the horse's face, then turned her side-on and spoke to her in a soothing voice running her hands down the animal's neck.

The last thing Alix needed was to get kicked, so she approached carefully with her breath held. But the beast only snorted and shifted its weight as she laid Cyrus's limp body across the saddle.

"We are close to Villecourbé and he does not have time for a leisurely walk through the forest," Alix said as she used her cloak to secure Cyrus to the horse's back. "Can you ride?"

The woman gave Cyrus an uncertain glance. "You may be better equipped to manage his weight. I'm not certain I can stop him from falling."

"I'm not leaving you here with a werewolf, and I can keep up with your horse. Just ride as fast as you can for the village. I will catch him if he falls. Right now we need speed."

After a moment of indecision, the brunette nodded once and swung herself up behind Cyrus. Alix had done what she could to ensure he did not flop around too much. The motion of the horse may worsen his injuries, but not more than being caught in the open when the werewolf returned.

And it *would* return. That fight was not merely an accidental encounter in the forest. They were being hunted.

"I'll be behind you," she told the woman. "Get him to the first safe place. Go!"

She pulled the blindfold off and the beast skipped to the side, uncomfortable with the strangely balanced weight. But the woman brought its head back around and dug her heels into its sides. With a snort the horse surged forward, hitting a canter within a few strides.

Alix put her head down and ran.

Clods of dirt flew past her on the left, kicked up by the horse's pounding hooves. Her heart beat in time to its pace, a panicked drumroll playing to the rhythm of *let him live, let him live, let him live.*

They charged down the road and Alix was forced to keep one eye on the forest, and the other on Cyrus. A flicker of movement caught her eye on the right, a mere flash of moonlight in the shadow, but to her well-trained senses, it was unmistakable.

The she-wolf was back. Her scent hit them a moment later, musky and bitter, touched with the tang of copper: the reek of a predator. The horse's fear leaked into the air like water through a broken dam.

She shied to the right, forcing the woman to lean hard and yank on the reins to haul the animal back onto the road. A branch whizzed by less than a foot from her head.

They weren't going to make it to Villecourbé.

Alix forced more speed from her legs, gaining ground until she ran along the horse's right side.

"We have to find a defensible position," she yelled over the thunder of hoof beats. "We cannot outrun her."

The woman did not glance at Alix, but her jaw set as if she understood the implication and did not like it.

She nodded and called back, "Lead the way!"

Breathing an internal sigh of relief, Alix pushed slightly ahead and scanned the tree line for a defensible position. Trees, rocks, and bushes blurred by in a wall of black and grey, interrupted by meadows, game trails, and smaller winding roads leading to campsites or cottages.

They needed someplace small and tight, where the wolf would not have space to take advantage of her speed. A cliff face loomed above the treeline to their left, its pale gray face broken by a jagged black fissure. That may be their best chance if they could make it. If the crack extended to the ground. If it was wide enough to fit through. *If.*

"Left!" Alix shouted, pointing.

The woman's chin jerked in an affirmative gesture.

Alix dashed forward and picked the clearest route possible, then cut left through the trees. The horse followed, breathing like a bellows. Running a horse at night was dangerous, even on a well-traveled road. But running a horse through the *woods* at night was as good as suicide.

She slowed to give horse and rider enough lead time to avoid obstacles and angled their flight toward the cliff thinking *please be there. Please, please be there.* She was so focused that she didn't realize she'd lost sight of the wolf until it was too late.

A low growl made the horse shy, thrashing its head as it hopped to the side. The woman's face twisted in concentration as she fought to hang on to both the reins and Cyrus's body, but the horse was too panicked to respond.

The woman stood in the stirrups to balance as she pulled back with all her weight, trying to bring the animal around. But the horse was mindless with fear, its ears laid flat as it twisted and hopped, turning to protect its vulnerable flanks.

The werewolf was close. Alix dug her heels into the turn and tried to change direction in time to protect the animal, but it was already too late. With helpless frustration, she watched as the werewolf leaped from the shadows. Its teeth flashed in the moonlight, and the horse screamed as it went down, hamstrung.

The monster bounded into the brush and Cyrus slipped from the woman's fingers before she was tossed from the saddle with a surprised cry. Alix had not been fast enough to save the horse, but she was close enough to leap and catch the woman.

She crouched between one step and the next and flung herself across the intervening space. When she crashed into the smaller woman, Alix wrapped her arms about the woman's waist and let her speed drag them out of the path of the falling horse.

She turned as they fell, taking the brunt of the impact when they hit with a crunch, the woman landing on Alix's stomach and chest and driving the air from her lungs.

For a few dizzy seconds the world spun, but Alix didn't have time to get her bearings. Cyrus lay tangled in the undergrowth at the side of the road, and his blonde hair caught the moonlight like a beacon. A perfect, defenseless target for the she-wolf.

Alix hauled herself up and dragged the woman to her feet. They ran for Cyrus even as the horse rolled to a stop in a cloud of dust and flying debris. The poor creature had broken a leg, and it twitched and groaned as they skidded to a stop over Cyrus's body.

It was hard to ignore the horse's pain even as she grabbed Cyrus's wrist and, with a mighty grunt, hauled him onto her shoulder. Her heart ached for the animal, but it may be the one thing that saved all three of them from death if she moved fast enough.

Fear, adrenaline, and pain turned the air around the injured horse into a cocktail of desire, one the werewolf should be powerless to ignore, even with the strange changes they noted over the last weeks. At least she could hope so, because it was the only thing that might give them a chance to reach cover.

"There's a cleft in the rock," Alix panted, gesturing with her chin. "Run!"

The woman sent a single heartbroken glance at her horse, then picked up her skirt and ran. Alix followed, bowed under the awkward weight of Cyrus's limp body. God's breath, the man was too heavy for this. But his heart still beat. He breathed. He lived.

For how much longer?

A horrible growl of pleasure rent the air behind them. The horse screamed and Alix's throat closed in grief even as she ran. She wished she could have put the horse out of its misery, but if she stopped its suffering, the werewolf would no longer be drawn to it.

She ran with straining eyes and blood pounding in her temples, staring ahead as if she could make the forest part by sheer willpower.

"There!" she yelled, her voice breaking with relief.

The fissure did extend to the ground, a black lightning strike that separated the two sides of the cliff face. They were close.

The woman leaped a tree root and turned left, aiming directly for the crack. It was no more than four feet wide at the bottom and partly clogged with shrubs and boulders.

It was perfect.

The awful sound of crunching bone and tearing flesh chased them the last few feet. Alix shouldered her way into the channel, letting branches and thorns scrape lines of pain down her arms and across her legs. She fought her way back far enough that, if the werewolf managed to get past them, it would not have enough room to maneuver.

Rock walls scraped her arms and shoulders as she lowered Cyrus to a relatively bare patch of ground. He was limp and cold. Her heart leaped into her throat and she ran her hands across his torso hoping to feel a breath or heartbeat.

Something scraped against her palm.

Her fingertips slid across the dented puncture wounds on the right side of his ribcage–there! Something hard protruded from one of the holes. Was it bone? Alix squinted at his injury, but it was too dark between the sheer cliff faces even for eyes as sensitive as hers.

Please don't be bone, she thought as she caught the object between her fingertips, pinched hard, and pulled. It slid out with a sucking sound, and Cyrus gasped in a deep, healthy breath. His heart thudded hard once, then again, and fell into a rhythm.

Her heart responded, matching the beat, and tears stung her eyes. She wanted to hold onto him, to feel the magic knit his flesh back together and be sure he would recover, but there was no time to examine him further.

As soon as the werewolf abandoned its grizzly meal, it would hunt them, and they'd be busy fighting for their lives. So she dropped the object into her pocket without looking at it and drew her silver knife.

The gruesome sound of tearing flesh faded to ominous silence.

Alix joined the woman at the narrow entrance of the cleft. She held a slender silver rapier in one hand as she peered into the dark. Where had that come from?

"She will attack again soon," Alix said, taking up a position on the woman's weak side.

"Yes," she agreed, but never took her eyes off the shadows.

"I am sorry about your horse."

"As am I."

"Your sword, is it silver?"

"It is."

Where would the average person obtain a silver sword? Alix let her eyes drift over the blade, noting the runes carved into the metal before returning to the wood, scanning shadows for movement.

"The artifice is impressive," she said. "I assume it imparts strength to the silver?"

"Among other things, yes. I will be certain to pass your praise along to my artificer. If ever I see her again, of course."

Alix had not believed herself capable of surprise at this point. But she heard herself say, "Her?" in a tone of voice that made the other woman chuckle.

"Delilah Irons. I have not seen her in some years, but if she has continued her practice, she will be the finest artificer west of Prague."

A low, threatening growl rolled through the wood like thunder.

"She's found us," the woman said, her voice far calmer than it should have been, given the dire nature of their circumstances.

Alix pulled in a surreptitious breath. Fear and adrenaline tainted the air, yes, but far less than an average mortal should have experienced. After what they had just been through, the scent of the woman's terror should have choked out every other smell.

It did not.

Mere weeks ago she'd been in a similar situation with Père Henri, and his fear had been so thick in the air she'd had to remind herself not to attack him. But the woman next to her apparently could not be bothered to exhibit a normal, mortal response.

What was this woman that a werewolf attack did not adequately scare her?

"You told me your artificer's name," Alix said, "but you have not told me yours."

"Gwen. Gwenevere, actually. Lady St. James Wainwright. But please, call me Gwen."

"And you must call me Alix."

"It is a pleasure to meet you, Alix."

"How does an English lady end up fighting werewolves in a French forest?"

She chuckled. "Luck, I suppose. Ah, there."

The tip of her sword lowered to point at the silver-grey light reflecting off the coat of the she-wolf stalking through the underbrush. The woman should not have been able to see that, not with dull mortal eyes.

"If you are not fast enough," Alix said, "or you need to rest, let me know before you fall back."

The werewolf turned, angling toward them, advancing like an alpinist taking switchbacks up a mountainside, her yellow eyes never leaving their position. Gwen set herself so her weight was evenly distributed, sword held in a firm but relaxed grip, her muscles primed to move.

She had training, then. As the growling grew louder and the wolf drew closer, Alix hoped Gwen's training would pay off, because this fight was going to be ugly.

"Get ready," she said.

The werewolf charged.

Gwen's sword flashed, faster than any mortal she'd ever seen, and the werewolf yelped and dodged to one side. In the light of the waxing moon, a long red furrow showed on the skin of the beast's forehead.

"You pinked her," Alix said, a note of approval in her voice.

"I've only made her more wary. I was aiming for her eyes."

"Either way, she will not charge in again so mindlessly."

Gwen shifted her stance and raised the tip of the rapier as the werewolf circled in the opposite direction, lips peeled back in a furious snarl, ears laid flat against her skull. "Remind me to be grateful for that if we survive."

Alix set her shoulders and bent her knees, ready to leap as the wolf prepared to dart in. "If we survive," she said, "I'll be grateful for us both."

27

Cyrus

"HE'S STARTING TO HEAL. We have to set the bone now or it will heal wrong."

The familiar voice swam through his barely conscious mind but he could not make it out, like peering through dark water and noting the shape of a fish but being unable to identify it.

A drumroll of pain pulsed deep in his leg, arrows shot through his chest with every breath, and a lingering electric fear screamed at him something was *wrong*. Wrong with what? Himself?

"Ready?" the voice asked.

A lightning bolt flashed up his leg and his mental landscape went white. He tried to draw away from the agony, to curl in on himself, but there was nowhere to go.

"Come on," the voice grunted. "Hold him!"

An audible snap. He screamed. At least, he thought he did. It was impossible to tell when all he could feel was pain and the landscape of his mind was nothing but a pulsing blur. Relief came a heartbeat later when the pain dulled into a throbbing fire.

"Chest wound next," the voice ordered.

Another voice said, "It is too dark to tell, but it appears to be only the intercostal spaces. And he is already healing. A bandage should do nicely."

Someone whimpered. The edges of his existence turned black and faded into nothing.

"His temperature is improving."

"That is a good sign."

"What are you doing here?"

"Washing my hands."

"What are you doing *here*, in the backcountry? How did you find us?"

"Ah," the sound of rough fabric rubbing. "I was visiting Loreau on my way back to England. The other travelers at the inn where we met spoke of the races, and I was intrigued. And I am in no hurry to return home."

"Where is your entourage? Why do you travel alone?"

Feminine laughter. It was a warm, good-natured sound that made Cyrus want to smile, but he didn't have access to his body. "Entourage? Nothing could be less desirable. I prefer to handle my own arrangements and safety without the responsibility of an entourage. After all, how would I explain to my chaperone that I needed to track down a werewolf and his partner?"

Unease uncoiled in his chest and sank claws of fear into his guts.

"How did you know?"

"Our silly bet at the inn. I am rather good at making intuitive guesses based on evidence, and your partner bears all the signs of lycanthropy. But the strongest proof was–I hope you will not take offense..he smells like a dog."

"If you know enough to guess what he is, you must also have known how dangerous it would be to follow us into the wilderness."

"The innkeeper in Loreau stole this from your pack. Or, to be more precise, he had one of his employees steal it while he insulted you."

"That was why he did not want us staying at the inn. Some innkeepers will make a tidy profit from petty theft or overcharging, but I did not think one would try so openly while the bag was at my feet."

"He was very good. I would not have realized it either, had my raven not alerted me."

"Your raven? No, don't explain it. This situation is strange enough without adding a familiar to the mix. How did you find us?"

"My dear, your angry footprints were as easy to follow as the road to Villecourbé. And, to be quite frank...the two of you were rather loud."

The words fuzzed around the edges, becoming harder to hold onto, and the familiar dark was wrapping itself around him once more.

"Why follow us? Why go out of your way to return this? It cost you more time and effort than the box is worth."

"Because I could. And you are decent people."

"Decent is not a word most people would use to describe a werewolf," Alix said.

"What else would you call someone who rescues orphaned children and provides for their well-being?"

The voices slipped away and unconsciousness welcomed him with open arms.

"What was that song?"

A heavy sigh. "I don't remember. Even the words escape me now. It has been a long time since I learned it."

"It was lovely. Is it a lullaby?"

"I think so. My maman used to sing it to me. I think she learned it from my Grand-mère, though I never heard her sing it."

"Memories are a funny thing, are they not?" A yawn. "I am going to go look for food. Can I bring you back anything?"

The voices were a faraway hum, like distant bees floating about the background of his mind. One voice was cultured with a British accent, the other low and rich. Cyrus recognized the words and understood them, but they did not seem to apply to him. Besides, it was hard to concentrate on the meaning of the words when his mind was so fuzzy.

He floated in hazy darkness, limbs heavy and tingling with the last vestiges of pain and spent magic. Identifying the voices felt important, but he was still lethargic from extended healing and some deep instinct told him he was safe. Leaving the magic to finish its business was a smarter choice than trying to puzzle out where he was and what happened.

"I'll take anything you can find. Thank you."

"I will bring back something for him, too. Hopefully, it will not be long before he can eat it."

"Cyrus."

His eyelids twitched. That was his name, and the low, honeyed voice spoke it with a kind of caress that made warmth uncoil in his chest. It was a much more pleasant sensation than the magical hangover.

"What?"

"Cyrus. His name is Cyrus."

"That's right. Cyrus, then."

A soft click, retreating footsteps, then silence. A cool hand brushed his forehead once, twice, three times. Humming, soft and melodious, filled his mind. The song sounded old, strange and familiar at the same time. It carried him away and beneath the velvet darkness of unconsciousness.

"I wish I remembered the words," the voice murmured sometime later.

Those words did not appear to be aimed at him but still pulled him up out of sleep like a fish on a line.

"But I have not thought of them in so long. I know I knew them, once. I remember Grand-mère speaking to Maman about it, but..." The hand continued brushing gentle strokes across his forehead. "I cannot recall what they said. It's unfair that recalling little things is so hard, but remembering the pain is as easy as breathing. As time passes I lose track of the everyday happenings that made life mine: habits of speech, conversations, small kindnesses, or the way Maman would raise one eyebrow when I was pert. I cannot even properly remember her face anymore. But remembering the night–" The voice stopped.

A heartbeat near him picked up, someone breathed faster, and the hand on his forehead paused.

"Remembering the night Grand-mère died is the easiest thing I will ever do. I can still see the smears of blood on the wall and smell the dead carcass of the wolf. Grand-mère may have been old, but she was quick and clever. The wolf was foolish to think she would be an easy target."

The cadence and rhythm of the voice changed, sounding distant and detached.

"She wasn't my real grandmother, you know. The story did not get much right, but that missing detail is the most irritating. If she was my family, her kindness would have been obligatory, no more than any grandparent would do for their grandchild.

"But she was simply a kind woman who lived on the edge of the forest and cared for hurt things. Animals, people, anyone, or anything who needed safety and a bit of love. It never mattered to her that the villagers did not accept us, or that the other children were scared of me. She took us in and defended us when no one else would. And the villagers had to keep the peace because she was the only cunning woman for miles. Who else would they go to for their tinctures and salves?"

Sad, ironic humor colored the tone of the speaker's voice, and a vision filled his mind of eyes the color of sunlight through whisky. He knew this voice.

"We would have starved if it were not for her. After meeting Grand-mère, we never went hungry again. She became family in every way but blood. She was the only safe place for an outcast girl and her mother in a world that shuns anyone different from them. She taught Maman about herbs and poultices, which plants to use fresh and which to dry, which to pick under a full moon, and which to gather young. Soon Maman was able to sell her wares in the other village markets to earn us some small income. I spent market time with Grand-mère, learning about the animals she cared for.

"In truth, she was my only friend. It is no wonder, then, that I can still see her face stretched in pain, still hear her voice begging for death."

Instead of resuming rubbing his forehead, a warm hand pressed his arm, and the bed near his elbow dipped and creaked as a weight settled on his chest. When she spoke again—he was certain now it was a woman—her voice vibrated against his ribs.

"She had taken sick in the spring and the illness settled in her lungs. Her chest rattled when she coughed, and it was hard for her to care for the animals. When she started getting thin, Maman mixed up a salve to ease her lungs and packed the market basket with fresh bread, honey, cheese, milk, and small beer. We only earned enough to survive, and I don't like to think of what she must have done to give away such a bounty. The villagers did not like selling to us and we never had much money, so she must have been very...persuasive.

"Then, Maman always did what she believed necessary. And if she was not ashamed to do what needed doing to help the people she loved, I will not disrespect her memory by being ashamed for her. I cannot say I would not have done the same.

"I knew even as a child that Maman gave too much. She was strong and had seen us through too many dangers to count, but I was frightened anyway. Despite what the story says, I had no intention of disobeying Maman. I never walked to Grand-mère's cottage alone. But it was cooking day, and the salves boiling in the hearth required constant supervision. If they did not cure properly, they could not be sold and we would lose what little income we had.

"So Maman held my face between her hands and said, 'You are fast and strong and brave, Alix. Besides, you know the villagers do not like to travel near sunset. You can withstand a bit of fear to help Grand-mère, yes?' I nodded because I could not speak, but her eyes told me she believed I could do it. 'Hungry people will take this from you by force if they can,' she said, 'so go quickly and quietly, and speak to no one. Do you understand me, Alix? Speak to no one, and come home to me safe'."

Alix.

Memories and consciousness came rushing back like water through a broken dam; Alix tossing a haunch of rabbit to him across the fire, Alix calmly protecting the farmer and his boy on the road despite the bullets tearing into her flesh, Alix sleeping with Mercedes in her arms, Alix stretched below him with her dark hair fanned on the moss and her cheeks pink with desire.

Alix, her face white with pain as the werewolf dragged her body across the ground. But she was here, and he was lying in bed. By some miracle, they both survived the fight, though bolts of pain pounded through his temples hard enough to make him wish he hadn't.

He wanted to sit up and gather her into his arms, but she was speaking again and if she thought he was awake, she'd stop.

"If I knew that was the last time I would see Maman's face, hear her voice, I would have...I suppose it does not matter now. But." She sighed "If I am refuting the tale, I should add that I met no strangers on the path to Grand-mère's house. No wolf, no cruel peasants, not even the children who usually threw rocks at me. I passed a woodcutter who did not so much as give me a second glance, and that was it.

"When I reached the cottage, the gate was open. I should have known something was wrong, as Grand-mère was so particular. Everything had a place in her world. That was the first sign. The scent was the second; heavy and putrid and tinged with dried blood that made my throat burn. But there were always so many animals in and near her cottage, that the smell could be easily explained.

"Perrault made everything sound so homey; a grandmother warm in her bed, cake, and a pot of butter on the stool. But when I pushed the door open..." Alix shuddered against him as her fingers clenched into a fist in the blankets. For a long time, she shook and nothing more. He should speak. It would be wrong to let her tell him this story when she thought him unconscious. And yet, with every word, little pieces of the mystery that was his partner fell into place.

And yet, she must have been deep in her memories not to hear the change in his heartbeat. And she trembled like a frightened child. He could not help wrapping his arms around her.

Alix startled and tried to pull away. "You're awake! Are you–how do you feel?"

"I'll keep," he said in a voice raspy with disuse. How long had he been out?

She tried leaning back to examine him, but he held her securely in place. *Moon and stars*, she felt good in his arms.

After a moment, she relaxed and let him hold her, but her voice was still hesitant when she said, "How long have you been awake?"

"A while," he hedged.

Her fingers tightened in the blanket covering his torso and her heartbeat sped. He must have heard more than she was comfortable with, which meant she was going to close down on him. Before she withdrew or pulled away he asked, "Is there any water nearby?"

"Oh! Yes."

He let her go this time, and a moment later she pressed a ceramic cup to his lips. Room-temperature water had never been so refreshing. Once the burning in his throat eased, he blinked a few times to clear the grittiness from his eyes and tried to bring his surroundings into focus.

A small, simple bedroom, rustic but clean and well cared for. His eyes slid to Alix and froze. Her hair was tangled, her clothes dirty and blood-stained. She hadn't even bothered to wash the spatters from her cheek. If she was still so messy, and standing while he was not, he must have been in bad shape.

Cyrus ran his fingers gingerly across his chest, remembering the sick popping noise as werewolf teeth sank between his ribs. Vague soreness remained, but nothing terrible.

He pushed himself into a sitting position, wincing as a sharp bolt of pain ran from his ankle to his knee. Ah, yes. His leg. Both bones snapped during the fight, and a broken leg would take longer to heal than torn flesh. Alix's lips flattened and her hands twitched as if she wanted to stop him from moving, but remained frozen to the spot.

"How long was I out?"

She swallowed. "Fifteen hours, at least."

So long and he was not fully healed? Even grievous wounds should have been nothing but a memory after fifteen hours. But it was hard to worry over his injuries when Alix radiated such a strange combination of worried energy and...shame? Self-consciousness? He needed to distract her. "Is this Villecourbé?"

"Yes."

"I don't remember leaving camp," he said, shaking his head. "How did we get here?"

"Do you remember the woman from the inn? The one you flirted with?"

"I did not flirt."

"You did."

"False accusations and lies."

Her lips thinned again, this time with unwilling amusement. "She happened to be in the last inn, though I still do not understand how I didn't smell her. In any case, she saw someone steal from my pack and tracked us after we left to return the property. I could not have dragged your carcass here without her help."

If Alix needed help, then she'd been too injured to carry him. "Are you alright?"

"If you consider our respective positions," she said, folding her arms as the hint of a smile curled one corner of her mouth, "I'm not the one you should be concerned about."

"It's no more than a scratch."

Her amusement faded behind a solemn expression, eyes roaming over him. "It was more than that. You weren't healing. Something was wrong with those werewolves. We found a tooth in your chest while dressing your wounds, and the magic did not begin healing you until we removed it. I've never seen such a thing."

The magic hadn't healed him? Cold sweat gathered at the base of his spine. Silver was dangerous to werewolves because of its unique relationship to magic and the moon. It was as if the moon's magic could not distinguish between itself and the silver. So it made sense for silver wounds to do more damage and take longer to heal.

But no other injury caused by mortal means, outside aconite poisoning, had the ability to withstand the magic.

Whatever was happening, it was dangerous on a scale far beyond what they'd guessed at the start of this hunt. And yet... purple smudges marred the skin beneath Alix's eyes and deep lines bracketed her mouth. She hadn't slept or bothered to clean herself. Why that seemed more important to him than the danger these monsters represented, he didn't bother considering, not while she stood there staring at him with concern shining in those wide amber eyes.

He only guessed one reason she would not even take the trouble to wash her face, and it made his chest tight. When he spoke, his voice was soft. "Were you worried for me, minx?"

She snorted, but her eyes gave her away. "Not at all. I just didn't want to explain to the Mother Superior that I let her newest employee get himself killed."

Two weeks ago such a response might have stung. She certainly sounded serious. But the corners of her eyes were tight, and her legs set as if she wanted to fight or run.

"Aye, of course. You made an oath, after all."

"Exactly."

"Exactly."

She cleared her throat and approached the bed with brusque efficiency, adjusting his blankets and pillow before pushing him down with both hands on his chest. "You need more rest. And the woman who helped us will bring you some food. I'll wake you when she gets here."

"I'll sleep better with you by my side."

Her eyes narrowed. "Are you using your injuries to manipulate me, wolf?"

"Aye," he laughed, "I'll use whatever advantages I have to tempt you into my arms."

Her lips twisted into something not quite a smile, an expression a mother might give an exasperating toddler, and it broke the tension keeping her body strung on the edge of breaking. She positioned her chair next to his bed once more. He obediently closed his eyes, but reached across the blanket and found her hand. She didn't resist when he laced his fingers through hers and let their joined hands rest above his heart.

He needed to know about his injuries, about the strange werewolves and the tooth she claimed slowed his healing magic, but all he wanted to do was sleep with her close by. And yet...

Cyrus closed his eyes and sucked in a deep breath, then let it out slowly. "I don't mean to insert myself or to pressure you to reveal what you don't want to share. But if you need someone to carry a few of your burdens, my shoulders are strong enough to bear them."

She had selflessly done as much for him. It was the very least he could offer her. Alix's breath caught and her heartbeat sped, like a deer scenting a wolf. Maybe she wasn't ready for such an offer?

"If it helps, I'll pretend to be asleep."

A small, unwilling chuckle made him turn his face toward her. Her laugh was warm and musical and he wanted to wrap himself around her and absorb every note, even as weariness settled on him like a blanket.

A moment later she said, in a small voice, "It does help."

He grunted, one of those sounds passed down from father to son for hundreds of years, one that meant anything depending on the circumstance and intonation. This time it meant, *I know and I don't mind.*

Laying perfectly still, fighting to stay awake, holding her hand as subtle nervous tremors ran through her fingers, he waited.

Come on, minx, he thought. *Trust me. I won't hurt you, I swear it.* But he said nothing, waiting to see if she would open herself while he was awake as she'd been willing to do while he slept.

"Since the time I saw you fall until the moment you woke up, I worried you might die. There was a time that wouldn't have bothered me. There was even a time when I would have happily done it, myself. I've been... I've been unfair to you, Cyrus. And cruel. I don't deserve your forgiveness, but I'm asking for it. Before you decide whether to give it, I think you deserve to know why."

Instead of gathering her against him and whispering into her hair that he'd forgiven her already, as he yearned to do, he tried to suppress the mad beating of his heart and remain downwind, stay still, do nothing to pressure her one way or another.

Alix was clever and capable and stubborn, but she was also wounded. If he tried to influence her at all, she'd turn and run like a deer into the woods. But he could not stop himself from saying, "If you decide to share your burdens, Alix, don't do it for me. You deserve to heal, and the only way to make it happen is if you choose freedom for yourself."

She didn't respond.

How could you be so bloody stupid? He berated himself. *Giving advice you cannot take as if you are not still as damaged as she? You've just bollocksed up the one chance you had of earning this woman's trust. Well done, you jackass.*

Then her fingers tightened in his, she took a quick breath, and stumbled over the words, "I murdered my grand-mère."

28

Alix

THE WORDS TUMBLED OUT like children running from a school building, afraid they'd get dragged back inside if they didn't escape quickly enough. They hung in the air, making the silence thick and heavy.

Not once in three hundred years had she admitted the truth aloud. It was like hearing the gavel of doom fall to pronounce her guilty. And yet...

Yet there was a hollow, echoing space in her chest where the secret used to be. Alix had been full-to-bursting for so long that the emptiness was a relief. Spurred on by the sensation, she let the memory pull her back nearly three hundred years and lost herself in the most horrible night of her life.

She stood in the open doorway without breathing, a nine-year-old statue clutching a market basket against her skinny chest to stop her heart from bursting out of her ribs.

Fresh blood tainted the air, wet and warm, and her throat burned with a combination of desire and disgust because blood was not the only scent in the fetid little cottage. Wet dog fur, vomit, and the heavy, sweet stink of death combined to turn the little cabin into a nightmare for Alix's senses.

But the smell, bad as it was, did not compare to the destruction: furniture was turned over and broken, herbs were scattered and floating in still pools of blood, broken shards of pottery and spoiled milk mixed with spatters on the wall, and the body of an elderly man lay at the center of it all.

A silver dagger protruded from his chest at an angle. His skin was yellow in death, like old candle wax, and a pair of clouded eyes stared at her from a face frozen in pain. Those eyes locked her in place, froze her to the spot, and stole the heat from her blood.

"Grand-mère?" Alix's voice was too small to overcome the horror of that room.

Where was she? There was so much blood, that it could not all have come from the man on the floor. A bolt of fear shocked her muscles into moving. "Grand-mère!"

She tiptoed through the room, carefully avoiding the destruction, listening as hard as she had ever listened in her life. There it was. A heartbeat. But far too fast for Grand-mère's old heart.

It galloped along while heavy breathing kept pace.

Alix stepped over a broken table leg into the only other room in the cottage, a small bedroom with a simple cot in the corner near a window. Grand-mère lay half on that cot, her homespun shawl stained and sopping as she held it against her thigh with one hand. Her other arm was bent at the wrong angle and hung loose at her side, and she shook so hard it was a wonder she hadn't slid off the bed.

"Grand-mère." The word slipped out like a prayer.

The old woman's face sagged in pain and exhaustion, but her eyes lifted to settle on Alix's face. When she spoke, her voice sounded like wind through bare trees. "Go home, darling. You cannot help me today."

She said the words as if it were any normal afternoon and Alix was only visiting to help feed the injured hawk.

What happened? Why was a dead man in the house? Did he break in to hurt you? Why haven't you found anyone to help you? She wanted to ask those questions, but what came out instead was, "But I brought you some bread and ale and Maman said..." *Her voice died away as she saw the full extent of Grand-mère's injuries. Her white hair was matted with blood and stuck to the side of her head. Bruises bloomed all over her pale skin. One eye was swollen nearly shut, and she looked too weak to stand.*

Grand-mère coughed like tearing paper. "Food will not help me today, darling." *She cleared her throat and winced.* "But you can do one thing for your grand-mère, eh?"

Alix nodded, uncertain of what to do. Did she run for Maman? Find clean cloth for Grand-mère's wounds?

"I need the silver—the silver knife. Did you see the man on the floor? Pull that knife out and bring"—*she coughed again, leaving little flecks of blood on her lips*—"bring it to me."

Every muscle in Alix's body tensed at the idea of touching the dead man. But Maman had said, 'You can withstand a bit of fear to help Grand-mère, yes?'

So Alix pinched her trembling lips between her teeth, took a deep breath, and tiptoed back into the other room. He lay twisted at the wrong angle, his chest pointed at the ceiling, his hips pointed at the opposite wall, and his open eyes staring blankly.

Her hands shook too hard to hold the basket. It slipped through her fingers and clattered to the ground. A jar of preserves rolled out and bumped across the floor, coming to a rest against his bloody hand.

'He is dead,' *she told herself.* 'He cannot feel anything. And he must have hurt Grand-mère. She is bleeding but you can help her.'

How the knife would help Alix did not know, but she latched onto the thought and gritted her teeth. She stepped forward, gripped the hilt in numb fingers, and closed her eyes.

'Just pull. That is all you must do. Pull.'

The knife slid out with a sucking sound and Alix stumbled backward, tripped over the dropped basket, and landed hard on her bottom. She sat in stunned silence, staring at the knife in her right hand as cold wetness soaked through her dress. When she raised her left hand, it was slick with blood.

Her meager lunch clawed back up her throat, but Alix clenched her teeth and pushed herself to stand. Grand-mère needed her. She could be sick later.

When she returned to the bedroom, the old woman looked as if she were running a fever. Bright red spots blazed on her cheeks, making the rest of her skin appear even paler. A fine sheen of sweat gleamed on her brow.

"Here, Grand-mère. I have it," Alix said, holding the knife toward her handle first.

But Grand-mère's hands appeared to have lost all their strength, because when she tried to take the knife, it slipped from her fingers once, twice, three times.

"Saints damn the moon and her children," Grand-mère panted.

She was breathing awfully fast, as if she'd just run all the way from town.

Alix wiped the blood on her skirt and placed the hilt in her grandmother's hand, then carefully wrapped her bony fingers around the silver until they were closed securely.

Grand-mère's face twisted in pain, but she said, "Good. Good girl. Now go home to your maman and don't stop. Tell her what happened. Don't look back. Just run. Run."

"But I–"

"Go!" the old woman barked, and some of the old strength was in her voice. "Do as you are told, for once."

Alix flinched and retreated a few steps toward the door. Part of her–a shamefully large part–wanted to run home screaming. But the other part, the part that loved her grandmother, wanted to throw herself at the woman and soothe her terrible hurts, to help in whatever way she could.

So she stood suspended between desires, unable to move. But that did not matter, because Grand-mère did not seem to see her anymore.

The old woman took a deep breath and drew the blade of the knife across her opposite wrist. But the knife slipped through her fingers and clattered to the floor.

"Dammit," Grand-mère growled.

All the hairs on Alix's body stood on end at that sound. It was not the kind of noise old women's throats were supposed to make. Alix rushed to the bedside and snatched the knife away, holding it protectively against her chest.

If she was going to use the knife to hurt herself, Alix would not let her have it.

"Alix? I told you to run. Do as-as you're told, girl!"

But Grand-mère was now shaking all over, and her breathing was rough and too fast. Her heart thundered and the angry red scratch on her wrist...was beginning to heal. Only Alix healed that fast. It was a secret she and Maman never shared with anyone, not even Grand-mère.

"Your wrist," was all she could say.

But the old woman did not reply. She arched off the bed with a scream, her withered muscles tight as a bowstring. After the spasm passed, the head of white hair was sweat-soaked and red, and the blue eyes were fixed on Alix's face. Only they were no longer blue.

'Yellow,' Alix thought, like a hawk or a wolf.

They focused on her, and Grand-mère took a deep breath, then shuddered and looked away. "It is too late," she said. "I cannot stop it. But you can. You can stop me. Come here."

The last thing Alix wanted to do was get closer to Grand-mère with the yellow eyes, but she bit her bottom lip till it bled and approached the bed.

A pale, shaking hand reached into the space between them. After a moment of hesitation, Alix took it. The old woman's skin was feverish.

"You must kill me, Alix darling."

Alix stumbled backward and her breath caught as if she'd been struck with a rock. "What? No!"

Grand-mère's voice was deeper than it had been, and she breathed so fast that most of the words were panted instead of spoken. "That man, he was not always a man. He was a-a"–she swallowed–"a werewolf."

A cold wave of dread drenched Alix from head to toe.

"I am alive because...he was slow and stupid. And old. But I am not stupid or slow. I killed him. But he mauled me first. When I turn into a werewolf, I will be more dangerous. I have spent my whole life saving things, and I could not say no when he came looking for shelter. Stupid."

There were too many things to say and not enough space in her chest or mouth or throat to say them. They bunched up and got stuck before Alix could push any of them out. But Grand-mère did not seem to want her to speak.

"You must kill me, Alix my darling."

The stink of death filled her nose and mouth, but it was the change in Grand-mère's voice that made Alix's heart try to pound out of her chest. It was deeper still, rasping. "You must kill me."

Alix's voice came out in a breathy whisper, the only thread of sound she could push past the blockage in her throat. "I cannot."

"You can. The gods have made you strong enough to give me this...this mercy. If you do not, I will try to hurt you. I don't want to hurt you."

Tears ran down Alix's face, leaving pale tracks in the blood smeared there. The handle of the silver knife was too big, and her hands were still slick and shaking. *"Grand-mère, I am frightened."*

"I know. I know. But I am dying, turning into...a monster. You can stop it. Please."

Werewolves killed indiscriminately. They were demons possessed by dark magic. Grand-mère was kind and good. She could not be a monster.

"I can't."

"You must."

"I cannot!"

Grand-mère flinched at her scream and closed her eyes. Alix could not help herself. She quivered like a newborn deer, but she could not hurt her grandmother. It was incomprehensible.

"Very well," Grand-mère said. Now her voice sounded merely like a tired old lady. Her body had gone still. Only her bony chest rose and fell, but instead of panting, she barely breathed at all.

Whatever magic changed Grand-mère's eyes must have burned itself out. But that meant she was dying.

"Go home. Do as I say. Run, Alix, and don't look back. And always remember that I..."

Her voice trailed off and her muscles relaxed. The cloth she held against her leg wound slipped out of her hand. *"Remember that I love..."*

It was a long time until her next breath. *"Run."*

A last shuddering inhale expanded her body ribcage, and then the air leaked back out in a long, rattling sigh.

"Grand-mère?" She was so still. Her skin looked wrong. *"Grand-mère!"*

But the old woman did not move.

She was dead.

The scent was unmistakable. Alix turned and vomited.

When her stomach was empty she stood for a long time staring at the body where Grand-mère once lived. But it was empty. A great weight of pain and grief rose up to drown her. Suddenly, Alix was more tired than she could ever remember being.

And she did not want to go tell Maman that the only person who cared for them was dead. She stumbled toward the bed and ensured Grand-mère was laid out properly.

How could she look so peaceful? She had died a terrible death and yet it was as if she were only sleeping. Aside from the waxy skin and lack of heartbeat, of course. She should go home and tell Maman what happened, but Alix had a terrible feeling that if she left Grand-mère, the old woman would disappear.

She could not bear for this to be the last time she saw the woman whose love protected her and Maman from a cruel world. So Alix climbed into the bed, squeezing between her grandmother's body and the wall, keeping the silver dagger pressed to her chest.

She took the bony hand and held it against her cheek. It was cold and heavy. Still, every good memory came dancing back with the touch. Alix grew up in the country, and while death was filled with sorrow, it was also a normal part of nature. She feared Grand-mère's body less than she missed the old woman's touch.

Tears stung her eyes, and it was hard to breathe, but Alix fell asleep in less than twenty heartbeats.

When she woke, it was not Grand-mère's cold body she saw in the first pale light of the moon, but the heaving chest of a werewolf.

29

Cyrus

WITH EVERY WORD, HIS stomach twisted into a knot so tight he doubted he would ever relax again. It was impossible not to imagine Alix as a young girl, clutching a bloody dagger to her chest, those amber eyes wide as her grandmother slowly became a monster.

But he couldn't stomach the thought of his distress making this moment harder for her. So, he forced himself to breathe evenly and tried to control the pained beating of his heart, despite the way her broken voice cut him.

"I did not understand then how an emotional shock could make one so tired," she said, "or I never would have looked for the comfort of sleep. But what did I know? I was a child, and nothing seemed scarier than the idea of telling Maman I let Grand-mère die. So I slept.

"I think the change woke me. When I opened my eyes, there was nothing but a cold wall on one side and a mound of matted fur on the other. In a strange way, she still smelled the same: lavender and honey, but overpowered by the musk of wolf pelt.

"Though I had never seen a werewolf and did not know how they changed, I knew it was her. She was still disoriented, twitching and snuffling as she grew used to her new body. It reminded me of a dog chasing rabbits in its dreams, so I thought she slept.

"I decided that if I was quiet, I could sneak away without waking her. The idea of running home to Maman was not nearly as scary with a werewolf at my back. I pressed myself against the wall, but my heart beat against my breastbone so hard I thought it would crack.

"I was halfway off the bed when she turned to look at me over her shoulder. My fear was thick in the air. Even I could smell it. Her eyes were twin moons in the dark, and though they were a different color, they were still hers, somehow...only maddened. The sight froze me."

A shiver of terrible anticipation ran down his spine.

"At first I thought she recognized me. The hope was almost as painful as the grief. But her lips curled away from her teeth and they were white in the moonlight. She growled at me, and in that moment I knew Grand-mère was gone.

"Much farther gone than simply being dead. It was enough to make me leap from the bed and run for the door. The wolf was faster. She sailed over my head and landed in the door with a snarl. I said, 'Grand-mère, it is me. Alix.'

"She could not hear me, of course. It was the full moon. And the magic used so much energy to heal her that she was starving. She could not have helped herself even if she wanted to."

That last line had the ring of something repeated so many times it was taken for granted. She could not have helped herself even if she wanted to. How often had Alix muttered that litany in the dark corners of her mind when she needed comfort? He imagined her lying in bed, curled around herself, repeating once more that the woman she loved only tried to kill her because she had no choice.

"What happened after is a blur in my memory. I can smell her fetid breath, I can feel the coarse hair of her coat and the burning pain as her claws raked down my arm. But, most of all, I can hear the crunching sound as the silver knife sank between her ribs."

His chest squeezed closed and his jaw locked against the urge to speak. The comfort she needed now would be found in the freedom of release, not in his words.

"I don't know how it happened. Grand-mère was old, past eighty, perhaps. It was a miracle she completed the change. She was newly reborn, uncertain in an unfamiliar body. And I had the strength and speed of terror to aid me.

"She screamed. It sounded so human. My hands were wet with blood and shaking as the magic abandoned her. I squeezed my eyes shut so I would not see her die. When I opened them, it was not the body of a werewolf that lay on the ground, but Grand-mère in her nightgown with a silver knife in her back and her cheek in a pool of blood.

"I killed the kindest woman I'd ever known. How could I go home and tell Maman what I'd done, that the villagers were right about me? For years we left town after town, always looking for somewhere safe, a place they would not run us out of. Grand-mère changed everything.

"She saved us, and I killed her. I could not go back. Maman would run away with me, but when she looked at me she would always see a murderer.

"So, I freed the animals from their cages, gathered what food I could in the market basket Maman sent with me, and disappeared into the woods. I slept beneath bushes and fallen trees in good weather, trusting Grand-mère's cloak to keep me warm.

"When the food ran out I hunted small animals and ate what berries and nuts I could scrounge. I stayed as far from villages as possible, though I was lonely and missed Maman terribly.

"Winter came, and though I learned much about surviving, the cold was bitter and I was not fast enough to hunt large animals. When Jean-Luc found me, I was almost frozen to the trunk of a pine.

"He thawed me out and brought me to the convent. I was wild and tried to run away several times, but he always caught me. Finally, one night after he tied my wrists to a heavy rock, he said, 'Don't you want revenge, girl? I think you have the fire to earn it, if you will stop wasting your energy and learn.'

"'Learn what?'

"'To hunt werewolves.'

"It was as if someone opened a door inside me. Instead of hating myself, I could place the blame where it belonged, on the real monsters who forced me to destroy my life by killing the woman I loved.

"I never looked back. I had a purpose. I may be a monster but at least I was a useful one. One of the *good* monsters." She chuckled but it was a humorless sound.

"And then you met me," he said.

"And then I met you."

He squeezed her hand and she squeezed back.

Thinking over the weeks they'd worked together made his stomach revolt. His presence must have hurt her with every step and every breath, a constant reminder of her past, her pain, and a challenge to the very story that kept her sane.

He had to be a monster, a worse monster than her, for her life to make sense.

If he were in her shoes, forced to work side-by-side with a vampire for weeks, he would not have shown half the restraint. Somehow she'd overcome her prejudice and learned to see him as a man.

Growing up, children of the moon had been respected and honored. He was different in a way that made him special and helped the people he loved. How would his life, his understanding of who he was, be different if he were shunned, instead? His father had been stern but he'd also been loving and present. Alix never mentioned her father, so she did not have even the protection of a strong man to rely on.

He wanted to ask her what manner of creature she was, what gave her the strength and speed to defend herself from a werewolf at nine years old, to live 300 years, but this moment was too fragile. And, despite his curiosity, he had to admit that it did not really matter.

She was Alix. That was all he cared about.

"Do I have permission to be awake, now?" he asked.

"If you have to ask–" she began, but he cut her off by rolling toward her, wrapping his arms around her waist, and hauling her up onto the bed.

She gave a little whoop of surprise but allowed him to tuck her body next to his, her back tight against his chest until they were as cozy as peas.

Then he said into her hair, "You are a marvel, Alix. I don't think you know how much."

She did not acknowledge the compliment, only said, "I hope you can forgive me. You were never to blame for my pain. And I am sorry. Not only for my cruelty to you but for anyone I might have...anyone you may have known that I..."

"Hush," he said and rested one finger gently over her lips. "You've nothing to apologize for, minx. You didn't know of my people or the differences in our magic. You've done nothing worse than a hundred other hunters, myself included."

"But you killed werewolves to protect mortals. I hunted them for revenge, to prove they were worse monsters than me."

He hooked one finger under her chin and turned her face toward him. Her eyes were shuttered, golden slits hidden beneath long lashes, as if she was afraid he would see all the way to her soul if she dared to look at him.

He waited, exerting no pressure other than patience. Her free hand went to her throat and fished out a dull red pendant necklace. She ran her fingers over it unconsciously. Finally, she held her breath and met his gaze, waiting for him to speak.

"I've seen you fight to protect people, and not only from monsters," he said. "You put yourself in danger for the good of others, and even help those without the strength to ask for it. You agreed to partner with me to save these villages, despite how my presence hurt you. And you keep your word, even when it's difficult. Those are not the actions of a monster."

She reached back to trace the planes of his face with her fingertips, her eyes soft and wondering. Despite being tired enough to drift off, a shiver of pleasure warmed him from the inside.

She closed her eyes, took a deep breath, and exhaled.

Tension drained from her body with the escaping air, and she settled against him. Her hair was soft beneath his chin, her scent was an amalgamation of dirt, blood, and sharp bite of fear sweat from the battle and subsequent flight to the village.

How those things should combine to create comfort, Cyrus didn't know. But he kept an arm wrapped around her waist and listened to her steady heartbeat as he drifted toward sleep. Hopefully this chance to speak left her feeling as free as he felt when she offered to take some of his burden.

Before he lost consciousness, Alix murmured, "Thank you."

###

"It seems to be a nice place, if a little dead," Cyrus noted as Gwen–Lady St. James, apparently–placed a tray of bread and soup on the small table.

The room was modest in every way, with simple furniture, plank floors, bare walls, and a single window; scrupulously clean and arranged, though underwhelming. But there was nothing underwhelming about the food.

A simple bean soup and brown bread shouldn't have been noteworthy, but herbs, butter, and yeast perfumed the air, and the broth had a complex, savory scent that made his mouth water immediately.

He tore into the bread and stuffed a chunk in his mouth, letting the crust crunch between his molars and groaning in pleasure. Moon and stars, he was hungry.

"The innkeeper did not want to let us stay," Alix said around a mouthful of stew.

Cyrus paused mid-chew. If she said they tried to deny her a room for being a faerie, he was going to punch something. "What made them change their mind?"

"I did, I'm afraid," Gwen said.

Alix introduced them shortly after he woke up, when the door opened and the crock of soup made his stomach growl. He was still weak, a side-effect of the healing magic, but not too weak to eat several bowls of soup and more than his share of bread.

Gwen gave him a charming, one-sided smile. It was hard to believe she not only followed them for miles through the countryside alone to return stolen property but had been brave and selfless enough to fight a werewolf alongside Alix.

He owed her his life. When they first met her at the inn while making arrangements for Mercedes, he'd been impressed with her mind and open temperament. Now he was impressed with her heart.

He swallowed the mouthful of bread and asked, "How'd you manage that?"

"She threatened the woman," Alix said, humor making her voice rich.

"I object to the use of such a vulgar term to describe my actions," Gwen said in a tone that implied she did not object in the slightest.

"But you did," Alix insisted.

"Well, of course, I did, but that doesn't mean we should couch it in such terms. I made a series of compelling arguments in favor of extending hospitality to paying customers."

Cyrus raised a brow. He doubted that very much.

She rolled her eyes. "Oh, fine. I told her if she did not give us rooms, we would leave you to bleed on the floor and use your blood to curse the place."

Cyrus's fingers tightened around his spoon. "She believed you?"

"Not at all. But she does think I'm mad and unpredictable."

Alix pointed at her with a crust of bread. "Yes, and she did not want you camping on her porch. Don't forget that part."

Gwen dismissed that with a wave of her fingers. "All's well that ends well, as they say. We shall be the best guests this inn has ever seen, and I will leave a substantial tip for her trouble. I'm certain she will forgive me. And if she doesn't, well...I think I can live with that. After all, this is to be our base of operations, correct?"

The swallow of soup stuck on the way down, and Cyrus pounded on his chest to clear it. "What do you mean, our?"

"You cannot expect me to leave knowing the village is in danger."

"I can, in fact," he said, scowling at her.

She may have saved Alix and himself with a bit of quick thinking, but she couldn't keep up with them as they–wait. They'd come to Villecourbé to investigate the rumor of plague as a cover for unexplained deaths. He doubted Alix told her the truth, so how had she come to such a conclusion?

Gwen had already proven to have unique insight, so he asked, "What do you mean the town is in danger?"

"We are in one of the more remote parts of the country where monsters are likely to hunt. I found two professionals less than five miles outside the village fighting three werewolves. Three. That alone is unheard of. There are five fresh graves in the village churchyard, and I overheard two shepherds in the tap room discussing dozens of sheep that have been savaged over the last two days.

That is more killings than a single werewolf on the move is likely to commit, given their nomadic nature. So, unless the dead werewolves are to blame for it all, which I doubt given the high numbers, there are more monsters outside this village and they are focusing their hunt here. Villecourbé is in very great danger."

Cyrus was gobsmacked. Given her observations when they'd first met he should not have been surprised. He exchanged a glance with Alix, then said, "You'd make a damn fine hunter, Lady Gwen."

"Just Gwen will do, thank you."

"Gwen, then. The problem is, these werewolves are unlike anything we've ever faced."

She pulled a pointed tooth from her pocket and held it at eye level, examining it with pursed lips. "I noticed that, yes."

"But you don't know what that means," Alix said, dropping her spoon into her empty soup bowl. "They retain more of their intelligence, they coordinate and work in groups, and silver does not affect them as it should. We"—she gestured between him and herself—"are specially equipped to deal with these creatures. You are not."

Gwen's pursed lips pulled to the side in an amused expression that wasn't quite a smile. "That is rather direct."

"We don't have time for anything else."

Alix was right. She may be clever and brave, but those qualities did not make up for speed and strength when facing predators like werewolves. The woman dropped the tooth back into her skirt pocket and regarded the two of them with cool intelligence.

"I understand this is your profession, and I cannot force you to allow me to help," she said. "But, without my aid, you would both be dead. All I ask is that you consider my offer. One more willing hand cannot hurt, and—to be quite frank—unless you intend to run me out of the village, you cannot stop me from staying."

His eyes widened, and Alix scowled.

"Do you mind if we discuss the matter?" Alix asked, unable to keep the amusement from her voice.

Gwen smiled magnanimously. "Of course not. I'd like to gather a bit more information about the place, in any case. If something dangerous does happen here, it will likely be during the full moon. The more we know before then, the better our plans will be."

She excused herself and left the two of them sitting in silence.

When the door closed, Alix said, "Absolutely not."

"If she wants to risk her life in service of others, she has a right to. She certainly helped us, and she's still alive."

"Because of circumstances outside our control. If the canyon had been any wider, she would be dead."

"Do you mean to say she was incompetent?"

Alix's brows lowered as she folded her arms over her chest. "No."

"Slow or stupid?"

"She was surprisingly competent with a blade and quick on her feet," she said, as if she hated admitting it. "But she is not physically capable of defending herself against these creatures."

"That werewolf tooth suggests otherwise."

"She is clever and skilled. I won't argue that point. But these creatures slaughtered an entire village."

"All the more reason to have someone intelligent and skilled on our side. Gwen seems to have gathered a substantial amount of information with very little effort, and every bit of it points to Villecourbé suffering the same fate as Mont Blanc. If what you say of her is true, she is certain to be of more help than any of the villagers.

"And she's right. We cannot force her out of the village if she decides to stay. Better to have her help than know she's out there alone following plans of her own."

As he spoke, her expression darkened. By the time he finished, her skin was flushed an angry red. Jaw clenched, she stood and gathered the dishes with the precise movements of someone tightly controlling their fury, then turned and left without replying.

Cyrus sat for the space of several baffled breaths, wondering how things had taken such a grim turn when the day started so well. Unfortunately, Gwen was right. Time was short, and he could not afford to let Alix nurse her anger until she dealt with whatever was bothering her.

Werewolves would descend upon the city in days. They had to work together to protect these people. With a soul-deep sigh, he pushed himself to his feet, ignored the lingering weakness in his muscles, and followed his partner.

30

Alix

PÈRE HENRI'S TEAR-FILLED EYES haunted Alix as she stormed out of the inn and into the afternoon sunlight. She pulled up her hood, wishing the cloak protected her from guilt the way it protected her from the sun. But nothing would save her from the hot knife of self-recrimination that stabbed her in the guts every time she remembered his face.

He lay dying in her arms, in extraordinary pain, and said, *There is always mercy for you.*

If she'd refused to take him hunting he might still be alive. He would be praying over his flock, welcoming their infants into the world and easing them through the grief of loss. Instead, his flesh rotted in the earth because she hadn't been able to save him.

Lady Gwen had the same large eyes and dark lashes as the dead priest, only she was far more competent. But no matter how capable the woman was, she wasn't a hunter. If the attack on this town was anything like Mont Blanc, the woman would end up fighting on her own at some point. Fighting for her life.

The idea of burying her made the knife twist.

"Alix."

She closed her eyes and pulled in a steadying breath as Cyrus hurried to catch up. The village was close to the same size as Mont Blanc, if nowhere near as wealthy. But that made sense given how secluded it was. She'd been walking for less than two minutes and she was halfway to the other side.

"Alix, wait."

With a resigned sigh, she stepped into the shade of the bakery and waited. He reached her a moment later. Beads of sweat glittered on his temples and slid down the side of his face. His hair had been tied back in a hasty tail, and damp curls clung to the nape of his neck.

"You should be resting," she said. "You aren't much use to me if you're too weak to fight."

His cheeks were red. Did he have a fever? A little spike of anxiety distracted her from the guilt.

"I'll not rest while you're angry," he said. "We won't make a very good team if you can't work with me."

"That isn't—I'm not angry with you."

One blonde brow raised. "Are you not? Because you glowered at me and stormed out of our room."

Alix ignored the warm, mutinous little glow that sprang to life in her belly at the words *our room*. How selfish was she that such a small thing could make her feel lighter when so much was at stake?

Her jaw clenched several times as she tried to respond without snapping at him. Pushing the words past her teeth proved impossible, so she blew out an explosive breath and clenched handfuls of her cloak, letting the fabric run between her fingers until the moment passed.

"The night I found you, I let a man die," she finally ground out. "He was the village priest and saw helping me as his duty. I needed a way to draw the werewolf out, so I allowed it. He was savaged before I could save him."

Pain drew a line between Cyrus's brows, and his hand twitched as if he wanted to reach out to her. "You couldn't have known there would be more than one werewolf. I was hunting them, and even I did not know."

"But I knew it would be dangerous. He died in my arms, with my knife in his heart, because I used him as bait."

"It was his choice."

She spun on him, cheeks hot enough to burn. "You think that matters? He did not know what he asked for. How could he? I was the expert, the one who should have kept him safe. Had I told him no, he would still be alive!"

She tightened her grip on the cloak to keep her fingers from shaking. What was wrong with her? Since meeting the damn wolf she'd suffered more emotional upheavals than she experienced in the last hundred years put together. The priest was just a mortal, and mortals died. She should be stronger than this by now, more composed.

Cyrus did not try to comfort her with trite platitudes. Instead, he said, "The past is not a guarantor of the future, Alix. And the man had a right—you might even say a responsibility—to protect the people under his care."

"Yes, and he was under *my* care, wasn't he? This lady will be, too, if she joins us. I don't want her death on my hands."

One more death, another in a long line that stained her soul as red as her cloak. For years that hadn't mattered much to her. But it did, now.

As if summoned, Lady Gwen's voice floated down the main road, clear and enthusiastic, and Alix had to close her eyes and fight not to picture the woman's broken body on the ground.

"Good news," she said. "I discovered who we must convince to rally the villagers."

The woman was too vibrant, too alive to die like the poor souls in Mont Blanc.

"Have you now?" Cyrus asked, and his voice shattered the unwanted visions.

Lady Gwen joined them, her brown eyes sparkling. "Indeed I have. The village has no mayor, as he was one of the recent casualties. But there is a well-respected council member the others are accustomed to deferring to. If we can convince her, the rest of them will follow."

"How did you learn this so quickly?" Alix asked.

Lady Gwen smirked. "Quite a lot gets accomplished when one employs a bit of charm. Come along. The sooner we start, the sooner these people can begin taking protective measures."

Gwen turned and strode back down the dirt road, her umbrella clenched in one hand like a sword, simple brown skirt swishing about her ankles.

"Did she just commandeer our hunt?" Cyrus asked, bemused.

Alix nodded, feeling as dumbstruck as Cyrus looked.

"I suppose that answers the question of whether she's helping us."

Alix sighed and followed the smaller woman down the street. "I suppose it does."

"Who's this, then?"

The elderly woman glared up at Alix from beneath the brim of a wide straw hat, her gnarled hands folded over the handle of the wooden rake she'd been using to clear pulled weeds from her kitchen garden. Her fingers were stained green with the juices of murdered plants and trembled from the effort of her work, but her brown eyes were as sharp as her voice.

A bolt of longing made Alix's heart jump. This woman was shorter than Grand-mère had been, with skin a deep, tawny brown, but the white hair and the clever eyes were the same. And something in her manner was alike. A kind of knowing hung in the air about her, as if she were a rock that split the river of time and recorded its passing.

She expected the woman to shy away, to avert her eyes in discomfort as soon as the unnatural aspects of Alix's presence registered on her subconscious mind, but the old woman only continued to stare defiantly.

Gwen said, "Madame Sophie, this is Alix La Rouge and her partner, Cyrus. They are the hunters we spoke of."

She tipped the brim of her hat back with one finger and regarded them, a badger trying to decide if the creature that disturbed its nest was better fought off or ignored. "La Rouge, eh? Heard of you. We haven't seen hunters in Villecourbé in fifty years, at least. You are here for the werewolf, I take it."

Alix blinked. "Yes, Madame Sophie."

"Just Sophie will do, thank you. I don't have enough time left for such formality."

"You know of the werewolves?" Cyrus asked.

"Not much happens here I do not know about, young man. Let's speak inside. It's too hot. Be a good lad and hop down into the cellar for some milk. It should still be cold. Then join us inside. Come with me, ladies. Let's make lunch."

The three of them exchanged amused glances, then followed orders. Gwen and Alix trailed Sophie into her cottage while Cyrus circled around to the cellar. Sophie's home was small but comfortable and neat, with bundles of drying herbs hanging from the rafters and hand-embroidered curtains blowing in the warm breeze.

They prepared bread, cheese, and sausage along with some late summer berries and cream, working in silent feminine companionship that made a warm glow of peace bloom in Alix's chest. A quiet life like this, she could get used to.

"Now," Sophie said as she lay wooden plates before each of them, "we will eat and you tell me why you think the villagers should be frightened of this werewolf."

Alix and Cyrus glanced at one another, brows raised.

"Have several villagers not died already?" Alix asked.

"Oh yes, but they were fools and we are better off without them."

Gwen choked on her milk, and Sophie patted her helpfully on the back. "They went hunting the beast, you see. Everyone knows if you stay indoors, the creature will move on to easier prey. No one has ventured out of doors at night since the mayor was killed."

"They went hunting it, you say?" Cyrus asked before popping a berry into his mouth and groaning with pleasure.

"Oh, yes," Sophie answered. "After it attacked the herd, several of the young men thought they would make heroes of themselves. They were troublemakers, anyway. It was the mayor that surprised me. I thought he had more sense. They found him a few days ago, torn up outside the north end of the village. Not a gut left in his belly."

Gwen swallowed, her face a bit green, and Alix let out a slow, silent breath. "You do not think that is enough to frighten the villagers?"

Sophie grunted and slathered butter on her bread. "If you put your hand in a dog's cage and get bitten, it is your own fault."

Alix set her utensils down and waited for Sophie to catch her eye.

"Madame Sophie, I think you may have misunderstood the situation. There is not one werewolf. There are many. And they will not leave Villecourbé if everyone stays inside."

The old woman's brows knotted together above her nose. "What do you mean, child? Werewolves do not hunt in packs."

"These do. We came to your village because a pack of werewolves destroyed Mont Blanc. Only a small girl survived because her parents gave their lives to fight off the creature who entered their home."

Sophie's cheeks went ashen. Her voice was thready and weak when she said, "Werewolves do not do such things."

Alix gave Cyrus a sideways, questioning look. He nodded and began unbuttoning his shirt.

"I'm sure you're very well made, young man," Sophie said, flapping a hand at him, "but I'm well past..."

Her voice died away as the open shirtfront exposed angry red scars. A series of large bite marks punctuated the side of his chest between his ribs. The magic healed him quickly, but the wounds were clearly fresh.

"We fought three werewolves just outside Villecourbé. They hunted and attacked us using strategy. And the walls of the houses did not stop them from killing the citizens of Mont Blanc. We hunt these wolves because something about them has changed. And if they attack your village the same way, they will kill everyone in it."

"Unless you protect yourselves," Alix added, placing one comforting hand on her frail forearm, hoping the addendum would stop Sophie from fainting.

The old woman swallowed, her skin going ashen. But her voice was firm when she said, "I think we had better open the wine."

Afternoon was wearing down to evening by the time they gathered the majority of the villagers in the square. They were sweaty, confused, and irritated about being dragged from the rest they deserved after a hot day's work.

Madame Sophie stood at the head of the square like a statue, still and commanding, her work-roughened hands clasping the handle of her trusty rake for support.

"I'll have silence, now!" Sophie called and thumped the butt of the rake on the dirt twice.

The milling citizens stopped chatting and directed their attention at Sophie and the three strangers standing next to her. A thrill of unease slid down Alix's spine. Several people stared at her with concerned expressions, then shuddered and dragged their eyes away.

Sophie raised one hand toward Cyrus and said, "These strangers are hunters, and they've come to warn us about the werewolves."

"A bit late!" someone shouted.

Uncomfortable chuckles and scowls followed that comment.

"Hold your tongue and use your ears, Pierre. I said were*wolves*. There are many, and they're going to attack our village."

The uneasy amusement faded as doubt spread greasy tendrils through the crowd. Madame Sophie did not suffer fools, and she was clever and frank. They knew she wasn't easily fooled, and if she said something dire, it was worth listening to. Gwen could not have chosen a better ally.

Sophie drew herself up and said, "These werewolves attacked another village and destroyed it. That's why the hunters are here. They think the same thing will happen to Villecourbé if we don't stop them."

Villagers looked to one another for confirmation, support, or denial, but none were forthcoming. Unlike the larger villages and towns, they did not have regular access to news. These people lived in the country, and they knew that if Madame Sophie was right, they were on their own.

"This is a scam," boomed a deep, scratchy voice in the back of the crowd. An elvin man pushed forward, his face bristling with a black beard and eyebrows that looked ready to attack anyone who stood too close. Well-developed muscles along his shoulders and arms singled him out as the village blacksmith, and the rest of the mortals looked at him with a mixture of relief and admiration.

"These hunters heard of our plight and want to wring money out of us. Well, I'm not stupid enough to fall for it. If we stay indoors at night, the beast will go off to find easier prey. Everyone knows it. All we have to do is get through the full moon and we'll be safe."

"Le Manteau Rouge doesn't flit around the countryside manipulating honest people for money," Sophie said, her sparse brows drawn low.

"The Red Cloak?" someone muttered. Astonished whispers spread through the crowd like wind in the treetops.

Alix tried hard not to fidget.

"Red Riding Hood? That's a fairytale," the black-bearded man scoffed.

Sophie grabbed Alix by the sleeve and dragged her forward to thrust her at the man. "Look at her, Hugh. Tell me she is a fairy tale."

Hugh turned a pair of skeptical green eyes on Alix, eyes shaded by heavy brows. His features were rougher than the average elf, hinting at a human somewhere in his lineage.

His mouth, what could be seen of it, curled in a sneer of contempt...until he spent a few seconds staring into her eyes. The predator buried deep within her sensed his fear the moment it bubbled to the surface.

This was the deeper reason she avoided moments like these. Being stared at like a monster was painful enough, a reminder that she would never have the sense of community and camaraderie these people took for granted. But when she scented his fear, her senses came to life.

His heartbeat thundered, breath scraped in and out of his lungs, and the air thickened with the electric shock of adrenaline. All of it was a temptation. Unwilling, she imagined herself springing forward, felt her teeth sink into the fragile flesh below his jaw, tasted the flood of sweet moisture, heard his pitiful cries like music...

Alix dragged her mind away and stumbled backward, fists clenched against the vision.

Hugh swallowed and retreated, eyes wide, hands trembling. He'd seen death in her eyes and had nothing else to say. His capitulation spurred the rest of the citizens to agree as Sophie laid out their plans to protect the village. While she spoke, looks of hope and determination replaced the unease on their faces.

"We can't start with these preparations until tomorrow," said a dwarven man with a braided mustache. "If the werewolves are breaking into homes, as you say, what can we do?"

Cyrus exchanged a look with Alix. She nodded.

"We can flee!" a woman at the front said. "Leave Villecourbé. We should take the children and go!" One of her work-roughened hands clutched the wrist of a young man, no more than thirteen years old, with freckles and eyes the color of a summer sky.

"We have what, three carts among us?" Sophie asked. "That isn't enough for all the children, let alone the rest of us."

"But we can get our children out! The rest of us can walk behind. Why wait?"

"We were attacked ten miles from here," Cyrus said. "You could try to flee, but we cannot guarantee you will be safe on the road."

"You cannot guarantee we won't be safe, either," the woman said, raising her chin. "I lost my husband to these damned mountains. I will not lose my son as well. You can stay if you like." She turned to face the rest of the crowd. "But I'll not wait to be butchered."

Sophie clutched the handle of her rake with both hands, her thumbnail digging little furrows along the well-oiled woodgrain. When she spoke, her voice was soft and resigned. "It is too late to leave tonight, in any case. Madame Lambert, wait till morning. If you must go, go then. And take with you whoever is willing. But we cannot spare any who stay to protect you."

Madame Lambert tightened her fingers around her son's wrist, gave the crowd a determined, hard-eyed stare, and dragged her son from the square.

Her fear infected the crowd like dye dropped in a glass of water, spreading with slow but inexorable tendrils. Alix felt the electric bite of it as the sour-sweet stink filled the air.

"We will roam the streets by night," Cyrus said, letting a bit more bass enter his voice. He stood tall, shoulders squared, his blonde hair shining in the last light of day. He looked like a holy knight protector from the stained glass windows of the convent, and the honesty in his voice made the crowd sigh in relief.

"Fear no noise by night," he said, "and keep your fires lit. Come the morning, those who wish to leave can go. The rest of us will prepare to make these monsters regret setting foot in your village."

Alix let Cyrus's confident voice sway her, too. They would protect the people of this village. They had to. That, or die trying.

Which meant it was time to clean her pistols.

31

Cyrus

Long after Alix left, Cyrus stood in the square answering questions. Citizens crowded like birds at a feeder, hungry for reassurance. Worried eyes stared up at him, set below brows pinched in concern, above mouths clamped shut to stop trembling lips.

He gave them what hope he could, speaking with a confidence he did not feel. Their only chance to keep themselves alive lay in believing they could win. Which meant believing in him.

Another village, dozens of lives, rested in his care.

When the last person hurried home, sending concerned glances at the darkening sky, Cyrus strode toward the inn. His muscles trembled and his stomach twisted against the fear raking his guts.

Since losing his family and everyone he loved, Cyrus hunted individual monsters alone, protecting mortals from the shadows. He never expected to be responsible for an entire village again. And he didn't know enough about their foe to guarantee their safety.

He needed a drink.

The inn door bounced off the wall when he pushed it open, making the innkeeper glance up with worried eyes. Cyrus leaned against the bar on his elbows, his head too heavy to hold up. "I need a pint of the strongest drink you have."

Without bothering to look up, he waited till a wooden mug thumped the bar near his hand, and downed the draft in a series of long swallows, not tasting whatever was inside. "One more."

After a surprised moment, the mug disappeared. He downed two more drafts in the same manner, then dropped several coins on the bar and took the stairs two at a time, his head comfortably fuzzy, emotions blunted. It wouldn't last, of course. The moon's magic burned it away too quickly, or he might have been tempted to spend the evening at the bar.

Alix sat at the little table bent over her silver pistols, her dark hair wet and hanging in a braid down her back. She worked a clean cloth in between the body and cylinder of the gun with the attention of a watchmaker.

"Do whatever you must to get ready," she said without looking up, then spun the chamber.

It rotated with a well-greased hum, shining in the lamp light before she snapped it back in place and worked the hammer to ensure everything functioned smoothly.

He held his arms out to his sides. "Everything I need is in here."

Her eyes flicked up to his face, hesitated, and narrowed. She pulled a breath through her nose and asked, "Have you been drinking?"

"Indeed, I have."

Her jaw worked for a moment. "Do you think that wise given what we are about to do?"

"I think it necessary."

"You are only barely healed."

"I've never felt better."

She blew out an irritated breath and began loading her pistols, dismissing him without a word. Fine, he could play at that game, as well. Lady Gwen also wielded a cloth, but she sat on the bed and ran the fabric along the length of a silver sword.

"That's a fine piece of work," he offered, standing close enough to see the runes engraved along the center of the slender blade. It was shorter than a rapier, but longer than a poignard, perfectly concealed within the umbrella she carried.

"It ought to be," she said, her voice amused. "It nearly cost me, quite literally, an arm and a leg."

He eyed her, noting a fine form, fit from physical activity. "You appear to have all your limbs."

"I did say nearly."

"So you did."

Alix's pistol snapped shut with an ominous click.

He rolled his eyes. "No need to threaten me, minx, I'm just making conversation. Biding my time, you might say, till we go out and skulk in the shadows on behalf of this lovely little village."

Gwen raised her head, her brown eyes sharp as she considered him. She slid the blade back into the umbrella shaft and said to Alix, "I'll be downstairs."

After the door closed, his partner sighed. "You've scared her off."

"I've done no such thing."

She stood, all lithe grace, and slid the pistols into the freshly cleaned holsters on her hips. Once her cloak was settled in place, she squared her shoulders. "What's wrong, wolf?"

"Not a thing," he said.

"Liar."

At the insult, a wave of heat rolled over him from forehead to toes. Her ability to strip him to the core with a few simple words was infuriating.

Did she truly want to know what was wrong with him? Aside from swallowing too much beer, he was tired, wounded in a way he hadn't experienced in ages, and tasked with the unexpected responsibility of protecting an entire village from the worst threat he'd seen in hundreds of years.

The last time a village relied on him for protection, he'd failed. His entire family died.

What was wrong?

He was scared. He should trust Alix with that truth, and spit the poison out before it tainted his insides. She'd been willing to shoulder his burdens in the past and trusted him with her own. But he couldn't say it. Speaking that weakness aloud would make it real.

He could not afford to be weak, not now. Not after three werewolves had almost killed them both. A vision of the wolf dragging Alix by the shoulder made fury and terror flame to life in his chest.

But fear, logical as it was, would cripple him.

Instead, he leaned into the anger. Anger was active and powerful. Anger got results. His voice was low and dangerous. "Haven't I warned you about insulting me?"

Alix raised a black brow and shifted her weight to a relaxed stance. She eyed him up and down, her gaze warm and tingling as a glass of whisky. But her expression was unimpressed, her voice dismissive. "Have you? It must not have been very memorable."

Blood thundered in his ears. "Perhaps you need another lesson?"

"If you think you can give it to me, you're welcome to try…wolf."

Cyrus sprang forward in a lunge that crossed the entire room and brought him up square against Alix, his chest inches from hers. She did not so much as flinch. Breath sawed in and out of his chest, and his fists clenched with knuckle-popping force...and that was it. He could do nothing else.

Every muscle, every fiber longed to move, to exorcise his fear and frustration so he could be free of the weight and pain of them. But he could no more try to hurt Alix than he could tear out his own heart.

She searched his face, the taunting expression melting into concern. "I thought you needed a good fight. You have one, if you want it. It might take the edge off. But maybe..." She traced his cheek with her fingertips, leaving tingling trails of fire across his skin.

Her lips parted and she leaned closer. Spearmint filled his nostrils, followed by the heady musk of her desire. The frantic energy in his muscles transformed, shifting into a hunger so deep it was inhuman.

"Perhaps you need a different kind of fight," she said, raising her chin until her lips were less than an inch from his. He stood transfixed, quivering on the edge of some great precipice as her breath bathed his face, her eyes both a challenge and invitation.

He heard himself speak words he hadn't intended to say in a low rasping growl that made the pulse in her neck flutter. "Don't. I don't think I can be gentle."

An answering gleam of heat smoldered in Alix's eyes, and her gaze dropped between his legs. "You cannot break me, wolf." Her lips curled in a wicked smile that made his cock harden in a painful rush. "But you can try."

How she ended up in his arms, Cyrus could not remember. But their mouths were sealed in a kiss so hot it made sweat run down his spine. She melded herself to him, her long legs wrapped around his hips to hold him close.

Not close enough.

He bit her neck with bruising force and slammed her back into the wall, pinning her with his body and jerking her trousers down over her hips. How she managed to tear his britches open he did not notice or care. The only thing that mattered was that her legs were open for him, her fingers were curled in his hair, and she moaned his name into his mouth.

The sound made him shiver as he positioned himself and drove home in a single thrust. Alix screamed and tightened her legs, pulling him deeper, wrenching his head to the side to sink her teeth into his neck.

A wave of ecstasy rolled down his body from her love bite and furious pleasure drove him forward. He wanted to lose himself in her body, in her kiss, in the sound of his name spoken in her husky voice.

His hips rocked forward in a punishing rhythm, her back slamming against the wall until the table rocked and the chair clattered to the side. They tore at one another with hands and lips and teeth, bruising and biting, and still, it was not enough.

"Deeper," Alix growled in his ear. "Harder."

Cyrus hooked his arms under Alix's knees and spread her legs open, planting his palms against the wall to support her weight on his forearms. She yanked him forward by the hips, pulling him into her body with a smack of flesh on flesh and a moan of pleasure.

His eyes rolled back in his head and the wall shook from the force of their coupling. Alix opened for him, accepted every bit of force, and begged for more. The world spun away, his breath sawed, his muscles burned, and tension built as his vision went black at the edges.

Only Alix existed, and he drove into her with the frantic desperation of a thirsty man falling into a river. Every emotion, even his past and his own name, were cut away like so much debris as he drowned in her body, her voice, the feel and taste of her.

Cyrus came with a shout, the sound muffled as he pressed his face into her neck and shoulder. But he did not stop moving. He thrust until Alix followed him into the dark, limp pleasure of completion. Her body went stiff, she gasped, shuddered, and relaxed with a long, lusty sigh.

Sanity returned with the steady inevitability of the tide. Alix lay limp against him, her head on his shoulder, nose pressed against his neck. Now and then her legs trembled. Had he not held her up, they would both be lying in a numb heap on the ground.

He withdrew from her body, watching his softened flesh, wet from their shared pleasure, slide free. Alix made a pleased purring noise and shivered. He lowered her, then wetted a hand towel from the unbroken basin and handed it to her.

She accepted it, brows furrowed, then glanced down at her body and blushed. "Ah...thank you."

He turned away to give her some privacy, waiting as the leather and metal sound of her belt being buckled said she was clean and covered. Shame welled up from somewhere deep in his gut, and he could not force himself to face her.

"I'm sorry," he choked out.

"For what?"

"For—for using you that way."

"Wolf," she sighed, "did I sound like I did not enjoy it?"

"I was...I didn't—oh, bloody fucking hell." He spun and glowered at her, expecting accusation but seeing only exasperated amusement. "I took you in anger," he said as if that was some kind of excuse for the way he'd used her.

"I know."

"You know? Alix—" He could not finish the sentence. The woman did not realize how dear she'd become to him, how fast she entered his blood. He wanted to give her pleasure and tenderness, not use her for his own relief. The darker side of his nature was kept in check with years of discipline, but their circumstances wore down his defenses. *She* wore down his defenses.

Alix closed the distance between them with two quick steps. "I would have given you a fight if you needed one. You did as much for me once. Don't think I didn't recognize the signs of it. You were about to jump out of your skin. This was a much more...enjoyable pastime."

The last was said with a sly curl of her mouth.

"Besides," she continued, buckling her pistol belt. When had he torn that off? "I needed it, too. I'm not looking forward to this."

Alix behaved as if he had not just slammed her against a wall and taken her with the kind of force he'd never used on any woman. When the buckle was secure, she looked up at him as if her statement fixed everything. But seeing the anguish on his features, she rolled her eyes and leaped at him.

He caught her on instinct. Alix wrapped her legs around his waist once more and flexed her hips to raise herself till she could look down at him while holding his face between both hands. Slowly, so slowly she barely seemed to move, she lowered her mouth and kissed him.

By the moon her lips were soft. Spearmint would haunt him for the rest of his life.

Her kiss held all the tenderness, the warmth his lovemaking—if one could even call it that—lacked. When she released him, her eyes glowed like sun-warmed honey. "Don't apologize for giving me pleasure, wolf. I enjoyed myself. Strangely enough, I find that I like you unhinged." Her expression sobered, and his stomach muscles clenched in anticipation of the scolding he deserved, but it did not come.

She rested her forehead on his, and her thumbs brushed across his cheeks. "I'm strong enough to help you bear your burdens, remember?"

A month ago she would have happily killed him. Now she was trying to comfort him. When he spoke, his voice was ragged. "I didn't hurt you?"

She scoffed and pulled down the collar of his shirt, her fingertips brushing a small half-circle on his skin where his neck met his shoulder. "As if you could. No, wolf. You did not hurt me. But it may take you a few days to heal this bruise." A featherlight kiss brushed the spot, sending goosebumps down his arms. "I can still see the marks of my teeth."

"Play with a vixen and you'll get bit, is that it?"

"Something like. Now, do you need to complain more, or shall we go protect this village?"

An unwilling smile tugged at the corner of his mouth. "You know, I think I like the softer side of a pleased minx."

"Maybe you should please her more often, then. But not tonight." She slipped from his arms, landed soundlessly on the floor, and grinned at him. "Tonight, it's time to hunt."

32

Alix

Icy wind howled down off the mountain peaks and ripped across the valley, dragging cold fingers through her hair and tearing leaves off the beech trees. Constant, droning rain turned the footpath into a muddy river and smothered the scent of anything but soaking earth and vegetation.

Alix patrolled the forest outside Villecourbé, moving through the night like a shadow. She was supposed to be hunting werewolf signs, but paying attention to anything—even the wind and the rain soaking through her cloak—was next to impossible while memories of Cyrus dominated her thoughts.

When he entered their room earlier, the air around him had crackled with the same restless energy she felt before a fight. She suspected what he must be feeling, knew how the futility of grief sank into and through every thought and heartbeat.

When the past loomed over the future like a vulture, promising to repeat itself with no clear hope of escape, she'd be filled with so much violent energy she'd do anything to be free of it.

What Cyrus needed at that moment was a good fight. He'd fucked her thoroughly, instead. There was no point in calling it anything else; it had been a violent, but necessary, release. Her cheeks heated in pleasure at the memory.

Mortals had delicate bodies, and a careless caress from someone like her could hurt them. Alix never had the freedom to touch or be touched without restraint. Her passion must be carefully controlled, so pleasure was merely a beneficial side-effect of her need for comfort and connection. If all she wanted was a climax, she had fingers and a few spare minutes whenever she needed them.

But Cyrus changed all that. He'd been too agitated for tenderness or careful consideration. His frenzied hunger might have scared her a few weeks ago. He'd been close to the edge, his wolf so near the surface that every instinct should have screamed at her to protect herself.

Instead, she responded with wanton abandon, challenging and pushing him.

Cyrus would not hurt her, she knew it on a level deeper than logic, even as those green eyes made her feel like a meal set before a starving man. And she'd been right. He hadn't hurt her.

But he'd used her hard...and she liked it—more than liked it.

His ferocity made her hot and wet and hungry. She wanted more of it, not less. And when his completion left him weak and panting, he'd ridden her until she found her own pleasure.

Every time she accepted him into her body, something fundamental changed in her. Freedom and comfort became a part of her daily existence because of him. That gave her access to a version of herself she did not know existed.

And yet, she hadn't been able to offer him the same. Their responsibility to this little collection of buildings and people weighed on him.

When he stood in the doorway vibrating with barely restrained energy, she saw the weight of it crushing him. Given his past, she understood why.

Their coupling had only dulled the worst of his emotions, giving him release and something else to focus on. Even furious passion wasn't enough to free him of the pressure of the future.

So she'd volunteered to patrol the forest instead of the town, though his senses were sharper than hers. He needed to stay near the people, to know he could protect them if something went wrong...because he hadn't been there last time.

After everything he'd done for her, she would give him that much.

So she crept through the undergrowth, careful not to slide in the building mud, and ignored the weather. The rain and wind made catching their scent or finding prints impossible, so she strained to hear any hint of movement through the constant hum of rain on leaves.

Wind tore a hole in the storm clouds and moonlight broke through, making sections of the forest glow with pillars of light. Storm pixies flickered in pools of water and zipped through the moonbeams.

The little creatures were curious and playful, often hovering over anything out of the ordinary. She'd used them often to hunt because they were intimately familiar with the forest and spotted inconsistencies far more easily than she.

But they were also shy. Alix crouched behind the broken stump of an old tree, sliding her fingers along the carvings left by generations of children, and watched from cover. They danced ecstatically through the raindrops and rode the wind in a twisting, churning murmuration, their lights flickering like silent laughter.

One pixie left the school and floated in and out of the closest moonbeam, riding gusts of wind back and forth with apparent glee, its pale blue light pulsing. Clouds reclaimed the moon and the forest went dark. The pixie turned to rejoin its kin but stopped to hover over a blackthorn bush still white with blossoms.

It descended in little bursts like a butterfly deciding whether to land on a flower. When it was mere inches from the bush it circled twice, then flashed off to disappear in the undergrowth.

Alix brushed rain from the hood of her cloak, made certain the oil-cloth flaps were secure over her pistols, and crept forward. The storm tore handfuls of petals from the blackthorn blooms, dragging them dozens of feet away and leaving them bruised in the mud.

She edged close, wary of the inch-long thorns disguised beneath leaves, and caught her breath. A handful of fur hung dripping from the thorns. It was deep red-brown and did not match any of the wolves they killed.

Alix hooked the fur on a finger and brought the strands to her nose. Rain could not disguise the oily musk of a werewolf up close. She examined the ground around the bush and found two sets of tracks filled with water, blurred and softened around the edges. The paws were larger than her hands, and neither belonged to a bear.

That meant at least two more werewolves patrolled the countryside around the village. If they were in the pack she and Cyrus hunted, there had been at least eight wolves at some point. Eight. That was enough to decimate the countryside.

How many mortals had they turned since Mont Blanc? How many more had they added to their number?

Following the tracks, Alix ran in a crouch, stepping on vegetation rather than mud, eyes locked on the ground for any sign of prints. But the rain had turned the dirt to soup. The trail faded away.

She flung the water out of her eyes and glared at her backtrail, which twisted along the mountainside till it disappeared in the direction of the village. Villecourbé twinkled in the valley below, windows and lamps glowing with welcome warmth.

A howl echoed off the mountainside and rebounded into the valley, the hollow sound chased by growling thunder in the distance. It came from the opposite peak, or somewhere close to it.

Was it a call or a signal?

A human-shaped shadow darted across her backtrail seconds later, heading down the mountainside at greater-than-human speed. Alix crouched behind a tree trunk and as another shadow, this one the size of a black bear, followed it downhill, ignoring the footpath yet moving as silently as a wraith.

She held her breath, but neither looked for her prints or scented the air. The howl had been a signal, then. Were they attacking the village before the full moon?

Alix hoped Cyrus and Gwen were ready as she unbuttoned the oilskin cover on her pistols and sprinted after them. They wove through the forest at blinding speeds, too fast for a clean shot.

Trailing less than three seconds behind the werewolf, Alix tracked it by catching glimpses of stray moonlight shining on its pale fur. It was not the werewolf with red fur. That made three more, plus the wolf howling earlier.

They cut left at the next footpath heading toward the village and slowed to a walk once Villecourbé was in sight. Alix slid into the shifting shadows and drew her pistols but kept them hidden beneath her cloak. Best not to get them wet until necessary.

The human shape was tall enough to be an elf, but their grace was predatory rather than elegant, and their shoulders were wider than what she'd expect of an average elf. Too fast for a human. She pulled in a surreptitious breath but the rain fell too hard for any scent to reach her.

A werewolf in human form? It was possible, if unlikely. Most werewolves had a hard time controlling their magic this close to a full moon.

Could it be one of Cyrus's kin? He was that fast in his mortal form.

She inched forward but kept herself out of striking distance. The man-shape turned to look down at the wolf, who raised its head and howled in a hollow keen that made goosebumps run up her forearms.

They were here to frighten the villagers. To surround them and cripple their minds with terror before the attack. She wasn't going to give them that chance. Alix raised her pistols, sighted, and fired.

Two gunshots split the air like thunder, one for each creature. The werewolf yelped and stumbled, and the man staggered but did not fall or cry out. Alix turned and ran, hoping to lead them away from the village. The squelching thump of paws followed her.

She cut into the trees, leaped onto a low branch some ten feet off the ground, and turned to fire. Two more shots hit the werewolf, one in the flank, and the other in the chest. But the beast did not stop or stumble. It gathered itself, took two running strides, and leaped.

Alix dropped as the beast flew over her head and landed several feet behind her. But the man was waiting beneath the tree. He wore a hood that shadowed his face, and clothing so dark it was almost lost in the night.

His fist shot out and gripped the front of her shirt to jerk her forward, but she planted both feet in his gut and launched herself backward. Her shirt tore away and she plowed into the rising werewolf, sending them tumbling through the undergrowth.

Her face and shoulder dragged through the mud, clogging her nose and one eye before she hit a tree next to the werewolf. Alix grabbed a handful of fur, twisted her hips, and pulled herself atop the writhing creature. She planted the barrel of her pistol against the back of its skull and pulled the trigger.

The beast collapsed under her without so much as a whimper, and she sprang to her feet with the pistol leveled at the cloaked man. One instant he was a dozen feet away, and the next he stood a long arm's reach from her.

A beam of moonlight broke through the canopy and shone into her eyes, blinding her. It was impossible to see his face or aim. She pulled the trigger anyway.

The thunder of huge running feet and a familiar growl followed the echoing gunshot. When the moon hid behind a cloud, the figure still stood in the same place as if transfixed. Had she hit him?

"You," the figure said in a deep, smooth voice that sent shivers of dread up her spine.

Cyrus barreled onto the path from the village, his tawny fur glowing even without moonlight. The figure's head snapped toward the oncoming werewolf, then back to Alix.

Cyrus gave chase and Alix stood for a moment, disoriented. Her knees wobbled. She tipped her face upward, catching the last falling raindrops on her cheeks, and took a deep steadying breath, turned, and ran.

Less than a mile later, with no sign of catching up to the fleeing shadow, a realization made Alix's blood go cold.

She slid to a stop, mud caking her boots, and shouted, "Cyrus!"

Seconds later the tawny wolf stood in front of her, head low and tail down, as if trying to make himself smaller for her benefit. Had she more time to think or feel anything other than panic, the gesture might have warmed her.

But fear made her voice thready when she said, "What if he's leading us away from the village?"

His green eyes widened, and then they were both flying through the forest. If something was wrong, they should have a signal from Lady Gwen. Unless the wolves already killed her.

Had she needlessly dragged him away from the people and sprung a trap? Her stomach twisted into a painful knot. But when they skidded to a stop on the high street outside the inn, everything was quiet.

A distant howl echoed through the valley. It was far away, perhaps several miles, but unease trickled across her skin, colder than the raindrops. An electric current filled the air, and Cyrus stood next to her in his human form a moment later.

He turned her by the shoulders and worried green eyes ran over her face, neck, and chest. "Are you hurt?"

"No," she said, glancing down at her torn shirt. It and her chemise hung in shreds from her shoulders, exposing the top of her corset and the bare skin of her chest.

Mud caked her right side and spattered her neck, but her mother's pendant still winked against her breasts like a drop of blood. Relief made her legs weak. If she'd lost the only piece of her mother she managed to keep after all these years, she didn't like to think of how she'd respond.

"What was that?" Cyrus asked, turning his gaze to the road out of the village.

"I don't know. I couldn't smell it. Could you?"

He shook his head. "We'll need to recover the body of the wolf you killed. Check it for clues."

They stood side-by-side and stared into the dark. The werewolves had help of some kind. Something faster than she, and strong enough to haul her off her feet without effort. Something that could take a silver bullet without flinching. Something werewolves obeyed.

There were more than common monsters in the woods, and the thought of walking back into those shadows was not very appealing.

"We are in trouble," she said, only realizing she'd spoken once she heard her own voice.

"Aye. Aye, we are."

Fifteen minutes later they stood staring at the dead man lying in the dirt outside the inn. Lantern light painted sharp shadows across his face and shone off the whites of his half-open eyes.

Luckily, the damage had been done to the back of his skull, and rain washed away the worst of the gore. She had insisted on carrying the werewolf corpse back herself, and her jaw was set in a stony line when she lowered him to the wet ground. The boy couldn't have been more than twenty years old when he died. He had a short, downy beard and the bare chest of a young man.

Had he volunteered to let the magic contaminate his soul, or had he been as innocent as the man she killed on the mountain? A shiver of disgust ran down her arms, and Alix wrapped her arms around her stomach. Searching his face for clues gave her no answer. But an amulet of some kind hung about his neck, half covered in mud and tied with a fraying leather thong.

Kneeling, Cyrus brushed the gunk away with a fingertip. Silver shone through the smeared dirt.

She crouched next to him as he untied the leather and dipped the dirty pendant into the rain barrel next to the porch. When he pulled the necklace free, water dripped from a familiar silver shape. Unease trickled down her spine, colder than rainwater.

She held out her hand, and Cyrus dropped the talisman onto her palm.

"This is the same symbol we found in the ogre's purse," he said.

She tilted her hand so lantern light glittered off every curve of the stylized *S* and the line that bisected it. "Coincidence?"

"The ogre was chewing a human bone. My guess is he stole it from a corpse, or the body of whoever he killed. For an ogre to plunder a body on the same mountain pass our werewolves used not days before, and end up with the same amulet as a member of the pack we're hunting? That is too unlikely to be a coincidence."

"Then I suppose the question is, where did the pendant come from in the first place?"

"Where, indeed?"

She stood and slipped the silver into her pocket, then rubbed her hands clean on her legs. It was impossible to scrub away the feeling of the young man's cold skin, but she couldn't help herself from trying. "Something is happening here. Something more than strange werewolves."

"Aye. But what?"

She shook her head and sighed at the futility of their position. "I suppose we'll find out tomorrow."

He eyed her from forehead to toes, taking in the mud and blood spatters, no doubt. When he spoke, he tried to sound casual, but his eyes were locked on the shredded neck of her shirt and chemise. "In the meantime, you'd better ask the innkeeper if you can borrow a shirt."

She fingered the ripped fabric but there was no saving it. "I'll wait. There are still several hours of night ahead of us. No use in cleaning up if I'm simply going to get dirty again."

A howl echoed off the mountaintops and rolled down the valley, chasing the thunder as clouds hurried west, leaving a clear sky behind them. The moon, one night from full, blazed down at them and lit the main street with cool, pale light, turning it into a silvery river of connected puddles.

"Maybe that's best," he agreed, eyeing the mud with distaste. "Why don't you take the next watch in the village? I'd like to sniff around a bit."

Alix narrowed her eyes at him. Being so far from the village would make him uneasy, that much was clear from the hesitation in his voice and the way his hands curled into fists at the suggestion. Not to mention the deep brackets around his mouth.

Something in the forest worried him enough to leave the people in her care, something he felt was his responsibility to find or face.

"Are you certain?" she asked, searching his eyes. "I don't mind the mud."

Tenderness softened his expression, drawing his brows up in the center and making his eyes shine. He swallowed back some emotion with an audible gulp and touched her cheek with two fingers, the feather-light touch making her shiver.

He said, "I can count on two hands the number of times someone thought of my feelings before their own comfort. Thank you."

Were those tears threatening to sting her eyes? She was not about to cry over a simple thank you. What was wrong with her? Alix shrugged off the ridiculous reaction and swallowed the lump forming in her throat. Her voice was suitably nonchalant when she said, "That's what partners do."

His hand dropped and he cleared his throat. "I see."

After a few heartbeats of uncomfortable silence, he continued, "I don't think the road will be safe for the villagers who try to leave in the morning. I've got a suspicion the wolves don't intend for anyone to leave

Villecourbé. I want to scout possible routes of escape, so someone must be here to protect these people."

Alix rested her palms on the butt of her revolvers and said, "The people will be safe."

"Good. Don't come back into the forest tonight, Alix. No matter what you hear. If something happens to me, you are the only thing standing between them and the monsters."

Her breath caught in her throat. Cyrus spoke as if he expected to die. She wanted to beg him to stay where they could protect one another, where Gwen's silver sword and the safety of buildings gave them a better chance against creatures like the shadow.

But she swallowed and nodded instead. "If you find them," she said, her voice cold, "kill them."

A small, feral smile curled one corner of his lips. "I will, my violent minx. Count on it."

He grabbed her chin in one hand, kissed her hard, then shimmered into his wolf form and loped into the woods.

Not the last time. She thought the silent prayer to any gods who might be listening as she clutched the red pendant. *Don't let this be the last time.*

33

Cyrus

As MORNING SUNLIGHT SPILLED over the mountain tops, villagers stood in a line outside the blacksmith holding bags, boxes, and trays, each waiting to donate their precious silver to the forge. Bracelets, rings, forks, and knives went into the crucible, and bullets came out.

There was depressingly little to be had.

Anyone not donating their silver was already busy fortifying the buildings they'd chosen to shelter in. They carried bags and boxes of supplies, makeshift weapons, and sharpened stakes without complaint. The foiled attack last night, if that's what it had been, scared the townspeople badly.

Cyrus strode into the square where the dissenters stood holding all the worldly possessions they were willing to flee with: small sacks clutched to their chests by white-knuckled hands.

Unfortunately, his news would not make them any calmer. He cleared his throat and fought not to fidget. "Last night on patrol I found several watch posts hidden along the route back to Loreau. The hiding spots had been used enough that even the storm could not wash all signs away. A healthy werewolf might spot a traveler from any of those positions and reach them within two or three minutes at a hard run. If you leave the village and the werewolves are watching, they will catch you."

They'd used those watch posts to terrorize the villagers last night, their haunting howls echoing a promise down the length of the valley: anyone who left the village would be taking their lives in their hands.

"You cannot guarantee that will happen," Madame Lambert pushed forward, her eyes wild. "You cannot guarantee they will do anything to us, not if we leave during daylight."

Cyrus took a deep breath to steady himself. He must respond to her calmly if these people were to trust him. "You are correct, Madame. I cannot guarantee it. I can only tell you what I've found. I don't believe the wolves intend to let us abandon this village. If Mont Blanc was any indication, they will savage this town and gather whoever lives through the change into their pack. As far as I know, La Manteau Rouge and I are the only hunters to respond to the danger for that very reason."

A wizened old human with skin as pale as a fish belly used his cane to make a path for himself to the front of the small gathering and glared up at Cyrus. "That doesn't make any sense. If as many people died as you say, hunters from all over France should be here."

"Only the living can hire hunters, grandfather."

Alix's low voice made a chill run up Cyrus's spine. He hadn't heard her approach, but her presence made the first few people back up a step.

"If no one survives to warn others," she continued, stopping at his side, "who will tell the hunters?"

A murmur ran through the crowd and they huddled closer together like sheep in a storm. He needed to calm them, and quickly.

"I cannot make you any guarantees," he said. "And I cannot stop you if you choose to flee. My only responsibility is to make you aware of the facts as I've gathered them. What you choose to do with them is yours."

After a moment of indecisive silence, Madame Lambert raised her chin and gripped her bag more tightly to her chest. "You lot can do as you like. Claude and I are leaving. We will warn Loreau and send anyone to your aid who will go. But we are not staying here."

She spun, grabbed her son by the coat sleeve, and stormed out of the square.

"She'll take her husband's wagon," the elderly man said. "Might as well ride on the back of it, if we can."

He followed her, and so did two or three others. The rest stood in confused silence before dispersing.

"That woman—" Cyrus began, but couldn't force himself to finish what he wanted to say.

"She's terrified," Alix said. "Her emotions are making the decisions, not her mind."

"She's going to get her son killed."

"Would a doe stand a better chance if she turned and faced the wolves? Fear will not allow her to stand still. I am surprised she made it through the night."

Cyrus sighed and ran a hand over his face. "We had better give them what advice we can before they go off to risk their fool lives."

But the small group of deserters were not deserting. They stood frozen outside a little barn, gathered around the un-hitched wagon.

"What are they doing?" Alix breathed.

He pushed forward, only to freeze alongside the townsfolk. The axle was broken, split through the middle like a broken matchstick. Snapping a piece of wood that thick must have taken terrible force.

"No," Madame Lambert choked, one hand on her throat.

Without warning, she sprinted to the road and down Main Street toward the other side of the village. Her terror infected the rest of them, and the villages followed her in a blind panic. But the axle of every wagon was in a similar state.

The sound of snapping such a sturdy piece of wood could only have been disguised if broken during thunderclaps the night before. Which meant something was in the village last night while he patrolled it, and he'd never known.

Dread condensed in Cyrus's stomach like a block of ice, heavy and cold. Madame Lambert stood trembling, while the others shouted and gestured helplessly at the wood or the sky. The message was clear.

There was no choice now but to protect the village.

Alix, Cyrus, Gwen, and Madame Sophie organized the citizens into work groups. They would block roads, lay traps, stock provisions, sharpen weapons, and prepare themselves for violence and death.

When the work was done, they'd take shelter in rooms secured by boarded-up windows with thick bars nailed across doors from the inside. They'd only un-bar the doors after dawn.

Several of the most experienced adults would stand guard, while the fastest waited to lead the others into the woods, should their plan fail.

But a few people refused to follow instructions.

"If you can put yourself in danger for my friends and family, I cannot do any less," Hugh said.

A cudgel of hard, oiled wood rested on one burly shoulder, his jaw thrust forward in a stubborn scowl.

Cyrus couldn't very well deny the man, not after telling Alix the priest had a right to defend his parishioners, and certainly not after allowing Lady St. James to help. So Hugh and several other villagers with a bit of experience and more bollocks than brains prepared to defend the streets. They sharpened their weapons and hauled debris and other obstacles into the roads.

Alix hefted a broken plough onto the barrier that would, hopefully, funnel the monsters down the high street, then wiped her sleeve across her forehead and glanced up at him from the corner of her eyes. "Will this work?"

She wanted reassurance, not answers. But he could not give it to her.

He checked the position of the sun and tried not to let concern color his voice. "It has to. This is everything we can throw at them on short notice."

"That creature from last night...I couldn't tell what it was. The hood was too deep, even for my eyes, and with the wind and rain? I don't know how to prepare for it and that makes me nervous."

If only he had answers. The storm confounded his senses, as well, washing away traces of the creature before he identified anything. He wanted reassurance as much as she did. It was one thing to risk his own life or to watch Alix risk hers. This was a profession they'd chosen.

It was something else entirely to risk the lives of these people.

"Perhaps we can identify it by the process of elimination."

Cyrus spun to see Gwen striding toward them. She hadn't been close enough to hear their conversation, not close enough for mortal ears. Hearing like that suggested elvish blood in her lineage, though she did not smell like an elf.

"I've considered that," Alix said. There was no trace of uncertainty in her voice when she continued, "But I do not have enough information.

It was fast and strong, had good night vision, and increased healing or the ability to ignore pain, or both. It also did not seem to be bothered by silver. But the list of possible monsters that fit that description is so long there is no way to prepare for all of the eventualities."

Gwen hefted the broken pieces of an old door onto the growing roadblock. "Which monsters are the most likely for our geographic location?"

"A hundred years ago that might have mattered, but now? As towns grow and better weapons are built, monsters are driven to migrate beyond their traditional territorial ranges. In fact, we fought an ogre coming over the pass and they are usually...wait."

Alix pulled the silver symbol from her pocket and offered it to Gwen. "We found this on the body of the werewolf I killed last night, and another in the ogre's purse."

Gwen plucked the talisman from Alix's palm and studied it in the light.

"This was made in bulk," she said slowly, turning the piece. "There are still lines here from the mold. Any craftsman worth their salt would have filed off the extra silver along the seam, so they were either made quickly or were not designed to be high-quality pieces. I would wager this is some kind of identification marker or talisman made on an assembly line."

"Do you recognize the symbol?" Alix asked, leaning in.

"No. Without context, there is no way to decipher the meaning. Where were these when you found them? I mean to say, how were they worn?"

"This was on a thong around the werewolf's neck," Cyrus said. "The other was loose in the purse."

"Then it is likely a marker or badge of some kind, given to someone as a token. Secret societies often do this. In New London, the self-professed king of the criminals is rumored to give those in his service a coin stamped with a cutthroat head."

"That's rather gruesome," Cyrus said.

"Indeed. But why is a werewolf wearing a silver amulet? How could the creature have worn such a thing without tremendous pain?"

Alix gave him a speculative glance. "Your family doesn't share the werewolves' aversion to silver."

He tried to control the tone of his voice but anger stained every word. "We still take damage from silver if wounded by it. We can wear and use it, with care. But these are not my kin."

Members of his family and others chosen by the moon died at the hands of hunters like Alix because of that misunderstanding. They should have made themselves known when the abominations began to spread, but fear spread faster than truth. By the time they realized the danger, biases against his kind were too deeply ingrained.

"Is it possible they are using some connection to your family? Distant relations, perhaps?" Gwen asked.

"There aren't enough of us left for this kind of destruction," he said.

"Do you mind if I ask...is the magic of your family hereditary, or do you achieve it by some other means?"

"The traditions and rituals are passed down through our families. I don't believe being chosen by the moon has anything to do with our blood. If it does, that knowledge has been lost."

Gwen's brows furrowed and she stared down at the amulet with so much concentration he wondered whether she was trying to set it on fire with her eyes.

Alix slapped her hands on her thighs, sending little clouds of dust rolling into the air. "Unless these answers hold a key to stopping the pack from tearing this village apart, they will have to wait. Sunset is close, and moonrise is only a few hours away."

The three of them exchanged a charged glance. The weight of inescapable violence was suddenly smothering. Men, women, and children of all races passed them as they prepared to protect themselves, their expressions determined but hopeful.

Anxiety pinned Cyrus's heart to his ribcage in a single, white-hot thrust. Could he protect them, or would he be responsible for the destruction of another village?

A scream of terror tore through the air. "Help!"

Cyrus was running before he had time to recognize the voice. Madame Lambert stood in the long shadows beneath the trees on the road out of Villecourbé, jumping and flailing her arms for attention. Blood stained the grey bodice of her dress.

"The fool tried to leave," Alix said under her breath.

Cyrus reached her first, though Alix and Gwen skidded to a stop next to him seconds later.

"It's Claude! Please help me!" Madame Lambert turned and ran into the forest. They followed her for a quarter of a mile before the coppery tang of fresh blood made Cyrus growl low in the back of his throat.

The woman was too overcome to hear. Claude lay in the bushes with his back against a tree trunk, his arms pressed over a hastily dressed wound in his belly.

"He tried to protect me," Madame Lambert moaned, her hands fluttering about the boy's wound. "He tried to save me. Oh, moon and stars, they'll kill us all. They'll kill us all. They'll kill us all..."

Gwen knelt beside the sobbing mother and pulled the traumatized woman into her arms as Alix examined the boy. He breathed in pained little gasps, his fingers bloody and clutching the clothes around his wound.

"We cannot treat this here," Alix said, her eyes wide and clear as glass as they locked on his. "Cyrus, he needs a proper physician."

"Is there a doctor in the village?" Gwen asked.

"He died," the woman gasped between sobs. "The monsters...it was the mayor..."

"He has time," Gwen said, placing one reassuring hand on the woman's shoulder. "Madame Lambert, look at me. This is not a fatal wound, not if he receives treatment. Do you hear me?"

The words did not calm the woman, but she raised her trembling chin and nodded.

"Someone needs to take the boy to Loreau," Gwen said.

"If we try to leave they'll kill us! They'll kill us!" The hysterical woman grabbed Gwen's shoulders, her face pale, her eyes so wide the whites shone all around her iris.

Gwen frowned at the woman, then slapped her once, hard, across the face. Madame Lambert flinched, her mouth hanging open for a startled moment. Then sanity returned to her eyes, her lips trembled, and she fell sobbing on her son's side.

"If this boy does not get treatment within the next day, he will almost certainly get sepsis," Alix said in a voice low enough for only his ears.

Cyrus ground his teeth in frustration. They could not let the boy die if his death could be prevented, and they could not spare a single competent person who might protect the villagers.

"I should have tied the woman to a post," he growled.

"I will take him," Gwen said.

Madame Lambert looked up, hope on her tear-streaked face. But horror crept back across her features and she said, "But the wolves are there. They will kill you. They will kill my son."

"They will have to kill me before they get to your son. And I am not so easy to kill, madame. Besides, if he stays here without treatment, he will certainly die."

"How can you hope to outrun them?"

Gwen said, "If there is a horse, I'll hide with the boy in the forest and wait for the first gunshots. Our best chance of making it through will be once the werewolves are fully engaged. They are less likely to chase us if you keep them busy."

"You will have to disguise your scent, and the scent of his blood," Cyrus said.

"That is far easier for two people than many," Alix said, though her expression was uncertain.

Lady Gwen stood and straightened her skirt, then gave the crying woman a final glance. "We have to try. It is that, or let the boy die."

Madame Lambert whimpered and clutched her son's hand.

"I'll go."

The harsh whisper made all four of them turn. Claude's face was pale and drawn tight with pain, but his eyes were determined.

"Keep Maman safe and take me. I'll go. I'll only be a burden if I stay. If you think"—he winced and his jaw locked against a wave of pain—"if you think you can get me out, I will go."

Claude had tried to protect his mother, and despite his injuries was trying to protect her, still. That was more than Cyrus had been able to do for his family. The boy deserved to live.

But werewolves under a full moon were more powerful, faster, and deadlier than at any other time. Their senses were sharper and the magic drove them mad. Unless the villagers made a true fight of it and engaged all of the wolves and the dark figure, Gwen and the boy would never make it out, no matter how fast their horse.

They'd have to put up one hell of a good fight. Cyrus knelt and hoisted the boy into his arms.

"We will give you every chance to get out," Cyrus said to Gwen. "But his wound needs to be cleaned and dressed well, or the blood will draw them from miles away. When that is done, I will help you hide. And may all the gods go with you."

34

Partners

Alix

FOR THE TENTH TIME that evening, the silver knife slid silently from its sheath. Alix turned it to catch the light of a nearby window, noting the fine sheen along the blade: wolfsbane oil. The knife was sharp, of course, made of silver and etched with artifice to keep it strong, but it was wolfsbane that made the blade truly dangerous.

She'd used enough oil over the years that it penetrated the inside of each sheath, so there was no danger of the oil wearing off the blade, but seeing it was still a relief. Her bullets had also been coated in the stuff. It was not a precaution she generally bothered with, but given the circumstances, safe was better than sorry.

Reassuring herself of her preparations only helped calm her nerves until she remembered they were all relying on the villagers' courage and ingenuity. Could they be trusted to be in position, to be prepared, not to flee when confronted with monsters from their nightmares?

They had no choice. And she had enough to worry about without trusting untrained civilians.

The sky was clear, and a bright-faced moon lit up the streets, casting jagged shadows across the road. Alix slipped through them like a wraith, following the patrol pattern they laid out earlier in the day. Hugh's body odor lingered in the still air along her route, less than fifteen minutes old. The smith kept to their plan, then.

Hopefully, that meant the others were as well. Cyrus could be trusted to follow the plan, but volunteers who spent their days farming and hunting deer?

Alix slid the knife back into the sheath and firmly turned her attention back to her job.

Sound floated far on the heavy night air, seeping through the thin walls of the houses, clear as if they came from mere feet away: the crying of frightened children, heavy boots pacing back and forth on creaky floorboards, the anxious tapping of toes or drumming of fingers.

She stalked down the high street on soundless feet listening to the villagers worry, her hands never far from the butt of her pistols. Imagining the people hiding, crouching in the dark and clutching one another while monsters stalked the night, made her jaw clench and her hands curl into fists.

The werewolves would have to go through her to reach the villagers...if the beasts ever showed up.

Hours passed. Crickets sang. The moon glared down at them. Stars wheeled overhead. But no growls or howls rent the night, no snapping branch or running feet alerted her to the presence of monsters.

Every movement, every casual night sound and every errant breeze made adrenaline blast through her like a lightning bolt. Was something else stalking the shadows? Something darker and more dangerous than her?

Worse, Gwen and Claude were waiting for the gunshot that would send them running toward Loreau, and every hour they hid in the forest increased the boy's chances of infection. She should be grateful there wasn't an attack. Being wrong about the pack's intentions was the best possible outcome for Villecourbé.

But she didn't think they were wrong. Which made the unexpected silence feel like still, dark water that hid unseen teeth and slimy tentacles.

Alix completed her third patrol. Her fourth. And nothing. Her mind wandered to the last kiss she shared with Cyrus, a brief, tender thing that was both a promise and a goodbye before he shimmered into his wolf form to patrol the wooded fringe of the village.

His fingers had slipped through the hair at her nape to cradle her head and hold her close, his lips brushing hers with the gentle hunger that felt so surprising and poignant in such a strong man.

"Be careful, minx," he'd said in a voice low as a prayer.

How had that stupid name become dear to her, a name she would desperately miss hearing if anything happened to him?

The click of a door handle turning was loud in the predawn silence and catapulted her thoughts back to the present. The first lightening of the eastern sky said dawn was a bare hour away. Why were people opening doors? They should be hiding till she or Cyrus told them it was safe to emerge.

A howl tore through the air, high and clear like the ringing of a trumpet. That wasn't an average werewolf. It was a warning. Cyrus spotted something.

Alix turned and sprinted toward the inn, following the first stage of their plan. She leaped for the lowest rafter on the ground floor and swung herself up to the roof. A few careful leaps put her on the second story where she could use the chimney for cover.

She flipped the covers off her pistols, slid a finger along the extra ammunition to reassure herself all was ready, and turned to peer through the dark.

Several villagers stood outside one of the safe buildings at the far end of the street, milling about and pointing at the sky as if safety were a mere hour away. And Hugh stood among them, urging people to leave the building.

That traitorous son of a dog!

The crack of a snapping tree trunk drew her eyes to the woodline on the opposite side of the village. Leaves and branches shivered in the canopy as if huge hands were shaking them. Cyrus was fighting.

A fist tightened around her heart, but Alix forced a deep breath to calm her nerves and scanned the open space between the forest and the village.

Twelve dark shapes slunk through the cropped grasses like alligators in a river, coming at the village from all directions. Twelve. Her throat closed. Twelve werewolves were akin to natural disaster, and she had a mere five—no four, gods be damned—mortals to help.

If she screamed at the people to get to safety, she'd warn the werewolves and alert them to her position. Mouth twisted in a grimace, Alix aimed at the closest wolf, waiting for it to reach pistol range.

The huge grey beast moved with the silent, predatory grace of a hunting cat. Her first shot took it between the eyes. She did not bother to wonder if the creature had been forced into the change or if the mortal inside that animal's body volunteered.

It fell before the crack of her shot echoed off the buildings.

The dark shapes scattered, leaping aside with blinding speed and taking cover behind buildings, rocks, and tree trunks. The fight was on.

Cyrus

He hit the trunk of the nearest tree and rebounded, digging his claws into the earth and springing at the creature's undefended flanks. The thick rope of hamstring snapped between his teeth and the werewolf tumbled to the ground with a whine of pain.

Cyrus tore out its throat before it could recover.

The creature had been strong and fast but had no fighting experience, not like the werewolves they'd faced outside Villecourbé. Those had been a team of assassins. This abomination was as unskilled as a puppy.

His stomach revolted at the possibility the mortal beneath the wolf's skin might be a young victim, but he swallowed his misgivings and turned toward the village.

A gunshot, like a crack of thunder, made the hair rise along his spine. His warning worked. The killing had begun. He sent up a silent, fervent prayer to the moon that Gwen and the boy were safe, and leaped toward the tree line.

Alix's voice floated toward him on a feeble breeze that also bore the rank musky scent of at least three different werewolves. "Get back inside! Bar the door!"

Why had the fools opened the doors?

No time to wonder. Cyrus crouched and slunk along the fence line of a kitchen garden, catching sight of a silvery pelt through the gaps in the fence posts. The beast was half his size, but its muzzle was already wet with blood. He stopped a growl in his throat, eased around the garden's edge, and sprang.

The beast turned in time to stop from being hamstrung, and its teeth flashed in an instinctive bite to protect its vulnerable haunches. Pain burned across his shoulder, but Cyrus ignored it and plowed forward.

Another gunshot cracked and several people gasped and whimpered from somewhere close by, but Cyrus ignored the sound and bit down.

Thick skin, fat, and fur protected a werewolf's throat, but only so long as the attacking werewolf wasn't as large as Cyrus. He clamped his jaws shut, felt wet heat stain his fur, locked his shoulders, and wrenched with his powerful neck muscles.

He left the creature bleeding and gasping on the ground, and leaped for cover, edging into the shadow of a building behind a hand cart.

Crouching to peer through the spokes of the wheels, he bit back a growl of fury. Hugh stood with his heavy maul raised, guarding the open door of the safe house from the frightened villagers who wanted back inside. That son of a—another gunshot, two more, and the light sound of feet hitting the ground.

Alix abandoned her position.

She would lead the creatures into the first trap, so Cyrus needed to get the villagers back into their safe house. He sprang from cover and raced down the street in three or four long strides, driving his shoulder into Hugh's bulky form before the man realized he was there.

The impact flung him across the intervening street and he hit the wall of the mercantile with a meaty crunch, his head snapping against the doorframe.

Cyrus ignored him and herded the screaming villagers toward the open door as Alix flashed down the street, a blur of red in the blue predawn light. Three werewolves were less than a second behind her.

One of them turned, saw Cyrus and the unprotected villagers, and leaped.

Alix

The cloak trailed behind her, pulling at her neck and shoulders, but Alix ran with speed borne of necessity. Her feet flew across the dirt road as she scanned the scene: Cyrus and the exposed villagers; a dead werewolf; Hugh lying in a limp pile against a building.

The impression of terrified faces and wide eyes burned into her memory, and she was past. Digging her heels into the dirt, she turned onto a side street and into the first trap, praying the other volunteers weren't as treacherous as Hugh.

The roadblock loomed ten feet beyond, and slavering werewolves not thirty feet behind. She reached under her cloak, pulled out the little earthenware jar that harbored a carefully protected ember, and leaped.

Alix sailed over the roadblock and hurled the clay pot at the pile of rotten wood and broken tools. The pitch they'd poured on the mass the day before caught, and the roadblock blazed to life. Flames roared ten feet into the air with a crackling whoosh.

The werewolves skidded to a stop, sitting back on their haunches to avoid the fire. Villagers leaped from the shadows with silver-tipped spears and rammed the weapons into the creatures with all the force of their work-hardened muscles.

Shrieks of pain sounded as Alix doubled back, rounding the building and drawing her pistols. Villagers had pinned two werewolves with spears that stuck out of their hides like medieval knights fighting dragons.

They tried to twist and bite at the wooden hafts but the villagers held them steady. All of their attention was focused on their prey, so the villagers did not see the third werewolf enter the street behind them.

The third beast lunged forward and caught one of the volunteers by the ankle, dragging him out of the fight. She raised and fired on instinct. Her first shot hit the creature in the shoulder, making it stumble and whine, releasing its grip long enough for the man to scrabble backward.

She darted toward the creature at full speed, not giving it time to regain its footing, and leaped in a spin that twisted her feet over her head, letting her keep her eyes locked on the monster. The silver bullet struck the base of the werewolf's skull, but the creature twisted just far enough that it wasn't the killing shot it should have been.

Alix hit the ground five feet from the wolf, holstered one pistol, and leaped again, drawing her silver knife. It spun toward her, fangs slashing, and opened up a long gash on her right thigh. Its teeth tore into the thick muscle as she struck.

The poisoned knife sank to the hilt at the base of the wolf's neck, slicing through tendon and bone alike. Its jaws loosened as it collapsed, pulling her down on top of its limp body. Alix rolled away, her blood pattering on the dirt when she came to her feet.

Released from the pressure of one of the spears, the smaller of the pinned werewolves spun, bit the wooden haft and wrenched the weapon aside. The wood snapped, flinging the volunteer off her feet and sending her rolling into the building behind her. She landed with a thump, her head smacked the wood, and her eyes glazed over.

Twisting with shocking speed, madness in its eyes, the werewolf lunged toward the other attacker. Alix lifted the pistol in her right hand and fired. But she was too late.

Cyrus

Gunshots. Not the evenly spaced, purposeful fire of someone in a controlled situation, but the frantic shots of someone in danger.

Alix.

Cyrus registered the sound and the frantic shouts of villagers as he forced the other wolf onto its belly by flexing his spine and twisting like a falling cat. He locked his jaw on the back of the wolf's neck and snapped it.

He rolled to his feet as the door closed behind the last villager. They hadn't waited to see who won but took advantage of the opportunity to flee. Good. Because he still had to kill the wolf twitching on the ground, and it wasn't going to be a pleasant sight.

Screams tore at his eardrums, piercing cries of fury and fear that made his stomach drop. He finished off the wounded werewolf—hoping to the moon it wasn't an innocent victim of the attack on Mont Blanc, and bolted around the corner, letting his ears and nose guide him.

Alix, four villagers, and two werewolves fought in the lurid orange light of a bonfire, black silhouettes against the piercing light. She'd sprung the first trap, but she was hard-pressed as she protected two villagers with spears from the darting attacks of a large werewolf.

Cyrus sprang forward and locked his jaws around the beast's hind leg. He planted his feet and wrenched the beast to the side, taking it off its feet. The two villagers still on their feet had no skill with their impromptu weapons, but they were intelligent enough to see the opening.

Both volunteers lunged forward and thrust their silver-tipped spears into the exposed belly of the werewolf. It screamed and thrashed, but the wounds were deep. He held the leg immobilized until the villagers dispatched the creature.

As soon as the beast was no longer a threat, he turned toward the other werewolf in time to see Alix sink her dagger into its side beneath the foreleg, twist, and wrench the blade free.

Alix stumbled to the side, her thigh wet with blood. His heart stuttered, but she righted herself and turned to lift a wounded man off the ground. He screamed and clutched his belly, but she ignored him and kicked in the closest door to deposit him inside. A woman stumbled toward them, her pupils unfocused.

Alix regarded her for a moment, shook her head, and pulled her toward the open door by a sleeve. Breaking one of the discarded spears in half, she handed the pointy end to the woman and said, "Hide and see to his wound, if you can. I'll return for you" before pulling the door closed and wedging the rest of the wood beneath the handle.

Screaming broke out again from the opposite side of town, and if he judged correctly, they came from the safe house near the inn. Alix broke a window with her elbow, reached inside, and pulled out the rifles hidden there, handing one to each man.

"Phase two," she said.

They took the weapons, sending worried glances at Cyrus as if he would attack them next, then sprinted out of the street without a backward glance. Two volunteers down. Six dead werewolves. Their odds were improving. He let his tongue loll out in a doggy grin.

Alix stared at him for a long moment, her eyes reflecting the firelight like amber gems. But screaming punctuated the crackling of the fire. Somewhere in the village, people were in trouble. She swallowed, nodded at him once, and turned to leave for phase two.

A figure in black stepped into the cross street. It moved with smooth, controlled calculation, floating more than walking. It turned toward them, pulled back its hood back, and smiled.

35

Partners

Cyrus

A CHILL SETTLED IN his bones, freezing his muscles as his heart faltered. The creature standing at the cross street was a vampire. His face was grotesquely beautiful in the firelight, like the burned-out ruins of an old church, or the bones of a tree long dead, weathered by the slow erosion of time.

But instead of the gentle wisdom of age, the vampire was surrounded by a sour blanket of hunger and the sharp, cunning wisdom of a spider luring flies to their death. His smile was delighted and made Cyrus's stomach curl in on itself in disgust.

It was a mimicry of emotion, the twisting of muscle and bone to approximate a smile, but the cold, cruel intelligence in his flat eyes made the expression entirely alien; a corruption so deep it was only a dim reflection of humanity.

Cyrus's muscles begged him to run, to fight, to do anything but stand and stare. Yet he could not force himself to move.

"I have waited a very long time to meet you, Alix La Rouge," the creature said.

That voice may as well have echoed from the chest of a crocodile. But it broke the spell. A red haze fell over his vision and Cyrus sprang forward without thinking, his instincts to protect—instincts given him by the moon herself—overpowering every human thought and emotion.

Werewolves were an abomination, true. But this creature was something else, entirely. It was a perversion of life, a mockery of it that infected everything it touched, an offense against life itself that must be destroyed.

The monster laughed and blurred, shooting away into the growing dawn so fast it was almost a blur. But Cyrus was made to run, to hunt, and to kill. His claws dug into the packed dirt of the road, and he *ran*.

Alix

Her heart pounded so hard it hurt and the rushing of blood drowned out every other sound. She stopped noticing the pain of her healing wound, the burning stink of the fire, the echoing screams of the villagers.

That creature had been a vampire, and not just any vampire, but an old one. Whatever humanity he might have had was long subsumed by the nature of vampiric magic. His humanity existed only as a shell, a costume. And he'd been looking for her.

Cyrus released a low, rumbling growl that reverberated in her chest, and sprang after the creature, and yet Alix could not move. She was not enthralled, that was impossible, but her body had shut down on its own.

The creature laughed as it led Cyrus away.

Away.

"Wait!" she called, but it was too late.

How were they supposed to destroy the rest of the werewolves if Cyrus was chasing the creature? She could not defend the village from so many without his help. Screams rose above the rooftops just as the first light of true dawn turned the mountain tops fiery red, and the thunder of three evenly spaced gunshots rolled through the town.

The volunteers were in place, and they would need her. She had to save the people, no matter where Cyrus was.

Alix drew both pistols and ran, trying not to dwell on the fact that their plan had gone so horribly awry. She took the side street and barely noticed the buildings that blurred past, the bodies already littering the street as werewolves turned back into humans in death.

The screams grew louder, coming from the town square.

Alix entered the square at a dead run and took in the scene in a heartbeat. Doors and windows had been broken and ripped off, not battered inward, as if the werewolves had rammed them with their shoulders. They were jerked outward by some mighty force that bent the handles and splintered the wood.

People crowded the square, screaming and huddled as they tried to defend themselves with the makeshift weapons prepared the day before. Several werewolves harried them, lunging and snapping, then leaped away.

It made no sense. They should have been mauling the townspeople, not herding them. But they stayed close enough to make getting a clean shot at moving targets without hitting an innocent person almost impossible.

Which rendered her sharpshooters, stationed on several buildings, useless. Her only choice was to kill the creatures one at a time until Cyrus returned.

Alix raised her pistols and fired.

Cyrus

The vampires he killed in the past did not prepare Cyrus for this creature. It was faster than anything he'd ever chased, and wilier even than Alix.

Alix.

A moment of sanity intruded on his hunt, the sound of gunshots and the vague memory of a job he was supposed to do. A dark-haired woman who needed him. But the call of the hunt overpowered every other concern.

He needed to rip and tear, to break and shake and destroy the terrible thing that threatened life. Trees flashed by, ferns whipped his face, but he gained on the monster by inches and feet.

Six feet.

Five.

Cyrus plowed into the vampire at full speed. The impact was terrific, and several bones in his shoulder and chest snapped with a series of dull, meaty crunches. But the injuries did not stop him from catching the monster in his jaws.

Snapping and snarling, his teeth tore through flesh that was not warm or supple, but hard and dry as seasoned wood. The sourness of rot filled his mouth but ignored that too. This creature must be destroyed.

"Curse the damned moon," the vampire snarled.

It twisted, breaking its own arm, and planted its feet against his stomach. The creature kicked, breaking several more of Cyrus's bones, these ones in his back. He flew backward like a stone from a sling and hit the ground rolling.

He tumbled, gritting his teeth against the aching throb of his injuries, and fetched up hard against a boulder. Snarling growls rumbled in his chest, making the ground vibrate, but he could not force himself to his feet. Muscles were torn, and moving would be next to impossible until they healed. He was vulnerable. A creature that strong could kill him with ease.

Cyrus kicked his back legs into a roll, craning his neck to search the forest. But the vampire was gone.

If the damned monster found disappearing so easy, why had it led him on such a chase? Why not simply...

The answer crashed upon him like a dropped piano.

By the bloody moon, it had led him out of town to get him out of the way. He was fast enough to catch and damage the vampire, which made him a threat. So the monster removed him from the battlefield by the simple expedient of triggering his prey drive.

The same mistake he made as a young man.

Cyrus's mind staggered beneath the weight of sudden, sinking horror. He'd doomed the people of Villecourbé.

Alix

Two werewolves fell, their brains spattering the buildings behind them as Alix fired. That left four more. Four. She could take four. But she needed to reload.

Alix aimed for the tightly packed crowd and leaped. They gasped and ducked as she sailed over them in a long, low dive, hit the ground on the other side, and rolled up into a run. If she could lead even one of the beasts away, she could kill it and reload from a rooftop.

She cut onto a side street and bolted toward another roadblock, but the creatures did not follow.

If the instinct to chase and hunt hadn't been activated, the blood on her clothing should have at least tempted them. But she found herself alone and flying through the streets. By the bloody moon, she was a fool. She should have known by now she could not trust her instincts when dealing with this new breed of werewolf.

With several muttered curses, Alix turned and reloaded on the run, trying not to fumble silver bullets as she pulled them from her belt. They dropped into the chambers with neat little clicks, the rhythm in time with her pounding feet and thudding heart.

Twelve more bullets, but these werewolves didn't go down under anything but a perfect shot. She needed to make each of them count.

Alix turned onto the high street, leaped another roadblock, and re-entered the square, pistols raised. There were...more werewolves? Her steps faltered. Not only were there two more werewolves, there were fewer townspeople.

And the gunfire from her hidden sharpshooters had stopped.

A wave of unease ran from the base of her spine to the back of her neck. Something was wrong.

"Alix, run!"

Madame Sophie? She peeked between the bodies of two huddling villagers Alix did not recognize. Someone threw a hand over the old woman's mouth and tried to force her down, but Sophie fought back, kicking and scratching until she was dragged to the ground.

Alix turned her pistols on the closest werewolves with a snarl, but before she could pull the trigger, a bullet hit her right shoulder. The impact was like being kicked by a mule, and she staggered to one side as another struck her left thigh.

She stumbled backward, her pistols wavering. The world slowed and every detail became painfully sharp and clear as her mind fought to catch up with what her senses already realized.

Hugh had not been the only traitor. Her eyes slid over the huddled mass of villagers, noting the gleam of silver around the necks of several villagers. Breath of god, they turned on their own neighbors.

Another bullet struck, this one stealing her breath and making her stumble backward. It was a trap. They'd forced the people into the square knowing she would protect them, and used the weapons she put in their hands.

Alix bit back a sob of frustration. She failed the people, failed the Mother Superior, and Mercedes. She failed Cyrus. At least he wasn't here.

Fire erupted on her left side, burning in white-hot streaks of pain from her collarbone to her hips and making breathing deeply impossible. Not even she could live through unlimited gunfire. Perhaps this was what she deserved after years of being the harbinger of death, to die in this half-empty village, her blood making mud of the dirt. There would be no one to bury her or cry over her grave.

Another bullet hit her shoulder and she spun until her legs gave out. Darkness closed in at the edge of her vision, making the staring faces of the terrified villagers blur into a shifting mass of color. At least Cyrus wasn't here. He might still live if he stayed away.

He *had* to live.

"Cyrus!" she screamed with what little air she had left. "Cyrus run!"

The world went dark.

Her finger throbbed in time with her heartbeat, a stinging pulse that did not subside even when she stuck her thumb in her mouth. Tears ran down her cheeks as she stared at the buzzing hive with fury burning in her cheeks.

"We will never harvest any honey if you don't get to work," Maman said, kneeling beside her and smiling beneath the brim of her wide straw hat. When she noticed Alix's face, she tsked and lifted the sheer veil that covered her face. "Did a bee sting you?"

"Of course it did," she said around her thumb. "I told you I didn't want to come to the hive. I hate bees! They always sting me!"

"Let me see."

Alix's thumb slid free with a little popping sound, and she whimpered as Maman turned her hand over to examine the sting. "Did you try to take the honey without caring for the bees first?"

Alix bit her lips together and looked away. "I thought if I was fast–"

Maman laughed, which Alix thought was terribly inappropriate and heartless given her injury, and lifted her water gourd from the strap on her belt. Pulling the stopper free, she dribbled a bit of water onto the ground, stirred up a bit of mud, and scooped up a teaspoon full of the wet stuff.

"Bees are kind little souls," Maman said as she pressed the mud onto Alix's finger. It took the edge off the sting, cooling it just enough to be bearable. "They work hard and give generously. But only if you respect them first. Did you give them the offering, as I told you?"

Alix clenched her jaw and shook her head. "It takes too long," she grumbled.

The sweet scent of honey was too tempting to wait while she added the herbs and fuel to the clay pot and created the spark and nursed the little flame.

"You cannot expect a reward you have not paid the price for, my darling."

"Bees hate me, Maman. Just like everyone else. They know I want their honey and they don't want me to have any. They sting me every time!"

Maman retrieved the clay pot from the ground where Alix left it in her haste to steal a bit of honey, and began slipping fuel into the opening on the side.

"Lavender and lemon peel," she sang, "pine needles and pitch" packing her own special mixture of offerings into the tiny-ovenlike space. The familiar, whimsical song was almost as soothing as the mud drying on her finger.

Maman took the small clay pot from her pouch, slid the twine off the lid, and tipped the little coal from their hearth into the smoker. It looked like a tobacco pipe had a baby with a vase. Smoke curled from the series of holes at one end.

"The bees love the smell of lavender," she said, smelling the smoke with a long, appreciative sigh.

"Why?" Alix asked.

"Well, don't you?"

"I suppose so."

She handed Alix the smoker and said, "If you offer the smoke to the bees, they'll give you a bit of their honey."

Alix lifted her gaze from the happily smoking little pot to the uncountable swarm of bees hovering in a cloud around the hive. One stinger for every bee. She shivered, her skin crawling at the very idea.

"No they won't," she insisted, backing away. "They always sting me." Just like the villagers did, only they used words and hateful expressions. "Maybe I don't want honey that much."

She tried to give Maman the smoker, but her mother pulled the veil over her face and tucked her hands behind her back.

"Perhaps the bees don't give you their honey because they are scared you will hurt them."

"They are the ones who hurt me!"

"They have been hurt by big creatures before. Bears and cruel people break into their hives and steal too much, they take without giving back. How do the bees know you will not do the same?"

Alix paused, her brows knitted together. She never thought that the bees might be as afraid of her as she was of them.

"The smoke," Maman said, "is how we tell the bees we mean them no harm."

Alix took a few steps toward the hive, then froze. Her sting had already stopped hurting, but memories of past stings made her eyes water and her limbs tremble. She could not get that close to the hive again. Her body would not move.

If she wanted something sweet, she could wait for blackberries. She didn't need honey.

Maman bent down, rested her clever hands on Alix's shoulders, and said in a low voice, "Change your thoughts, change your behavior. Change your behavior, change your future. Just because a bee stung you in the past doesn't mean it will sting you in the future."

"Bees never sting you."

Maman frowned, then reached into the collar of her white beekeeping dress and pulled out her necklace. The winking red gem was in Alix's *earliest memories, laying against the smooth skin of her mother's chest as she knitted by the fire.*

"This," Maman said, "is my secret. It was blessed by a witch to keep me safe from bees."

Alix's eyes widened. "I knew it! I knew you had some magic!"

With a few deft motions, Maman unclasped the chain and fastened it about Alix's neck. "You have magic, too, my darling. But perhaps you need to wait a while so you can learn to trust it. And while you wait, you can use mine. Now, you know what to do?"

Alix stared at the hive and the bees dancing around it. One hand involuntarily went to the necklace, and she squeezed the pendant until her knuckles turned white, her heart thundering. "Yes," she said and took a deep breath. "I know what to do."

She took slow, careful steps toward the hive, and the low buzzing of bees filled her ears. It grew louder, sounds sharpening, becoming more rhythmic and staccato. Words solidified in the bee buzz until she thought she could understand what they said. The first trace of imagined honey was sweet on her tongue, but something was wrong with it.

It was warm, too warm.

When she pulled the top from the hive, it wasn't brimming with golden honey.

It was soaked in blood.

Alix screamed.

36

Alix

WARM, WET FLUID PATTERED against her lips in a constant drip, drip, drip. Was it raining? She tried to turn her face away but gasped in pain. Every muscle and joint burned with a fatigue deeper and hungrier than mere exhaustion. It was hollow, greedy, and demanding, sucking energy even from the marrow of her bones. Breath of god, she was ravenous.

Liquid dripped into her mouth, thick and sweet as honey, and a current of power ran through her body like a lightning strike. She stiffened, muscles clenching so hard the world went white. The rich, wet heat filled her mouth, and trickled down her dry throat, whetting a thirst so desperate she blindly lunged toward the source with a low growl, mouth open like a baby bird.

She was so empty, so tired, so damned hungry.

Alix swallowed a mouthful, then another, every nerve ending in her body lighting up with pleasure and energy. With an almost audible clinking of gears, her mind ground back into motion. This heady sensation of being alive was terribly familiar and came from only one place: blood.

Alix flung herself backward and spit, hacking up the last mouthful and blinking as her eyes watered. Disgust warred with her hunger and twisted her still-empty stomach into a knot. She wiped her mouth with both hands and coughed until her gorge rose.

"So, it is true," said a deep, smooth voice.

Alix scrambled backward until her shoulder blades hit something hard. She'd been so desperate to rid herself of the sick, wonderful flavor she had not gotten her bearings when she finally opened her eyes. But that voice...

She blinked and fought to bring the world into focus, blinking in brief flashes of recognition as her brain tried to catch up: a rough wood building, small, grey with age and exposure. A large porch of some kind. Blue sky. Mountains. A view down into a—what? A quarry? Chains.

No, manacles. Shackles locked around her wrists and set into a plate bolted onto the side of the building next to her head. Terror rose up alongside her confusion to choke her. Alix wrapped her weak fingers around the chain and flung herself away from the wall. The chains snapped tight. She could break these. They weren't that thick and they were poorly constructed, as if someone made them in a hurry.

She jerked her arms backward with a sharp, snapping motion...but nothing happened. With a cry of alarm, she pulled again, the edges of the cuffs biting into the skin of her wrists. Not so much as a crack.

"There is no use in that, dear heart. You will only hurt yourself." That deep voice, again, too smooth and sweet to be human.

Alix looked up to see the vampire looming over her, his black hood and cloak making him a shadow, even in the sunlight. His horrible, beautiful face was arranged in lines of fond amusement.

Memories came flooding back: Hugh dragging villagers from the safety of their houses, people cowering together in the square surrounded by werewolves, the silver amulets hanging on leather thongs about their necks.

Bullets tearing through her flesh.

"It was a trap," she growled. For a moment her anger was strong enough to make her forget the gnawing hunger and exhaustion. "You planted traitors in the town."

The vampire knelt so they were eye to eye. Honey-colored eyes stared at her from the depths of his hood, and when he spoke it was slow and melodious, with a casual tone that belied their respective situations. "Fighting fair against the Red Cloak would have been foolish. Your reputation precedes you after all. I merely took precautions. I have worked far too long to risk failing now."

Alix closed her eyes and fought to control her wild emotions, but it was difficult when memories of townsfolk cowering in the square dominated her mind. They'd been held hostage by their own neighbors as werewolves snapped and snarled.

How could anyone with a conscience do such a thing?

"You enthralled them," she said, her voice weak.

"No, nothing so complex as that. I promised them power. A gift I shall give them tonight. And you get to watch. Won't that be fun?"

"Power? You mean...you mean turn them into vampires?"

"So they can compete with me for food and resources? No. Even if I could control them, young vampires are too much trouble to raise." He pointed one elegantly gnarled finger between the balusters to the pit below.

The quarry had gone dry some years ago, but it was deep with steep sides and several terraced stairs where the rock was cut. On the right-hand side, in the center of a pit with fifteen-foot-high sides, stood a terrified man. Tremors ran through his body, as if simply keeping himself from fleeing in terror required every ounce of his will.

And no wonder. A werewolf circled him, yellow eyes locked on the man, strands of drool dangling from his open jaw and lolling tongue.

"No," she breathed.

Her muscles bunched as if she could leap over the edge of the platform and come to the man's defense. But she'd used every bit of her strength trying to break the chains. She could not even stand.

The vampire said, "Do not worry, dear heart. He doesn't need to be saved. He chose this, after all. Watch."

That was what he meant about power. The werewolves hadn't simply attacked villages, they infiltrated them and offered power to those willing to turn traitor and make the change. And those selfish bastards opened doors and exposed their neighbors to death and destruction.

When the werewolf attacked, the man screamed and flailed in mindless terror. His cries echoed up from the pit, bouncing off the trees until they seemed to come from everywhere at once.

Alix squeezed her eyes shut and tried to ignore the sounds, but it was impossible. The wet tearing of flesh, the piteous cries, the ecstatic growls...

A pair of cold hands, cold as a trout drawn from a mountain stream, locked around the sides of her face and forced her to turn toward the attack. Two fingers pried her eyelids open.

"Watch," he commanded. "This is where things become...interesting."

The beast lunged, flashing across the distance before the man could so much as flinch, and sank its teeth into his thigh for the second time. The high, warbling scream bounced off the quarry walls and faded into the trees, but not before the wolf shook the man like a dog shaking a hare.

The violent motion tore his flesh, leaving a gaping wound where only punctures had been. Bright red blood spurted from the injury in time with the man's panicked heartbeat. His artery was severed.

Bile burned the back of Alix's throat as the lingering taste of blood made her mouth water. The werewolf backed away, whining, its muscles tense and quivering. It wanted to finish the job.

"Impressive self-control, isn't it?" the vampire said, effecting a wistful tone. "It took quite a long time to train Remi not to kill them all. So many lost opportunities in the beginning. He is still the only werewolf who has enough control not to kill them outright."

Alix heard him and registered his meaning, but her attention was focused on the man–a man she had not noticed–running toward the violent scene with something in his hand. She squinted, trying to make out the slender shape, but it was too far away, even for her eyes.

He knelt next to the injured man, who reached out and clung to him with both hands, and jabbed the object at the man's uninjured leg.

"A syringe?" she asked without thinking.

"You recognize it?" Why did he sound pleased about that? "Yes, it is. Filled with an alchemical form of colloidal silver mixed with trace amounts of aconite. It must be administered instants before the change, you see, so the magic learns to fight the silver and attenuate the wolfs-bane."

The man shook uncontrollably and fell to the side clutching the wound in both hands.

"But the silver should stop the change," Alix said, remembering the knife vibrating in her hand as Père Henri's heart struggled to change despite the silver. The magic hadn't been able to overcome the blade.

"It does if the dose is too high. But the right amount initiates a form of magical phagocytosis. That is, it trains the body to attack and destroy the silver. I borrowed the idea from a promising young scientist named Metchnikoff."

Alix blinked and shook her head. The world swam in a wavy, blurry haze, and she had to brace herself on both hands not to tip over.

The friendly, educational tone of the vampires's conversation made him sound like a professor or priest, not a murderous monster. Listening to him speak was more surreal than the twisting colors of the world around her.

Exhaustion rose up like fog on a dark night, making everything soft and hazy. Her eyes rolled back and her elbows gave out.

"No, not yet," he said, and pressed the cool lip of a ceramic cup against her mouth. The scent of blood made her eyes pop open and saliva pool around her tongue. Her throat was achingly dry and Alix had to lock her teeth against the violent longing to suck in great mouthfuls.

She turned away and held her breath against the sweet, coppery scent.

He took her face in one large hand, fingers and thumb digging into her jaw muscles and forcing her mouth open. Not since she was nine years old had Alix been at the mercy of anyone stronger than she. That was more frightening than the pain. She whimpered and thrashed against his hold but she had as much chance as a kitten fighting a hawk.

"Keeping you alive long enough for your body to heal has been nearly as difficult as creating these new werewolves," he complained. "I had to let your magic rob your body of its resources trying to heal you while giving you enough blood to keep you alive, but not enough to allow you to regain strength. A delicate balance, particularly after I removed the bullets.

"Your body needs sustenance. Right now, it is eating itself. Most vampires die when this happens. Did you know that? Your human side is keeping you alive, if barely. You are stronger that way than we are."

He released her.

She spit and coughed, trying to retch the blood back up, but her body hoarded it and ran the energy through her veins like a river in flood. Satisfied, the vampire turned away from her and back to the spectacle in the quarry. Another man, this one tall and slender with pointed elf ears, was escorted–or driven–to the pit by a werewolf.

"Brilliant, is it not? They become harder to kill if they survive the change, and build some tolerance to silver, as well. It is not perfect, not yet. Which is why I need more subjects. But I may be only a few more test groups from perfecting the process."

Screams, thrashing, growls and running feet. Alix tried to look away, but could not drag her eyes from the horror of it. The process was a crude, violent mockery of science, nothing like the methodical procedures of the Sisters, who experimented year after year, looking for a cure.

The body was dragged out of the pit, and another man–Hugh–was escorted into it. Alix thrashed against her chains, but her struggles were too weak to matter.

The vampire's laugh sounded like wind through a graveyard, in-human and full of the stink of death. "You cannot save them. Your magic has cannibalized your body to heal those wounds. Your body is eating itself slowly, Alix La Rouge. It will take you days and weeks to starve. You will be far too weak to help anyone. Unless, of course, you take what I will give you."

"I will accept nothing from you," she snarled.

He ran cold fingertips down her cheek. "Oh, I think you will. It will be instinctive, at that point. I mean to drive you quite mad, you see. That, or to kill you. But I would much rather keep you alive and by my side. It is time for monsters to take their proper place in this world, and you have been the most prolific monster in the last several hundred years. No one has killed more than you. Not even me."

Sickness that had nothing to do with the blood made Alix's throat tighten. She tried to swallow, but her throat was gummy and thick. Tears spilled freely down her cheeks.

Footsteps, punctuated by grunts of pain and a racing heart, approached. One pair of feet thumped across the deck, and another pair dragged on the wood.

A burly woman with a silver pendant around her neck dragged the first wounded man toward them. A blood trail left red streaks on the wood behind them.

"He is still alive, my lord," she said, letting the injured man crumple to the deck. "Strong, this one."

"We shall see," the vampire said, kneeling.

He examined the wound, then took the man by his shoulders and said, "Look at me."

The man's face was waxy and grey, his eyelids purple. When he opened them, his eyes were dazed but he managed to focus on the vampire. The lines of pain carved deep into his face eased, like prints in the sand when a wave washes them away.

A contented expression settled in place, and his shoulders relaxed. He fell limp into the vampire's arms.

"There's a good boy," the vampire said.

He pulled a syringe from a cloak pocket and jabbed it through the man's clothes at the shoulder, pressing a plunger down. More silver? He replaced the syringe and removed a pendant, the twin of the one hanging around the woman's neck, and slid it over the man's head almost gently.

"As inside, so outside," he said. Then flicked his fingers at the woman. "Find somewhere for the body. Unless—" He turned to Alix, his eyes glittering. "Unless you'd like a drink?"

She turned away and let her head hang on her shoulders. The suggestion had made her mouth water, and she hated herself for it.

"Don't expect me to help with your experiment," she said, infusing as much disgust as she could into the word.

He laughed. "Oh, you will, dear heart. In fact, you already have. You are, after all, my most successful experiment."

She turned her head enough that her loose hair fell away from her face, letting her glare at him between lank strands. A spiteful curse perched on the tip of her tongue, but she didn't have the strength to let it fly. Instead, she shook her head.

The vampire eased forward, never taking his eyes off hers, until he captured her face in both hands and raised her chin. "Yes, dear one. You are stronger than the rest. I believe you are destined for great things. Of all my children, you were the only one born alive."

37

Partners

Cyrus

By the time his bones healed enough to run, it was too late. There were far more werewolves than he could fight on his own, and they herded the townspeople out of the village and force-marched them up the mountainside.

The track was wide and sturdy, dug deep by years of heavy traffic from loaded wagons. But Cyrus avoided the road, keeping to the undergrowth and using every shadow and creaking branch to disguise his movement despite the desperate tension in every muscle urging him to run.

The pack was forced to walk at human speed rather than the comfortable lope of a wolf, which meant Cyrus's progress was torturously slow. He wanted to charge up the hill, tear the monsters apart, and make certain Alix was safe.

Instead, he stayed far enough behind not to alert the wolves, peering at them between breaks in the foliage. Now and then he caught flashes of Alix's red cloak as a dark figure–he could not determine if it was the vampire or someone else–carried her limp body up the hill.

Never in his long life had stealth required more patience or been harder to come by. Her blood perfumed every breeze, lighter and sweeter than that of a regular human. Somewhere along the way, he'd forgotten to care about that. She was simply Alix, and that was all that mattered.

And right now she could be dead and he wouldn't know it. The uncertainty turned every stealthy step into an exercise in self-control.

He may be able to rescue her now if he was willing to sacrifice the villagers. May the moon forgive him, he wanted to. He could creep in, scoop Alix up, and run her out of the mountains like he had after she'd been shot. Of course, he'd have to set his wolf free to accomplish it, something he'd never allowed himself to do.

Mortals were breakable, after all, and it was his job to protect their lives, not end them. Unfortunately, even if he betrayed everything he believed in to save her, there were still too many werewolves and humans with guns to guarantee success.

If he wanted to rescue Alix, he was going to have to be smart and patient, pick the enemy apart one by one until a manageable number remained. So, Cyrus maintained his distance and his discipline, even if he only held on by the tips of his claws.

They crested a rise that skirted the right flank of the mountains to the west, following a long spur that angled back toward the peak. The road curved to the right, guarded by evergreens on either side, then opened up to a long bare slope of exposed rock and scrubby vegetation.

Several weathered buildings with wooden shingles stood butted up to an outcrop of grey stone. Aspens, still ragged from the storm, dotted with open hillside. Beyond that, a great swath of the mountain had been cut away in descending strips, like giant stairs leading into the earth. A quarry? No wonder the tracks on the dirt road were dug so deeply.

Villecourbé must have been built to house the miners. No wonder the town appeared so prosperous while it died slowly. It had been built for an industry that no longer existed. And when desperate people were given a chance at power...could he really blame them?

Yes. Yes, he bloody well could.

Cyrus sank down on his haunches behind a shrub growing out of the crack in a cart-sized boulder, and settled in to watch. So long as the wind remained in the north, his scent shouldn't alert the patrolling beasts.

Werewolves herded villagers into the largest of the buildings, and two took up station outside the only doors in and out. Four men wearing silver amulets around their necks broke away and followed a footpath out of the village toward the quarry.

And the dark-cloaked figure carried Alix to the smallest of the three structures. He climbed a set of stairs that led to a balcony of sorts, and lay her on the rough wood planks. The balusters made seeing details from that distance difficult, but the metallic snap of chains locking in place was unmistakable.

His jaw locked against the growl bubbling in his throat.

The dark cloaked figure entered the building and returned seconds later, leading a weakly struggling young man. Judging by his height and slender form, he could not be more than fifteen years old, and his pale skin was chalk-white with fear.

The boy leaned back and away from the iron grip around his wrist but could do nothing to stop the forward momentum. Dark Cloak stopped, turned on the boy, and locked eyes with him. His struggles ceased and his muscles went slack, body swaying like an aspen in the breeze.

Dark Cloak was the vampire, then. And he'd just enthralled the boy. Cyrus turned his face away as the boy released a muffled scream of shock, followed by a moan of ecstasy. A vampire bite was laced with potent magic.

Old vampires who were crafty and powerful enough to live in large cities like Paris and Prague were rumored to have dozens of thralls. They were addicted to the vampire's bite and willingly returned month after month to be fed upon.

Some found the experience so addicting, they willingly killed themselves being fed upon too often.

His stomach threatened revolt. Vampires were among the most abhorrent monsters. As much as he hated werewolves for corrupting the moon's magic, vampires were worse. They were anathema, parasites who fed on the source of life to sustain death.

In his memory, greasy smoke trails rose into a grey sky, and his ears buzzed with the silence that blanketed the ruins of a home where laughter and friendly chat once filled the air.

The only sound was his claws ripping at the earth to dig a grave deep enough to hold them all.

He'd only managed to catch and kill a very few vampires over the years. All had been young and foolish. He suspected the Dark Cloak was neither. After nearly a minute, the dull thud of a body hitting the ground made a shiver of disgust run up Cyrus's legs.

He chanced a glance, tilting his head to see between the balusters that lined the balcony, but saw only the fragmented forms of Alix and the Dark Cloak. That, and the limp hand and arm of the young man lying prone. Cyrus knew enough of death to recognize a corpse.

What was the vampire doing to Alix? He needed a better view. Sick at his helplessness, he slunk into the trees and looked for a better position.

He was getting Alix out of here and away from that monster no matter what it cost.

From his position atop the rise behind the quarry, Cyrus watched the werewolves kill three men and drag their bodies back to, what he assumed, was the overseer's cabin.

The werewolves prowled the outskirts of the operation in twenty-minute rotations, and the mortals wearing silver amulets stayed close to the buildings, rifles glowing orange when they caught the late evening light. If the pattern held, Cyrus would start killing them tonight.

Once or twice Alix's voice, angry and cutting, floated toward him on the breeze.

She was still alive and fighting. And if he was quick and quiet tonight, she'd remain that way.

Alix

Her heart pounded hard enough to crack her breastbone and a thousand disconnected thoughts whirled through her mind so fast it made her dizzy. She must have misunderstood him. After all, how could she hear anything clearly over the blood rushing in her ears?

In a trembling voice, she demanded, "What did you say?"

The vampire's lips curled in an expression approximating a smile. "Do not pretend you didn't hear me, Daughter."

Pain sat like an elephant on her ribcage, crushing her breath out in a broken moan. She bit the sound back and clenched her teeth. No. He was lying, trying to weaken her, to break her mind. Vampires loved to seduce their prey, to feed on their pain as much as their blood.

Alix refused to give him that pleasure. She used what strength of will she had left to steel her mind and spat, "You are a liar."

"Of course I am. But I have no reason to lie about this. I am rather proud of you, in fact. You became a competent killer on your own. Do you know how long it took me to turn these creatures into worthy tools?" He gestured toward the prowling wolves patrolling the edge of the quarry. "They are faster than humans. Stronger. They live longer. But for a hundred years, I could not find a way to let them keep their minds intact."

"Why? Why would you even desire such a thing?"

He ignored her question and pointed to a human male being hauled into the pit. "Now, look at them."

The man shook with fear as his eyes darted from side to side, searching for an escape. His fingers dug into the fabric of his shirt as he backed away.

"Mortals are cowardly, weak, and short-lived. They are greedy, selfish, and stupid. They will betray everything they claim to hold dear, even risk death, for a chance to inherit power."

The werewolf lunged, the sound of its jaws snapping echoing up from the depths. The man screamed.

Mouth twisted in disdain, golden eyes focused on the macabre tableau, the vampire said, "Why should they control this world?"

"Werewolves are no better," she forced herself to say, but the words tasted like ash in her mouth.

He examined her face, watching her expressions the way a hunter watches a deer, waiting for it to step out of the brush for a clean shot. "Not even you believe that, dear heart. You have seen enough of mortal behavior to know the truth. Werewolves, at least, have the excuse of the magic corrupting their minds. What excuse do mortals have for wars and murders and a thousand petty cruelties?"

Alix closed her eyes tight and clenched her fists. Truth burned with a clear, bright pain that lies could never replicate.

"Werewolves do nothing but what their nature demanded of them and what the magic compels. But the children who threw rocks at you did so merely because you were different. The villagers who chased you and your mother into the forest, leaving you to starve, did so because they were superstitious and fearful."

Every word was like a burning arrow shot directly into her soul. Visions of her youth flashed across her mind, hot and sharp as the rocks that struck her. How did he know these things? Could he read her mind?

He mistook her silence for agreement. "Do you know how many mortals are killed by beasts of burden? Horses are responsible for more deaths than any ten bears, wolves, or tigers. But mortals continue to employ them because they are useful, once they are broken. Werewolves are also useful, once they've been improved."

"Making them more capable of murder is not an improvement," she said, but her heart wasn't in the argument. Too many emotions and questions warred within her, emotions she could not examine and questions she did not dare to ask.

"Of course it is. Mortals have no more right to control this world than monsters. And if it were not for their technology, they would still be huddling in caves around fires, afraid of the creatures that lurked in the dark."

"The way the deer fears the wolf?" Sarcasm and spite made her voice sharp.

"You think I aim to create a world filled with fear, uncivilized as the forest? No, dear heart. I am content with a gentler world than that. I want the mortals to see us for what we truly are: shepherds for the sheep. Let them live under our guidance and protection, and be used for our purposes when nature demands it."

A cold chill slid down Alix's spine. The hunger of a predator she understood. But this plan of benevolent murder? To shepherd mortals and cull them, like sheep to slaughter? It required the sick, cold calculation of a creature without emotion or empathy. In a way, the idea was more horrible than simply hunting and killing.

He touched her cheek with cold fingers and lifted her chin, forcing her to look into his face as the sound of another body being dragged onto the balcony—and the sweet scent of fresh blood—made her stomach clench with need. "I will create this world, a world where monsters no longer live in fear, crouched at the edges in the dark. We will be lords of this world. And you will be at my side to see it."

Cyrus

The first werewolf died before moonrise. He stalked it to the edge of the territory they protected and waited in the shadows. These wolves were far younger and less experienced than he, and they could not maintain their transformation for as long.

The signs of impending failure screamed at him across the distance: uncontrollable shivering as it tried to keep hold of the magic, drooling and rolling eyes. All he had to do was wait. Its gait became slower, its balance more tenuous, until at last the werewolf broke.

It whined and twisted, spine curling as its bones began to shift for the transformation. Most werewolves were safely in dens or homes when they shifted, having only spent hours or, more rarely, a day, in their beast form. This wolf had been pushed to its limit, and its body required restoration.

Shifting was the most vulnerable time for these creatures. Which made it the perfect time to attack. The beast did not even notice Cyrus as he stalked forward. After what they had done in the village, it did not trouble him overmuch that the creature was half in its mortal form when he attacked.

That only made the kill faster.

Every time Alix cried out, he cared less about the blood that stained his fur or the sour flavor of it in his mouth.

One down.

Cyrus crept soundlessly into the woods to hunt for the next.

Alix

The moon smiled benevolently down at her, broad-faced and silent. Alix stared at it for a long time before she realized she was awake. A howl—in warning, she thought, rent the night air. Seconds later the stink of werewolf fur made her wrinkle her nose, though she did not dare to shift her body enough to see. The soft thump of heavy footfalls made her weak muscles tense to roll away, but she forced herself to lie still.

Electricity filled the air, followed by the muffled crunching and popping of bones and muscles shifting. These transformations were nothing like the elegant shimmer Cyrus underwent when he changed forms.

She pictured him in her mind, upright and golden, as heatwaves formed around his body, leaving a tawny wolf in his place. Her heartbeat slowed, and she took a slow, secret breath.

"Another body," a woman's voice said breathlessly. "One of the young ones. That is three, tonight."

The vampire swore. "Tighten the patrols."

"I have done so, my lord."

Two swift steps and the vampire loomed over her, blocking out the moon and making her vision of Cyrus waver and disappear. He lifted her by the front of her cloak and said, "Who is this creature that hunts with you?"

Did she have anything to lose by speaking his name? Perhaps Cyrus's people had weaknesses she wasn't aware of. There was no way to know if his name would give the vampire an advantage over him, so Alix only smiled.

The vampire's lip curled, and he dropped her. Turning to the naked woman he said, "Bring me one of the children."

38

Partners

Alix

THE DWARVEN BOY WAS no more than six years old, small and sturdy, with a shock of red hair and freckles. Instead of cowering in fear, he glared at the woman who dragged him up the stairs. But Alix's heart dropped into her stomach.

The vampire took the boy's arm from the woman and hauled him toward where Alix slumped against the wall of the building. He may have looked fierce, but his little heart beat like a hummingbird's.

"What is the name of the creature who hunts with you?" the vampire demanded.

Alix pressed trembling lips together. Cyrus was the only hope of escape, not only for her—unless she pulled off some kind of miracle in her weakened state—but for every hostage in that building.

The vampire tightened his grip on the boy's wrist, and he winced, his skin turning white with pain. "What. Is. His. Name?"

Alix closed her eyes against the sight and locked her jaw, her fingers curled so tightly into fists it felt as if her knuckles would break through her skin.

A soft, wet tearing sound and a gasp of surprised pain. The scent of fresh blood was so close it made her mouth water. Her eyes flew open with sick horror to see the boy's wrist mere inches from her face, blood dripping from a clean set of teeth marks.

He began to cry, all his defiance melting beneath the heat of pain and fear. Tears filled Alix's eyes—tears of guilt, of disgust that she had to swallow back the spit that filled her mouth at the scent of his blood—but she blinked them away.

"What is his name, daughter?"

Alix swallowed, her throat working as the muscles had to fight back the words clamoring to escape. Cyrus was their one hope, the most likely savior. She had to protect him. The boy's lips trembled even as he hung, almost limp, from the pleasure of the vampire's bite.

"You will release the boy and return him to his family with no further harm," she rasped.

One corner of the vampire's mouth curled. "I swear it."

The words pressed up her throat and through her lips, scraping her mouth raw. She could only pray the name would mean nothing to him as she said, "Cyrus Campbell."

The vampire stood frozen for several infinite heartbeats. Then, with almost hypnotic slowness, he gave the boy back to the naked woman. "Return him unharmed, and tighten the patrols."

She obeyed without a word. A tear slipped down Alix's cheek.

Cyrus

He could tell by the way the creature moved, by its size and the way it scented the air, that it was older and more competent than the others he killed that night.

Alix had been silent for several hours. He tried not to think of what that might mean as he stalked the patrolling wolf.

The beast knew he was there. Hackles rose along its spine as it lifted its nose to the breeze. He needed to end this fight quickly.

Alix

The vampire was silent for so long Alix wondered whether it was still conscious. She closed her eyes and let her head fall back against the wood, pulling in a shaky breath. Her muscles were barely strong enough to keep her upright and her stomach was so hollow it threatened to collapse in on itself.

If she did not eat something, and soon, her body would devour her muscles and leave her nothing to fight back with.

"Campbell," the vampire muttered. "I thought I killed them all."

Alix's eyes flew open. "What?"

A howl of mixed pain and fury rose into the night. The werewolves nearby raised their heads, ears pricked, then bolted toward the sound. It cut off as abruptly as it began. A werewolf was dead.

Cyrus.

Cyrus

He shifted to his mortal form, shed his bloody clothes, and bolted through the trees toward a stream he crossed earlier that night. He smelled different as a mortal. This may be enough to throw them off his trail.

The water stung his skin and made his feet numb, but he followed the stream up the mountainside long enough to mask his scent before shifting again. His sensitive ears picked up no trace of pursuing wolves, but his gut told him they weren't far behind.

A pine tree ahead stood at least a dozen feet taller than its neighbors, and the lowest branch was low enough for his purpose. He picked up speed and launched himself at the tree, shifting mid-leap and hitting the branch in his human form.

The impact drove the air from his lungs and made a wave of dizziness roll over him, but he clung to the rough bark with both hands and pulled. Scrapes burned the skin of his stomach, but nothing drew blood.

Cyrus eased onto the limb and began climbing as werewolves darted through the forest beneath him.

Alix

Every inch of exposed skin stung, and she barely had the strength to lift her arms far enough to cover her head. When he'd taken her cloak and the rest of her clothes, leaving her in nothing but her torn chemise, the vampire had said, "It does not need to be this way, daughter. Join me now and I will not have to break you."

"No."

He'd sighed, purely for the drama of it, she was certain. "What do you owe these mortals? What have they ever done to make this world a welcoming place for you?"

Alix turned her face away and held onto her chain with both hands as he tore the clothing off her body. Now the sun beat down with unrelenting fury, and her skin was red and tender. There was no place to hide.

He had forced drops of blood into her mouth just before dawn. She fought back, but it was no use. All she could do now was try not to wonder where the blood came from. It crusted the side of her face, and she didn't bother wasting strength to wipe it away.

The vampire merely stood and watched, waiting.

Now and then, one of the werewolves dragged a mauled villager onto the balcony. They were all dirty and bloody, their faces drawn in pain with lines bracketing their mouths. The vampire would peel back their eyelids to check their pupils, look at the color of their gums, and give them another injection.

Or not.

The ones who did not get injections always died. Her mind was too fuzzy to wonder whether that was because they would not survive the change, or if he did not wish them to.

Blisters rose on her skin, stinging and weeping when they broke. Her lips were so dry they cracked and bled. She ran her tongue along the cracks, hungry for even a small bit of moisture.

###

"It is one wolf!" the vampire roared. "Find him!"

Alix's eyes fluttered open. How long had she been asleep? Hours? Days? Time was a blur, a hazy stream punctuated by screaming mortals, echoing howls, burning sun, and memories that plagued her even while awake.

What was wakefulness, anyway? Telling the difference between awake and asleep was getting harder.

Blood. The scent pulled at her like the tide to the moon, pulled enough to make her roll toward it as her mouth watered and her stomach cramped with stabbing pain.

She squinted against the sunlight to see the dark shape of the vampire dragging a limp form behind him. Dark hair matted with dirt and dried blood.

Hugh.

The vampire dropped him at her feet and the big blacksmith hit the boards with a pained cry.

"The time has come, dear heart. I thought he would be easiest for your first time."

Alix blinked, fighting back the hunger that threatened to overwhelm her. It clawed up her throat and sent desperation coiling in sick waves through her guts. The hot, moist flutter of his terrified heart was—

"No."

The vampire ignored her rasping denial, grabbed Hugh by the back of his neck, and dragged his body closer, until his scent overpowered every conscious thought.

"He betrayed you," the vampire purred in her ear. "He betrayed his neighbors. He is not strong enough to complete the change, and death is coming for him. Why not give him justice as well?"

He did deserve to die. She remembered him blocking the doorway, forcing his neighbors to stand exposed in the street. She imagined him telling them all was safe so they would unbar the door.

A growl rumbled in her chest and she licked her lips even as she turned her face away.

"I cannot continue feeding you like a babe with my own blood," the vampire said. "And if you don't feed soon, you will die."

"Then I'll die."

Sweetness bloomed in the air and her body jerked in convulsive desire. An iron grip locked on the back of her neck and twisted her upper body until her nose was inches away from Hugh's throat.

A neat cut bled just below the corner of his jaw, and clean runnels of life-giving fluid left red streaks down the column of his throat. Inches away. So close.

If she fed from Hugh, would it strengthen her enough to fight back? To rip the bolted plate from the wall of the building and use it to crush the vampire? She pushed back against his hand, away from Hugh's throat, her muscles quivering under the strain.

"Come, dear heart," the vampire said. "You need to be strong. And this traitor must die."

"No," Hugh moaned. "No, *please*."

Fury turned her small, dark world into a red haze. Where were his pleas when he sacrificed his neighbors to the werewolves in exchange for power? What about Claude and Madame Sophie? The poor dwarven boy who bled on this deck? Where were his pleas for them?

"Kill him," the vampire whispered. "He deserves it."

He smelled so good, so damnably, gut-wrenchingly desirable.

The vampire tightened his grip on her neck and smashed her face against Hugh's throat. His blood smeared her nose and cheek, and before she could make any conscious decision, she was swallowing great mouthfuls of warm, wet liquid that lit up every nerve ending from the top of her head to the soles of her feet.

The world came to brilliant life, the darkness slipped away, and her thoughts became sharp as the blade of her silver knife. Her fingers dug into the resisting flesh of Hugh's shoulders as she drew swallow after swallow, a constant purr of pleasure rumbling in her chest.

Why had she denied herself this for so long? Her body felt strong, alive. She could—her meal was torn from her grasp and flung across the balcony to land in a limp heap.

For a moment, Alix sat stunned, blood running from the sides of her mouth down her throat to stain the torn white chemise. Her skin no longer burned, and the night was nearly as clear as day.

The vampire crouched in front of her with a satisfied smile on his terribly beautiful face. "Not too much," he warned, then reached out to dab at her lip with a handkerchief.

Alix flinched away, her eyes wide with horror. No heartbeat came from the limp body on the floorboards.

"What have you done?" she choked.

"Helped you take the first step to become who you were meant to be."

The blacksmith was dead. "I killed him."

"You did."

"Oh god, I *killed* him."

"Which god?" the vampire asked. "I don't believe any of them are interested. Nor would they care about a waste of flesh like him. He served his purpose."

Alix threw herself backward with blood-fueled strength and yanked on the chain with all her might, planting her heels on the wood and wrenching on the shackles with the force of her whole body.

A bolt popped free just before the vampire tackled her, slamming her to the ground with a huff of expelled air and pinning her wrists to the ground. "You are strong, daughter, and even from such a small bit of weak human blood. Just imagine what you could do with a steady diet of richer blood?"

She writhed and bucked, desperate to free herself, but he was too strong.

"You are not ready for this fight. When you are, I will teach you what it means to be a vampire. But not yet. First, you must help me catch a werewolf."

"I will not help you do anything!"

"But you already have. You've proven my experiment a success. And you've killed Hugh for me. Does the flavor of his blood not linger in your mouth? The power of it run through your veins?"

A weak sob escaped her lips. After three hundred years of fighting her instincts, of trying to prove to herself and the world she was more than her blood destined her to be...she'd failed.

She was a monster.

When the vampire stood, Alix did not even try to stand or fight. The steady gaze of the waning moon fell upon her where she lay, alone and empty, with blood on her hands.

Alix curled into a ball, wrapped her arms around her knees, and cried.

Cyrus

He waited till long after the sound of hushed footfalls faded into silence. Waited for the crickets and birds to feel safe enough to resume their nightly symphony.

When nothing more than dirt and leaves perfumed the forest air, Cyrus stood, balancing on the branch he'd used for shelter, and surveyed the forest.

They'd lost his scent, searched the forest for half a mile in every direction, and dispersed. He still had at least two hours of moonlight left, and though he'd had almost no sleep in the last three days, he could not stop now.

The breeze picked up, ruffling the pine needles and making the sharp, resinous scent of pitch stick in his nostrils. The stuff was stuck to his hands, feet, and stomach. Such was the price of sheltering in a pine tree.

But the breeze carried with it another sound, something soft, and heartbreaking. He knew that sound down to his very bones. It was the sound Alix made when she cried in his arms, believing herself a monster.

It was the sound she made the night he'd fallen in love with her.

She was still alive. And she was breaking.

39

Partners

Alix

SOMETIME DURING THE NIGHT, the vampire had carried her down to the quarry and chained her to a bolt as thick as her forearm. It was mere steps away from a sheer drop into the deepest part of the pit, where men had been mauled...when? Days before?

The circular ring at the end of the chain meant it had likely been used at some point to lower supplies into the pit. Now it was used to secure a half-vampire monster. She could not find the will even to fight back.

Bare stone sucked the warmth from her body, and Alix lay shivering as the vampire built a bonfire a dozen steps away, too far to feel its warmth. The sun rose pink above the mountaintop by the time it was done. Villagers were marched out of the bunkhouse to stand in a line along the edge of the balcony, leaning over the rail to watch as the remaining men, five that Alix counted, began placing a series of blocks into the quickly developing coals.

The vampire directed the affair until he deemed everything in order, then he crouched next to her as the sky turned a vibrant shade of blue and the last morning clouds burned away.

He pushed the dark hood off and lifted his face to the diffuse morning light, pulling in a deep breath through his nostrils. "Most vampires never live long enough to rejoin the sunlit world. Did you know that? They are killed, either by other vampires or by hunters like yourself. It was my hunger for the sun that started all this." He gestured to the mortals bent over the fire, the few remaining werewolves, and the cowering villagers.

"Quite a legacy," she said, lacing the words with as much sarcastic acid as she could muster.

He was unfazed. "More than you realize. Hundreds of years of labor. It began with destroying the last of the clan werewolves. Being chosen by the moon provided them far more power, enough to kill young vampires with relative ease. They were too resistant to change to see the benefit of my vision, too committed to protecting mortals even though their people were killed by hunters as indiscriminately as mine."

A wave of guilt made Alix want to sink into the earth. They were killed by hunters like her.

"So, they had to be removed. I thought I succeeded. I have encountered a few random moon children since then, those who have discovered the old rites and offered their offspring to the moon. But none of the old blood. Not until now. He is quite determined to save you, do you know that? Seven of my wolves have been killed."

His tone was conversational, but there was a sharp edge beneath the words. With a quick jerk, he pulled Alix to her feet by the chain connecting her wrists, making the metal bite deep enough to send rivulets of blood running down to her fingertips.

"Bring the pole," he said to someone over her shoulder.

Two humans with silver amulets around their necks carried a log some fifteen feet long between them. They slid one end into a post hole, then stood the log on its end. Like a stake.

"That will end soon, however. And we can resume our steady march of progress. That is a good line, isn't it? Cannot remember where I heard it, but it has stuck with me."

As he spoke, he pulled her backward, toward the pole, and his plan made itself clear in a burst of crystalline clarity. Alix twisted away, desperation lending strength and speed to her atrophied muscles. But the vampire was too fast.

He caught the chain and jerked her off her feet. Alix hit the ground, her head bouncing off an exposed rock hard enough to send stars whirling across her vision. By the time the world resolved itself, she stood with her arms above her head, chained to the pole with three thick iron bands.

"No!" she screamed, pulling and grunting as iron cut into her skin, but the metal would not budge. He was going to use her as a lure to capture Cyrus.

Cyrus

The scream echoed off the trees and stopped his heart.

Alix.

That was not a scream of anger or defiance but of pain. Cyrus hurtled through the trees, barely seeing where he was going as ferns and tree trunks flashed by in a blur. He skidded to a stop on a promontory that jutted out of the mountainside just far enough for a view of the camp.

He found the outcrop the night before and had used it to check on her several times during the intervening hours. He scanned the buildings but saw only rows of villagers standing along the rail of the balcony, holding tight to the balustrade as guns were pointed at their backs.

Where was Alix? His eyes were not so keen as hers but he should still be able to see...

A bright spot of white caught his eye, and he stopped breathing. They held her chained to a pole near the deepest quarry pit, her chemise stained with dirt and...blood.

Blood smeared her face and neck, and bruises bloomed along her bare arms. Why hadn't she healed? What had they done to her? He swallowed the growl threatening to rumble up his throat.

He could not save her if the werewolves caught him.

But the sight of her exposed and vulnerable, imprisoned like a—he pulled in a deep, calming breath. He needed to carry out his plan, to finish picking off the werewolves so he had a chance of freeing her.

Turning his face away and padding back into the forest was the hardest thing he could remember doing.

"Campbell!"

The deep voice resonated off the mountain like a tuning fork, and every hair on Cyrus's back stood on end. He crouched, taking shelter in the shifting shade of a gorse bush, and peered down the mountainside through its branches.

"Campbell!" the voice called again. It was the vampire. It stood next to Alix, and sunlight gleamed off a silver blade in his right hand.

Alix

The vampire leaned in, resting his elbow on the wood near her head as if it were a doorframe and they were having an intimate conversation.

"When I began experimenting with creating half-vampires," he said, his voice low enough not to carry, "I wasn't certain if it could be done. Oh, there were rumors, of course, but those were mostly fear and superstition.

"So far as I know, except for you, it has never been accomplished. Mortal women never lived through copulation. Their bodies were too weak. It required quite a bit of training on my part. I was forced to curtail my own pleasure to merely keep them alive. And when the women did catch, the pregnancy would kill them, or the child was born dead. I had nearly given up when I found your mother."

He hooked a finger beneath the chain around her neck and pulled until the pendant popped free and the stone lay on her chest. The sun cleared the mountaintops and hit her full in the face, making the blood-red gem glow.

"She was strong," he said with a semblance of affection, "and more determined than the others. I cared for her during the pregnancy, monitoring her health and your growth very closely, keeping detailed notes. But your mother was cleverer than the others had been, and ten months is a long time to remain vigilant.

"She managed to subvert one of my guards, who helped her escape. I found you both, of course. It wasn't difficult to follow the trail of a lone woman no village would accept. I waited and I watched. Your mother truly was an extraordinary mortal, you know. Far softer on you than I would have liked, but much better equipped to raise a half-human than I."

He considered the blade for a moment, plucking the edge with a fingernail. It made a dull ringing noise. "This is very well made. And sharp. I took the trouble of removing the aconite. I hope you don't mind."

Then he pressed the edge against her shoulder and ran a long, deep cut down her arm to her elbow. Alix screamed.

Cyrus

The sound of her pain tore through him like shards of glass.

Knowing what the vampire meant to do did not stop Cyrus from turning toward the work camp and running with every ounce of speed he could force from his overworked muscles. When he was halfway to the camp, she screamed again.

Alix

"You were much stronger than I expected," he said, trailing one finger through the blood dripping down her arm. The cut had already begun to heal, though far too slowly, but the pain still made the limb pulse and burn.

"Unless I took you from your mother, I had no way to test your strength. And it was useless taking you unless you were strong enough to fulfill my purpose. And so, I was at a standstill, cursed merely to watch.

"Then the old woman started protecting you both. She was clever, planted all the right herbs, and protected her threshold. I was never able to get close to you, so long as she was there. Until that hapless werewolf appeared, anyway."

He trailed the tip of the knife across her collarbones from one side to the other, absently sucking her blood off one finger. "When you killed the old woman for me, I knew it was time. Until the bloody hunter found you. I crossed paths with that one before. It wasn't worth the fight, not when I could simply wait him out. Hmm." He tapped the tip of the knife against his lips as he considered her chest, then rested the cold metal against her skin just beneath her left collarbone. "How about here? If we are going to give you scars, they may as well be aesthetic."

Alix gritted her teeth against the scream. She refused to be a tool to draw Cyrus to his death. But the sound forced past her lips anyway.

She would heal. The wound would require more of her body's resources to restore itself, and she would be weak again, but she would heal. She repeated that to herself as the vampire considered where to place the next cut.

"I cannot say I regret letting the hunters have you," he continued in a conversational tone. "After all, they trained you well. Your skill surpasses any common hunter, and you have more successful kills than—well, anyone. You've made yourself quite a valuable resource.

"Unfortunately, you also made yourself difficult to track, and I had my experiments to see to. That made capturing you the most efficient path forward. I wasn't certain it was you tracking me, of course. Not until I saw your mother's jewel last night." He flicked a finger at her chest. "That is when I knew for certain. I will never forget the way it winked against her throat when I took her, like a drop of blood in the moonlight. I believe her fiancé gave it to her. Not that it did the poor soul any good. She was thoroughly ruined when I finished with her."

He brushed her tangled hair from her face the way one might wipe dust from an interesting statue. "You look a great deal like her, you know.

Your slender nose, the curve of your lips. Everything except your eyes. Those are mine."

Another cut, this along the line of her jaw as he held her face in place with one hand. She couldn't have fought him even if she had the strength. Alix stood locked in place with chains, bleeding from several cuts, her tears mixing with blood.

White spots swam before her eyes and memories rolled through her mind like summer storms breaking against the mountainside. Maman curled in her bed, crying in the night when she thought Alix was asleep. The scars on Maman's chest and belly when the two of them washed with hot water from the kettle, deeper and more ragged than the stretching marks on her belly.

Haggard lines beneath her eyes and bracketing her mouth when they fled yet another village in the dead of night. Lines of worry between her brows when she treated Alix's blistered sunburns with lavender oil. The indomitable determination in her eyes when she started building their next life from scratch.

Every blurred memory of her strength and sacrifice came back to haunt Alix in a rush, clobbering her with the truth of what her mother had done to care for the child of a monster, the offspring of an evil creature that forced itself upon her.

A high-pitched keen came from somewhere in the vicinity of her chest, just below the spot where her mother's jewel rested against her breast.

She could no longer hide behind her weakened body or the lie that if she protected mortals, she was somehow less of a monster. She could not earn forgiveness or redeem something that had been spoiled from the start.

Darkness closed around her, threatening the edges of her vision.

"Ah, at last. There he is."

The vampire's eyes—her father's eyes—swept past her just as she heard the thumping feet and labored breathing touched with a growl. No. He had come.

"Cyrus, run!" She shouted.

Her father backhanded her, and the world tipped drunkenly to the side. Gunshots cracked, rolling like thunder. Someone screamed. Many someones screamed. Running feet. Blood.

By the time her vision cleared, they were carrying Cyrus to the edge of the pit. His limbs lay at wrong angles, and his tawny fur was matted with blood from a dozen gunshots.

"Don't worry. They didn't use silver bullets," her father said, wiping a smear of blood from his face. "Not for what I have in mind."

His cloak was torn and injuries peppered his body. Cyrus had not gone down easy, but with fire coming down from the balcony and the werewolves waiting in the quarry, he did not stand a chance.

Neither of them did.

They were going to die.

40

Enemies

Cyrus

HE HIT THE FLOOR of the pit with bone-breaking force and blackness swirled in to drag him under. Flashes of memory illuminated his mind like lightning strikes: Alix chained to the pole, blood staining her white chemise, her long dark hair plastered to her body in tangles, amber eyes filled with pain so deep he could not stand to remember it.

His mother, smiling.

A stringer of fresh fish gleaming in the afternoon sun.

Lyrus laughing as he darted between trees during a game of tag.

Effie's little hand, bloodstained in the grass.

Darkness, deep and soft as velvet, wrapped welcoming arms around him.

Magic consumed all his remaining resources, commandeering them as fuel for his healing body. So, when Cyrus woke, he was hungry enough to swallow dirt if there had been more than bare rock beneath him.

His muscles shook with effort and his stomach cramped to protect itself from the hollow, stabbing pain. He sucked in a deep breath at one particularly deep shock, and the scent of Alix's blood raked through his sinuses.

She was nearby, and he wasn't strong enough to help her.

He shifted to his wolf form, leaped at the walls of the pit, and hit the unforgiving stone, his claws scraping the exposed rock as he slid down once, twice, three times.

When he struck the bottom of the pit for the fifth time, Cyrus stood gasping, his muscles trembling with fatigue.

A figure in black appeared at the edge of the pit, staring down at him like a visitor in the zoo. The vampire. Cyrus's hackles rose and a snarl echoed rumbled in his chest.

"The last Campbell," the vampire said with a note of satisfaction in his deep voice. "I am grateful my daughter brought us together at last."

Cyrus shook his head as if to clear water from his ears. Daughter? Was his weakness affecting his hearing? Vampires did not reproduce through any means that would give them children.

Despite the danger, Cyrus shifted to his human form and nearly collapsed. Once he regained his balance, he set his legs apart and shouted, "Who are you that you know my name?"

"Do you not know me? I suppose it has been a rather long time since I visited the Campbells. Perhaps you've forgotten my last appearance. But I doubt it. I imagine it is not easy to forget losing one's family, but I am no judge of human emotions."

His mind went absolutely blank and his body froze.

"I destroyed the few remaining survivors over the years. Couldn't have them ruining my plans. But I never found you. We have my daughter to thank for that fortuitous circumstance."

Cyrus could not speak, only mouth *who?* as his brain tried furiously to process so much information through the haze of shock and exhaustion.

As if in answer, the vampire bent, took hold of something, and stood again. Alix hung from his outstretched arm, her feet dangling off the ground like a landed trout. She would have appeared unconscious if not for her haunted eyes.

"Quite extraordinary, isn't she? The only one of her kind, as far as I know. I have great hope for her future."

"She isn't—" The truth of it came back to him in a hundred memories. Her speed, strength, her ability to heal, to go without sleep, and that damn red cloak she always wore, even in the summer heat.

Somewhere along the way he'd stopped caring about the answer to the riddle of what she was, content to let her keep her own secrets. The world was not a safe place for monsters after all.

But he had never dreamed she might be a vampire hybrid. They were impossible, nothing more than superstition. Except one stared down at him, and the truth of it was in her eyes.

"You..." he choked as the words stuck in his throat. "You knew. You lied to me. Even...even after I—"

His knees went weak and the ground rushed up to meet him. A hundred daggers forged of betrayed trust pierced him from every angle and he collapsed under the pain of them.

"Cyrus."

His name was a prayer on her lips, but instead of crawling toward her, he scrambled backward, scraping his palms on the rock.

"No!" the shout started low and picked up volume until it scraped his throat raw. He fetched up against the wall on the far side of the pit, chest heaving.

He told her of his family's murder and she held him as he cried. She kept the truth from him, let him love the kind of monster that destroyed his life and stole more than he was capable of expressing.

She had lain in his arms knowing the truth and said nothing.

"You mustn't blame her," the vampire said, eyeing his offspring with sick paternal pride. "This sort of thing is what she was bred for. A monster must be a monster, after all. As you will soon learn."

While he focused on Alix and the vampire, the remaining werewolves and mortals wearing silver amulets had gathered along the lip of the pit. Three werewolves and five mortals, not counting those guarding the villagers.

"No!" Alix screamed, but he barely heard her over the ringing in his ears.

They were coming to kill him.

Alix

Cyrus fought like a demon despite his weakness, but there were too many. The wolves harried, biting at his hamstrings and then slashing his neck and shoulders when he turned to protect himself.

The mortals attacked from a distance, jabbing the spears into his unprotected sides as he spun. By the time the werewolves were done with him, Cyrus was so weak he barely breathed.

Alix fought against her bonds, wrenching her body and tearing her skin on the poorly constructed manacles. The bones in her wrist broke under the pressure.

As Cyrus lay bleeding on the stone, she hung from her bonds with blood dripping from her fingertips.

"This is not a battle worth fighting, dear heart," her father said. "You must keep your strength. You will need it."

He curled his fingers in her hair and lifted her head, giving her a perfect view of Cyrus as he lay shivering and bleeding on the stone.

Cyrus

Time ceased to exist. There were only fangs, pain, the empty black pit in his chest, and a pair of amber eyes staring at him. Sometimes they belonged to the devil who destroyed his life.

Sometimes they belonged to *her*.

Sometimes he dreamed of killing her, of ripping her flesh until she screamed with the same sound his soul made when he was conscious enough to remember all he'd lost.

And sometimes he dreamed of her opening her arms and drowning him in her embrace.

But always, he hurt. Every fiber, every cord, every hollow place inside him hurt beyond the words he had to express it. It was as if Cyrus was gone, and only anger lived beneath his skin.

No matter how fast he turned, how viciously he attacked, there were too many of them. He killed one human attacker, but another took his place. The man's spear scored a deep gash across Cyrus's shoulder that paralyzed the limb as his magic fought to heal it with diminishing resources.

He didn't sleep, he merely stopped being conscious. Night fell, dawn broke, stars wheeled. Whenever he woke, they were there waiting. He ceased seeing them as people. They became spears, teeth, and claws.

So, when they threw the old man into the pit, alone and armed with a wooden spear, he killed the wretch with a few vicious snaps. As the last breath rattled in the man's bony chest, Cyrus released his grip on humanity, and let himself fade away into the wolf.

Alix

They tortured him for days. She watched Cyrus fight and kill too many times to remember, every day fading into a never-ending blur of snarls and death. Now and then they threw him parts of a deer carcass because he refused to eat the bodies of those he killed.

She thought she knew why they insisted on prolonging his life but tried not to think of it too much. Not yet. That pain would be forced upon her soon enough. Until then, she endured the burning sun, the cracked lips, the dry, swollen eyes, and the sight of the man she loved as he murdered innocent people.

He was mindless by the time he killed the first mortal. Alix knew it. But seeing it happen through the haze of pain and guilt that blurred her own vision was enough to break her.

Even if there had been hope of an escape, Cyrus would never forgive himself for what he'd done. For what they'd forced him to do. And if he ever cared about her, even a little, that was gone as surely as he was, both consumed by the madness of trying to stay alive.

"Now you see," her father said, after Cyrus killed the third mortal, "that even those who claim righteousness are, in their hearts, monsters. Look at him."

Cyrus was busy tearing apart the hind quarter of a deer, his face wet with blood and his fur so dirty and matted he was hardly recognizable. He had not shifted back to his human form since learning what she really was.

"Would he want to live this way, you think?"

Her voice was barely a whisper. "No."

"If his people were not so stiff necked, they might have helped me create a world where no monster ever suffers such a fate. Where we are not forced to hide in the shadows, scraping a life for ourselves from what crumbs fall from their table."

Cold fingers turned her head away from the gruesome sight in the pit, and her eyes focused on his, so like her own.

In a soft, earnest voice, he asked her the question he'd been asking her every day since Cyrus entered the pit. "Will you help me create such a world, daughter? You never have to live without family again. You will never be alone, forced to hide what you are. You will be welcome and valued by those who share your nature. Say you'll join me, and all this will end. I will even give you your wolf, nicely tamed, to answer your beck and call."

The depth of her longing for that reality was terrifying. Those were the words she'd been desperate to hear every day of her long life. To be safe, welcome, and wanted was more than she dared hope for.

And the only time they'd ever felt possible was when Cyrus said them to her in the forest.

She'd given her heart to him then, even if she hadn't realized it.

Alix opened her mouth to answer, hesitated, and spat in her father's face. The spittle slid down his cheek, which spasmed as his lip curled in a furious sneer.

He backhanded her with enough force to blacken the world. Her head hung limp for a moment, pulling against the chain around her chest.

"Fine," he snarled. "Perhaps you are not quite ready to give up your hope of a human life. Perhaps"—he gripped her face with one hand and forced her to look down into the pit—"you need one last object lesson in what makes you a monster."

When they released the chains, she fell into a limp heap on the rock. Her father rolled her body with the toe of his boot, then knelt on her chest, pinning her arms with his knees.

Holding her head up with one hand, he pressed a cup of blood against her lips. She spit it back in his face, so he pinched her nose shut with one hand and forced her mouth open with the other. Fluid, already cold and coagulating, slopped into her mouth until she swallowed convulsively. Strength returned to her body in a rush. But it wasn't enough.

Not nearly enough.

Once she'd swallowed the last mouthful, he jerked her up by one arm, still choking, and said, "If you are too human to save your own life, you aren't worthy of the future I want to build for you" and shoved her off the ledge.

Alix hung in the air for a stomach-dropping second and hit the floor of the pit hard enough to break her ankles. White-hot pain shot up her legs and made her feet go numb.

But the blood was already at work in her veins, sharpening her senses and healing what could be healed. But it would not repair her broken bones fast enough to save her from Cyrus.

He lifted his head when she hit the stone, and narrowed mindless eyes on her from the other side of the pit. Bones and decomposing bodies littered the ground between them.

"Cyrus," she said, breathless both from pain and from desperate hope. Would he recognize her?

His lips pulled back in a snarl that shook the ground.

She scooted backward, propelled by her hands and hips, until her back struck the wall behind her. "Cyrus, it's me."

He advanced in a hunting crouch, his head held low, the green flames of his eyes—eyes that looked on her once with longing and tenderness—burned a hole through her chest.

He was going to kill her.

41

Enemies

Cyrus

ANOTHER ENEMY FELL FROM the sky, but this one—a female—stared at him with the same yellow eyes that haunted his troubled sleep. They were the eyes of a predator, hawk's eyes, and so familiar it made his brain hurt.

Familiar or not, she would try to kill him, just as all the others had.

Abandoning his meal, Cyrus crept forward, careful not to startle her. If he could kill her quickly, he might finish eating before the next enemy appeared. He was still far too weak to defend himself properly and, despite the constant pain...he wanted to live.

He had to be quick and careful.

"Cyrus," she said, and the low, honeyed sound sent a shiver down his back. He ignored the sensation and gave her one last chance to flee, growling a warning and showing his teeth.

But, despite the electric bite of fear floating in the air, the yellow-eyed female did not try to escape. Instead, she scooted to the side, running her hands across the rock. Foolish. There were no weapons here, only pain and death. Best to end it quickly.

When he was in striking distance, he feinted to one side, then lunged. But she rolled away, faster than his other enemies, and his teeth snapped together hard enough to sting.

He spun, but she had already scuttled halfway across the pit, her yellow eyes locked on him. What was shining on her face? Something about the wet lines made his chest hurt, but he ignored that, too. It was creeping toward his meal, food he could not afford to lose if he wanted to survive.

Instead of stalking the creature, he attacked.

Alix

Tears streamed down her cheeks and blurred her vision, but she did not have time to wipe them away. They'd pushed him too far and his instincts for self-preservation had taken over. To him, she was no more than a threat, one best dealt with quickly.

Alix pushed herself across the stone with every bit of speed she could manage, scraping her palms on the jagged rock. Another foot and she could reach a spear discarded by one of Cyrus's many attackers.

Before her fingers brushed the wood, he snarled and leaped across ten feet of space in the blink of an eye. Alix curled forward to pass beneath his flying body. The cold, slimy bone of a deer leg dug into her ribs as she rolled, and Alix grabbed for it blindly as she turned.

Coming to her feet, half-healed legs screaming in pain, she crouched, holding the bone like a knife. The end had been broken off, and the shards of splintered bone were as sharp as any spear.

Cyrus recovered, spinning to face her, his eyes flashing to her makeshift weapon. His growl stopped the breath in her lungs. She'd seen him fight like this more than once, saw him dismember creatures three times her size, and she wasn't strong enough to stop him.

"Cyrus," she pleaded, feeling her way gingerly backward with slow steps. "Listen to me. I know you're in there."

He continued to advance, head held low, slobber dripping from his exposed fangs, a constant rumbling growl vibrating in his huge chest.

"I've seen you comfort orphaned children," she said, "remember Mercedes? I've seen you laugh with strangers and show mercy to creatures who did not deserve your pity. Cyrus. Please, you are *not* a monster."

Did he flinch? It was impossible to tell. Whether he did or not, he continued to stalk her. She fought to stay just outside his range, but he would back her into one of the walls at some point. She could not outlast him like this, not while he was fed and she'd been nearly starved. Getting through to him might be her only chance.

"We have to save the villagers. Do you see them up there, Cyrus? They are scared and hungry. If we don't protect them, no one will. I cannot rescue them on my own. Please, come back to me."

One great ear cocked to the side. Was she breaking through the barrier protecting his mind from all the abuse? An ember of hope flared to life in her chest.

"Come back to me," she whispered, staring into his eyes and continuing to back away slowly enough to avoid startling him.

Her heel came down on a pebble. The thumb-sized rock rolled along her sole and her foot slid from beneath her. Alix cried out, arms flailing to steady herself as her weakened ankle gave out. Cyrus's ears flattened and he struck, bounding forward in two great strides with his jaws held wide.

She turned the fall into a spin, trying to lean outside his attack, but his teeth sank into her left forearm. On instinct, she pulled against his hold. It tore the muscle of her forearm, but let her use his weight as leverage to right herself and thrust the sharp end of the bone into his side.

He yipped in surprised pain and released her arm to turn and snap at the bone jutting from his flesh, giving her a precious moment of respite. Alix turned and sprinted across the pit. Pain shot up her legs with every step, and the puncture marks on her forearm oozed pale blood. She wasn't healing fast enough, and Cyrus was on her heels.

She ducked to one side, snatching a fallen spear and trying to ignore the thought of Cyrus's teeth sinking into her fragile neck.

"Well struck, daughter," her father called, a note of jolly amusement making rage boil in her chest. "Perhaps you are worthy of the station I designed you for, after all. Make a slave of him. Or kill him. Prove yourself and you may join me."

She bolted toward the cliff wall at full speed, Cyrus mere heartbeats behind her, his breath hot on her back. Teeth gritted against the pain, Alix leaped, planted her feet against the wall, and pushed. She sailed backward in an arcing flip, watching Cyrus skid beneath her to avoid crashing into the wall.

When she landed, white-hot pain shot up her legs, making her knees weak. She used the butt of the spear to stop herself from toppling over, then held it in a low guard as Cyrus regained his feet and turned to face her.

The bone had opened a deep gash in his side and blood dripped from the ends of his matted fur onto the rock. *Pat, pat, pat.*

Her father said, "You have the advantage. Take him now. Release your true nature, the dark parts you have been too afraid to acknowledge. That is where your strength lies."

"I am not a monster," Alix heard herself say, the words slipping out like an unconscious prayer. "I am not a monster. I am not a monster."

"Yes you are!" he shouted. "Until you accept that, you will always be forced to hide from both sides of what you are. Embrace it, daughter. Be what you were born to be."

Cyrus lunged and she tried to parry, pushing him aside with the shaft of the spear. But he twisted, catching the wood between his teeth to wrench it away. She clung to the weapon as he leaned into her, planted her feet, and twisted her shoulders.

The torque of her full body turned Cyrus's head like a cowhand wrestling a steer, forcing his nose upward and his head to twist to one side. Alix bore down and set one heel behind his opposite foot. With a scream of pain, Cyrus lost his footing and they rolled. Alix came down hard atop him, pressing the wood back into his mouth, forcing his jaws too far apart to let him bite down.

His head was trapped between her and the rock, pinned by the thick shaft of wood between his jaws. All she had to do was let go long enough to reach his throat. Much of her strength was gone, but a crushed windpipe would give her plenty of time to recover the spear and thrust it up beneath his ribcage.

She could kill him.

In a moment of suspended reckoning, Alix met Cyrus's gaze as his green eyes widened in pain. He must have seen his death in her face, because he flailed madly, curling to bring his back legs up and kick her off.

But Alix leaped free before he could dislodge her. She quivered with exhaustion, chest heaving, hands trembling. She had been a breath away from killing the man she loved. Time slowed, passing like honey dripping from the hives her mother had loved.

If she killed Cyrus she might live. She may even save the villagers if she was lucky. But it would not be a life worth having, not if the best person she had ever known died at her hands. His death would also kill whatever human parts of her remained.

Peace washed over her, calming her heartbeat and softening the hard edges of the word. If the only way out of this pit was either to kill the one person who valued her for who she wanted to be, or die, it was an easy decision to make.

Cyrus rolled to his feet and snarled at her, his eyes mad with pain.

She faced him and held her hands out to her sides. Fear melted away like frost beneath the sunrise as she said, "I am not a monster."

He leaped.

Several hundred pounds of fury crashed into her chest with no resistance. Alix heard her ribs break, saw stars as her head bounced off the rocks, and let the pain wash through and over her, unrestrained.

She would rather die here, this way, than become the creature her father created her to be. Cyrus pinned her by the simple expedient of crushing her body with his own. Air whooshed out of her lungs in a giddy rush.

His teeth closed around her throat.

Alix let her eyes fall closed as the pressure of his jaws made the edges of her vision darken. Before the world went black, she whispered three words.

"I love you."

Cyrus

The female's fragile throat rested between his jaws, weak as a baby bird. All he had to do was clamp down, and he would be safe. The tips of his teeth broke the skin and its blood ran across his tongue, too sweet for mortal blood.

The scent of—what was that? Spearmint?

A hundred memories, each as sharp as a shard of broken glass, flashed through his mind. Arms reached out to him, dappled by sunlight breaking through the forest canopy. A small circular scar below a collarbone. Long-lashed eyes half closed in pleasure. His name a prayer whispered into the night.

Cyrus froze.

Alix.

Her voice echoed through his mind, a memory of his desperate flight through the forest while terror for her clenched an iron fist around his heart. He had been certain he was too late to save her when her voice rang through the trees, as clear as a bell.

Cyrus, run!

She'd tried to save him. Why was she here?

Memories fell into his mind like stones in a pond, these ones heavy enough to crush his soul. Spears and teeth, the stink of stale sweat and voided bowels. By the blessed face of the moon, how many people had he killed? Deer meat soured in his stomach as guilt and self-loathing twisted around his intestines.

He had lived his life believing himself something better, more pure than the average werewolf. His mission to protect life made him special. *Chosen.* But he was a monster after all. And he had nearly killed Alix. No matter how badly her lie hurt, she deserved life, perhaps more than anyone he'd ever known.

That he'd been capable of hurting her made his gorge rise. He had to get her out of there. But the walls of the pit were surrounded with werewolves, armed men, and that damned vampire.

Half starved, he wouldn't be of much help, not until he had a chance to recover. And Alix should have healed by now, but she'd been starved too, by the look of her.

They had one chance to save the villagers and themselves. And even if it killed him, he would give it to her.

Alix

Once more, she was trapped by the body of a huge werewolf, helpless and small, and unable to breathe. Alix blinked. She was breathing, though it hurt like the very devil. And she knew that scent.

Cyrus.

His teeth rested gently against her throat, and his chest vibrated with a deep growl that shook her bones. She should have been dead by now, but he wasn't hurting her.

Tentatively, she curled her fingers in the fur of his chest. Cyrus released her just enough to turn his head and pressed the side of his neck against her face. He whined softly enough that only she would hear it. The heat of his artery, so close to the surface of his skin, pulsed against her in time with his heartbeat.

He grunted, an impatient noise, and pushed his neck more firmly against her face. The truth of what he was doing lit up the dark corners of her mind like a lightning flash. He still covered her body, as if he were strangling her. From above, she was lost beneath him. But he was offering her the only thing that might save them both.

Her hands shook against his chest. Alix had never drunk from a living creature save for Hugh...and she'd killed him. She could not kill Cyrus. She refused to kill him.

He growled, conveying both impatience and urgency. *This is our only chance,* that growl said. If she thought too much, she would never be able to do it. Alix closed her eyes, buried her face in Cyrus's fur, and sank her teeth into his neck.

While she'd never found the scent of his blood appealing, Cyrus was old and his blood was rich with the power of the moon. It felt as if she'd swallowed a thunderstorm, strength whirling in gusts that snapped her bones back into place. Muscles knit, skin closed, and air filled her lungs.

His groan vibrated through her chest, as he started shaking. His heart faltered and his breath caught. If she did not stop now, she would kill him. But with the power of his blood, she could do anything: destroy the monster that forced her into this world, save the villagers who still lived, build herself a safe place where no one could ever hurt her again.

The soft, whimpering sigh that escaped Cyrus was a slap to the face.

Alix wrenched her head away, gasping, and Cyrus fell limp atop her. Her heart clenched. Had she killed him? Pushing him to the side just enough to see the wound, she watched as his skin began to knit closed. Blood stopped flowing. He took a shuddering breath.

Cyrus was weak, fearfully weak...but he would live. He'd given her everything he had left despite the way she'd betrayed him. And she was going to make damned sure his sacrifice was worthwhile.

Carefully, Alix pushed Cyrus to the side, sliding from beneath his body. She vibrated with power, every muscle tense as a coiled spring. When she stood, the faces of the villagers who stared down at her were slack with shock.

But her father stood silent beneath his black hood, and said, "Are you ready to release your fear and embrace what you truly are?"

Something deep inside her, a piece of her soul she'd never wanted to admit was missing, snapped into place. Yes, he was her father. And now that her mind was clear, she saw the truth: she'd been created in violence and lived her life by it, but never fully surrendered to the darkness lurking inside her.

She walked a tightrope to straddle both sides of her nature, never human enough to be accepted, never monster enough to be without fear. Forever alone and on the outside, unsafe in both worlds because she never allowed herself a place in either.

The life she dreamed for herself, the one she would only be worthy of if she redeemed herself, did not exist. And, as much as she hated to admit it, there was power in the darkness.

No matter how much she wanted it, Alix would never be human. It was a truth she could no longer ignore. Not if she wanted to live. Not if she wanted Cyrus to live.

She looked up at her father and said, "Yes. I am ready."

He held out his arms, an inhuman smile stretching his skin across his bones. "Welcome, daughter of my blood."

Her father was right. She was a monster. And he was about to learn what happened to those who created monsters.

42

Alix

No one bothered to lower a rope or offer a hand. Instead, they kept their rifles trained on her chest as she strode toward the cliff encircling the pit.

It would take more than bullets to stop her this time. The power in Cyrus's blood was too potent. It coursed through her veins like a river in flood. Every detail stood out sharp in the late morning sunlight, from the luminescent shine and delicate veins of a dragonfly's wing as it sped by, to the rancid stink of the men and werewolves standing dozens of feet away.

And her body felt light, as if Cyrus's gift counteracted gravity somehow and she floated rather than walked. He sacrificed too much to save her life. She had to finish this and get him out alive.

With a casual glance at the rim of the pit, she gauged the distance, crouched, and leaped. Her muscles exploded like taught rubber bands, and she flew upward with the ease of a cat leaping to a windowsill. When she landed on the lip before her father, he flinched backward a fraction of an inch.

The rifle barrels tracked her as she stepped forward to place herself within feet of the man who abused her mother, tortured the man she loved, and revealed the truth about what she really was.

He smiled, lay his hands on her shoulders, and squeezed hard enough to bruise. The gesture was both a benediction and a warning. "The reign of mortals over this world is coming to an end," he announced. "Together, we will usher in the Fall of Night."

Howls and shouts of celebration reverberated off the stone. He pulled a silver pendant from a cloak pocket and made to place it around her neck. She took the braided leather cord before he could bestow it, and turned the amulet over on her palm.

"A symbol of our purpose," he said. "Protection and recognition for those who join our cause."

She raised an eyebrow. "Protection and...control?"

"Perhaps."

Whatever this talisman did, it was the last thing she wanted around her neck. A plan had been forming in her mind from the moment Cyrus's blood slipped past her lips, and she could not succeed if he had even a small measure of control over her. She must begin by playing her part to have any hope of saving the villagers and Cyrus.

She let her eyes flick toward the balcony of the overseer's cottage above, where the villagers stood in a neat line. "What of them?"

"They can join us, or become food. Either way, they are useful."

"Can I choose mine now? I am still rather hungry."

"Werewolf blood not enough for you?"

"It doesn't taste very good."

"I don't imagine it does. Choose your meal, then. But first—"

Faster than Alix would have thought possible, her father clamped a familiar set of manacles around her wrists. Her heart thudded once, hard, but she kept her face blank as she said, "Killing the man I loved did not earn your trust?"

"Were you foolish enough to believe it would? You have strength of spirit. That makes you valuable. It also will make you hard to break. Changing your mind fully will not be so easily accomplished as a few days without food. But I am patient. We will repeat the process when necessary."

"You mean to starve me again?"

"If I must. However, there are other, more interesting ways to break someone. I hope you will not force me to employ them. Remember this: I am not stupid, daughter. I will hurt you, even to kill you, if it is necessary. The sooner you learn that, the easier our relationship will be."

Alix nodded, dropping her head in submission.

"Come along," he said. "Choose your next meal. Then we can begin."

He knew. Whatever she did wouldn't be a surprise, not entirely. So she'd have to be fast and brutal. She had to use her frustration and anger instead of hiding it. But surprise would have made her job far easier.

If she ground her teeth in frustration, he would hear it. If her heart raced in anger, he would know. So Alix breathed in slow, calm breaths, and followed her father up to the overseer's cabin. She could escape now, she was certain of it. And she might even be able to save Cyrus if she could get him to change back to his human form.

But saving the villagers was another matter. That required a bit of guile.

Her eyes flicked over every enemy as she walked. Three wolves guarding the edge of the quarry, two more who patrolled the perimeter of the camp, and two armed humans were the only members left of the small army her father built. How many did Cyrus kill?

Grief for him squeezed her heart, but she could not afford to feel that now.

She stepped up onto the balcony, noting the tattered remains of her cloak lying next to the chain piled near the wall. When this was over, she was going to melt the damn thing down.

Madame Sophie stepped forward, ignoring the moans of protest and grasping the hands of her fellow captives as they tried to pull her back into line. Her jaw was set, her bony fists clenched at her sides.

"Take me," she said, raising her chin. "Old blood is strong blood, and I lived a full life. Take me and let the others go."

She was dirty and far too thin, her white hair hanging ragged to float above her shoulders. But she had an unbreakable will. Like Grand-mère.

Alix took one long stride forward to meet the old woman, placing herself between the two guards with rifles who stood at either end of the line of captives. "You would trade your life for these people?"

"I would," Madame Sophie said, her eyes leveling an accusation. "I thought you would, too."

Alix gave her the most meaningful glance she could manage. "I did, madame. Now it is your turn"—her eyes flicked to the left-hand guard and stayed for a fraction of a second—"to give yours for me."

Madame Sophie's lips thinned, then she swallowed and nodded. Alix searched the crowd of shaking mortals and settled on a relatively young, strong-looking man who might withstand what she intended to do.

"You," she said. "Come here."

He looked to the left and right, as if she couldn't possibly mean him, then swallowed and stepped forward, staring at her like a deer might stare down a hunting hound.

She wore only a torn, bloody chemise that was so thin it may as well have been transparent. From his position, she probably looked as frightening as the monsters holding them hostage. But it was her eyes he could not escape from.

She could not enthrall someone, but she held his gaze with all her might as she slid her hands up his chest, curled her fingers securely in the front of his shirt, and leaned forward.

"Don't be afraid," she whispered.

There was no time for hesitation or second-guessing. If she did not steel herself now, and embrace the monstrous side of her nature, she wouldn't act with the conviction of purpose required to pull off something this insane.

Moving so fast her bones hurt, she turned, spun, and flung the man fifteen feet, screaming at the other captives, "Get down!"

He crashed into the gunman on the left and bore the man down. They hit the ground with a tremendous crash, knocking the rifle from the gunman's hands. It skittered across the wood and tumbled down the far stairs.

Her father blurred toward her, hands outstretched, but Alix was already moving. She ducked beneath his grasp and spun, wrenching her wrists apart. The chain snapped with a metallic ping. Chains flew, bouncing off the rails and building as she launched herself at the other guard.

He raised the rifle and fired, but his mortal reaction time was pitifully slow. Alix hit him in the chest with both feet, and his ribcage snapped with a sound like breaking matchsticks.

The thrill of violence, a thing she'd always kept in check, swept through her. Battle lust awakened every sense and nerve ending to almost painful clarity when piled atop the power Cyrus gave her.

The shot went wide, tearing a chunk from the balustrade as villagers ran screaming.

She let herself fall flat, landing on her back as her father's extended hand swiped through the air above her with bone-crushing force, just where her head would have been if she'd landed in a crouch.

There was no redemption after this. He would do his best to kill her. But she had to ignore him and stop the remaining were-wolves–who were bounding up from the pit toward the road–before they killed the fleeing villagers.

Rolling in a backward somersault, Alix coiled and then straight-ened, planting her palms on the boards and launching both feet at her father's hips. He bounded to the side to avoid the strike, and she landed, continuing the motion with a backflip that carried her off the overseer's porch and into the road.

Villagers sprinted toward the forest, screaming and clutching one another for support. But werewolves blockaded their escape, a row of piercing teeth and two-inch-long claws. There were too many of them to fight alone, and she had no weapons, nothing with which to protect the fleeing captives.

Not unless she let the monster out.

Days of starvation and exposure roared into her mind and chest, setting her afire. In a fraction of a second, memories accosted her: every ray of the sun that burned her exposed skin, every scream of terrified and dying mortals echoed in her ears as the man she loved was tortured into madness again.

Worse, the horror of knowing her father, who should have pro-tected, cared for, and loved her, had created her as a tool. He never wanted a daughter...he wanted a weapon.

And Cyrus was lying motionless in the pit.

The barriers she built and maintained over hundreds of years, barriers meant to protect herself and others from the darkness in her soul, crumbled to dust.

Alix bounded forward with a burst of speed and a scream of fury. A red haze fell over the world and her heart thundered in her ears. Time ceased to exist. She descended upon the monsters like a storm unleashed: striking, kicking, sinking her teeth into tender flesh.

Blood filled her mouth before she spat the gore into the dirt and spun into another attack.

The werewolves healed quickly–too quickly–but Alix had become a thunderstorm, a hurricane, a tidal wave that refused to be stopped or slowed. She vaulted over one wolf and launched herself toward the other with her shoulder held low. It spun toward her, mouth open and teeth gleaming, but it wasn't fast enough to realize it was already dead.

Alix did not punch the beast so much as reach through it. When she tore her fist out of its side, a rope of greyish intestines slipped through the gaping wound her hand made. It wasn't a fight. Alix murdered the werewolves with the single-minded ferocity of a mother bear protecting starving cubs.

One werewolf fell. Then another. Two down. One was left standing as the other three hurtled toward them from the quarry. Her muscles sang at the promise of battle, of blood. A grin stretched across her face as she bared her teeth.

"I will kill her."

The words locked Alix's muscles. She hesitated just long enough to be swept off her feet by the last werewolf, its head knocking her legs out from under her as it spun. She tumbled backward, caught herself, and looked up to see her father holding Madame Sophie by the throat.

The third werewolf, deciding its master had the situation under control, left to pursue the fleeing villagers. If she tried to chase it down and stop the beast from killing more people, her father would snap the old woman's neck.

"You are not willing to be ruthless in pursuit of your goals," her father said, tightening his grip until Madame Sophie gasped. "Your idealism will always be a weakness, daughter. Let us see if we can beat it out of you. Lie down and stretch your arms to the side. If you move, I'll break her neck."

"Do it," the old woman said between clenched teeth. "Alix will have no reason to hold back once I am gone. My life is a worthy sacrifice to secure your death."

If her father heard the old woman, he did not react, merely stared her down with knowing eyes. The three werewolves who had been guarding the quarry bounded onto the road. They created a perimeter, circling the three of them with raised hackles and their heads held low.

She had seen common wolves do the same thing to elk separated from the herd. If she moved, one would dart in to hamstring her while the others distracted her from the front. Her gaze fluttered across each enemy, mind working for solutions and finding none.

"He will kill me either way," Madame Sophie croaked.

Her father shook the old woman once, hard enough to make her teeth rattle. "Now, if you please. Or I will give her to the wolves for a toy."

Jaw locked in helpless fury, Alix held out her arms and began to lower herself to the ground. Her father winced, his hands jerked toward the back of his head, and a gunshot roared across the open space between the treeline and the quarry.

Madame Sophie slowly crumpled as a familiar voice rang out like the chiming of church bells. "Get down!"

Alix lunged forward, wrapped her arms around Madame Sophie, and bore them both to the ground. A silver ball the size of her fist hit the dirt near her father's feet. The two closest werewolves stopped and stared.

It was one of the grenades Sister Mary Paul had given her. The one she gave to Lady Gwen to keep her and Claude safe on their flight to Loreau. Swearing, Alix rolled away to cover Madame Sophie with her body.

The ball clicked, the top and bottom turned in opposite directions, and then exploded with a resonant, metallic pop that made her ears ring. Small beads of silver burst in a cloud, buzzing by her ears like angry bees. They peppered the area, hitting every surface so fast it sounded like a handful of rocks hitting the water all at once.

A handful of white-hot pinpricks burned on her shoulder and back, but she stayed on top of Sophie, covering her with her body as werewolves stumbled and screamed, and her father cursed.

Grabbing a fistful of dirt, Alix leaped to her feet and flung it in her father's face before racing toward the werewolves. The creatures writhed in pain, pierced by so much silver even their newfound resistance could not save them from the agony of it.

Alix aimed at the closest wolf, forcing every ounce of speed from her legs, and swung the flat of her hand in a curving strike aimed for the creature's windpipe. The impact reverberated up her arm and to her shoulder, followed by a shockwave of pain as the bones in her left hand broke. But the wolf's windpipe was crushed, its neck broken.

The thunder of gunfire erupted, and the other werewolf dropped to its haunches, snarling in pain. She tried to turn toward the final wolf, but a force slammed into her back and ripped her off her feet, tearing her chemise. Alix turned into the force, letting it guide her backward. Instead of hitting the ground in a heap, she landed in a roll, coming to her feet to face her father.

Another gunshot, another screaming wolf, and the thump of a heavy body hitting the ground. Alix did not look. Not while her father stalked her.

"I exposed your strength. I gave you a world without fear," he snarled. "And this is how you repay me? Perhaps you are not worth keeping alive."

"No. Cyrus gave me that. I just didn't realize it until it was too late." She slid into a fighting crouch, weight balanced, feet shoulder-width apart, hands up. "The only thing you gave me was scars. Let me return the favor."

She shot forward in a blur.

They fought like a whirlwind, like leaves twisting in a breeze, so fast Alix would never have been able to properly track his movements without Cyrus's blood. She sidestepped a kick, parried a looping blow, and launched a series of attacks that forced her father back on his heels.

He was stronger and faster than her, even with the benefit of Cyrus's gift. His responses were almost too fast to track...but they were sloppy. Strong, but not sharp or well executed. He left openings that should not have been there. He overextended. He ignored his balance.

Alix realized, in a startling instant, that her father was no fighter. In his long life, he'd likely been faster and cleverer than any opponent. He did not need to spend decades honing martial skills, not when a casual blow could kill someone.

But Alix had been fighting for her life for three hundred years. She'd trained in every martial art form available to her and learned lessons on the deadly end of fang and claw. And while she wanted very much to live, if Cyrus and the villagers were safe, she wasn't afraid to die.

She could beat him.

But not without a weapon of some kind.

Another gunshot cracked and Alix slid outside an open-handed strike, lifted her shin to slide a kick aside, and ducked beneath a wild swing. As she ducked to the inside, she landed a hard left hook to her father's ribs. But if he felt the blow, he didn't show it.

Instead, he leaned back to deliver a front kick that sent Alix tumbling backward. He sprang after her and wrapped his hands around her neck, bearing them both to the ground. Breath rushed out of Alix as she landed on her back in the dirt next to the crater, arms splayed wide to catch herself.

Her father landed on her chest and shook her like a dog trying to break a chicken's neck. "I spent months planning these attacks," he growled through clenched teeth. "Just to lure you in."

Her fingers scraped along the dirt.

"I spent years perfecting these techniques." He squeezed and the edges of her vision went black, constricting the world down to a tunnel.

She groped blindly, finding nothing but dust and pebbles.

"Only for you to throw it in my face!" He leaned down until his breath was hot on her ear. "But now I know it can be done. I will conquer this world with an army of your brothers and sisters."

Three more gunshots, evenly spaced, rang out as the world began to go dark. Alix's fingers slid across something cold and twisted. At last. The sharp edge cut a line down the outside of one finger as she grasped it in her right hand.

With her remaining strength, Alix pressed her heels into the ground, lifted her hips, and twisted her lower body hard to the left. Her father was so focused on strangling her that he let his balance slip, and her leverage toppled them both to the side.

He flung his arms out for balance, but she followed the momentum of the spin, clutching his shirt in her left hand, and forcing him down as they changed positions. As soon as Alix rolled into the dominant position, she struck.

The twisted bit of silver shrapnel slid between his fourth and fifth rib like a diver parting the water.

He gasped and bucked, swinging one arm in a defensive blow, but Alix only leaned back out of his reach and thrust the slender shard of metal in further.

Blood washed her fingers, slipping out of the widening wound like the first streams of water to break past a dam. But her father would not stay down long, even with a heart injury, unless she stopped the organ altogether.

Her own eyes stared back at her from her father's face, wide with shock and fear. The blood covering her fingers was the last blood on this earth that connected her to any other living being. And she was about to destroy him. Hesitation could get her killed, and yet...

A low growl vibrated the air behind her, and a familiar scent made a frisson of electricity fizzle over her skin. The hair on her forearms stood up. Perhaps this blood was not the only blood binding her to someone else.

Cyrus approached with the inexorable strides of doom, his eyes alight with consuming fire. And Lady Gwen strode next to him, the butt of a rifle pressed against her shoulder.

He had given her the strength to save them all, not only because of his blood but because of the person his love helped her become. In return for the gift of his kindness, Cyrus had been tortured. The least she could do was offer him a chance to put an end to the past that tormented him.

"No," her father wheezed. "My research, my methods must not be lost. The new world depends on them. A world where we will not be monsters but lords."

Alix smiled at her father, but there was no joy in it. "Once upon a time, I thought a world without monsters would be a better world. Now, I'm not so certain. But a world without you? That is worth being a monster for."

She stepped aside and turned to Cyrus. "Your family deserves vengeance, wolf."

Her father's tawny eyes widened in disbelief as Cyrus closed the distance on silent paws. They remained wide when his head rolled several feet away, staring at the sky and the blazing sun he would never see again.

43

Cyrus

TWENTY PEOPLE WERE DEAD or missing. They did not count the traitors. By consensus, those bodies were piled in the overseer's cabin to be burned alongside the attackers.

Villagers hauled them up the hill two at a time, silent and solemn as gravediggers, their eyes haunted. Everyone was tired, but they worked with single-minded determination to cleanse the quarry of the horrors that stained the wood and stone of the place.

No one would have blamed them for walking home and leaving the bodies to rot, but Cyrus suspected they did not want to bring the taint of the place back with them, where there was already a mess to be cleaned.

But no one wanted to recover what was left in the pit.

Cyrus avoided looking at it. As they had taken count of the survivors, the weight of their deaths—many of them at his hands—settled around his neck like a millstone. A shiver of disgust ran up his spine and made his stomach heave. He dropped the armload of dry kindling on the deck and braced himself on the rail, breathing through his teeth.

He barely remembered them. It was like looking through a dirty window during a thunderstorm and only seeing the landscape during lightning flashes. But what he did remember made the gore in the pit—his stomach crawled up his throat and tried to escape.

Cyrus bent over the rail and heaved until his eyes watered and his stomach muscles burned. Nothing came up. He was hollow inside.

The fire they lit that night chewed through the dry wood as if it were the pit of hell starving for lost souls. It glowed in the eyes of every villager and made the skin of his face sting from a long stone's throw away.

He wondered what it would feel like to walk into it.

At some point, they'd begun the long walk back to the Villecourbé. He stumbled down the hill at the end of the column, not wanting to make the villagers more uncomfortable by proximity. After all, they'd seen him murder their neighbors. They should not be forced to endure his company.

Their wary glances and pounding hearts made the weight on his shoulders almost unbearable. How had Alix endured such suspicion and fear for so long without becoming... His mouth went dry at the word he could not even force himself to think, not without running off into the woods and never coming back.

She'd saved both their lives, he should at least be able to speak to her. Yet he avoided her gaze, though he watched the sway of her dark hair as she guided the villagers down the mountain.

Somewhere between one thought and the next he found himself back at the inn, staring down at a familiar bed. He was far past tired, had left exhausted behind hours ago, and wasn't even certain if he was, in fact, still alive. Yet he could not force his hand to pull back the blanket or even allow his body to collapse onto the mattress.

He simply stood and stared.

Someone else drew back the blanket, and warm hands turned and guided him down, coaxing his body to do the work his mind was unable to complete. The familiar scent of spearmint teased his memory, and he caught the wrist on instinct.

"Lie with me?" he asked.

A warm body slid in next to him, molding to his side. Arms wrapped around his torso. One leg slid over his. And a head settled on his chest to rest over his heart. Sleep rolled over him.

Bacon. Oatmeal. Honey. Bread. Butter. His nose teased him awake and his stomach screamed with hollow desperation, but Cyrus was too disoriented to move. Where was he? For a moment fear sunk its claws into his stomach. Had he only dreamed of burning the bodies of his tormentors? Was he still in the pit?

"How did you revive him?"

Alix's voice.

She was close. He was in the inn, but she wasn't in his room, the echoes weren't right for that. Maybe next door? He sighed in relief and muscles he hadn't realized were tense relaxed.

Lady Gwen's clipped accent replied, "Would you believe I did it with a potion?"

"If you mean a tincture or alchemical solution, yes. If you mean a potion from a witch, I would ask you to prove it."

"It is more like a potion than anything else I can name. A cunning woman outside a small village in Germany gave it to me. She was terribly skilled with healing herbs, though I hesitate to call her a witch. In any case, I discovered who was pillaging her storehouse, and she thanked me with a bottle of something she called wakefulness. She would not tell me what was in it, but I found a mere sip fortifying in the extreme."

"The Sisters have something like that," Alix said, "though it is not of much use to me. But I would have sworn your possessions were lost when we escaped the werewolves. How did you recover it?"

"On my way out of Loreau, I crossed paths with a rogue carrying a familiar pair of saddlebags."

"That was lucky."

"Oh, it wasn't luck. It was Aristotle."

Another voice, masculine but not human, said, "He's a pretty bird."

"This is Aristotle?"

Gwen laughed, a merry sound that would have made him smile if he still had access to his emotions. "The pretty bird doesn't like to follow instructions. He was supposed to stay at the inn when I left to find you.

Once Claude was safely in the doctor's hands, I hurried to the inn to ensure Aristotle had not stolen everything in sight, only to discover the innkeeper was very sorry, but my bird had escaped at the first opportunity."

"You make him sound like trouble."

"Indeed, he is. He was carrying out a campaign of attrition by diving at the man with my saddlebags and grabbing fistfuls of his hair. The poor fellow was nearly bald when I found him. I offered to help with his raven problem in exchange for a few items from the saddle. He was quite happy with the bargain."

"You let him keep the saddlebags?"

"Yes, well, it seemed fair compensation for the scalp lacerations and lost hair. Besides, I had a new saddle and he clearly hadn't eaten much in the last few weeks."

At the mention of food, Cyrus forced his eyes open and sat up. A tray of breakfast sat untouched on the single table. It was cold, but the smells dragged him out of bed and across the room. He demolished the food, ceasing to think, hear, or feel anything but his slowly filling stomach.

The food ran out long before he was content.

What should he do now? Carry the plates downstairs? Go back to sleep? Walk out of Villecourbé and just keep walking?

He stared at the wall in indecision, watching with detached interest as patterns formed in the wood grain. A seal blinked at him from knot eyes formed by a whorl in the growth pattern. An agonized face screamed at him from another.

"Cyrus?"

He flinched, then cleared his throat. "Aye?"

The door handle turned and Alix stood in the doorway. Her dark hair hung in a long braid over her shoulder, and she wore a simple grey dress, likely borrowed from one of the local women. A familiar red pendant necklace winked on her chest like a drop of blood.

"May I come in?" she asked.

He thought, *no*, but said, "Of course."

She closed the door softly and sat on the bed, folding her hands in her lap as if she would not be able to keep them still, otherwise. "I had them draw a bath for you downstairs. I thought you might like to wash up."

"Thank you."

She nodded, but her jaw clenched and unclenched several times. Her discomfort made the air in the room too thick to breathe.

Cyrus cleared his throat and said, "Are you...well?"

"Mmm," she said but didn't meet his eyes. "You?"

"I'm–" He stopped, blinked, and decided not to finish the sentence. How *was* he? Looking at Alix across the room he was struck by her beauty, but could not draw his eyes away from several new scars on her arms and throat.

Part of him (the greater part, or the lesser?) wanted to pull her into his arms and bury his face in her hair. He could forget the world in her embrace, in her body, and cherish the fact that they were both alive. She'd saved all of their lives and given him the chance to avenge his family.

But the other part, a deep and secret part, wanted to curl up in a corner and scream at her to leave.

Those golden eyes watched him with empathy that should have touched his soul, but all he could think of was whether those eyes–her father's eyes–were the last thing his family saw before they died. In his memory, they stared down at him while he savaged the very people he swore to protect.

There it was. The uncomfortable truth he refused to face.

"No," he said, at last. "I don't think so."

Her lips pressed into an unhappy line, but she nodded in a gesture that seemed to say either I understand, or me, too, or both. Grief was written in every line of her body. He should say something, offer comfort. She must have suffered in ways he could not guess.

Though he remembered nothing of what happened outside the pit after the vampire told him the truth, bits and pieces of violence haunted every thought.

He would have given his soul to erase them.

Alix dropped her head as if she could no longer meet his eyes and traced the tips of her fingers unconsciously over a recently healed bullet wound on the outside of her arm. He wanted to apologize for blaming her, for not trusting her after all they'd been through, for not being there when she needed him, but all that came out of his mouth was, "I'm sorry about your father."

Her head snapped up and the fierce expression on her face stopped his breath.

She snarled, "Don't you dare be sorry," but tears welled in her eyes and spilled down her cheeks.

He'd never been able to resist those tears.

Two strides brought him across the room, and she was in his arms, a trembling glass sculpture beneath a hundred pounding fists. They were two figures carved to match, her head fitting neatly beneath his chin.

Warmth threatened to dislodge his heart from where it clung to his ribs. If that happened, it would drop into his stomach and drown.

Was that better or worse?

"I am sorry about your father," she whispered against his chest. "Your family. And everything my family cost you. I am sorry I did not tell you what...what I was. What I am."

I forgive you. I forgive you. *Say it.*

It wasn't her fault. She was a victim as much as he was. If there was any justice in the world, she would not even feel the need to apologize for a situation she had no hand in creating. But the words would not come out.

Alix leaned back to look up at him. Teardrops on the tips of her lashes caught the window light and glowed as she searched his face, looking for something she did not find.

Her lips trembled for a moment before her jaw firmed and she took a measured step out of his arms. She nodded at him once in a gesture of what? Respect? A goodbye? It was impossible to tell through the haze that settled on him.

After the trauma of the last week, he should not have had the capacity for more heartbreak. But he discovered as Alix walked away from him and a sharp pain shot through his chest, that he most definitely did.

No one in the village would hear of Lady Gwen riding away without a full stock of provisions. Her horse shifted his weight and groaned in protest as the last bit of food was stuffed into the saddle bags and a warm wool blanket strapped behind the saddle.

"Bear up, my lad," she said, patting the beast affectionately on the neck. "I'll find you a few apples when we get to the convent."

The horse turned solemn brown eyes on her and pricked his ears, then began snuffling at her pockets. Which was a good distraction from the enormous raven who sailed down to perch on the cantle.

Cyrus remembered Lady Gwen calling him Aristotle, but the bird seemed less like a philosopher and more like a thief as it eyed the various sacks strapped to the saddle. After a quick glance to see if anyone was looking, it began picking at a knot with the tip of its beak.

"You have an interesting ride before you, with that wee beastie at your back," Cyrus said, offering the lady a hand up.

She grasped his fingers with surprising strength and flowed gracefully into the saddle. "He does keep me on my toes," she agreed. "Are you certain you will not join us?"

Cyrus fought not to look at Alix, who was busy saying goodbye to Madame Sophie. "They need help to repair the damage, now that—now there are fewer people here to work."

Her eyes clouded at what he didn't say. That there were fewer people in Villecourbé because of him.

She leaned down to take his hand and pressed it between both of hers. "I am glad to have met you. If you ever visit New London, there are a few stray cats I could use some help getting rid of."

He barked a surprised laugh, kissed her cheek, and watched as she turned the horse's head and let the beast amble down the main street toward the west.

Alix was in the middle of being hugged by Madame Sophie. Her spine was stiff in surprise at the physical affection. But she thawed enough to embrace the old woman before excusing herself and joining him in front of the inn.

They stood for a moment, staring, but unspoken words filled the space between them like toxic fumes. Alix spoke the way one might wave a hand to clear the air. "You will return to the convent to retrieve your pay?"

"Aye, once I've helped with repairs here."

She nodded and glanced down, her jaw working as if she were either fighting words back or trying to force herself to speak. Every fiber of muscle in his body tensed with the desire to kiss away her worry, but he could not allow himself to touch her.

He clenched his fists until his knuckles felt like they'd burst through his skin.

"I will be there for a month," she said at last, looking up with a hard glint in her eyes. "A month."

His heart squeezed. A month. He nodded to let her know he understood, and said, "Stay safe, Alix La Rouge."

Somehow, since they'd started talking, their bodies had drifted together. She stood not a foot from him, the scent of her making his head spin, her heartbeat echoing in his ears.

He raised a hand as if to touch her cheek, but blood was smeared across his knuckles and dripped from his fingertips in his memory. With clenched teeth, he blinked the vision away, dropped his hand, and took a careful step backward.

When Alix spoke, her voice sounded like the last leaf clinging to a bare branch. "And you, Cyrus Campbell."

44

Cyrus

FENCES NEEDED TO BE mended. Windows replaced. Roofs patched. Walls rebuilt. Wagons fitted with new wheels. Firewood chopped. The list of chores was endless and Cyrus attacked each one like his salvation waited on the other side.

He worked. He ate. He slept. The sun beat down on his bare back and burned the skin of his neck. His stomach growled and thirst burned in his throat, but he still had two more rows of firewood to stack.

A handkerchief slapped his shoulder with a little *fwap*. Madame Sophie stood at his elbow, her lined face set in determined creases. "That's enough for one day, boy. Come get something to eat."

"As soon as I stack the last rows of firewood to cure," he said, but she batted the log out of his hand and pushed him toward the front of the cottage with her shoulder. "If you stack any more wood, it will be holding the roof up instead of my walls. Besides, I didn't spend an hour on supper for it to sit cold on the table again."

Cyrus gave in and promised to be there as soon as he washed his hands and face. But once Madame Sophie was out of sight, he stared at the rows of neatly stacked wood beneath the eaves and felt the first hints of desperation growing in his gut.

When he worked, the memories sat quietly in the back of his mind. But as soon as an idle moment for thought arose, they awoke and prowled around his head like hungry mountain cats looking for something to devour.

He'd tried to chase them away with drink but, thanks to the magic, his body burned the liquor off too quickly to be useful. It wasn't a good solution...unless he never stopped drinking, which sounded tempting. But he had to sleep at some point, and he always woke sober.

Even so, no matter how hard he worked or how much he drank, the hole in his chest yawned with empty hunger. Whenever he turned around, he expected to see Alix watching him with her hands on her hips and a clever retort on her lips.

He hadn't realized that a hundred little things: her voice, the sound of her heartbeat, a glimpse of black hair shining in the sun, the way she rubbed the fabric of her cloak between her fingers when she thought, had slipped quietly into his heart and filled every crack.

And now that she was gone...

Cyrus yanked off his gloves, swearing, and stuffed them into his back pocket as he washed his hands and face in the icy water from the rain barrel. If Madame Sophie caught him at her table with dirty fingernails, there would be hell to pay.

But when he entered the small dining room, there was no food on the table. Only a long-handled silver knife. He froze.

"I have a question for you," Madame Sophie's rasping voice came from behind him, not unkind but firm as granite. "How you answer it will determine how that knife gets used. Have a seat."

If he wasn't certain of the old woman's character, he would have turned and left. Still, Cyrus sank warily into a chair and eyed his hostess.

She dropped into her chair with a groan and folded her hands on the table. "I've watched you torture yourself for the last two weeks. You work yourself to exhaustion day after day, you rarely speak, never smile, and your eyes look like they're staring up at me from the bottom of a grave."

He forced his jaw to unlock long enough to say, "That wasn't a question, Madame."

"I'm getting there, don't rush old women. It's bad manners."

An unwilling smile forced itself onto his lips. What would she say if she knew he was at least two hundred years older than her?

Madame Sophie did not give him the chance to ask. She said, "You are in pain, and given what happened, I think anyone would understand that."

His throat tightened until breathing was almost impossible.

"But you cannot continue living as you are," she said. "If you do, you will be dead in a month. So this is my question for you, young man: shall I use that knife on the bread I baked this morning, or would you rather use it on yourself?"

Sunlight filtered through the curtains, shining dully on the polished metal.

"If you don't like the knife, there is a cliff halfway through the pass"—she pointed with one gnarled finger—"in that direction. It's two hundred feet or so straight down. Not even you would survive such a fall."

He swallowed past the lump in his throat and rubbed sweating palms on his trousers. "Are you hoping for my death, Madame?"

"It doesn't matter whether I hope for it or not. Death is where you're headed. I'm old enough to recognize the signs. Quick or slow, the choice is yours. Unless you care enough to keep yourself alive, that is."

A dozen scenes, half a dozen screams and pleas for mercy, ran through his mind like train cars. He bunched the fabric of his trousers in his fists to stop his hands from shaking.

It wasn't only the memories, not only the truth of what he'd done. It was the fearful glances, the distance, the forced smiles and whispers when he passed.

His voice came out in an anguished whisper. "I don't think I can live with what I've done."

Madame Sophie snorted and folded her arms. "And why not? You think you are the first man to kill someone?"

"They were innocent," he choked, barely fighting back the bile that rose in his throat.

"Oh, were they? And how do you know that?"

He stared at her helplessly.

"How do you know who they were? They may have been murderers, rapists, liars, abusers, cheats...how do you know? Maybe they weren't. Maybe they were only average, petty mortals. But they might have become any one of those things in the right circumstances, someday long after you saved our village."

"Maybe they were not innocent. But they were under my protection. And I failed them in the—" His voice dried up, and it took several moments to force the rest of the words out. "I murdered them."

She nodded and dropped her eyes. "Yes. Yes, you did. But you were not the one who threw them in the pit. As far as they were concerned, you may as well have been a forest fire or a flash flood. The state you were in..." She took a deep breath. "That wasn't your fault, boy. But the question is the same. Can you live with it? There's no reason to torture yourself. Choose life or a quick death."

He traced the line of the knife blade with one finger. "How? How can I live with being a monster?"

There. He'd said it aloud. The truth he had not been able to acknowledge. Before the pit, he had been a werewolf. He'd failed his family and his village, yes. And he'd spend several lifetimes making up for it.

But he hadn't been a monster, not like this.

"The world is full of monsters, you fool. Why do you think you are the only one?"

He blinked at her.

"Oh, Cyrus," she growled, standing up to pace into the kitchen. A moment later she returned with bowls of soup and bread and plunked them down on the polished table. "You want to know how to live after what you've done? You move to a small village, you build yourself a little cottage, and you spend your days helping and protecting the people there."

His mouth popped open, and not because the food smelled like a bit of heaven. "You...are you—"

"I won't tell you," she interrupted, resuming her seat and laying a napkin on her lap. "It's no business of yours. Listen to the important part: you build a life, boy. A beautiful life. A life that redeems what you've done if you can. You buy those lives, you earn them with every bit of good you can do. And you bloody damn stop feeling sorry for yourself. *You're* still alive."

With that, she dug into her soup with a will, stopping after several bites to sigh and close her eyes in pleasure. "That is good."

This small woman with barely eighty years behind her struck the steel of her wisdom against his pain and sent sparks of hope dancing in his soul. The first flickers, a promise of the fire that might be kindled, cast weak light on the truth he hadn't been able to see.

He found himself asking, "What do I do?"

"Pull your head out of that admittedly shapely ass and go find your girl."

A bark of surprised laughter made him feel, somehow, fifty pounds lighter. Madame Sophie gave him a knowing smile and held her hand out for the knife. "Shall I cut the bread?"

45

Alix

THE TRIP BACK TO the convent of St. Christophe took more than twice as long when traveling with a human. Alix needed less than half as much sleep as Lady Gwen, so two nights out of three, she either hunted the darkened forest for monster signs or lay sleepless by the fire, staring at the stars.

Cast across the blanket of night like handfuls of diamonds, they shone with cold, distant light, removed from the violence and pain of the world. She envied them. How would it be not to feel? To be so steady that others might plot their course through danger merely by noting where you stood?

Unlike the stars, Alix felt everything but had no compass to guide her through the tangled web of emotion. Resentment was the only feeling not confused by a dozen others. Until meeting Cyrus she'd been, if not exactly happy, content with the life she was used to.

Her expectation of the future was simple. Her goals were small and achievable.

But now...she wanted. She knew what a fuller life could feel like, and the thought of returning to the emptiness made sleep nearly impossible, even when her body cried out for it. She resented him for that. And she resented her father for not being what a father should be.

Both of them forced knowledge on her that she would have been happier without.

And she grieved for them both: for all her father stole from her, and all Cyrus promised her.

But she did not grieve for her father as she grieved for Cyrus and the unseen scars he now carried, scars she may as well have scraped into his soul with her own hands. As much as she wanted to stay with him, asking him to face that pain day after day to ease her own suffering was cruel.

Alix had enough of cruelty.

So she kept her head down and led Lady Gwen back toward the convent one league at a time, despite feeling that every step wore down what was left of her soul a little at a time.

The only bearable part of the journey was her companion.

"If you were to ask me a week before," the smaller woman said as she turned an intricate gold astrolabe over in her gloved hands, "I would have told you ghosts could not exist, let alone be handsome. But"—she tossed Alix the little tool with a casual flick–"here is proof."

Alix caught the device and examined it. The ghost story might be a tale told merely to amuse–it was hard to be certain with Gwen–but the astrolabe was real enough, and captivating. "I'm glad you managed to recover it from your saddle bags," she said, handing it back.

Lady Gwen rode with casual grace, content to let the horse guide itself along the road while she bent to accept the astrolabe and carefully return it to her pocket. "As am I. It has quite a unique provenance. After all, how many women can say a ghost captain gifted them a priceless artifact?"

"A handsome ghost captain," Alix added, a smile tugging her lips up at one corner.

Gwen winked. "Of course, we mustn't forget the most important detail. Though I will admit, he was not so handsome as Cyrus."

Alix's smile withered. Out of habit, her hand twitched toward her cloak, only to remember the garment had been burned inside the overseer's cabin. Madame Sophie loaned her a hood and cowl, but it wasn't the same. So she stuffed her hands into her pockets instead.

Lady Gwen continued as if she hadn't noticed Alix's sudden change in attitude. "It is rare to meet a man so handsome who is also kind and thoughtful. While we prepared the village I actually saw him rescue a kitten. The little beast tried to hide in one of our roadblocks and crouched inside crying for its mother.

"Cyrus dug it out and carried it around on his shoulder until mama cat came looking for it. I thought that sort of thing only happened in romantic fiction."

Alix made a noncommittal noise and set her jaw. Maybe she'd scout ahead for a while to calm her nerves.

"And such a good-natured sense of humor," Gwen said, shaking her head. "Most people do not laugh enough, but to find someone who can laugh even in the face of danger is a true gift. Did you know–"

"I know who he is!" Alix blurted.

If she had to hear one more word in praise of Cyrus she was going to scream or flee into the woods or both.

Gwen pulled her horse to a stop and turned in her saddle to gaze down at Alix, her brown eyes warm with compassion. "Do you? Then what are you still doing here with me?"

The heat drained out of her cheeks and Alix slumped. "He does not want me."

"Is that so? Then I know nothing of men, for I must confess, I have never seen a man look at a woman the way Cyrus looks at you."

A fist of grief tightened around Alix's throat. "Maybe once he looked at me with desire, but I destroyed that by keeping the truth from him even after I knew what happened to his family. I held onto the warmth of him with both hands knowing he would eventually..." Cast her away, as everyone else did. Because she could not trust him with the truth of what she was.

"It was selfish," she finished at last. "I knew it and did it anyway. And he cannot forgive me."

"Did you ask him?"

"Of course I–" Alix paused. Had she? She replayed their conversation in her mind. She told him she was sorry. That wasn't exactly asking for forgiveness but it was close enough. Wasn't it?

Gwen's voice was soft. "How do you know if you didn't ask him?"

"He won't forgive me."

"How do you know?"

Because I can't forgive myself.

She did not say the words aloud but they hung in the still forest air, heavy as rainclouds. How hard had she tried to earn his forgiveness? Had she even tried at all?

"Granted, my personal understanding of men is about as deep as a mud puddle, which is to say deep enough to know who I'd like to take to my bed for the night, and no deeper. But I suspect the situation would change substantially if you'd pluck up the courage and tell him the truth."

"What truth?"

"That you love him."

Alix may as well have been struck by lightning. Every muscle, thought, and even the blood in her veins froze in an agony of hope that hurt so deeply she was afraid to move.

"It wouldn't change anything," she said, the words escaping on a barely-there breath.

Gwen climbed off her horse and held Alix's face gently between her hands. Despite being several inches shorter, she had the kind of magnetic presence that demanded respect. More compelling was the evident kindness in the woman's eyes. Alix found she could not look away.

Gently as a butterfly lighting on a flower, she ran her thumbs across Alix's cheeks, brushing away tears Alix hadn't realized she had been crying.

She blinked down at the smaller woman in something like awe. No one but Cyrus had ever touched her so familiarly without permission, without restraint. Without fear. The warmth of her concern brought a little life back to Alix's limbs.

Was this what it felt like to have a friend?

Gwen held her there for several heartbeats merely with the force of her eyes before asking softly, "If he said it, would it change anything for you?"

Yes. God's breath, if Cyrus told her he loved her, it would change everything. It didn't matter that three simple words couldn't change the past, or earn forgiveness. Just the thought of it sent a thrill of horror or joy or both up her spine.

Of course, she'd done nothing worth earning the love of a man like Cyrus but if such a thing was within her reach, despite everything she'd done and everything she'd been through...it would be worth fighting for. Even if he turned her away again, at least she would have fought as hard for him as she fought for everyone else.

At least, she thought with a pounding heart, she would have fought for herself.

Heat sped from her chest and flushed both cheeks, warmth racing through her veins to every muscle. Each thump of her heart whispered *run, run, run.*

Alix caught Gwen up by the waist and deposited her in the saddle. "You have weapons?"

She patted the bundle strapped to her saddle and smiled.

"Good. You're only a day short of the inn if you follow this road. If I don't meet you there in a week, I'll see you at the convent." Alix turned to leave, then paused and looked back over her shoulder. "Thank you. For everything."

Gwen waved her off with a laugh. "Stop talking and start running."

The moon chased the sun across the sky once, twice, and still she ran. The initial hope that lit a fire inside her had dwindled, threatened by the persistent fear that this desperate move would only hurt both of them.

And still, she ran.

Her muscles burned and her eyes swam, her throat was as dry as the crumbling dirt on the edges of the road.

And still she ran.

Twilight leeched the color from the world one long shadow at a time, drawing it up and into the indigo sky where stars peeked through. Alix stumbled to a stop, her chest heaving. The world tilted drunkenly to one side, and she had to brace herself on the trunk of a tree until she caught her breath.

Pixies flickered in the underbrush, but Alix barely noticed their green lights dancing. She sank to the ground and drew her knees up, tilting her head back against the bark to watch the moon between swaying branches.

She'd run for three days without stopping and it only occurred to her now that she had no way to know whether Cyrus was still in Villecourbé, if he left to accept his pay from the Sisters, or if he was in France at all. A few days would take him east to Switzerland, and a few more south to Italy.

What if he went looking for at the convent only to discover she never arrived?

A thousand doubts made her empty stomach sick. She was a fool. She'd abandoned perhaps her first real friend on a barely traveled path in the wilds of France to chase a man who as much as told her he did not want her.

Hadn't his refusal been enough?

She turned her forehead into her shoulder, wiping away the sweat beaded there. This was a fool's errand. Life taught her very clearly not to reach for things never meant for her. Monsters did not deserve love.

After a bit of rest, she would turn back and meet Gwen at the inn. Then she'd find Mercedes a good school, one where the little girl would be safe and could make something of herself. After that?

A twig snapped and Alix's heart leaped into her throat. She swore at herself internally as she rolled quietly to the side and into the shadow of a berry bush. A careful breath revealed no unnatural scents, but the wind was against her. Her pistols had been destroyed by the vampire, but Madame Sophie had saved her knife.

Alix drew the blade silently and crouched, listening while berating herself. She'd been so focused on returning to Cyrus that she'd gotten lazy. Another example of why thoughts of love were not for the likes of her.

There. Footsteps. Quiet ones. Someone who knew how to move. It may be no more than a passing traveler, but Alix adjusted her grip on the hilt of her knife anyway. If it was an average mortal, she'd allow them to pass undisturbed. If not...

The wind changed, dragging with it the scent of the approaching traveler. An electric shock of recognition catapulted Alix to her feet and she found herself leaping onto the road before making a conscious choice to do so.

Cyrus stood on the hard-packed dirt, moonlight turning his loose hair into pale silver. Her heart crashed against her breastbone as her eyes devoured every familiar inch of him. A short beard obscured his jaw, and his hands were curled into fists at his side. Even in the moonlight, the travel stains on his trousers and jacket were visible.

Moving slowly, Cyrus pulled open the collar of his white shirt, exposing the upper swell of his chest muscle above his heart. "I deserve your anger and more. If you're going to kill me, do it quickly."

46

Alix

ALIX BLINKED, CONFUSED, THEN realized she still held the silver knife. She'd leaped out of the bushes at the poor man in the dead of night. She straightened and sheathed the weapon, wishing desperately that she had taken the time to bathe.

She wiped her hands on her trousers and said the first thing that came to her lips. "What are you doing here?"

"I might ask you the same question. Why aren't you at the convent."

"I was on my way, but…" Her voice trailed off and her mouth went dry. The heartfelt words she rehearsed countless times over the last two days evaporated up like dewdrops in the sun. So she said the only thing she could think of. "I came back for you."

His brows rose, but his right hand stayed curled against his chest, gripping the fabric above his heart as if a blade had been planted there. "For me?"

"Yes."

"Why?"

This was the moment. She felt herself teetering on the edge of the life she wanted to leave behind, and two possible futures. In one, she spilled her heart over the ground, and he picked up the pieces and put them back together in a shape more beautiful than what had been broken.

In the other, he left her on her knees to gather whatever was worth saving.

The latter possibility terrified her. She opened her mouth but found no words.

Cyrus crossed the distance between them and bent, scrutinizing her face. "Bloody hell, you're so exhausted it's a miracle you're still on your feet."

"I'm fine," she said, but her reply was automatic.

Cyrus wasn't listening. He took her by the wrist and led her off the road, weaving through the undergrowth with the certainty of a fox heading toward its den. Alix stopped when he dragged her toward the cave-like entrance of a huge slab of stone leaning against the rock face of a low hill. It formed a kind of lean-to twice the size of an average tent, though tall enough at the center for Cyrus to stand comfortably.

Another cave.

They'd begun their acquaintance in a cave. The irony that they may end it in one was not lost on her. She hesitated in the shadows. He did not force her into the space, merely let go of her wrist and began the familiar routine of setting up camp. They'd completed this task together so many times that Alix found herself falling into the pattern, despite her reluctance.

Within minutes, bedrolls had been laid out and a fire crackled against the stone, reflecting heat and light into the small space and warming the moss enough to make the air fragrant. Cyrus crouched over his pack and began pulling out bread, cheese, and sausage. All had been neatly wrapped in paper but the smell made her stomach cramp and gurgle. Loudly.

"God's breath, minx, how long has it been since you ate?"

Alix sank to a crouch, ran her hands through her hair to loosen the braid roughed by so many hours of running, and re-plaited it while she thought. "A couple of days."

He grunted. "No wonder you look like hell. Here."

She accepted the food and ate without comment. When she'd finished everything and was licking grease from her fingers, Cyrus held out another serving.

"What about you?" she asked, though her mouth watered at the sight.

"I've eaten well. Madame Sophie packed my bag to twice this size before I left."

When her stomach felt like it might burst, Alix pulled out her canteen and sipped what water was left, watching Cyrus re-pack his travel bag. The comfort of simply being with him like this had stolen into her without her realizing it, and her eyes pricked with the realization that this may be the last time she'd ever know such peace.

A flash of red fabric between Cyrus's fingers made her catch her breath. Hearing the sound, he looked up, and a flush of nearly the same color burned in his cheeks. He dug out a bundle of fine red wool tied with twine.

"I happened across a merchant on my way," he said, running one finger across the twine. "She had several colors and when I saw this one...well, I knew you'd lost your cloak. She didn't have any embroidery thread but–" He held out the bundle almost shyly.

Alix accepted it with shaking hands. It was fine, indeed. Her fingers ran over the fibers in wonder. Soft, tightly felted, and heavy, it would hang around her shoulders like comforting arms.

No one had ever given her a gift.

She held the bundle against her chest like a shield and said, "I never asked your forgiveness. I apologized, but it just–it wasn't enough. That's why I ran for days to find you. I couldn't wait and hope you'd come to the convent. I needed to ask you if you'll forgive me for not telling you what I was, even if–"

"Alix," he interrupted, leaning close and raising one hand as if he meant to touch her. But his fingers stopped short and he shoved his hands into his pockets before looking down. "No, minx. Your secret kept you safe. It was your right not to share it."

"I didn't keep the secret for my safety," she admitted, staring down at the fabric. A thoughtful gift that represented all the things Cyrus was to her. If there was ever a time to tell the truth, it was now. "Well, at first I did. It was habit and you were an enemy. But once I knew you and learned about your past, I kept it because I..." Her throat closed around the words. Why hadn't he touched her? This would be so much easier if she had the comfort of his touch to promise her that these words would not leave her alone in the woods. When she finally spoke, her voice came out small and weak. "I kept the secret because I wanted you. Just for a while, for whatever time we had. If you knew I was the kind of monster that killed your family, you would never look at me the same. And I liked the way you looked at me."

Cyrus was so quiet he might as well have disappeared. She lifted her gaze just to be sure he was still there and found him watching her, his eyes nearly gold in the firelight. All she could say was, "I wanted to keep it, the feeling of being wanted. Even if meant lying to you. And I hope you can forgive me for it."

Cyrus's Adam's apple bobbed in a painful swallow. "You wanted to be wanted?"

"Yes."

"By me."

Her chin trembled, the first tremor in a landslide that would bring her self-control crumbling down if she didn't fight it back. "Yes. I wanted to tell you. The guilt gnawed at me but I was too selfish to listen."

Slowly enough that she would withdraw if she chose, he raised his hands and gripped her upper arms. His fingers trembled against her skin. With a shock, she realized he wasn't afraid she would pull away. He was afraid of his own reaction. A surge of nervous energy raised goosebumps on her arms.

"You are the least selfish person I've ever known," he said. "And while I appreciate the gesture, I don't want your apologies. And you have no need of my forgiveness. I need to ask yours. No, to beg for it."

Cyrus knelt in front of her, and the motion gave Alix a moment of vertigo so strong she almost lost her balance. It was only his hands gripping hers that kept her from toppling to the side.

"I was willfully blind," he grated, his brows lowering in self-recrimination. "Happy to think of myself as something pure, as the hero chosen by the moon to fight monsters. I never realized that...I was the monster."

"Cyrus," she whispered, but he kept talking.

"I treated my pain as if it were more important than your honesty. As if all the times you proved to me what kind of person you were could be thrown away because of a secret you had every right to keep. My betrayal was worse than anything you could have done. And it left me open to becoming the thing I've hated my entire life."

"That wasn't your fault. They tortured you," she said.

"Aye. And they tortured you. Did you kill innocent men because of it?"

She shook her head but she wasn't certain if it was a denial of her virtue or of his guilt.

"I've been chewing on my shame for the last two weeks and it's made me so sick I cannot stand it. I don't know if I can live with what I've done. But I know this." He grabbed her wrists and kissed her palms, then pressed both of her hands against his chest. The wild beating of his heart vibrated up her arms and echoed in her soul. "The only hope I have of making their deaths mean something is to honor their memories by living a worthy life. And I cannot imagine a worthy life for myself without you in it."

Either the entire world condensed hard enough to squeeze all the breath from her lungs, or her chest had expanded so far that she could not gulp enough air to fill it. Her fingers tingled with thousands of pinpricks, and her vision swam.

"What are you saying?" she whispered.

Cyrus slid his fingers into her hair, cupping the back of her skull and drawing her forward until his breath was warm on her lips. "I'm saying that I love you, Alix La Rouge. I am haunted by the memory of you. I see glimpses of your face in every person I pass." He kissed her cheek, a featherlight brush of his lips. "The color of your hair in moonlit shadows"—he kissed her forehead—"the feel of your skin"—her other cheek—"the taste of your mouth. You are burned into my soul. And I will count this life shallow and empty without you in it."

He traced the lines of her face as if she were a sculpture he created with every caress. And, in a way, she was. His words, the way his deep voice broke, the warmth in his eyes, all of it reshaped her into a person she never believed she had the ability to become.

"Will you forgive me, minx? For leaving you alone to bear the burden of Villecourbé and my own selfishness? If you cannot, tell me now, for I don't think I can—"

Alix leaned forward and kissed him, pressing the bundle of cloth between their bodies. He made a sound, almost of pain, and pulled away just enough to say against her lips, "I know I've done something unforgivable. It's made me question everything about who I am. I don't deserve your—"

She stopped his apology with her fingertips and let her forehead rest against his. Closing her eyes, holding him close with one hand, and listening to the sound of their mingled breaths, she drew strength from some deep reservoir that only seemed accessible when Cyrus was near.

She could get through this. She had to.

"I've believed myself a monster my entire life. I was conceived in violence and born to desire blood. Everyone saw it in me. I thought that was why they hated me. And when I killed my grandmother, I proved them right. They do not fear me at the convent, but they see me as a useful and dangerous tool, not a person. I never believed I could be more, deserve more, than that. Until you."

"But I—your father, I—"

"I would have killed him if you did not. Your family deserved justice. But he taught me one valuable thing. Our darkness carries a strength of its own. If we fear it and hide it away, it festers, like an open wound. But if we acknowledge it, train it, break it to our purpose, it becomes a well-trained beast to be called upon at need."

He choked out something that wasn't quite a laugh. "I would rather not need it."

"As would I. But I think...that is not always a choice given to us. Circumstances require a choice, but we cannot choose a path if we aren't aware of it. If I had not chosen to embrace my darkness, none of us would be alive."

"Aye, but you *chose*. What if my darkness overwhelmed me because it is who I am?"

"Have you any proof of that? In three hundred years? No. You were taken off guard because you did not believe darkness lived within you. The only reason I had a choice is that I have lived with mine every day of my life.

"If you believe me capable of good, you must believe it of yourself. And if you cannot, trust me to believe it for you."

Their eyes met and locked and something clicked inside her chest. A key turning in a lock. A door cracking open. While on their journey, sitting awake as Gwen slept had left her nothing but time to think. She planned a hundred things she wanted to say and rehearsed them in her mind. But the words that poured out now came from her heart.

"I choose who I will be. I choose it a hundred times every day in small ways. I lived in the dark because I believed that was the only option. Now I know it is merely a land I can visit when I choose. And, I hope those choices will pile up until they weigh the scale in my favor. Perhaps, in the end, I will have chosen right enough times to become the person I want to be.

"But the only choice I care about right now is the one that puts me in your arms."

A trembling smile pulled at his lips, and he repeated her earlier words as softly as she had said them. "What are you saying?"

"That I don't mind being a monster if I am *your* monster. And I plan to haunt you until the day I die."

He laughed but the sound was so close to a sob that she reached up to trace the lines of his face with her fingertips, finding his cheeks wet. "I'm saying that I love you, Cyrus Campbell. More fiercely than I've ever loved anything. So unless you plan to chase me away, you had better kiss me."

He dragged her into his arms before the words were fully out of her mouth.

Cyrus turned as they fell backward onto the bedroll, one arm around her shoulder and the other catching their combined weight. He dragged her beneath him and pinned her, letting her take his weight slowly as he lowered them both onto the blanket. Alix barely noticed. All of her attention focused on the taste of him.

It was like drinking wine for the first time, heady and sweet. Her thoughts and worries swirled away, melted into a series of observations sharp enough to embed themselves deep into the fabric of her being.

His broad hand running down the length of her body to lift her hips. His weight settling between her thighs. The soft pulling of his lips and tongue, as if he were sipping from her mouth. The heat, the pressure, the delicious stretching as he pressed into her. Her name growled low and the way the sound of it vibrated from his chest into hers. His brows drawing together, sweat beading his upper lip, the line of his throat as he threw his head back, the way the muscles of his back clenched as his need grew sharp enough to make him groan.

Cyrus shaking in her arms, spent and slick with sweat. Her name once more, this time a prayer whispered against her neck. The safe circle of his arms. Her body melting. Coming apart. Floating away.

And, finally, the whoosh of his deep, contented breathing, and the music of his heartbeat beneath her cheek.

Sunlight broke through the canopy in luminous pillars, turning the silver-grey leaves into glowing gems that quivered in delight. Dewdrops trembling at the edges of leaves warmed in the sun until finally evaporating. Ephemeral tendrils of mist rose from the vegetation like the spirit of the forest made visible.

"It's like the first day of creation," Cyrus whispered.

"Mmm," Alix agreed, and cuddled deeper into his arms, pressing her cheek against the flat muscle of his chest.

It felt like that, new and fresh, as if her life before last night was merely a dream, a prelude to the promise of a sunny morning and all the day might bring. Amazing how the love of one man turned the world into something new.

And she a new creature, someone able to appreciate it, to take the promise in both hands and make of it what she would. What she chose.

Cyrus tightened his arms around her, and Alix smiled.

THE END

Read the exclusive epilogue on Ream

To read more about Alix and Cyrus, continue with The Gwen St. James Affair

47

About the Author

NICOLE MCKEON IS DEFINITELY a human. A regular human who eats food, sleeps, and likes dogs. Like all regular humans. She is certainly not a fae creature masquerading as a person. Those don't exist. Who told you that?

Her books will NOT suck you out of your world and leave you stranded in precarious situations with magical characters so she can absorb your energy and increase her power.

People will say anything these days. Just read one of her books. Tell your friends. You'll be fine. Trust me.

48

Other titles by this author include

SERIES: The Gwen St. James Affair

- Vanished

- Moonstruck

- Spellbound

- Bedeviled

- Forsaken—releasing in 2024

Companion novels in The Gwen St. James Affair

- The Cutthroat King—releasing in 2024

SERIES: The Eververse Chronicles

The Founding Trilogy

- The Laws of Founding

- The Founding Lie

- The Founding War